THE FEW

THE FEW

A NOVEL

HAKAN GÜNDAY

Translated by Alexander Dawe

Arcade Publishing • New York

Visit our website at www.arcadepub.com.

10 9 8 7 6 5 4 3 2 1

Names: Gunday, Hakan, 1976- author.
Title: The few : a novel / Hakan Gunday.
Other titles: Az. English
Description: First English-language edition. | New York : Arcade Publishing, 2018.
Identifiers: LCCN 2017046188 (print) | LCCN 2017047754 (ebook) | ISBN 9781628727104 (ebook) | ISBN 9781628727098 (hardcover : alk. paper)
Subjects: LCSH: Youth--Turkey--Social conditions--Fiction.
Classification: LCC PL248.G766 (ebook) | LCC PL248.G766 A9313 2018 (print) | DDC 894/.3534--dc23

Jacket design by Erin Seaward-Hiatt
Cover illustration: iStockphoto

Printed in the United States of America

For Nevzat Çelik

We are not many, certainly
We are not on the side of the many
We will never be on the side of the many . . .

—Nevzat Çelik, *İtirazın İki Şartı*
(Two Requirements of Protest)

DERDÂ

She was six years old and she was going to die that way. She was shaking but she was too scared to stop looking at the bug. A ceiling as vast as a field of sunflowers but all she saw was the bug. A bug the size of a sunflower seed. Its sharp legs were covered with hair and its antennae were as thin as eyelashes. Its body was so still it could have been a photograph of an insect and in the thick darkness it could have been a jet-black stain on the gray concrete. Black, the color of the girl's eyes, bleary with fear.

She pulled the blanket up to her chin and held it tight in her sweaty fists. Any second the insect could fall on her face. She was on the top bunk of a ladderless bunk bed. The ceiling was less than half a meter above her. If she fell asleep her mouth would slip open and the insect would drop and slip through her teeth. Or first it would drop onto her blanket and crawl over her face and go up one of her nostrils and nibble away at whatever it could find. She quickly rolled over and peered over the bed trying to guess how far off the ground she was. But it wasn't long enough to figure it out. She couldn't make out the floor, so she turned back to the ceiling to watch the bug.

Of course it wasn't the first time she'd seen an insect. She'd seen them on the walls at home, and on the walls in other people's homes, too. She'd never set foot in any house without at least one bug on the wall. Her father told her they came up from the stream. She'd seen big insects that came up from the stream too. They crawled up onto the ceiling but they were too heavy and fell onto the stove. There were also little bugs—lice—that made them cut her hair off. She'd seen bugs that scurried away, disappearing into the walls, and others that waited patiently to be killed under the sacks of beets. She'd even seen a rat. And once, a wolf. A wolf a hundred times bigger than the bug with black eyes. But she wasn't afraid of any of them. She never trembled or cried. But she hadn't been alone. Although she wasn't alone now either. There were thirty-five other kids in the dormitory. But they didn't count. She didn't know any of their names and it was too late to find out now. They were all asleep. She listened to their sleep. She could hear their breath get blocked in their stuffy noses. Kids wheezing in their sleep as they tossed and turned, kids flipping their pillows over as they tried to find a cool spot, kids scratching one foot with the heel of the other. No one was worried about the bug.

She had to move. She had to get down off the top bunk before the bug fell on her. But how? Why wasn't there a ladder? The kid sleeping on the bottom bunk had pushed her up but she told her she'd have to do it herself next time. She sounded angry.

She pulled the blanket over her face. But the wool had become scratchy over the years and it scratched her cheek like thorns, and anyway, she knew it was a mistake to cover her head. Now she couldn't see the bug. But it was still there. Just because you couldn't see it didn't mean it wasn't there. Why hide where you couldn't watch the enemy? It was much more dangerous. The bug could do anything and nobody would know. There was no surveillance.

Her face was dripping with sweat. The chicken pox rash on her temples started to itch. Her heart was pounding and her breath couldn't keep up. She had to get away. She had to get away from that bug. She felt so alone. She had to find a way out, a way to get down. There had to be a way. Some way down. And then she decided. She chose the easy way out, the quick fix, the whatever happens happens. She threw off the blanket and she pushed herself into the void. She jumped into the emptiness.

When her forehead hit the floor it made the sound of a single clap. No one heard her neck break. When she hit the concrete her heart, beating like a hummingbird's wings, stopped cold. She was six years old. And the crack in the ceiling, in the darkness, in her fear, that resembled a black bug was only a year older. It had been transforming into an insect every night for seven years. Once the corridor light was turned on and the ward's door swung open it was nothing but a crack in the ceiling again.

Derdâ's eyes opened at the sound of the clap and she saw the girl lying on the floor, her neck snapped back. Though it was dark and she couldn't make out the face she knew who it was. A few hours ago she'd looked her in the eye and told her she had to sleep on the top bunk. She'd helped her clamber up and then told her she'd cut her tongue out if she complained. She'd said it loud enough for everyone to hear. Now the girl was lying on the floor right in front of her. She must have fallen. Or did she jump?

She took her hand out from under her pillow and nudged the girl's arm. No reaction. She poked her shoulder. She looked up and scanned the ward from between the bunk bed's iron bars to see if anyone else was awake. Not one head had popped up; relieved, she slowly got out of bed and kneeled next to the girl. She took her by the shoulders and turned her over; she was as light as a cat. Her little face was covered in blood. Derdâ lifted her head and looked around. Sure that no one was awake, she started to cry, biting her lower lip to muffle the sound. She sobbed in silence so no one would wake up.

The little girl was from Yatırca. Yatırca, infamous for its state-funded militia and its informants. Yatırca, as the children called it, the village of spies; Yatırca, those sons of bitches. It was forbidden to help anyone from Yatırca. Not even if they were dead. Derdâ didn't tell the teacher on duty or do anything that night. She only cried. Slowly she moved away from the girl's body and quietly slipped back into bed. She herself was from Yatırca and it had taken four years to make the other kids at school forget it.

The blanket hung down from the top bunk, a big triangle whose tip touched the floor. In the darkness Derdâ imagined the blanket was a sail and the bed was a boat. A sailboat that traveled by night. She had seen something like it once in a picture book. A book where colorful boats with white sails sailed over a deep blue sea. Little girls in yellow raincoats stood on deck, smiling as they sailed toward the horizon. A book where all the girls were happy. But it was just a book, some stupid book. Probably the dumbest book in the world, a bunch of crock. Those girls didn't really exist. If they did, the book would be full of their happy photographs, not those phony watercolors.

"Lord, let me die in my dreams," she whispered.

She was about to correct herself, and say "in my sleep," but the boat of her bed sank into sleep. She was eleven years old. Ten and one.

"The dirty little Yatırca girl's dead!"

Derdâ woke up wishing she had died in her sleep. She kept listening.

"She fell and split her head open! And that idiot Derdâ's still asleep! Wake up! Get up!"

She knew that voice. It was Nazenin. Her father died six years ago. He was shot during an attack on a police station. The whole town demanded his dead body back, but their protest was forced to disband when Special Forces tanks rolled into town. So the organization took the matter of retrieving the corpse into their own hands. After nightfall they launched a rocket. But the terrible irony was that the rocket didn't hit its target—the regional gendarme headquarters—but the building right next to it: Nazenin's house. A slight error in calculation and two walls of their own dead man's home were brought down and a sleeping baby was blown to pieces. In the end nobody could reclaim the body. There wasn't even one to be reclaimed because it was buried into a pit near the police station and nature refused to give it back. The regional head of the organization apologized profusely to Nazenin's family, but in the end they only paid half the promised blood money. People in the town paid the other half in the time-old currencies of honor and esteem. A loan from Ziraat Bank helped them rebuild the two walls, and later two more rooms were added to the house using the compensation money the family received as victims of an act of terror. Nazenin, the oldest daughter of the household, received her share of prominence and was selected resident supervisor in her ward of the regional boarding school. And the whole town agreed that it was lucky the baby was a girl and there would be no blood feud.

Derdâ opened her eyes when Nazenin shook her.

"The girl from Yatırca fell off the bed last night. Wake up, Miss Yeşim is calling you."

She couldn't speak so she just nodded her head. She sat up and set her feet on the floor but quickly pulled them away. She lifted her head and looked at Nazenin towering above her and heard just what she expected to hear.

"Clean that up!"

There was blood on the bottom of her feet.

"Didn't I tell you that girl was to sleep on the bottom bunk?"

Yeşim was posted to the regional boarding school five months before. When she first saw the enormous school building she recoiled in fear, and when she had learned there were only four teachers responsible for four hundred and thirty students she had trouble convincing her feet to move forward. But what could she do? She had to wait another five years to be reappointed to another school.

"I'm talking to you. Do you hear me?"

If only she worked at a school where she could say, "I'm going to speak to your parents!" But here if she called in the students' legal guardians, they came toting AK-47s and asked her if she had any problems with their protection, "dear miss teacher," with every implication that they could stop "looking after her" whenever they wanted. There were no lazy, naughty, bad students in this school. The parents considered the teachers agents of the state who brainwashed their children. They'd even claim teachers came and snatched their babies out of their arms. The children whose fathers were martyred taking arms against government forces were then subjected to torture, being taught social sciences, mathematics, and Turkish. Homework and written exams were forms of abuse. Why should a girl who at fourteen years old was beyond marriageable age associate with male teachers? They should be home married to men of that age. And these schools flaunted their religious beliefs. But what else could you do with them? The organization couldn't always watch over you. If you were abandoned there was nowhere to run but the state. Children found playing with rabid dogs in front of houses made out of dung were thrown into Yeşim's arms. And she received them with open arms. And then with no shame whatsoever she grabbed you by the shoulders and shook you.

"Derdâ, answer me! Do you understand what you've done?"

But was there a Derdâ who could answer? Was there anything left? What part of her was eleven years old? Her legs, her nails, her sunken cheeks? What part of her was still a child? The strands of hair that escaped from her braids like wisps of steam, the cracked soles of her feet that would never heal?

"All right, Derdâ. It's all right. Go to the dining hall and have breakfast. And wash your hands and face."

Twenty-six-year-old Yeşim was as much a teacher as Derdâ was a child. She released her grip from Derdâ's frail shoulders. In a final attempt she grabbed her chin and lifted her face. Maybe if she could look her in the eye . . . a house cat and a street cat staring each other down, barely a hand's distance apart. Yeşim gave up. Derdâ's sealed lips won.

"We'll talk later."

Yeşim watched the little girl disappear out the door as she opened the top drawer of her desk and took out a pack of cigarettes. She pulled out a cigarette and a lighter. She lit the cigarette and the smoke poured out of her mouth and covered her face. Her eyes welled up. At the first drag she considered running away. She thought of stepping out of the building, passing through the garden, walking out of the iron gates, and running to the village; then from town she'd catch a minibus and get the fuck out of here. A few more drags and she'd returned. She stubbed the cigarette out in a glass ashtray. But it didn't go out; smoke kept rising from the crushed butt. She tried again. Then again, her fingertips turning black. Ash got stuck under her nails. But the cigarette was still smoking. She didn't look at it anymore. She closed her eyes and just sat, waiting. Whatever, it didn't matter what happened anymore. Earthquake, fire, avalanche, any disaster. A pen with a divine tip to write a full stop to everything. She waited. And then it happened.

The rickety door to her office opened without a knock. It was Nezih, the assistant director. He poked his head into the room and looked through his glasses at the young teacher slumped in her seat, her eyes closed, and this during office hours.

"Miss Yeşim, are you sleeping?"

Her eyes blinked opened.

"The girl's family can't come. The village road is blocked. For the time being the body will be stored in the meat refrigerator in the kitchen, until the gendarme comes. Ok, enough now, go down to the dining hall. The children shouldn't be left unsupervised."

This was unlike any of the disasters she'd been contemplating, but a dead child kept in the meat refrigerator was grisly enough to be disastrous. Whatever she had in her chest contracted. Her stomach and abdomen turned hard as stone. Her body felt heavy, like she had swallowed a stone. She didn't stand up but she just knew Nezih would insist. And he did.

"Yeşim Hanım, we don't have the time to wait for you. Let's go."

Smoke was still wafting up out of the ashtray. She watched the rising smoke disperse. She thought, *So this is how people lose themselves.* And then she stopped thinking. She picked up the glass ashtray and hurled it at Nezih. It smashed into the door and Nezih retreated into the corridor. Yeşim grabbed a heavy stapler and hurled it at him. Then a penholder, a notepad, a 500-page book. And then the exam sheets were fluttering around the room like wild birds, crashing into each other before they fell. Nezih called to her from behind the door.

"Yeşim Hanım! Yeşim! Hey!"

But Yeşim wasn't listening. Her eyes halted on the desk set, a gift from her mother. A fountain pen, a ballpoint pen, and a letter opener. She held the letter opener high and plunged it down into her stomach. There would be no more problems if she died. But unfortunately, she survived.

On the day a student died and a teacher tried to kill herself, the school was trying to make its guest in camouflage feel welcome. The gendarmes were telling jokes but the students weren't laughing. The captain pretended to listen to the headmaster. Nezih rubbed his temples but he didn't have a headache. Derdâ chewed her food but she couldn't swallow. Yeşim lay on the infirmary's only cot wanting to die, but still very much alive.

Decisions were made, orders were given. The gendarme would take Yeşim and the child's body to town where they would receive professional attention. It was an unusual situation. The school's center of gravity had shifted as the children were left unsupervised.

Like a boat rocked by a sudden wave it swayed to the left and to the right, but Derdâ was the only one in the schoolyard who felt nauseated. The others kept their balance, but Derdâ fell like she was falling into the sea. She didn't drown, but they rolled her facedown so she wouldn't swallow her tongue. It didn't seem like she'd collapsed, it seemed like she'd just lain down.

When she came to she smelled Yeşim. She lifted her head to look for her teacher. But the infirmary was empty. She was lying on the cot where Yeşim had been. She couldn't hold her head up for very long. She rubbed her head into the pillow, crushing her hair into the pillow, but there wasn't a sound. Even if there was, Derdâ wouldn't have heard through her tears.

In one day she had caused both a death and a suicide. She squeezed her eyes shut but still she saw Yeşim and the girl from Yatırca. Maybe Derdâ didn't have an extra kidney, but she had double the consciences and the extra pains that came with them. She might not go down in medical history as the first person to have a double conscience, but still it was all too much for her little body. She felt like she would never be able to get out of bed.

"They're going to put me in prison," she whispered. "The gendarme will figure it out and they'll throw me in prison!"

But even before the gendarme there was another institution to be afraid of. The oldest institution in the world. Family. Or at least half of it. Mother. She didn't have a father. He had left for Istanbul four days after he'd gotten her mother pregnant and he never came back. That was twelve years ago. At least he was thoughtful enough to leave her mother pregnant so she wouldn't be left alone.

They'd married in the presence of God, an imam, and two witnesses, but then everyone else left and she was left with only God. And God would only come help her at the end of her life. It was her one and only prayer. "God, please take my life away so that I will be saved!" Eventually God would hear her—the miracle of death comes to us all—but she was not a patient woman. She married Derdâ off before the girl even had breasts. She was all out of patience. She'd waited eleven years. For the first two years they'd stayed with her husband's family, cursing her all the way for not having a boy. The rest of those years were spent cleaning the teachers' residence in town where she'd escaped with her daughter. But she felt dirty. And she was wasting time. Her twisted body was sick of following a bucket up and down the three floors of the teachers' residence, sick of destroying her knees, grinding them against the floor, sick of the bleach gnawing away at her hands. She wanted to get back to the village. Build a house, get a few animals.

Her daughter didn't want to stay at school anyway. If she did, she wouldn't have fainted like that in the school garden, now would she? The assistant director would not have called her to tell her to come and see her daughter. That scumbag assistant director, does he have any idea how much the minibus costs? Is he the one scrubbing the teachers' toilets? Is he the one coughing his lungs out from inhaling all that hydrochloric acid? She'd take her daughter out of school. If they tried to stop her, she'd kidnap her. She'd find a way. Then they'd go back to the village. In the end, she was one of us after all. Maybe she didn't have any money, but she did have Derdâ. Her relatives would help her find a way. Who wouldn't want an innocent eleven-year-old girl? If only they gave her a house and a few animals, she'd let Derdâ go just like that. She'd marry and make her mother comfortable. After all, a child owes it to her mother.

"Sister Saniye!"

She peeled her head away from the minibus window. She shook her thoughts away and gave the driver her fare. As they drove through the school gates she decided that on the way back Derdâ would sit on her lap so she wouldn't have to pay for her.

"Sister, your daughter's ill. But don't worry, it's nothing serious. Forgive us for making you come out all this way. But the girl will be so pleased just to see you."

Nezih spoke to Saniye. Then it was Saniye's turn. It was her turn to speak.

"Let me take my daughter, sir. I'll take her back to the village for a week. So she can rest. She'll feel better and then I'll bring her back."

Nezih's mind was on Yeşim. He was thinking that some people just never get used to it. Some people just never get used to this part of the country. *It was obvious,* he thought, *there was a strangeness about her from the day she arrived. She wasn't right in the head. Why else would someone try to kill themself?*

"What do you say, sir?"

"How's that?"

"The girl, let me take her to the village for a week."

"To the village? To Yatırca? But the road's blocked."

"No, I'll take her to Kurudere."

Nezih wasn't interested and he didn't extend the conversation any longer than he had to. His mind was on Yeşim. On her breasts to be more precise. He was thinking of that night he had touched them. That night in Yeşim's room when he sat on the chair by the side of her bed. That night he pressed one hand over the girl's mouth and pressed the other on her breasts. That night he looked into Yeşim's eyes and whispered, "I'll have you shot, they won't even be able to find your corpse!" That night Yeşim trembled in icy fear. He was thinking of that dark room where he came on the girl's face and told her as he left not to worry, that he wouldn't fuck her. But Yeşim was gone. Who was he going to touch now? Who was going to be a good girl and go clean her face off and act like nothing happened? Who could be more of a coward than Yeşim? The girls in their last year? Or the younger girls? Nazenin passed him by. Nazenin with her blond hair. *Why not?* he thought. He felt better.

"All right, take the girl. But make sure she's back in a week."

"God bless you, sir."

Nezih didn't like having his hand kissed. He held Saniye by her shoulders and made her stand up. *A beautiful woman,* he thought. *If only she didn't smell like bleach.*

Derdâ couldn't understand. She asked again.

"A whole week?"

Saniye was taking the girl's belongings out of her closet in the ward and packing them into two bags. She looked at Derdâ.

"The assistant principal gave us permission."

"But I have school work."

Saniye looked into Derdâ's eyes.

"You can catch up when you come back."

"So I'll be back a week from today?"

14

Saniye looked deep into Derdâ's eyes.

"Yes, my girl, what should we do in the village? I got a week off myself."

Better than being arrested, Derdâ thought. *Better than being taken away by the gendarmes.* She thought of her school books. She was having some problems with fractions. She'd have lots of time in the village to figure them out.

"Wait, let me go get my books from the classroom."

This time Saniye remained silent. She only looked up as the girl left, staring at the girl's long braid that bounced and swayed with every step. *They will like her,* she said to herself. And she smiled.

The classroom was empty. Derdâ opened her desk and took out her books and notebooks. She carefully slipped them into her bag. She hated it when the corners of the pages got bent. She was about to pack her math book when Nazenin came in.

"Where are you going?"

"My mother came. We're going to the village," said Derdâ. Whenever she was alone with Nazenin she felt a concentrated fear pounding in her forehead. She started to pack quickly so the fear wouldn't burst. She didn't even notice she was crumpling the pages.

"When are you coming back?"

"A week from today."

Nazenin was acting strangely. Her voice didn't have a trace of its usual violence. Usually it was like getting punched when she spoke to you. She never had to use her fists. But now she was only watching. Silently. Derdâ was trying to zip up her over-loaded bag, and she just watched. Nazenin was fifteen years old. In some places that's the same as twenty-five.

"You're coming back, right?" she asked.

Derdâ didn't know how to react to this sudden interest. She hadn't yet learned how to speak confidently.

"Of course I'm coming back. My mother said so. I'm coming back next week."

Derdâ slung her bag over her shoulder and took a step. But Nazenin blocked her path at just a comfortable slap distance away. Nazenin was a thick book taller than Derdâ but Derdâ stood up tall to make up the difference. For a few heartbeats Derdâ saw Nazenin, and Nazenin saw all the girls like Derdâ who had left. Not one had come back. And not one had ever known she wasn't coming back. She would go, too, when the day came. She would follow her uncle and never come back to this school ever again. She would leave. Leave and never come back. Nazenin stepped out of the way. Derdâ walked away. She wondered whether she should turn back and wave. But the thought scared her and she couldn't do it.

"Hey, Yatırca girl!"

Derdâ froze. She turned around. She saw a hand. A hand in the air. Nazenin's palm. A wave. And Derdâ smiled for the first time that day, maybe even that week.

Derdâ took small steps so she wouldn't slip on the slushy snow. Her legs ached and her ears were already red from the cold. She was listening to her mother.

"You wanted to bring all those books and now look, you can't walk."

"Are we going to Kurudere?"

"We're going to your aunt's. Do you remember your Aunt Mübarek? That's where we're going."

They had to get to the main road and get on the minibus before the biting cold went to their heads. Saniye warmed herself by talking.

"What happened at school today? They were all talking about something, but I didn't understand what."

Derdâ stared out in front of her. She wanted to press her face into her mother's chest. Out of shame, and because of the cold.

"There was a girl from our village. She fell off the bed and died. The gendarmes came. And Teacher Yeşim . . ."

But those who warm themselves up by talking don't listen. Saniye had already lifted her arms in the air and was fluttering like a silly bird to flag down a passing minibus.

When the white door slid open the warmth of the bodies inside hit their faces. They stepped up the single step and sat down. Derdâ didn't have to sit in her mother's lap after all because the driver didn't ask for Derdâ's fare. He was a distant relative of Saniye's. One of those endless, useless, good-for-nothing relatives.

The snow that had piled up on their collars melted and slid down the backs of their necks. The warm smell of the breath of fifteen people packed into a small minibus made them sleepy.

Their eyelids lowered and their frozen eyelashes melted and softened. Derdâ was sitting at the very back between her mother and an old man. Her head made pillows of their shoulders. The little girl fell asleep. As she slept she got smaller. And as she got smaller she had nightmares. She held the dead girl from Yatırca in her arms and cried until she woke up. When she woke up she didn't remember anything.

"Sister Saniye!"

They were in Kurudere.

Kurudere looked more like a rugged, undulating piece of land than a village. Smoke rose up from the windowed humps and stained the white sky. There were no streets or addresses in Kurudere. There were only man-made humps huddling close together for protection from the cold. And people lived inside, although just barely. Forty-three households, all right under each other's noses. The Kender branch of the Aleyzam tribe. The broken one. The good-for-nothing one. A place good for the carcasses of dead ants and nothing else. Where Sheik Gazi didn't even bother to stop by. A very dry stream. So dry that it wasn't really there. Maybe it never had been. Or maybe, seeing the village, it had changed course.

People don't speak in Kurudere. They grumble when they're angry and they mutter when they pray; between there is silence. And ravens. And the loudspeaker of the mosque: "People of Kurudere, His Highness Sheik Gazi Hoca Efendi is going to visit Girinti village. We will go welcome him. The minibuses will leave at nine o'clock tomorrow morning." Then crackling from the speaker and perhaps a cough or two from the imam. Then silence again. As if nothing existed. As if everyone were holding their breath. Forty-three households. Forty-three homes, each like a cracked jar full of mystery.

"Sister, it's us."

Mübarek looked at Saniye and Derdâ looked at Mübarek. Mübarek was so fat you couldn't see the door behind her, though the doors in Kurudere were so small you had to bend over to go inside. A head poked out from behind Mübarek. A girl about Derdâ's age who came up to the fat woman's chest came out.

"What's going on, Saniye?" said Mübarek, or rather, grumbled.

"Aren't you going to invite us in? Let us in so we can sit down for a while."

Mübarek moved out of the way like a door opening, and the four of them went into one of the humps. It was like being buried alive.

"She's grown so much!" said Saniye as she stroked Fehime's head. She was Mübarek's youngest daughter.

"She's eleven," said Mübarek.

"Derdâ's eleven, too."

Mübarek got right to the point.

"What are you here for, Saniye?"

Saniye was ready. She had thought about what she was going to say on the minibus.

"They kicked us out of the teachers' residence. And the girl's sick. I have no one else to turn to, where could I go? I don't have anyone but you."

Mübarek's response was ready, too, but was threadbare from being used for so many years.

"You should have thought about that before you married that guy from Yatırca. What happened to that dog—any news?"

"No, sister. No news, nothing. I hope he's dead."

"*İnşallah!*"

They fell silent. They looked at each other. Mostly Fehime. She looked at Saniye. She looked at Derdâ. They examined each other like animals until the tea was ready.

As Fehime poured the tea, Mübarek switched legs; the one she'd been sitting on had gone numb. She said, "Let's wait until Ebcet comes home. Maybe he knows someone at the teachers' residence."

Saniye looked at Fehime as she warmed her hands around her tea glass.

"Fehime, show Derdâ around the village."

Fehime saw her mother nod approval and she walked toward the door. Derdâ followed her. When the door closed behind them Saniye began to speak.

"I want her to get married. Do you know anyone? That's why I brought her here."

Mübarek's mouth gaped open in laughter; she looked like a hippopotamus. Then she closed her mouth and spoke: "So? First you send the girl to school, and now you want a husband for her! Who would want a girl who's been to school? Poor girl, she's no good anymore!"

Saniye had already considered this, but what could she have done? They had nothing; she had to send her away to state school. To boarding school. Would she give her up to the state if she could have looked after her herself?

"What could I have done, sister? I had no choice but to send her away. But it's over now. I got her back. She's not going back to school. What's the situation here? Is there anyone suitable, someone with means?"

Mübarek leaned back against the wall covered in carpets. She thought as she stared at the ceiling: What if Ebcet wanted Saniye? What if Saniye stayed here for good? What if Saniye doesn't have

20

enough money to go anywhere else? If Derdâ marries someone decent, Saniye will get the bride's price and she'll leave. Then she spoke and told Saniye one by one what the ceiling had told her.

Fehime saw the hem of Derdâ's school uniform hanging down from under her coat. She knew the color well. It was the color of school.

"Do you know how to read?"

Derdâ took some snow in her hands, pressed it into a ball, and threw it between two humps.

"Of course I know how to read. I'm in fifth year. Don't you go to school?"

Fehime was trying to scrape off the snow stuck under her rubber boots with a broken branch.

"No."

They fell silent. There was nothing else to say.

"Do you think it would work?"

Saniye was excited. She could practically see a few animals and a house already.

"Of course it would. It'll be spring in a few weeks. They'll all come. They'll come to kiss Sheik Gazi's hand."

Saniye was even more excited.

"So they really come from so far away?"

"Of course they do. Just be patient. I'll talk to Ebcet, too. He'll find a way."

Saniye's heart was pounding.

"You swear it's true?"

"I swear, they come every year. They get girls from the village and leave. And they pay lots of money. But tell me something. Let's say you get the money—what will you do?"

"Forgive me, sister, but I wouldn't stay here."

Mübarek felt happy for the first time since her sister arrived. She was so happy that she stood up and filled Saniye's empty tea glass herself.

"I'll go to Tomurcuk . . . Animals . . . House . . . A nice spot . . ."

Mübarek didn't listen. She didn't care about the rest.

Ebcet studied the newcomers closely as he drew the first drag of his cigarette. Mübarek and Saniye had settled themselves in a dark corner of the room like cockroaches, whispering to one another. Derdâ was teaching Fehime how to write her name. *Why the hell did they have to come now?* thought Ebcet. Two more mouths to feed. He hardly earned enough to feed himself. What were they going to eat, this woman and her bastard daughter? If he threw them out, he would be disgraced in the eyes of the villagers. What did Sheik Gazi say? You should be a father to the fatherless. But how? The snack shop was not doing well. Sales were down since the gendarme started cracking down on smuggled cigarettes. Nobody's business was good in the village. His thoughts made him worry and he stood up. Everybody fell silent. Except Mübarek.

"Do you want something?"

"Come with me."

Mübarek followed her husband. They left the house and went out into the cold. Ebcet lit another cigarette off the one he was smoking.

"When are they leaving?"

"That's what I wanted to tell you," said Mübarek. "Saniye wants Derdâ to marry. Maybe you could tell Sheik Gazi's son. Someone might come up."

Ebcet held the smoke in his throat and looked at Mübarek in the dark. God had seen him! He exhaled all his worries with the smoke leaving his mouth.

"All right, I'll speak to him. How old is she?"

"Eleven," said Mübarek.

"*Maşallah*," said Ebcet.

The approach to Girinti village looked like a car lot. People from all over had come to see Sheik Gazi. They gathered together in the village square kissing the old people's hands and offering each other cigarettes. They hardly had time to speak. Then a six-year-old boy shouted, "They're here!"

A caravan of four cars twice as long as normal cars pulled up into the village. The crowd swarmed the cars. The villagers had already decided among themselves who would be the first to kiss the Gazi's feet. The chosen ones waited for the doors to open. Which car was Sheik Gazi in? Who would be the one lucky enough to kiss his feet first? Which door would he come out of? No one could see a damn thing through the tinted windows!

When Ebcet cried "Allah" all the people waiting to kiss the Gazi's feet glared at him with blind jealousy, forgetting entirely about the person that was about to step out of the just-opened door. Sheik Gazi was slow to get out of the car; he was eighty-one, after all. His feet came first and Ebcet caught them before they could touch the ground and kissed them, though he couldn't see exactly what he was kissing, the end of his robe or the leather of his shoe. Then he felt a hand on his head. Sheik Gazi's hand. Ecbet was still kneeling. The old man supported himself against his head like a walking stick and slowly got out of the car. But Ebcet's mission wasn't done. He stood up and took hold of Sheik Gazi's hands, kissing them before touching them to his forehead. Both hands. Tears ran from his eyes. Once more God had smiled on this poor servant! He knew that everyone was watching him. They all wished they were him. The whole Aleyzam tribe, the whole Hikmet Tariqat, everyone. Two thin hands took his cheeks and raised his head. Then he looked into Sheik Gazi's eyes. Time stopped for a few seconds. Then the same hands lowered Ebcet's head and Sheik Gazi touched his lips on the forehead before him. Roses bloomed on Ebcet's brow.

Gido Agha, sixty-one, was the head of the Aleyzam tribe. He controlled a large share of the diesel oil the tribe smuggled over the Iranian border. He didn't trust Sheik Gazi, an old, senile man that he nevertheless had to tolerate. The Aleyzam tribe was a flock of men that had worked as government-sponsored militia for five years before flipping sides and becoming terrorists fighting against the government, choosing sides according to the political climate at the time. Gido Agha was their shepherd. He lived in a villa the size of ten houses. Like every other house in the region, it had a room reserved for honored guests. Sheik Gazi had already dozed off in the guest room, still in his white robe and turban. He was very old. He hardly spoke, or listened for that matter. His function was that of a flag; he was placed somewhere prominent for these village visits, and used as a focal point for people to gather around. While Sheik Gazi billowed in the wind, his son Hıdır Arif handled the affairs of the Tariqat.

Tayyar was the only one in the room who was standing. He was a judo master, made more of muscle and sinew than flesh and bones. He stood behind Sheik Gazi, his eyes recording everything like two cameras; the intensity of his gaze suggested he was trying to detect dust particles in the air. He was six foot four and weighed well over two hundred pounds. His arms bulged out from under his robe but his forehead was too narrow for his face. He had a mangled nose and fingers thick like the barrel of a gun. He kept his hands clasped under his sash. He was Sheik Gazi's adopted son and he'd been with him since he was seven. He was Palestinian. His mother, father, and four sisters were killed by Israeli bombs, and when three million Palestinians fled in the aftermath of the Six-Day War, members of the Hikmet Tariqat helped him cross the border into Turkey and introduced him to Sheik Gazi. His dark, seven-year-old eyes had deeply affected the Sheik, who said, "Cry as much as you want my child, for you will never weep again."

From that day on he was sheltered in the shadow of Sheik Gazi, growing up under his wing. He became the eyes, mouth, and fist of his spiritual father, visiting every city and town in the country, whispering the words of Sheik Gazi into the ears of members of the Hikmet Tariqat, communicating his orders and his demands. As the years passed, Sheik Gazi became more and more withdrawn and Tayyar became the old man's sole messenger, traveling the world to never cry again.

The Hikmet Tariqat differed from other religious sects in the region because their sheik was homeless. Hikmet Tariqat members did not have a particular medrese, nor did they frequent any dervish lodge. Homeless Sheik Gazi was born a refugee to the world and he would die one, too. He didn't own a home and he wasn't an officially registered resident of anywhere. He moved from one disciple's home to another every three months, living on whatever was offered him. Homelessness was the founding principle of the Hikmet Tariqat. In their eyes, borders between states were fictitious. They didn't believe in nation states. There were only believers and non-believers. Their members were scattered all over the world. Homeless. Although being homeless didn't mean one couldn't own property; there were not a few title deeds in Hıdır Arif's name. Hıdır Arif lived in Istanbul but also spent time in London, waiting for his father to die. Most of the year he was in Istanbul, in a neighborhood called Çemendağ. He owned 221 of the 226 buildings in the neighborhood. The remaining five had been built illegally without municipal permission. His plan was to apply pressure on the municipality to have those five buildings demolished as soon as possible. There was also a mosque in Çemendağ. But Hıdır Arif did his best to ensure that the mosque couldn't reach the Hikmet Tariqat members.

But more than anything else Hıdır Arif was a businessman. A businessman who owned a supermarket chain in London and livestock somewhere near Hamburg, and who managed construction projects in Istanbul. He was busy. And it made him angry when he had to leave everything at the drop of a hat to parade his father through villages like a circus animal. But the believers couldn't rest easy until they'd seen their flag. When they were restless they called Hıdır Arif to complain: "We paid the last installment, but our houses still aren't finished." They complained all the time. Endless complaints. Men like Ebcet, now kneeling before him, never stopped bothering him. What did the fool want from him now?

"I have a girl, my niece. She's eleven. An appropriate . . ."

"You have a photograph?" asked Hıdır Arif.

Lost in his own troubles, Ebcet wasn't listening and didn't understand.

"What?"

Hıdır Arif sighed and repeated his question; a businessman needed patience.

"Take her photograph and send it to me. We'll look into it."

"May God bless you, may God grant . . ."

"Alright then," said Hıdır Arif and he cast his eyes about the room. He noticed the wrinkles on Gido Agha's face, like knife wounds, and then the saliva dribbling from his father's lips. He watched the men genuflecting before him, whispering into each other's ears. Hıdır Arif was forty-four. He had three wives and eight children. He'd graduated from Princeton with a degree in economics. He left for the United States sixteen years ago, swearing never to return to Turkey. Why would he? To sit beside a good-for-nothing like Gido Agha in a cesspool of a town like Girinti? This wasn't for him—villages and villagers. *I'll transfer everything to London, and I'll never come back*, he thought. Then he thought of the view of the Thames from his office in London and he smiled. Gido noticed it and gave Hıdır Arif a tough but friendly tap on the knee.

Squatting on the ground with her face in her hands, Fehime bit her lips as she watched Derdâ being photographed. She was tired of feeling jealous. She'd have to get used to watching; she was condemned to do it all her life. She'd watch until she lost her mind, her insanity rising until she died. Like all the other village girls, Fehime was nothing but a pair of eyes, eyes that opened at birth and closed at death. Her mouth, her voice, served no purpose at all.

Checking that no one else was around, Ebcet said, "Uncover your head." Derdâ undid her black headscarf and left it around her neck. A long black braid of hair slid down her back like an exotic snake. Ebcet had bought his camera from the only white goods shop in town and they had warned him: "There has to be enough light—it won't work without light." Now under a dull sky, Ebcet did his best to position Derdâ's face toward the light. At the same time, he thought of how her buyer would reimburse him for the camera. Not only would he pay him for the machine, but he'd have to be the one to shoulder the sin of making an eleven-year-old girl uncover her head. And of course that would mean more money.

It was the first time Derdâ had had her picture taken and she didn't know if she should smile or not. But she wanted to so in the end she couldn't help it and smiled. Ebcet couldn't help himself and slapped her.

"You'll make me a sinner! Now go inside!" Fehime couldn't help but laugh and he barked, "You, too!"

The girls quickly disappeared behind the door. Ebcet mumbled to himself as he turned the camera over in his hands: "How do you turn this damn thing off?"

The time when taking a picture was considered sinful was long gone.

A month had passed since the pictures were taken. It was spring. The snow was melting, and patches of the earth were emerging over the countryside.

"Don't cry anymore. Don't you see that I'm sick, too? But you don't even care. Here, have some soup. Come on now," Saniye said.

Saniye set the bowl down beside Derdâ and left the room. She found Mübarek burying potatoes in the ash at the bottom of the stove and said, "The girl's sick as well."

"She'll get used to it."

"She's so thin, she'll die. She won't eat."

"She'll eat, she'll have to. There's not much time left anyway. They'll be here next week. And then you'll find peace . . ." She stopped herself before she said, "and so will I."

The next morning Derdâ woke up and figured it must be the day she was returning to school; she woke up early, got her things together, then waited an hour for her mother to open her eyes. In that hour, she thought about the girl from Yatırca, about her teacher Yeşim, and only when she thought of how Nazenin had waved to her as she left could she drive away the knot in her throat. But her reverie abruptly came to an end when Saniye woke up and saw her.

"Where do you think you're going?" she snapped.

"Aren't we going back to school?"

She felt like she'd died and come back to life when Saniye said, "You won't be going to school anymore."

Saniye stood up. "Let me have a look at you." She went into Derdâ's room and saw that the soup bowl was empty. She was pleased. The little girl wasn't going to starve herself to death. But then she noticed a stain on the wall. A dripping stain. She'd thrown her soup at the wall. She slapped Derdâ with the back of her hand.

From then on, the girl was kept prisoner. She lived deep in the corner of the room. An iron ring circled her ankle and was attached to an iron chain. The chain was fastened to a ring nailed into the wall. Four times Derdâ had tried to escape. But they'd always found her. Everyone was tired of her causing trouble so they chained her to the wall. She'd heard she was going to be married off. So there was something else for Fehime to be jealous about. Fehime bit her lips even more when she learned where Derdâ would be going after she got married. Not that she knew where such a place even was. She only knew it was somewhere far from here.

Saniye felt remorseful for striking her. She knew she only had a week to train Derdâ, and they'd send her back if she was violent toward her husband. She knelt down beside the little girl and hugged her.

"Don't be scared, my child. I'm only thinking of you. I'm doing all of this for your own well-being. Look at the state we are in. How can I look after you? I also married when I was your age."

But she was lying—she got married at thirteen.

"Mother," Derdâ said. "I'll never see you again."

"That's not true. I'll come visit you. You'll go first and then I'll come to see you later."

She was telling the truth. At least she believed she was, because she had the shortest lasting but most infectious human malady: hope.

29

They cried together and this helped. Derdâ didn't throw her second bowl of soup against the wall. She even ate some bread. Mübarek was right. The girl was adjusting. Like everyone else in the world who kept on living even though they knew all too well that one day they would die.

The following day Derdâ's chain was removed and the mark around her ankle rubbed with balm. Two days later Mübarek took her measurements and sewed a dress from some dark red fabric that Ebcet had brought. Fehime went quiet and never spoke again. Three days later Derdâ's braid was undone and her hair was washed and combed. Four days later Derdâ burned her notebooks and books in the stove. Five days later Ebcet was arrested by the gendarme for selling contraband cigarettes. Six days later he was set free. Seven days later, late in the afternoon, there was a knock on the door.

A young man and an old man in religious robes entered the house. The old man's beard reached down to his chest, but the young man's beard was only a little below his chin. Ebcet kissed the old man's hand and the two men exchanged greetings. The young man remained silent. "He doesn't speak," said the old man. They sat around the low wooden table. Mübarek and Saniye served soup. They waited for the women to leave the room before they began to speak.

The old man's name was Ubeydullah and the young man's name was Bezir and he was his son. Ubeydullah spoke and Ebcet and Bezir listened.

"We cannot stay long, Ebcet. With God's permission, we will take the girl and go to Istanbul. The marriage will take place there. We'll return after we handle some business there. No one takes proper care of our shops while we're away. We need to get there as soon as possible."

Was it time to call Derdâ in and show her to them? How much would they pay? Ebcet nodded his head as he calculated possible figures. But first he had to exchange social graces.

"How is the High Sheik? Did you have a chance to see him? Is he in good health?"

"He is in fine health. You do have an ID card for the girl, correct?"

The very words were a comfort to Ebcet. Ubeydullah was obviously as eager to finish the job as he was.

"Yes. Everything is in order as agreed. Shall I call her in?"

"No," Ubeydullah said. He took an envelope from beneath his robe and handed it to Ebcet. "First, take this."

Ebcet took the envelope. What was he supposed to do? Should he count the money then and there? It was his first time selling a girl. His own two daughters had committed suicide seven years ago. On the same day. The very same morning. Side by side. With the very same rifle. First one, then the other. And Fehime's turn had not yet come. Seeing him hesitate, Ubeydullah laughed.

"Come on, open it. Open it and see."

How easy it was to do business with such a worldly man! Ebcet opened the envelope and counted the banknotes one by one, shifting them from one hand to the other. His breathing quickened as he counted. It was all there in his hand. The cost of the camera, the atonement for the sin he had committed, Saniye's share, his own share. He didn't know what to say. He began to mutter, "May God make it so . . ."

When Ubeydullah stood up, Bezir followed his father.

"We should be going. We have a long journey ahead of us."

Before Ubeydullah could finish, Ebcet turned toward the inner room and shouted, "Mübarek! Bring her in."

The door swung open and Derdâ stepped into the room. Mübarek held her by her shoulders and pushed her forward.

Only Derdâ's eyes were visible. First she looked at Ubeydullah. She felt fear well up inside her. Then she saw Bezir. And the fear redoubled. She turned her head and held her hand out to her mother now standing beside her. Saniye took her hand and then let it go. Derdâ had a few things packed in her school bag: her dark red dress, underwear, and a pair of shoes. Bezir took the bag from Saniye and followed Ubeydullah to the door. He didn't look at Derdâ once. Mübarek shoved Derdâ forward and then turned and looked at Saniye. They were both crying, but tears couldn't change anything now.

Bezir opened the back door of the car and stood waiting for Ubeydullah to get Derdâ's ID card from Ebcet. Derdâ took a few steps forward then collapsed an arm's distance from the car. She was wearing a black chador, so no one could see the stain.

It was eleven-year-old Derdâ's first period. The bleeding was so heavy her blood pressure plummeted and she fainted. Ubeydullah and Bezir went to stay with a relative in Girinti and would return two days later. Saniye washed Derdâ and put her to sleep. Ebcet was preparing an apology for Ubeydullah, he worried that the old man would be displeased by this unfortunate incident and might abandon the agreement. But the old man said, "It is auspicious," and he felt relieved, tucking the envelope full of money under his pillow.

The second visit was even shorter than the first. They came, got Derdâ, and left. Now her blood was flowing. She had nothing else to shed. Not even a tear fell from her eyes as she looked at her mother for the last time.

It took them fifteen hours to reach Istanbul and another hour to reach Çemendağ. They stopped three times on the way but Derdâ never once ate. They didn't say more than sixteen words in the sixteen hours on the road. Derdâ didn't sleep at all. She looked out the window and fiddled with her black gloves. She took them off and put them on again and again without the men in the front noticing. She made a fist and put her glove on and flapped the empty fingers around. Finally, the door opened and she got out of the car.

They went up to the fourth floor of an apartment building. It was Derdâ's first ride in an elevator. Two doors on the fourth floor were already cracked open when they arrived, a collection of heads peering out from behind each door. Women kissed Ubeydullah's hand and took Bezir's bags before disappearing inside. Men and women filed into separate apartments. For a moment, it seemed that everyone had forgotten Derdâ standing by the elevator, but the woman saw her and pulled her inside. Derdâ entered the women's apartment.

The women surrounded her and took off her chador to examine her. Derdâ felt totally numb. One of them asked her name but Derdâ told her it was none of her business and they all laughed at her. But the woman got her revenge when Derdâ went to the bathroom. She followed her in and slapped Derdâ across the face. Derdâ tried to lock the bathroom door, but saw there wasn't a key in the keyhole to turn. Doors only locked from the outside in the Hikmet Tariqat. The master of the house was the sole keeper of the keys.

They had been traveling all night so Ubeydullah and Bezir slept until noon prayer. Derdâ wasn't tired but the women insisted. They showed her to a bedroom and closed the door behind her, and Derdâ closed her eyes. She opened them when she heard the key turning in the door. She looked up at the ceiling. She could make out fractions in the patterns in the cement. She tried to add and subtract them. When she started thinking about her mother she shut her eyes immediately. Derdâ gave up on her mother in that bed.

Ubeydullah and Regaip walked down Çemendağ's main street and entered the apartment building. They went up to the fourth floor and into the men's apartment. In the living room men sat on their knees, listening to the imam recite the Koran. Ubeydullah told Regaip to sit down beside Bezir, who didn't even turn to look at him. There was a knock on the door and someone opened it.

Derdâ entered the living room with a woman no older than she was. She told Derdâ to sit down. The imam's voice filled the silent room. Then he fell silent. He opened the marriage registry, found an empty page, and carefully inscribed the name Derdâ. He looked up at Regaip, and Ubeydullah said, "Regaip." The imam inscribed his name, too. Then he added the names of the witnesses and completed his list with the name of the groom,

Bezir. He asked them the amount of money agreed upon, using the customary Islamic euphemisms. Ubeydullah told him how much he had paid for the girl. The imam looked at Regaip, who nodded his head in agreement.

Then the imam began to read verses from the Koran when suddenly he looked at Regaip and chanted a long sentence which began, "By the order of God and the laws and decrees of our Prophet . . . being her representative, do you accept to give Derdâ . . . to her suitor Bezir as wife?" Regaip said, "Yes." He repeated the question twice more. Twice more the reply was yes. The imam turned to Bezir and intoned another very long sentence ending, "Will you take her?" and for the first time in days Bezir spoke. He never said much, and now he only repeated the same word three times: "Yes."

"I now pronounce you man and wife," declared the imam. He cleared his throat and began reciting more verses from the Koran.

While all of this was happening, Derdâ stared at her knees covered in a black cloth and carefully studied the lion figure in the carpet below her knees. The lion was lying near three trees, watching her. Derdâ stared into the lion's eyes until the woman behind her reached over and touched her shoulder. And just as she was dreaming of the lion leaping out of the carpet and devouring everyone, she lifted her head and saw a hand stretched out to her lips. It was Regaip's right hand.

Ubeydullah spoke. "Come, kiss your father's hand."

She kissed the hand and brought it to her forehead, wondering if what she had just heard was true. Was Regaip really her father? She'd never seen him before, and she couldn't stop staring. But her gaze was unreciprocated; Regaip stood up after Bezir and left the room. Just as she was about to cry, "Father, take me with you!" another hand was extended to her lips. By the time she finished kissing Ubeydullah's hand, her father was already gone. She kissed several more hands and touched them to her forehead. No one seemed to notice that Derdâ was running a fever well over a hundred degrees. The little girl's forehead burned like a stove.

For two days Derdâ was taken in and out of various government offices. She had more photographs taken, but she no longer smiled. For two nights she burned with fever, which broke only after a night of heavy sweating. The women woke her up the next morning and told her to wear her long dark red trench coat, and to cover just her head with a scarf. They brought her to a car. Bezir drove and Ubeydullah sat beside him. They drove along narrow streets and avenues and as the car slowed near a bus stop Derdâ wanted to open the door and run, but instead the door flew open and Regaip got in and sat down beside her. It was the fourth time she had seen Regaip. Derdâ watched her father silently. He stared ahead into space. Derdâ brought her lips to his ear and whispered, "Father." Regaip brought his index finger to his lips.

Derdâ didn't give up. She whispered again, "Take me away from here."

Ubeydullah turned around and said, "You know what to say, don't you?"

Regaip held onto the headrest in front of him and straightened himself, saying "Yes, yes, I know."

Derdâ had no intention of giving up. She whispered again, "Father, why didn't you ever come?"

Regaip waited for a garbage truck to pull up beside them. The traffic was heavy and when the truck revved into gear, he spoke into the girl's ear, pretending to cough.

"I'm not your father."

Derdâ didn't whisper again. She just stared into the leather back of Bezir's seat. She planned to jump out of the car the next time they stopped at an intersection, but the child lock was on.

Derdâ uncovered her head when Ubeydullah told her to. They were in the waiting room of a building with high ceilings. When their names were announced, they stood up and went through the designated door. A security guard led them along a corridor, stopped in front of a door, and pushed a button on the wall. Two seconds later a green light flashed under the button. Their guide opened the door and showed them in—three men and one little girl. A man in a suit sat behind an enormous desk. Smiling, he stood up and held his hand out to Ubeydullah. He didn't shake hands with anyone else. When he sat back he asked in broken Turkish, "Are the papers ready?" Ubeydullah said they were.

Ubeydullah then introduced Regaip, a future employee in his furniture company, and his daughter, Derdâ, to the commercial attaché to the UK. The attaché looked at Derdâ and told her there were very good schools in his country. After forms were filled out and a few questions were answered, it was settled that both father and daughter would be given a five-year visa. As the attaché picked up his phone to communicate the necessary orders, he offered his guests something to drink. Ubeydullah declined but the attaché took a piece of chocolate from a jar on his desk and offered it to Derdâ. The little girl took it and looked at Ubeydullah. The old man nodded his head and she unwrapped the chocolate, put it in her mouth, and started chewing. Suddenly she grimaced and vomited the chocolate and everything else in her stomach onto the coffee table in front of the attaché's desk. After three days she still felt nauseated from high fever. She vomited onto the cover page of one of three magazines on the coffee table between Ubeydullah's and Bezir's knees, the one with the Queen of England emblazoned on the cover.

Ubeydullah was the angriest. No surprise considering that he was the one who most passionately swore his loyalty to the Queen of England twenty-six years ago when he became a British citizen. As they were both British nationals, Bezir and the attaché were not overly put out.

Regaip took Derdâ in his arms and carried her out of the consulate, wiping the wet hair out of her eyes and off her brow and pressing her head to his chest, like he was a father who had abandoned his child before she was even born. Maybe that was why Derdâ had hope. She opened her eyes and said, "Father." This time Regaip didn't deny it. But he didn't admit it either. He didn't say a word running to the car with Derdâ in his arms.

When they arrived in Çemendağ, they stopped at the Sheik Gazi clinic where they entrusted Derdâ to female doctors before performing their noon prayers in the small mosque in the clinic's garden. Rising after his prayers, Ubeydullah said to Regaip, "That's all we need from you now. You'll go your own way, and we'll go ours." But Regaip had no intention of going anywhere.

"Take me with you!"

Ubeydullah had not expected this. He assumed he'd paid Regaip enough to satisfy him.

"Where?" he asked, surprised.

"To wherever you're going."

Hearing Regaip's tone, Bezir took two quick steps forward. One sudden move and he could have broken Regaip's arm, but he stopped when he felt Ubeydullah's hand on his chest.

The old man fixed his gaze on Regaip and slowly intoned, "We have an agreement. We take the girl and go. And you stay."

Steadying his eyes on Bezir, waiting for his father's signal to attack, Regaip asked, "And if I go to the police?" He said the words slowly, calmly, but not as an obvious threat.

"What is it you want? Tell me!" Ubeydullah shouted, unable to restrain himself. He was tired from standing for so long; he leaned on Bezir's shoulder for support. Negotiating was what he did best, but now his voice was trembling. Normally he could negotiate for anything and with anyone, with the devil, with God, with anyone.

"I'll go with you and then I'll disappear. That's all. I don't want anything else. Take me to England with you, and then I'll go my own way."

"You pay for your own ticket," Ubeydullah interrupted. He was in no state to come up with any other way to silence him. He was tired and he was concerned about the health of a young girl he'd just bought for his son. He was worried about his factories, the ones he called his shops. He was worn out by this wretched man's insistence and by the thought of having gone to such pains for his son. *Now what*, he thought. *The swine will come with us and will surely cause us grief. Will I be dogged by this man until the girl comes of age? Should I give him a job? Maybe it would be better to keep him close, so I can keep track of him. But I won't pay for his ticket! He'll pay himself! God damn him. The sly bastard.*

He stopped himself and said, "How do I know you won't cause trouble? If you're just going to cause trouble, then don't come. You'll never leave my sight and you'll work for me, understood?"

"We'll see."

"What's your line of work?" Ubeydullah asked.

"Don't have one. I was a ranger in the government militia."

Though a keen negotiator, Ubeydullah's patience was at the limit. "What were you doing in Istanbul then?"

Regaip's lips curled into a frozen smile and his tongue lashed like a razor between his teeth. "I killed people. When your men found me, I'd just been let out of jail."

Killers did not intimidate Ubeydullah. When it came to sheer violence, there were hundreds of men around him who could outdo Regaip. Only thieves scared Ubeydullah. He didn't hesitate a moment more.

"All right then," he said. "You'll be a bodyguard."

"We'll see," Regaip said, deliberately aggravating the men even more. "Let's just get there first and then we'll see."

Bezir's right hand seized Regaip's neck like a knife thrown at a target and yanked the man up into the air. Regaip could hardly breathe, struggling to balance on his toes. People in the clinic garden turned to look but when Ubeydullah shouted "Bezir!" he released Regaip's neck as fast as he'd grabbed it.

Coughing, Regaip forced a smile and said, "You want to kill me? You wouldn't kill your own father-in law, would you?"

Regaip insisted they all travel together so they couldn't double-cross him. But when he couldn't get a seat on their plane, they all had to travel the next day and Ubeydullah had to forfeit his tickets. The police kept close surveillance on Ubeydullah. Now they had an extra day to kill, so he told Bezir to drive them to a cemetery. There Ubeydullah recited verses from the Koran at the grave of Yakup Hodja Efendi, Sheik Gazi's brother. Yakup had been nomadic just like his brother, moving from one place to another all his life, and was buried where he had died. There was a wooden fountain beside his tomb, so the whole thing looked like a small mausoleum. At least that was the intention. If they could have, they'd have made a tomb out of the man himself. Just the way it was with his brother.

Derdâ was tasked with pulling out all the weeds covering the grave. When the car pulled into the cemetery a boy about Derdâ's age watched it drive down the cemetery's lane. Now he approached them with two tanks of water.

"Shall I pour some water, uncle?"

Ubeydullah frowned at the boy and continued to loudly recite from the Koran before quickly falling off into his typical mumbling. But sensing that the boy wasn't going to leave them alone, he lifted his head and signaled to the grave with his eyes.

The boy stepped toward the grave and carefully began to pour water over the grave where Derdâ had already cleared, watching the water seep into the soil. Derdâ angrily continued to pull out the weeds, and the boy poured water into the holes left in the earth. They moved in silence around the grave. There were other members of the Hikmet Tariqat who had come to the cemetery to visit the graves of their relatives and Bezir stood silently listening to their stories. Whatever it was they were telling him couldn't have been very interesting because he kept looking around over his shoulders.

The boy had finished watering the grave and went to fill the marble basin at its base. Though he rarely saw birds come to drink from the basin, he wanted to diligently fulfill his task to ensure a good tip. He opened the second tank and began to fill the basin. Then he saw a pair of hands stretching out to the tank's spout, held close together as if in handcuffs. They were covered with dirt. The boy raised his head and his eyes met Derdâ's for the first time. He shifted the barrel and began pouring water over her hands. Derdâ washed her two white hands under the stream of water. This kept them close to one another, in fact too close.

"Thank you," Derdâ said.

The boy was about to say "you're welcome" when a hand seized him by the collar and dragged him away. Then Bezir lifted him into the air and tossed him like a stone. Ubeydullah lifted his head, looked at his son, and began reciting the Koran even more loudly; Bezir understood. He took a few coins from his pocket and gave them to the boy dusting himself off. He stood up and picked up his tanks. First he shot a glance at Bezir and then he looked at Derdâ. Then he turned and walked away. Ubeydullah closed the Koran in his hand, still mumbling, and then pronounced a clear "Amen" for everyone to hear.

Ubeydullah imagined he was performing prayers in his house in London as he walked through the maze of steel benches at the airport, running his prayer beads through his fingers. Bezir and Regaip carried the suitcases, and Derdâ walked behind them with her schoolbag flung over her hated black chador. Her mouth gaped open in surprise as she took in the immensity of the building. It was the first time she'd been to an airport.

But her wonder came to an end when she remembered how much she despised each and every person she had known in her short life. Now there were people everywhere. She was surrounded by them, by all these people, people hurrying past her. They were racing past her, going the same direction, not seeing the girl dressed in black. *Why don't they understand*, Derdâ thought. *I am walking beside them. I am here with them. But nobody cares. They don't even see me. They're blind. Or maybe it's this black robe, my cloak of invisibility.*

Three hours later a stewardess peered down into the only visible part of Derdâ's face and smiled at her with pity before helping her fasten her seat belt. Half an hour later the plane's wheels disappeared into its white belly, Derdâ looked down at Istanbul, and the plane flew away like a migrant bird.

For a while she thought of the girl from Yatırca and her teacher Yeşim. As if they were right there before her eyes. One cried as the other spoke to her. And then slowly their faces faded away. She'd learned the word from Nazenin and she said it just like her. She said it to herself in her mind, in one sharp exhalation: *Fuck!* It felt good. So she said it again, *Fuck, fuck, fuck!* and an imperceptible smile flickered on her face. No one could hear her. *Just people*, she thought. *They can't see me, they can't hear me. I'll say it a thousand times for every one of them. Fuck, fuck, fuck, fuck, fuck, fuck, fuck,* "fuck, fuck, fuck . . ." A few of them she even whispered out loud, only to mock the people mute to her profanity. She pronounced the "k" a little more loudly. Ubeydullah was sitting next to her and noticed the little girl moving her lips. He was pleased, assuming she was either praying out of fear or reciting a verse from the Koran—Ebcet had told Ubeydullah that Derdâ had been sent to a Koran course when she was five.

When she had recited a thousand *fucks*, she tilted her head back and looked at the buttons above her. She noticed a circular stain in the overhead light. She looked more closely. It was a fly, still alive. Somehow it had gotten inside the cover and it got stuck inside. It buzzed helplessly behind the little plastic cover, unable to escape. Derdâ felt no pity, felt nothing at all, and switched on the lamp.

Derdâ watched everything with intense curiosity. A minivan had picked them up at Heathrow Airport and they were pulling onto the ring road. Derdâ sat by the window. Though she hadn't spent much time in cars, she'd already decided it was the best spot. But it wasn't because a window seat let her watch the scenery. In a window seat there was one less person next to her. Derdâ was learning. The fewer the better. But now the scenery was new. She gazed out over green fields and marveled at the farm houses along the highway. It was all like the pictures in the books she'd once read. She looked at everything. Signs, people in passing cars, clouds, and giant power plants. Her eyes burned from looking so much, they ached from the sensory overload.

They were driving at ninety kilometers per hour but she didn't want to leave a single image behind. Nothing escaped her eagle eye. Sometimes she missed things as they sped by—a building or a bridge—but she immediately turned her head. Back. But she turned too quickly, loosened the black chador wrapped tightly around her, and everything went black. She wanted to pull the cloth tight around her cheeks by adjusting the pin under her chin but she couldn't—she was afraid she might miss something in the passing scenery.

She was fascinated by everything she saw, her eyes moist with pleasure and surprise, hardly blinking. Traffic picked up when they arrived in London. Just when Derdâ came eye to eye with a punk begging on the sidewalk, Bezir reached over her to a black tube above the window—Derdâ hadn't even noticed such a thing was there—and yanked down a tinted plastic curtain. The window went dark. The world was invisible. Derdâ lowered her head and looked at her knees. She closed her eyes and thought about everything she'd seen on the way in from the airport. She imagined the images just as they had been in her mind's eye.

When they woke her from her daydreams they were in Finsbury Park, the headquarters of the Hikmet Tariqat in London. The English version of Çemendağ. Finsbury Park, where property prices plummeted with the rise of Muslim immigrants, where the English became poorer and increasingly racist every day and Muslims got richer and richer, slowly taking over the neighborhood.

The minivan pulled away with Regaip inside. The others entered a twelve-story apartment building, half occupied by members of the Hikmet Tariqat. By the time they reached his flat on the eleventh floor, countless people had come out to kiss Ubeydullah's hand. Then he placed his hand on Bezir's shoulder.

"You go up to your flat. They'll send the girl."

Ubeydullah's wife Rahime and several other women brought Derdâ into the bathroom. "Do you know how to perform ablutions?" she asked.

"Yes."

The women weren't convinced. They wanted her to show them. Right then and there. Derdâ undressed and performed her ablutions in the exact way Mübarek had taught her to do them. In the Hikmet Tariqat style. The women were satisfied. One smiled and said, "Look, I'm Sister Rahime, I was your age when I came here, so don't be afraid." She took Derdâ's hand and led her to one of the two apartments on the twelfth floor. She rang the doorbell to the flat closest to the stairwell and then left, going back down the stairs. She heard the door open and turned to look at Derdâ, who remained motionless for a few seconds before passing through the door.

Bezir's apartment had three rooms with wall-to-wall carpeting. Carpets with lions. In the living room there was only a couch, two armchairs, a lectern that could have well been a hundred years old, and a poster of the Kaaba in a black frame. One of the rooms was completely empty, and in the other room there was only a large wardrobe. The only mirror in the house was in the bathroom. One bedroom was significantly larger than the others. In it there was a double bed pushed up against the wall, accessible only from one side—from the marks in the carpet it was apparent it had just been moved into the room.

Bezir walked over to the poster of the Kaaba. There were two prayer rugs on the floor, one beside the other. He stood over one and signaled for Derdâ to come. The little girl stood over the other rug and with their bodies facing the picture of Kaaba on the wall, set in the direction of Mecca, they began to pray together. Thick curtains covered the windows. It was midnight in London. Derdâ watched Bezir out of the corner of her eye and prayed he didn't know that she wasn't really praying.

Bezir slowly rolled up the rugs and set them on the couch. Then he took Derda by the hand and led her to the bedroom. Never taking his eyes off the little girl he pulled his gown over his shoulders and, pointing at her chador, he told Derdâ to take it off. She did and then he told her to lie down. Then he pointed to the wall.

"Come here."

He remained standing, watching Derdâ, now only in her underwear. She was trembling. They both were trembling. Bezir spoke for the last time that night: "*Bismillahirrahmanirrahim.*"

And he fucked Derdâ until the morning dawned in London.

It was the longest night in the history of London. Even the sun was too embarrassed to rise; morning came late that day.

Bezir got in the elevator, examining the teeth marks on his hands, and left. Derdâ was lying in the bathtub covered in blood, hardly able to breathe. "Clean yourself up," Bezir had told her. He'd carried her to the bathtub and left her there, as if laying her in a grave. Derdâ was naked. She was too scared to find out where the blood was coming from. In any case, she couldn't even move her head. All her strength was gone. She'd resisted all night long. Pulling, pushing, and biting the hands covering her mouth to muffle her screams. But to no avail. There was dried blood under her fingernails. Her arms and legs were covered in bruises. The bruises covering her arms and legs made her look like a leopard—and after just one single night of being battered. Battered and shriveled up. She couldn't even cry.

She heard someone at the front door. Someone was trying different keys in the lock. Finally, a key turned in the lock, the door opened, and a woman called out: "Derdâ! Derdâ!"

Rahime came into the bathroom and saw the girl. Without registering any surprise, she turned on the tap and tested the water temperature. Derdâ watched as if her eyes had sunk deep into their sockets, as if she were looking at the world from somewhere deep inside the depths of her body. She couldn't speak, she couldn't give sound to the words on the tip of her tongue. She could only look. She looked at Rahime's hand under the running water as if she was looking through the wrong end of binoculars. After making sure the water was warm, Rahime pulled her hand away and flicked the drops off her finger tips. Then she turned on the shower and Derdâ felt water falling on her legs. She moaned. It was all she could do. Warm water poured down over her body like rain, over her feet, her arms, her hands, her neck.

"Close your eyes," Rahime said, smiling.

Derdâ didn't hear her. She didn't understand. There was a humming in her ears. She involuntarily closed her eyes as rain drops fell into her mouth. Water struck her face, lashes of water, like a hundred fishing lines, streaming out of holes in the shower head. It looked like she was crying. But she wasn't.

As the water washed away the blood, her wounds became apparent. Blood had flown from between her thin legs, something between those legs had been dismembered, something had been torn, something was dead. Though the water cleaned away the blood stains, purple tattoos remained all over Derdâ's body. Parts of her were damaged, parts of her were broken, but certain things were newly born. She had purple eyes. Now Derdâ had an eye on her back, though she couldn't use it yet. In time, she would learn how to open that eye.

She wanted to eat the soup set before her but she just couldn't. Rahime took the spoon from her hand, blew on it to cool the soup, and poured it through Derdâ's lips. After a few spoonfuls, an "ah" passed through Derdâ's lips. It then became a capital "A." And she multiplied them: "AAAA!"

Eventually only intermittent breathing interrupted the wail: "AAAAAAAA...AAAAAAAA...AAAAAAA..."

Her lips didn't close until Ulviye from the fourth-floor apartment came up to give her an injection of diazepam. She couldn't close her lips. She wasn't aware of her screaming, her eleven years compressed into a wail. And then she fell asleep.

When she woke up she was sixteen. Lying on the couch, she looked up at the ceiling in the silence of a warm afternoon. She was startled by a noise from behind the door. She stood up and covered herself in her black chador. She couldn't see through the peephole because the lens had fallen off balance, so she opened the door a little and peeked out.

First, she saw a leaf. A big leaf on a big house plant in a big pot. Then she saw an armchair, a black leather armchair. Then she saw Stanley, a tall, thin man. He was pushing a glass coffee table to the side of the corridor to open a passageway for a man in blue overalls carrying two boxes to get into Stanley's new apartment. Pushing the low table aside, he stood up and looked at the other furniture around him. Then he saw the head and shoulder of his neighbor, Derdâ, peering at him from behind the door. He didn't smile or say hello. He just stared at her jet-black eyes framed in pitch-black cloth. Derdâ disappeared immediately as if something had pulled her back. She shut the door as if taking refuge behind it.

Evidently, they had found a tenant for the flat opposite, which had been empty for five years. This meant that from then on Derdâ would have to cover herself when she swept the threshold or when she saw Bezir off at the elevator in the morning. This was the first thing that came to mind. To cover herself so that she'd be invisible to a stranger. She knelt down and put her ear against the door to listen for signs of life. She heard noises. Soft, loud, and sudden noises. She tried to match the sounds to different pieces of furniture. If she knew that none of her assumptions were true, who knows if she would've stayed there with her body pressed up against the door until the door outside was shut and the corridor was silent. Maybe she wouldn't have cared at all, but Derdâ had nothing else to do. She'd lived in this flat on the twelfth floor for five years. The only difference between this apartment and her room in Kurudere was that there was no longer an iron ring around her ankle. Now the ring encircled her whole body.

She only left the flat on Fridays. It was exactly sixteen steps to the eleventh floor where Rahime held open the door. All the women there were members of the Hikmet Tariqat and they came there to listen to a speech called *sohbet*, a kind of religious conversation. At first Derdâ couldn't understand why it was called a conversation. As far as she knew, a conversation was two-way. But after some time, she stopped caring. She only made sure not to sit beside the old man, Vezir, who whined out the *Hadith* with saliva sputtering out from his mouth. Whenever the old man spoke he made a terrible noise accompanied by ample spit. He could go on and on for three hours, his eyes closed over the final hour.

The women huddled together on the floor to make enough space for everyone else. Derdâ liked the spot between the big yellow armchair and the wall. She always went down a few minutes before the *sohbet* began. She liked to feel hidden. For the last two years she wore her two-piece black chador when she went down to the *sohbet* (normally she preferred the single-piece chador with an elastic band at its waist) and secretly kept her left hand in her baggy *şalvar* pants, her middle finger inside her. As the women in the room listened intently, weeping and often

50

bursting into flights of hysteria, Derdâ came at least three times during the three-hour *sohbet*, moaning every time.

She was like everyone else in the crowd, her voice part of the general hum. Moving her curled finger to caress the walls of her vagina, she fantasized about being held down and fucked by a dozen anonymous men. But she never rushed into the final episode of her fantasy, the summit of her pleasure. In the final fantasy, a miracle had rendered Bezir motionless. He seethed with anger as he was forced to watch his wife's face contort with pleasure. At every *sohbet* she imagined another way Bezir would be unable to move. Sometimes he was paralyzed by an illness, sometimes his hands and feet were bound, sometimes he was held down by three men. Derdâ stared at Bezir's suffering face while she moaned. Then the *sohbet* ended and everyone returned to their own apartments. Bezir arrived two hours later and sat down with Derdâ on the floor around a low wooden table. He ate his dinner without chewing, saving his teeth for Derdâ.

Any other teenage girl would have picked at her eyebrows, peeled the dry skin off her lips, or gnawed the insides of her cheeks during the *sohbet* sessions. But Derdâ's personal protest would not be through pain. She had enough of that from others. So many only wanted to cause her harm. She wouldn't be one of them. So she found pleasure in her silent scream. It was her only revenge. She pleasured herself in a world of suffering. This was the only way to deny she was a victim. At least to herself.

Ubeydullah never knew that Bezir beat Derdâ; Rahime never told him what she had seen in the bathtub. In fact, Ubeydullah took a liking to Derdâ. He felt compassion for her. On those rare occasions when he came over, he'd call her his daughter. But he couldn't see what was under her chador. He couldn't see the welts on her knees (the work of belt buckles) or the bruises on her shoulders (the marks of fists).

Bezir beat her because speaking was too difficult. He beat her because kickboxing still couldn't control his anger. A teacher in the school he'd attended briefly encouraged him to try kickboxing, but sixteen years of practicing the art hadn't managed to tame the beast. He beat her because years had gone by and Derdâ still hadn't gotten pregnant.

Derdâ heard the door open across the hall and she jumped up and pressed her ear to the door, closing her eyes. A thin, tall man with short-cropped hair appeared in her mind's eye. *His eyes,* she thought, *were they blue?* She couldn't say. But she knew that one of her fantasy men would have a face at the next *sohbet.* At least that she was sure of.

Bezir had to go to Istanbul for four days. Derdâ was overjoyed at the thought of being alone, if only for a few days. But her joy was cut short when she was told she would pass all waking hours with Rahime.

Rahime was always smiling. It was like her face had been fixed with glue. She always smiled. She smiled when she ate, she smiled when she prayed. She smiled when she looked at Derdâ. A smile was a permanent fixture on her face. She had something she wanted to tell Derdâ.

"Do you know why Bezir went to Istanbul?"

"For business."

Rahime narrowed her smile.

"Is that what he told you?"

"Yes," Derdâ answered.

Rahime's smile grew larger.

"Ah, my girl, if only you knew. Don't tell anyone you heard this from me, but he went to find a girl."

Derdâ's response was too sudden.

"Will he leave me then?"

"Do you want him to?"

She knew her answer to this question was important, and could result in a terrible beating four days later.

"No, no," said Derdâ.

This time Rahime laughed, her smile broadening.

"Stupid girl! Why wouldn't he be looking for another girl? When he has a wife like you. You're an idiot, a moron!"

Derdâ turned her head and narrowed her eyes. She looked at Rahime, who was covering her mouth with her hands trying to control her laughter. Then it dawned on her—something was not right about Rahime. She was insane. Thirty-two-year-old Rahime was out of her mind, and Derdâ was the first person to notice. Her only daughter to Ubeydullah was only fourteen when she was married off as the third wife to Azamet, the eldest man in the neighboring apartment block. Rahime knew she'd never see her daughter again, and that she wouldn't recognize her even if she did. She gave up trying to understand anything about the world.

Derdâ listened to Rahime natter on about her private conversations with God until the evening prayer. Always smiling, she whispered to Derdâ, "Nobody else can hear. He only speaks with me. He says that he'll take me to his paradise."

Every once in a while, she stopped speaking as if she just remembered something, her smile frozen on her face, then several absent seconds later she started up again.

"'Rahime,' he says to me. 'You're my favorite servant. I believe only in the sincerity of your prayers. The others are all liars . . .'"

She made Derdâ swear again and again not to tell anyone about her conversations. Almost every two hours.

"You won't tell anyone, will you?"

She brought out her Koran.

"Put your hand on it," she said. "And swear!"

They had dinner and Derdâ returned to her apartment to sleep. She began to slowly climb the stairs, the key to her prison on a rope around her neck. As she was unlocking the door, the elevator arrived at the fourteenth floor and Derdâ froze, the key still unturned in the lock. The elevator doors slid open and Derdâ couldn't help but look over her shoulder. Stanley stepped out of the elevator in a leather overcoat with black kohl around his eyes. He looked at her, looming over her in his giant, steel-tipped, knee-high Dr. Martens. His blue eyes were like the sky behind black clouds.

Like a black ghost, Derdâ slowly turned around, leaving the key in the lock, to look at Stanley. The yellow ceiling lamp suddenly went out, enveloping them in darkness. They were both invisible. Derdâ thought of running to him and throwing her arms around him. Stanley would return her embrace and they would rush into the elevator and travel to eternity. But there was something Derdâ had forgotten: it was impossible for them to escape in the dark. When Stanley stepped forward the motion-sensor triggered the hall light. They were still staring at each other, less than six feet between them. The light went off again and this time Derdâ stepped forward, moving so quickly that Stanley surely heard the rustle of her chador. Years older than Derdâ, Stanley acknowledged her with a curt nod and turned toward his door. Though drunk, he managed to insert his key and in one swift movement he opened the door and disappeared inside. The corridor light went off and when it came back on his door was already closed.

That night Derdâ slept on the floor by the door, hoping she might hear a sound from the corridor. When she woke up she stepped outside, glancing at Stanley's door. It seemed more like a wall with nothing beyond it. Bowing her head, she went downstairs. Rahime opened the door before the doorbell's singsong melody had finished.

"You know Ulviye, right?" Rahime asked her.

Derdâ nodded.

"She says she speaks to God, too, you know? She told me the other day, the lying bitch!"

Derdâ didn't want to miss the chance to swear and so she too used the word, fully stressing each letter's sound.

"Bitch!"

Rahime was delighted to hear her repeat the word and she smiled so broadly that her lips nearly reached her cheek bones.

Derdâ spent twelve hours performing her ablutions and prayers, cooking, eating, and pretending to listen to Rahime before she left for her apartment. On every step up to her floor she stopped and listened for the elevator. Silence. She walked up three steps and then down two, then up one more before counting to fifty—but not a sound from the elevator. After the first eight steps, she gave up on waiting and hurried into her apartment without even looking at Stanley's door.

For the first few hours that night in the apartment she sat in an armchair she had moved to the window and watched London in the dark. Then she stood up and slowly undressed. Naked, she took a step forward and pressed the tips of her fingers and her nipples onto the window overlooking the city. A naked Derdâ stood at the window of a dark flat on the twelfth floor with her arms spread wide open. Her brow was also up against the glass as she stared at the lights in the distance. At first, she was worried that someone might see her, but soon she was wishing someone would. That night Derdâ stood against her bedroom window like a white flag. That night Derdâ was naked like a cry in the dark. But nobody heard her. The window was soundproof. Nobody could see how crudely her body had been beaten. No one saw all the bruises. No one informed the police, and no one even noticed her display of exhibitionism. Derdâ fell asleep naked.

Her eyelids blinked opened as a black silhouette shifted over her. Realizing someone was in the room, she opened her eyes and quickly sat up, holding a pillow tightly over her breasts. Rahime was sitting on the edge of the bed looking at Derdâ's naked shoulders, smiling. At first Derdâ couldn't understand how she'd gotten in, and then she was confused as to where she was. Remembering that Rahime had her keys struck her mind like a stone hurled with hatred. Who knew how long she'd been there. Just next to her in bed. It was morning and the curtains were a shade brighter in the sun. Maybe she had seen her the night before?

"Once I was beautiful like you."

Derdâ let out a deep sigh. Rahime stroked Derdâ's shoulder with the palm of her hand and continued to speak: "But look at me now. What has become of me?"

Rahime lay down on the bed in her chador. And putting her head on Derdâ's chest, she wept. Derdâ caressed the cloth covering her head—it was only thing she could do to console her.

The day was quiet and no one performed prayers. Toward evening, Rahime came to see Derdâ with a shoebox. She whispered, "Do you know what's inside?"

Without waiting for an answer, she opened the box and took out an object wrapped in scarves. She untied the scarves and presented Derdâ with a small, metal radio.

She turned on the radio and whispered, "Don't ever tell anyone, ever!" Siouxsie and the Banshees were singing "Peek-a-Boo."

Rahime laughed and said, "I don't understand a thing but it's just so good, isn't it?" Derdâ laughed, too.

They listened to music and danced until midnight in the only way they knew how. They mostly held hands and jumped up and down, turned themselves around, and bumped into each other. They were doing the pogo, though neither of them knew it.

But it was exasperating for Derdâ to have to swear every half an hour with her hand on the Koran: "I won't tell anyone about the radio."

Derdâ woke with a knot in her throat that wouldn't go away. She couldn't swallow. It was like a small steel ball was lodged in her throat; she could hardly breathe. It was the last day before Bezir came back and she just couldn't relax. Each passing moment brought the day closer to its end, each passing second. That was why she had a knot in her throat.

She was thinking of her next-door neighbor's eyes; she imagined the blue around his pupils, hovering there just before her. Then his pale face came into focus around his eyes, and as it became clearer and clearer, Bezir's dark face faded away and with it the knot in her throat. She considered knocking on her neighbor's door. *I could tell him to take me away? Beg him to kidnap me?* But how would she speak to him? In what language? Then she realized she could communicate with him through pictures. She could draw out her thoughts. Everything: How she came to the apartment five years ago, and the way Bezir tortured her. How they would leave the apartment together and never come back. They would simply walk out the front door, hand in hand. She'd draw him a picture of a heart, an enormous heart.

She jumped out of the bed and raced into the living room. Bezir's notebook and fountain pen were on his lectern. He was studying Arabic. She grabbed the notebook and the pen and stretched out on the floor. She opened a blank page and she drew a self-portrait. It was easy—a black snowman. Then she drew Bezir beside her—a white snowman with a beard. Next to them she drew their apartment building. Then she wrote the year, the year she came to England. Then she drew a straight line below the two figures, and her basic graphic novel moved to its second scene. Now the white snowman was holding a thick club, and the black snowman was on the ground. She needed a red pen to draw the blood, but she couldn't find one in the house. She ran to the kitchen and got the bread knife. She slowly drew the knife back and forth over her finger like a saw. A red line appeared on the surface of her skin. She returned to the living room and rubbed her own blood over the black snowman. In the third scene, she carefully drew a blue-eyed man leading Derdâ out of the apartment building. And in the final scene she drew a heart and colored it in with the last drop of blood she could squeeze out of her finger.

She tore the pages out of the notebook, got dressed, and left the apartment. Rahime opened the door, still holding her Koran.

"What do you want?" Rahime demanded. She'd forgotten everything: that Bezir was gone and that during his absence Derdâ was supposed to spend the days with her. She'd forgotten all about the songs they'd listened to together the other night, everything. Derdâ tried to smooth things over and said that she had just come over for some bread.

"We don't have any," Rahime snapped. "I don't have anything for lying bitches like you!"

Derdâ smiled as Rahime slammed the door shut. She hurried back upstairs. She was so excited about her plan that she was afraid she might abandon the whole thing if she stopped to think about it for even a second. So she didn't. She ran straight to her neighbor's door and rang the doorbell.

She heard footsteps, and the door swung open. Stanley had just woken up—he had heavy, dark circles under his eyes from all the meth he'd done the night before. He was wearing nothing but leather pants, with the top button undone. His torso was covered in tattoos. Hardly any skin was left uncolored. Derdâ took a step back, her pictures trembling in her hands. She was afraid of all the devils she'd just seen in the tattoos. But she thought of Bezir and how he'd be coming back soon and she held out her pictures. Stanley took them and closed the door.

She didn't know what to do. She stood silently in front of the closed door. She waited for a few minutes before she went back to her apartment with a final glance over her shoulder at Stanley's door as she stepped inside.

Night fell over London. Derdâ could see the lights racing over the city streets from the bedroom window. She sat in the armchair with her knees pulled up to her chest, looking out over London, but not really seeing anything. She was afraid. *What if he shows the pictures to Bezir?* she thought as she gnawed at the insides of her cheeks. She stared at her reflection in the glass for hours, thinking about killing herself. She could just open the window and jump.

She stood up and realized that she'd forgotten to take off her chador. It was still wrapped around her like a second skin. She hadn't even taken off her gloves. She couldn't be bothered. She took a step forward and opened the window. She felt the first drops of newly falling rain on her face. She looked down to the ground twelve floors below and then out into the distance. Suddenly there was a heavy knock on the door. The doorbell was broken.

Feeling empty, Derdâ left the open window and slowly walked through the living room and down the corridor toward the door. She opened the door listlessly, not even lifting her head to see who was there. But there on the floor she saw a pair of Dr. Martens and as she slowly lifted her head she saw a pair of legs covered in black leather, a black T-shirt, and finally Stanley's face. Her eyes met his blue eyes. They were looking over Derdâ, peering into the darkness of her apartment, as if looking for someone, trying to understand if anyone else was home. He placed his hands on either side of the doorframe and leaned forward, looming over Derdâ, as he tried to get a better look inside the flat.

"Is anyone else here?" he asked in English. Derdâ involuntarily turned her head and looked into the apartment. Then she understood. She turned and said in Turkish, "No, nobody's here," opening her palm to Stanley to emphasize it. Though a little surprised by the gesture, Stanley understood what she meant. He took Derdâ by the wrist and pulled her out of the apartment, just like she had drawn in her graphic novel. Derdâ hardly had time to reach out and shut the door. *I'm leaving*, she thought. *At last, I'm leaving.* But they didn't go far. They passed the stairs and then the elevator and went into Stanley's apartment.

They passed through an empty entrance hall and down a dark corridor and stepped into a large bedroom. Derdâ knew the layout even though she'd never been here before. She knew it like the back of her hand—it was the exact same layout as the apartment she'd been living in for the past five years. In her bedroom Bezir kept the bed up against the wall. In Stanley's room, there were black curtains hanging from chains, and there was a black leather armchair beside a double mattress on the floor— the one Derdâ had seen when she first moved in. The walls were covered with foldout posters from *Torture* magazine. Looking closely at the posters, Derdâ saw what the men and women were doing to each other and she dropped Stanley's hand and stepped back. Her instinct told her to get out. Stanley put his hands on her shoulders and smiled. He slowly held up his hand and gestured for her to stay. Then he caressed her head. Derdâ began to pull off the cloth covering her face but Stanley stopped her. The tall man shook his head. He didn't want to see her face. Derdâ understood. But what did he want? She'd find out soon enough.

Stanley took off his T-shirt, lifted one of the pillows on the mattress, and pulled out a rubber bat. Then he knelt down on the bed and gave it to Derdâ. She took the bat, and Stanley lowered his eyes. Then he unzipped his pants and brought them to his knees. He braced himself against the mattress and looked up at Derdâ like a dog. Derdâ could see a hard piece of flesh jutting out from his midsection, and she noticed bruises around his swollen spine. Caressing the protrusion between his legs as he balanced on his knees, Stanley looked up at Derdâ and begged her with his eyes. He was waiting for the first blow. In a sudden movement, she slammed the bat down on his back.

Her eyes went dark with terror and Derdâ ran out of the room.

But three hours later she was back, beating Stanley so much that the paint on the bat began to peel off.

Stick was a pub on a corner deep in the backstreets of Camden Town, a neighborhood fueled by the underground scene of madmen and degenerates. Stanley stood behind the bar absently wiping a beer mug with a towel as filthy and pathetic as a floor mat as he talked to Mitch, who sat on a stool at the bar. Mitch was American. He had come to London because where he was from most people thought S&M was a brand of soda. He'd found Severin in the personals of *Torture* magazine and he quickly made himself her slave. But it didn't work out. She woke up one morning and told him she was a lesbian. Set free from his bondage with her, Mitch lost his grip on reality and sank into a dark void. He was listening to Stanley's story, wiping beer off his chin with the back of his hand and adjusting the monocle over his left eye. It was attached to an earring in his left ear by a thin chain.

"But you should see her, man, she's beautiful! It's hard to explain, I don't know. You know these Arab women—totally in black. You can only see their eyes. She's one of them, probably Turkish. I mean, there are lots of them in the building, the custodian told me. He's a Turk, too, I think. Whatever, she has a husband or a brother . . . some guy with a beard. They live in the flat across from mine. I'd seen the girl a couple of times before, but of course we'd never spoke. But yesterday she comes and knocks on my door."

"How old you think she is?" Mitch asked.

"How should I know? But she must be pretty young. At least she seems young."

Hearing this much was enough to turn Mitch on. But he wasn't sure if he should start stroking himself through the hole in his pocket—Stanley might get annoyed if he realized he was doing it. He stopped himself and asked him for another beer.

Stanley took his dirty glass and refilled it with beer and put it down in front of Mitch. It was ten o'clock in the morning and Mitch was the only customer in Stick. They kept talking.

"What was I saying? Yeah, she just came over and knocked on the door. She had these pictures. I took them and looked them over. She'd obviously drawn them herself."

Mitch was already a little drunk. Excited, he said, "Didn't you ask her in?"

"Patience," Stanley said. "Listen, she'd drawn all this stuff on paper she'd ripped out of a notebook—a man hitting a woman, and something even stranger, there was a heart, painted in red, but guess what—I think it was real blood."

"Fuck," Mitch moaned. He thought of Severin. She always got sick when she saw blood. "Fuck," he said again.

Stanley laughed and went on.

"I'm serious. Whatever, so I wait until evening to make sure the guy with the beard wasn't around. I kept checking the scene through my peephole. The man never turns up. So I go and knock on the door. She opens it and I look into the apartment and it seems like she's there alone."

"Did she say anything? I mean, didn't you talk to each other?" asked Mitch.

"No, no, she doesn't know any English. Anyway, so I took her over to my place. You won't believe it, Mitch, it was like a dream! An incredible dream!"

"Did you see her face?"

"Are you crazy? What's the fun if I see her face? I didn't see her face at all. Not even her hands. She was wearing black gloves."

"Yeah, I know," Mitch said. "They go to the Tesco on my street. Five women all dressed in black. They walk up and down the aisles like ghosts. I was behind one of them at the cash register once. She was wearing those long black gloves . . ."

Mitch went quiet. He tried to imagine all the Muslim women in the world with every part of their bodies, even their faces, covered. Then he said, "If you ask me, they're probably the sexiest women in the whole world."

"Who?"

"Muslim women. See, they must be just too sexy, and that's why they cover themselves like that. The message they're giving us is, if we uncovered ourselves you guys would lose control. You get it? They're saying to men, look, if we took off these clothes, you'd lose your minds! Yeah, that's it . . . I've never thought of it like that before . . . but that's just how it is! Otherwise, why would a woman cover herself like that, unless she was the hottest woman in the world? They're probably afraid of being raped. Think of it this way, have you ever seen a beautiful naked woman? Not one. It's like Muslim women are some kind of weapon, like a lethal weapon, so lethal that they're always kept wrapped up. They're like nuclear bombs, man. Never fired but it's enough just to know they're there. If they ever uncovered, it'd be the end of the world. They'd enslave everyone. Maybe they're actually enslaved Amazons . . ."

They broke out laughing. But suddenly Stanley became serious.

"She just really turns me on with that black chador. And this isn't just a fantasy of mine. It's the real thing! They're nothing like the idiots around here who wear ironed skirts during the day and latex masks at night. These women are always in that black robe. And they're proud to be wrapped up in it. It's like they don't even need to walk, they just glide, you know?"

"Right on," Mitch said, thinking of Severin again. Severin worked in some shitty bank wearing some standard suit. "Then what happened, what did you do?" he asked Stanley.

Stanley took off his T-shirt and turned around. His back looked just like Derdâ's—covered in dark purple bruises. Mitch stretched out his trembling alcoholic hand and touched them. When Stanley turned around he was pleased to see Mitch's mouth wide open in surprise.

Stanley locked the front door and went into the women's bathroom with his American friend and came into his mouth. He hadn't cleaned the men's room yet.

When he reopened the bar, Regaip was the first person to walk in. The moment Stanley saw him he bolted to the back of the pub, knocking over chairs as he went. He thought he could lock himself in the toilet stall where he'd made the American get down on his knees not too long ago but he was wrong. Regaip broke the door down with one powerful kick, grabbed Stanley by the back of the neck, and forced his head down into the toilet bowl and flushed. For a few moments they remained still as the water flushed over Stanley's head. Then Regaip yanked Stanley's head out of the bowl and smashed it into the wall. Stanley waved his hands in the air and said, "Alright, alright . . ." Regaip took a step back and waited. Stanley reached into his back pocket, took out two hundred pounds, and handed the money to Regaip. It was half of what he owed him for this month's meth. Regaip took the money and said, in English, "I'll be back for the rest next week."

He turned around and walked out of the bar. When he saw Mitch cowering behind the bar, pitifully brandishing an empty whisky bottle in the air—clearly too afraid to actually hit someone with it—Regaip shouted out, "Motherfucking fags!" in Turkish and calmly walked out of the pub. But once on the sidewalk he suddenly stopped, turned around, and walked back into the pub. His voice was even louder this time, and still in Turkish.

"You're going to hit me with that, are you, you bastard?!"

Mitch's eyebrows shot up when he saw that Regaip had come back for him and his monocle fell from his face and dangled ludicrously from his earlobe, nearly ripping it open.

Bezir asked her one more time: "What did you say?"

"Shopping. Can I go with Sister Rahime? They always forget some things when they shop for us."

Bezir asked her again, this time in three clear parts. "You? You want to go out? With Sister Rahime?"

This was enough. Derdâ wasn't going to insist. He'd made his point.

"No," she said. "Never mind, they always shop for us, too."

Bezir sat on the couch, leaning back with one leg folded under him.

"Now are you going to tell me about the armchair?"

"What armchair?" Derdâ said.

"That one. You moved it."

He pointed at the armchair that Derdâ had put in front of the window when he was away—for four days and four nights. Now it was back in its normal place opposite the couch. Derdâ didn't know what to say.

She stuttered as she spoke: "May . . . may . . . maybe I pulled it over there when I was vacuuming the floors . . ."

Bezir smiled.

"Is that so?"

He pulled out his leg, stood up, slowly placed his hand on the back of Derdâ's neck, and squeezed, but not too hard.

"Come with me," he said.

He brought Derdâ to the window. The curtains were drawn. She had no idea what he was planning to do. She felt a sudden rush of fear.

Then she felt a heaviness on the back of her neck as Bezir forced her down to her knees. He knelt down beside her and forced Derdâ flat onto the floor, pressing her face into the carpet.

He asked her, "Then what the hell is this?"

Derdâ couldn't see anything, only individual strands in the carpet. Bezir realized this and lifted her head up a little. But she still couldn't see anything but the carpet, nothing more.

"What is it?" she finally managed to say. "What I am supposed to see?"

Bezir pointed to a small indent.

"You see this! This!" he screamed as he dragged the girl's head over to the other indent thirty inches to the right.

"You see this, too!"

Then another indent.

"And this one here!"

Then the last one.

"And this!"

Still on her knees, he forced Derdâ to look at each indent the armchair had left in the carpet, rubbing her face in them.

"I don't know," Derdâ cried. "I really don't know!"

She started to cry. Bezir hated it when she cried.

"Who then? Someone else? Was someone else in here? Did someone else move the armchair over here! Did someone else draw the curtains to look outside? Did you let someone in here? Is that what you're telling me? Is that why you want to go shopping? You want to go see him?"

Bezir wasn't shouting now. He spoke in a stiff, muffled voice, because Ubeydullah had told him before that he was making too much noise. He'd even asked if he was doing anything to the girl.

Then suddenly Bezir released his grip on her neck. Bezir didn't have much time. He was late for work. He went to the front hall, slipped on his shoes, and left. Derdâ remained flat on the carpet for some time. When she finally raised her head, she saw Bezir's lectern. Her eyes searched for the notebook she'd used for her pictures, but it wasn't there. *Did Bezir notice that, too?* she thought as she stood up. She'd find out that evening when he came home.

She paced back and forth in the living room until noon and then left the apartment and knocked on her neighbor's door. Stanley wasn't working that day. Without even looking at his face, Derdâ stepped into the apartment and walked straight to Stanley's bedroom. Stanley followed. Derdâ bent over his bed and took the bat out from under the pillow. Stanley raised his index finger to tell her to wait. He took a three-piece studded collar from one of the chains hanging from the ceiling and fastened it around Derdâ's neck. He took a step back to look at the girl in black now wearing an S&M studded choke collar. He was in awe. Then he slowly undressed and assumed a new position. This time he remained standing with his hands together above his head. His eyes closed. As the hard plastic bat came down on his back and the back of his legs, his penis became more and more erect. He remained still until a translucent liquid spurted out from the tip of his erect member and as he opened his eyes he opened his palm to Derdâ, who stopped beating him. Stanley leaned over and picked up a bracelet lined with nails and slipped it inside-out over his cock slick with come. The nails ran over his flesh as he moved the bracelet up and down. He looked up at Derdâ and she understood right away what Stanley wanted her to do. Her black-gloved hand clutched the bracelet and moved it up and down exactly twelve times. This time the liquid was tinted with blood.

Derdâ threw the plastic bat down on the bed and started to search the house. She was looking for something—a book, any book. And soon enough she found what she was looking for—not a book but a magazine, a TV guide. She opened it to a random page and showed it to Stanley who followed her about the house eagerly as he got dressed. Enunciating loudly, she said, "English," in an attempt to make herself totally clear. She always felt that her voice was barely audible beneath the cloth over her mouth. She pointed at the pictures in the magazine and said again, "English!"

"I don't get it. What do you want?" Stanley asked.

Derdâ pretended to write something in the air and Stanley brought her a pen. On the back cover, there was an ad for handbags. In the ad, a naked woman bent over with both her hands on her calves, her breasts covered with the advertised bag and the brand name written exactly where her legs came together. Derdâ put the pen on the bag and scribbled. Then she circled the woman's eyes and scribbled some more, all the while saying, "English!"

She realized something was missing—so she added a question mark at the end of all her lines and then Stanley finally understood. He took the magazine from Derdâ, and pointed at the naked woman and repeated the word in English several times.

"Woman," Derdâ repeated after him.

That day Stanley came twice and Derdâ learned thirty-six new words.

"There's the famous Big Ben," Hıdır Arif said.

But Gido Agha wasn't listening. He'd just bought into a heroin ring and he couldn't think of anything else. Smuggling heroin was eight times as lucrative as smuggling diesel oil.

He'd come to London to negotiate with his fellow country-men—Turks who'd lived in London for a long time. Although he'd negotiated with men from villages he'd never heard of before, he still considered them his people for they were weaned on the milk of their Kurdish mothers. But he never discussed business with women. He'd told his compatriots in London that he wouldn't take the heroin over the Bulgarian border. He said they would have to take it from there; he couldn't get involved with transportation after that. They agreed, but said because the costs would be higher his cut would be smaller. Gido Agha wasn't pleased. And so Big Ben just drifted by unnoticed. He was only really interested in buildings that were his.

But then Hıdır Arif wasn't happy there either, on the Thames in a none-too-small boat that they had rented for the day. But all the same, they couldn't pretend they didn't know each other just because they were thousands of kilometers away from their homeland. They had lots of things in common—around two hundred thousand things. That was the population on the expanse of land in southeastern Turkey that they each ruled sep-arately. Hıdır Arif knew from his father that it was best not to get involved in the affairs of Gido Agha, and although he knew what he was up to, he didn't say a word about it to him directly.

Likewise, Gido didn't involve himself in Hikmet Tariqat affairs. They shared the people—their flesh and blood belonged to the Aleyzam tribe, and their souls to the Hikmet Tariqat. It was a fair deal that went back nearly a hundred years. Gido looked after the business affairs of the organization, and Hıdır Arif kept a list of those people who went to the mountains to join the rebel fighters.

Hıdır Arif didn't give a damn about which flag flew over his land. He knew well that people became the living dead with-out faith. So Hikmet Tariqat rule would carry on even if China took over. "Kurdistan, the Turkish Republic, People's Republic of China, what difference does it make?" he used to say to his father, Sheik Gazi—when he could still hear, that is. Hıdır Arif was a Princeton-educated citizen of the world. He knew no boundaries except those made by religion. If a Muslims without Borders was ever formed, he saw himself as its leader. But still, he preferred certain nationalities over others. For example, he admired the pretension of the Arabs. If they wanted to cover the Kaaba with gold, he'd be one of the first to support the project. He loved pretension; he'd once paid half a million dollars for a five-hundred-gram stone he hardly believed was a part of *Hacer-ül-Esved*, and he made sure every guest who came into his study saw it—a jet-black stone seemingly suspended in the center of a glass sphere etched with a map of the world, a stone in the center of the world instead of magma. The sphere was mounted on a steel column and it was the first thing people saw when they entered the room, as if basked in an elaborate lighting system. Hıdır Arif could select his color of choice for the sphere with a remote control. His favorite was green, the color typical of Islamic mausoleums.

As they approached Waterloo Bridge, Gido Agha said, "There's a man, maybe you know him."

"Who?" Hıdır Arif asked.

"Bedir, or Bezir, something like that. He lives here. You know what he does?"

The other boats on the Thames and Waterloo Bridge were teeming with tourists. Many of them held cameras, snapping photos of everything around them—photos they would probably never look at again. Someone on the bridge saw the old bearded man in an Islamic robe and turban and snapped a photo of him before his luxury yacht sailed under the bridge. He figured he was the political leader of some country in the Middle East.

The man next to him on the bridge said, "Forget that guy, I know who he is. Get a photo of the one we're after."

The two men in trench coats were MI5 officers, members of the British Security Service. They had been assigned to collect information on Gido Agha, currently residing in the Waldorf, one of the most expensive hotels in the city. Gido could have come to Britain like any other tourist and left the same way, but the fact was he visited people the MI5 had been watching for months and this made him a new suspect. So now he was being watched under tight surveillance, too.

A Scotsman with a bushy red beard and a kilt elbowed the MI5 officers out of his way, grumbling, "Out of my way. Can't you see I'm working this part of the bridge?"

And as he resumed blowing vigorously on his bagpipe the officers had no choice but to move out of his way. A double-decker bus emblazoned with a full advertisement for the new James Bond film barreled past them as they stepped back toward the street. There was James Bond in a tuxedo, his hair blown like a motorcycle helmet, and bikini-clad girls draped over his shoulders. The two agents looked at the poster and then each other, at their dark coats and what remained of their hair—there was less and less of it every year—billowing in a gust of wind. Their eyes were bloodshot from so much overtime. They had bought their Chinese-made shoes on sale. They couldn't help but sense that the Scottish bagpipe player—now comfortably blowing a Scottish air on his bagpipe—was shooting them an evil glare.

"Fuck James Bond," one of them cursed, and they walked away.

Meanwhile, Hıdır Arif was trying to remember where he'd heard the name before. He needed more details.

"Which group is he associated with?"

He meant to ask whether he was from the tribe or the sect. More precisely, he was asking where his true allegiance lay.

"He's one of yours," said Gido.

"Praise God," said Hıdır Arif, nodding his head. "I know the name but from where? Anyway, why are you interested in him?"

"Don't ask . . ." Gido said, lowering his eyes to the muddy waters of the Thames. "We have some business together."

Hıdır Arif didn't ask any more. So he wouldn't learn that Bezir had established a small organization of Muslim kickboxers in London and that he had managed to hook hundreds of non-Muslims on heroin, justifying himself by saying, "in the service of God any kind of jihad is permissible." Hıdır Arif didn't ask any more. And so he didn't find out that Bezir had reinvested all the money he'd earned from drug dealing in heroin, as he couldn't touch that dirty *haram* money, and that he'd developed a kickbox move that could break the knees of drug dealers who sold heroin to Muslims in one just blow. Even if Hıdır Arif had asked despite Gido's countermand, he still wouldn't have learned the truth about Bezir.

Gido himself knew nothing of all this. His men only told him that there was a man from the Hikmet Tariqat who'd gone gonzo. They told him to take care of him. They'd heard it from Dulluhan, one of the four brothers who were proud to control 75 percent of the heroin that came through the UK. The Daltons of London. Their problem with Bezir was that he bought heroin from the Russians. In other words, from the 25 percent that didn't belong to them.

"We'll look into it," Gido told them. And that was when the MI5 got their first picture of him. The shot was taken from a window on the fourth floor of the apartment building right across the Dalton headquarters in Westminster.

They moved to the stern of the yacht and sat down to eat.

Hıdır Arif said, "Right! I remember the man. Bezir, he's Ubeydullah's son. He's a good boy. He looks after his father's furniture factory."

He didn't say that five years ago he'd acted as an intermediary for him, when he bought an eleven-year-old girl to be his wife.

He carried on carefully: "That's right. He married a girl from Kurudere. Now I remember. In any case, what do you need him for?"

Gido was put out that *rakı* wasn't served with the meal.

Lifting his head, he said, "Just give me his address. And tell me this. Is he useful?"

Hıdır Arif had expected this. That it might come to this. This son of a bitch Gido might hurt the guy. He made a quick calculation in his head. The outcome was to Bezir's disadvantage. *God forgive*, he said to himself.

"No, he's not."

"Good," said Gido. He felt much better after that. Then he looked up. "What were you saying, something big to see around here, where is it?"

Hıdır Arif swore under his breath and said, "We already passed it. That was the clock tower, Big Ben."

And just as they were about to eat, a woman came crashing down into the long wooden table between them. Looking up, they saw that they'd just passed under Tower Bridge. The woman had jumped off the bridge, falling directly onto their boat. And, presumably according to plan, she was dead. The table had been split in two, and Rahime was splayed out on the floor covered in blood, holding a small radio. It was still on. It was stronger than human flesh. "If It Be Your Will" was still playing. Rahime wasn't wearing her black chador. She'd uncovered herself on the last day of her life. Perhaps she'd had nothing left to hide.

The following day one of the MI5 officers was reading the headline news. "Fuck James Bond!" he grumbled. Pictures of Gido's bewildered face taken from every angle on a boat covered with the blood of a suicide were all over the front pages. Another paper had an interview with Hıdır Arif:

"We're not safe in this country! What if this woman had fallen directly onto us? Can't they at least put a safety net under these bridges! They bleed us for taxes! I have every intention to sue those responsible for this. But God has saved us and we are alive today. I would just like to say to my Muslim brothers that I am fine and there's no need to worry."

Kaşıkatlı Seyit Muharrem's poem, dated 1842 and titled "*Hikmet-ül Arz*," was the foundational text of the Hikmet Tariqat:

> *Your trial will end with your appointed death*
> *Dismiss your feeble state and disdain finality*
> *You may take lives in self-defense*
> *But you must never take your own*
>
> *As long as you exist you will stay*
> *In life and in peace of mind*
> *Not cruelty nor blasphemy nor adultery*
> *But suicide is the greatest sin in this world*
>
> *Do you not know to whom your breath belongs?*
> *Do you not prostrate yourself until you are underground?*
> *Not lies nor hypocrisy nor lust*
> *But suicide is the only betrayal of God*

As you have come when you were called
So you will go upon being called
If you rebel and cast your own rope
You will vanish in a void blacker than coal

So the first victory in your trial, do not forget,
It is to be patient till your appointed death . . .

Like all organizations that derive their power from the masses and then create a functional set of rules to command them, the Hikmet Tariqat held that committing suicide meant eternal damnation. The existence and preservation of the Tariqat depended on the existence of its members. And those who died not in the name of the cause but in their own name were good for nothing. That's why the Tariqat members rejected Rahime's corpse. She had committed suicide and in her final breath her face was unveiled for the world to see. But even more damning than that was the fact that in her selfish act she almost killed a superior being—Hıdır Arif—and the sect could not forgive that.

It didn't take long to think the matter through before rejecting Rahime in every way. But Ubeydullah honored his late wife. "There will be a funerary prayer. If necessary, I'll do it myself!" he said to himself, because all his supporters had left him. As a result of the general opinion on Rahime's suicide, his otherwise busy, social world suddenly went cold.

Bezir went with Ubeydullah to collect Rahime's body from the hospital morgue. She was buried in a Muslim cemetery in North London. Bezir arranged everything to please his father. He arranged everything according to Muslim tradition, from the funeral shroud to the washing of the body. After the funeral,

Ubeydullah was no longer at peace in his apartment. His heart ached and he felt a new shortness of breath.

Derdâ begged Bezir to take her to the funeral. In a rage, Bezir slapped her across the face so hard that she fell to the floor. She cried; she cried like she never cried before. She screamed and pounded the carpet with the palms of her hands. She had no strength left to bear such oppression. She stood up and ran to the window. She opened it and screamed, "I'll jump! I swear, I'll jump!"

Bezir stared at her, silent. Then he turned to leave, but at the door he paused and then walked back into the living room and stood in the doorway staring at Derdâ, her one leg suspended outside the building. Silence. It was as if he was waiting for her to jump and die. Suddenly his massive frame buckled and Ubeydullah appeared behind him. The old man had punched his son's back with untold violence. Bezir turned and fell to the floor, not because of the power or pain of the sudden blow, but because he had been hit by his father. He hunched his shoulders and lowered his head, and though well over two hundred pounds, Bezir looked like a little ball crumpled up on the floor.

Ubeydullah was crying like a child. He'd loved Rahime. He'd lost his first wife to breast cancer and Bezir was his only son. Though he was thirty-six years older than Rahime, he had loved her dearly all the same. In a way that he loved all human beings—with compassion. He loved her both as his wife and as a child. He might have been the reason she took her own life, but he had loved her. Ubeydullah didn't know any other kind of life. He'd never known any other way to act toward a woman. Now he could only cry and strike Bezir with trembling hands. It was as if Bezir had thrown Rahime off the bridge himself and Ubeydullah was taking his revenge. But the truth was Ubeydullah's violence was meant for no one else but himself.

"Never again!" he cried, gasping for breath. "If you ever touch this girl again, I'll kill you. Do you hear me? With God as my witness, I'll kill you! You might be my son but I will kill you!"

He continued to drive his fists into his son until he collapsed to the floor. Bezir sprang to his feet and grabbed his father. He raced out of the apartment. Derdâ ran after him. Bezir took the stairs—he'd forgotten all about the elevator. He held his father close to him; in a way that only a son could know, he knew that he was on the verge of death. The old man had never had such difficulty breathing before.

"God!" Bezir cried. "Oh, God!"

Tears filled his narrowed eyes and there was a thin trail of saliva from his lower lip to his chin. He didn't notice Derdâ behind him. He didn't see anything at all—only a door, a double door at the entrance to the building. He kicked it open and ran through the garden to the parking lot. Derdâ hardly had time to realize that this was the very door she'd come through five years ago. It was the first time she'd left the building in five years. She also had tears in her eyes. She didn't know why, maybe for everything, for the past five years, for Ubeydullah, for Rahime, for herself.

For a moment, she couldn't see Bezir. She was confused by her surroundings. The open sky made her head spin. But quickly adjusting to the light, she found her husband in the parking lot and ran over to him. Bezir was strapping his father in the back seat. Derdâ tried to open the front door but couldn't. She didn't know how. For a moment, their eyes met above the car. Bezir's and Derdâ's eyes. They saw each other crying. Derdâ's vision came into focus: it was the first time she'd seen her husband cry.

Bezir shut the back door and walked around the car. Derdâ took two steps back and covered her eyes with her hands in self-defense.

"Get in," said Bezir.

Opening her eyes, she saw that he'd opened the door. She got in the car. Bezir sat next to her in the driver's seat and started the engine. They pulled out onto the street. Ubeydullah moaned in the back seat, regaining consciousness.

"Promise me, Bezir!"

"Dad!" Bezir said. "For God's sake!"

He couldn't bring himself to swear that he'd never hit Derdâ again. He pounded his calloused palms onto the steering wheel.

"Dad, for God's sake . . ." he kept saying.

Ubeydullah was insistent.

"I can't swear!" he whimpered, but Ubeydullah didn't hear him and pushed him further.

"Swear! Swear that you'll never hit her again! Swear . . ."

He stopped mid-sentence. His anger, his life, everything was suddenly cut short. Overcome by the labor of beating, his heart stopped like a bullet lodged into his flesh. It would have passed clear through him, but his son wouldn't give in. He wouldn't let the bullet pass through . . .

Ubeydullah died at the second intersection, just four intersections away from the hospital. Derdâ knew he was dead.

"He isn't moving!" she cried, shaking the old man's inert body. Bezir slammed on the brakes and a taxi crashed into the back of the car. Derdâ's forehead slammed into the dashboard. Bezir jumped out of the car, opened the back door, and pulled his father out of the car. Ubeydullah crumpled on the ground like a blanket. Bezir knelt down by the car and took his father in his arms. His voice echoed off of the buildings at the intersection: "God!"

Bezir didn't touch Derdâ for forty days after his father's death. He didn't even know she was there. He didn't leave the house for forty days. He was hardly aware of his own body. He didn't eat, he only drank water. When his kickboxer friends came over, he locked his wife in the bedroom and held meetings in the living room. At nights he sat in a corner of the room and cried with his hands over his face.

Meanwhile, Derdâ wrote a short letter using the English she'd recently learned, folded it seven times, and pushed it under Stanley's door. She finished the letter with the words "do not come."

Derdâ couldn't decide whether she pitied Bezir or simply despised him. One morning she thought she felt something like pity and approached Bezir who was sitting on the bed silently sobbing. She put her hand on his shoulder. The sleeve of her chador was partially rolled up and she could see the dark brown skin over her wrist. Then she saw scars—the work of Bezir's hands. She remembered everything he'd ever done to her and pulled back her hand. Bezir continued to sob and Derdâ returned to not caring.

On the forty-first day, Bezir got dressed and left the house. His mourning was done—now it was time for rage. With his profits from the heroin trade he would have the Afghans make him bombs. He'd set them off in underground stations during rush hour. He'd fuck England, home of infidels. This was the plan he'd worked out over the last forty days as he wept and grieved. A plan to fuck England! He was going to avenge his father. He wasn't able to seek retribution in himself; he had to take it out on the rest of the world. But the fact was that he was the only person in the world truly responsible for his father's death. Bezir was like his father in this way. He was just like Ubeydullah, a man who beat his own son because he couldn't beat himself.

Stanley opened the door for Derdâ and smiled as he showed her in. She went straight into the living room, where she turned to Stanley and said, "Money!"

Stanley's expression turned sour and he said, "I don't have any."

Derdâ shook her head, walked to the window, and pointed. She pointed at London, she pointed at all the people living there.

"I . . ." she said as she waved her hand as if batting away a ghost. Then she pointed out again and said, "They . . ." and pretended to pull something out of the air and said, "money."

Stanley finally understood. And then he remembered the first gift he had given Derdâ, whom he now considered his master.

"Wait!" he said and ran to the bedroom. He came back holding an English- Turkish/Turkish-English dictionary. When Derdâ saw the small book, she understood what it was and leapt on it like a dolphin. She then summarized what she wanted to say in the following words:

"I . . . beat . . . man . . . then . . . money . . . take . . . because . . . I . . ." She couldn't find the exact word she was looking for but found one just as good: "Queen."

Stanley smiled and said, "Yes, you're my queen."

Derdâ's intelligence belied her insular life. She slapped Stanley's cheek just like Bezir used to slap her. Then she caressed it and placed her hand on Stanley's shoulder, nearly a foot higher than her own, and she applied pressure. Half of his face was now bright red. Stanley didn't resist and lowered himself to his knees and looked up at Derdâ. But this wasn't enough. She pushed harder until his forehead was on the ground. There were no carpets in Stanley's flat. She forced his nose down into the parquet floor. Then Derdâ lifted her left foot and stepped on the back of Stanley's neck, forcing his entire body to grovel beneath her.

"I . . ." she said, unable to remember the verb she was looking for, and she rifled through the dictionary. "Take . . . money . . . and then . . . give . . . you . . ."

Stanley moved his head slightly. And Derdâ rubbed her foot up and down his neck. Stanley managed to pull down his pants, despite his awkward position. He brought his hands down to his crotch and rolled over onto his side exposing his gaping, completely hairless hole to Derdâ. First, Derdâ inserted one of her fingers, and then another. Good thing that she had three more pairs of black gloves at home, because this glove would soon be filthy.

Derdâ hadn't had any contact with money for five years. Bezir never left money at home and he only kept credit cards and coins in his wallet. So, after English, what Derdâ needed most was money. And if there were more people like Stanley in London, she could definitely make money. She'd make them suffer as much as they wanted. She'd oppress them and humiliate them as much as they wanted. When it came to this kind of stuff she was better informed than anyone. She'd suffered all her life.

And she wouldn't even have to take her chador off while she worked. Derdâ was right. After all, they were living in London. There were probably thousands of people like Stanley who went to work every day and came home at night imagining things that people beside them at the bus stop could never dream of. Among them were postmen and lords, all willing to empty their wallets only to be—if for just half an hour—the slave to a sixteen-year-old girl dressed all in black, only her eyes peeking out from behind the dark cloth.

Derdâ's first customer was Mitch. He was nervous when he came over to Stanley's house. But the fear turned him on. Derdâ stood with her hands behind her back in front of the living room window; in her single-piece black chador she looked like a dark club. She was even shorter than Mitch had imagined and her small size—almost that of a child—fired his fantasies as he imagined Gulliver being tortured by the Lilliputians. Mitch was as heavy as Bezir—he weighed over two hundred pounds—but he was nothing but a tub of lard.

Derdâ was also turned on. She was used to Stanley's body and she wondered how she would deal with this redhead fatso squeezed in a leather jacket. Mitch's forehead was dripping with sweat and his eyes darted nervously about the room. Derdâ knew that her face was covered and that no matter how stimulated she felt, no one would be able to tell. Then she thought of Kurudere; she thought of the chain in Kurudere.

Mitch stood beside Stanley at the door to the living room. He gave a light nod to Derdâ. These guys were the perfect Laurel and Hardy combination, but Derdâ had never heard of them anyway. Calmly, she stepped between them without even glancing at their faces. Stanley and Mitch looked at each other in surprise. They followed Derdâ down the corridor and into the bedroom. They found her gripping one of the chains hanging from the ceiling; she was waiting for them. She'd attached an unbuckled leather belt to the end of the chain. She pointed at Mitch. He trundled up to her, as bumbling as Oliver Hardy.

Derdâ tightly wrapped the whip around her hand and whipped Mitch with a long leather whip for a full hour. Mitch's feet were bound in chains, Stanley's dirty Cramps T-shirt covered his head, and a studded choke collar was around his neck. Derdâ noticed Mitch's hands were still free and so she chained them, too. She was becoming quite the professional.

Derdâ lucked out by having a blubbery seal like Mitch as her first customer; he was turned on by even the slightest smell in the air, and she quickly learned the patterns of his reactions and desires. In the game of S&M no one is drawn to an indecisive master. Nothing turns a slave on more than an unbendable, iron will. In fact, it was just like what happened in real life. This was pure improvisation based on everyday scenarios. It was no different than a town's eventual liberation from an enemy occupation. In this kind of play, the master embodied life in all its cruelty and the slave was a solitary human being. After all, every

84

human being is beaten down by life, and rarely rewarded. It was that simple.

The walls of Stanley's bedroom echoed with cries of pain and pleasure, but the leather and steel accessories there were mere details, details to help victims get in the mood. In the real world there were telephone cards, briefcases, neckties, handbags that came with free perfume samples, glasses you wore just because they looked cool, color contacts, hair dyes, brochures for epil-ation at discount prices, and sports equipment bought to lose weight in the privacy of your own home but kept stashed away in the bedroom. The ears of bad children that get used to being yanked as they're yanked more and more, the steady rise in radi-ation levels, two-bedroom ground floor apartments bought on thirty-year payment plans; doing all the shopping on installment plans, the rule of law, police batons, food that gives you cancer, cigarettes that do the same—not to mention all the secondhand smoke—and the porcelain caps on the divinely radiant smiles of political and religious leaders. Words like "please" and "thank you" and the entreaties and apologies that always follow the very real violence of the real world. So it wasn't unhealthy for a per-son to accept his or her relationship with life for what it was—mostly painful, rarely pleasurable—and play the game according to its rules.

As some psychologists vapidly say to patients who partic-ipate in nights of S&M—it's only about understanding what's what. These tendencies aren't only the traumatic consequences of molestation or violation experienced in childhood. It was life itself that was traumatic, all of it, the whole damn thing. And especially all those things which on the surface don't really seem traumatic—like being born. In other words, postpartum depres-sion isn't a psychological illness particular to new mothers; a state of depression was life itself, the compulsion to go on living, in spite of life.

Stanley watched Mitch and Derdâ until he couldn't stand it anymore. He got up, took off his clothes, and then bent over Mitch's greasy, tattooed back and pushed himself inside him. Derdâ began beating both of them at the same time. She'd beaten Mitch so badly that he probably wouldn't be able to walk after it was all done. He put his clothes on and pulled out a twenty-pound note from his leather jacket and tossed it onto Stanley's bed. Derdâ wasn't amused. Despite the dark and ugly decor in the room, she found the gesture distasteful. Maybe she just didn't think it was respectful to toss money like that at the queen. *From now on, it'll be different*, she thought, and she turned to Stanley who had finally come to his senses.

"Your name?"

"Stanley."

Thus, she finally learned the name of the blue-eyed man she'd dreamed would save her from Bezir. Stanley would save her, although not quite in the way she initially imagined. *Stanley will collect the money from now on,* she thought. *I won't touch it.* Like most people with powerful imaginations, Derdâ had no understanding of money.

After the redheaded walrus left the apartment, she gave Stanley—as she'd promised—one of the two ten-pound notes. Derdâ went home and examined the bank note; she was curious about the woman wearing the crown. She'd seen her somewhere before. Once upon a time she'd thrown up on that face.

Six days later, Mitch came back—this time with a camera. They'd told Derdâ about the plan in advance. They had her kneel before Bezir's lectern, intently focused on the open Koran, the heavy-framed photograph of the Kaaba featured prominently before her. Then Stanley came into the living room in a full latex suit. That's when they'd start rolling film. They had it all planned out.

Derdâ remained motionless for a few minutes on her knees before the lectern. Then she began to slowly sway from side to side as she moved her lips, pretending to recite from the Koran, although her words were unintelligible. Then Stanley entered the room. His hands were handcuffed behind his back. He stopped two paces away from the lectern. Derdâ's eyes rose slowly to meet his. She shut the Koran and stood up. As she rose she picked up a forty-centimeter-long rubber horse whip she had beside the Koran. She approached Stanley, then unzipped one of the many zippers slashed across his latex suit. A piece of uncircumcised flesh rolled out. Stanley did everything in his power to remain flaccid. Derdâ lifted lightly the tip of the lifeless flesh with her whip and Mitch zoomed in on Derdâ's eyes for a close-up. Derdâ shook her head and coolly said, "No, no, no." Then she snipped the air with her fingers as scissors. She opened and closed them three times.

Stanley's flesh was quickly swelling with blood and Derdâ snapped it with the end of her whip. Then she squinted at the sign on the armchair behind Mitch. She'd written her line on a large piece of paper and practiced it over and over with Stanley. It was barely intelligible through her thick Turkish accent.

"I will circumcise you," she said. In Derdâ's thick foreign accent the words were all the more sexy.

From then on, neither Derdâ of Yatırca nor Stanley of London spoke. They only groaned. One threatened and the other groaned in fear. What happens between East and West, happened then between Derdâ and Stanley. Threat and supplication. Punishment and reward. Apathy and violence. Sadism and masochism.

Mitch knew he was holding a masterpiece when he burned the CD in his cramped flat. He was right. Within a week the forty-four-minute film of a man's circumcision by a covered Muslim woman would be the rage through all the dark clubs and the dark houses of London. They would be awestruck by Derdâ. Remembering what he'd once said to Stanley, Mitch wrote on the CD: "A Muslim Woman Is a Nuclear Bomb."

Derdâ's take from her first film—admittedly the title was a little long—was only five hundred pounds, although the film had earned Mitch and Stanley 4,300 pound sterling. It was the first time she was ripped off in the performance world. In the real world, she was deceived all the time but she never knew. Five hundred pounds made her feel like the richest woman in the world. But cheating his master to buy more meth made him feel guilty, and he needed something stronger to silence his pangs of conscience—he needed heroin.

In three weeks Derdâ appeared in four more of Mitch's films and had sixteen new customers arranged by Stanley. She gave them the most unforgettable thirty minutes of their lives. She had no inkling she'd become a star lighting up the dark face of London, whose eyes searched everywhere for her. She was a woman of mystery. They paced behind all the covered women on the streets hoping they might find her. And they laid plans to track her down. But Derdâ didn't care. All she wanted was to disappear into London with the 3,600 pounds she had stashed in the hood above the stove and her English vocabulary—now close to four hundred words—that she kept locked in her memory. She had to escape from the apartment building. She was ready. The time had come. She'd just go. She wasn't scared. What could happen out there that was any more dangerous than what happened in her own apartment? But she had to plan carefully. First, she had to finish her association with Stanley. Bezir might go see his neighbor and make him talk, and if Stanley knew where she was, it would all be in over. It wouldn't be hard to make Stanley talk. So she wouldn't say anything to Stanley or Mitch. She'd asked their help for just one thing. Two weeks ago, she asked them to buy her clothes and a pair of shoes. That was all.

Derdâ would just disappear. She didn't think she'd have trouble finding somewhere to stay. And she'd find a job, too. Maybe she'd move to another city in England, or to another country, somewhere far from Bezir. Anywhere really. Meanwhile, Bezir had completely changed—he'd grown distant and even more silent. And he didn't beat Derdâ anymore. He never laid a hand on her. Sometimes he didn't come home for days on end. All of this made Derdâ worry about timing her escape. Best to disappear as soon as possible.

That night she couldn't sleep. Two hours before the early morning prayer she slipped out of bed as silently as a snake. She watched Bezir for any sign of movement as she quietly backed out of the room. She put her black chador on over her nightgown in the other bedroom, then went to the kitchen. She got her money and dictionary out of the stove hood. Then, with a last look at her dark apartment, she opened the door and slipped outside and left the door halfway shut behind her. She couldn't make the slightest sound; she wouldn't use the elevator. With a final glance at Stanley's door she started tiptoeing down the steps. Then she remembered something. She went back up to the twelfth floor and opened the fire hose box just opposite the elevator. She'd oiled the hinge the day before so she knew it wouldn't creak. She pulled a bag out from above the thick, red, tightly wrapped hose—she'd almost forgotten all about it. She'd stashed her new clothes here. Then she turned around and walked away, never to return.

Twelve floors later she found herself at the building's main door, the same one she'd raced through to follow Bezir carrying Ubeydullah in his arms. It was ten minutes later before she figured out how to open it. You had to press the white button on the wall to automatically open the door. She started at the heavy clank of the lock, then she pushed open the heavy door and darted out.

She walked down the dark garden path and stepped onto the sidewalk. Which way? The street seemed so long. She looked right and then left. She saw an indistinct figure in the distance, a man with his hands shoved in his jacket pockets coming toward her. Derdâ was filled with fear. She turned and started to run the other way.

The indistinct figure stopped where the garden path met the sidewalk. He waved at Derdâ to come back and looked up at the building. Then he set off down the garden path. When he arrived at the entrance, he took a piece of paper out of his pocket and used his lighter to check the address and building number. He entered the four-digit password onto the security panel beside the door. There was a metallic clank and he pulled the door open.

The elevator was waiting at the ground floor. He stepped in and pressed the button for the twelfth floor. The elevator door slowly opened and the ceiling light switched on automatically. He checked the numbers on both doors in the hall. He approached the door near the stairs and pulled a screwdriver out of his jacket's inner pocket. As he lowered it to the lock, he realized the door was ajar. He slowly nudged it open and peered into the dark apartment. He put the screwdriver back in his pocket and drew a gun before he stepped into the apartment. He crept down the corridor, passing the living room and the kitchen. Both were empty. The bathroom was empty, too. There was a closed door at the end of the corridor. He reached out for the handle but before he got there the door swung open. He was face to face with Bezir.

In a flash Regaip pulled the trigger, killing Bezir instantly. He was afraid, at least partly. He did it because he'd once served in the government militia. He did it out of the memory of a fight years ago when he was almost choked to death. But when he couldn't find Derdâ he cursed himself for killing his only source of information. Bezir had to have known where she was. He would've satisfied Gido and he would've found his daughter, too, who was now a widow and nowhere to be found. *I'll find her soon enough,* he thought, *it wasn't fated to end this way.*

Regaip couldn't know that in the days to come others would say the very same thing—it wasn't fated to end this way. He didn't know that ten men would gather in a kickbox club and decide to abandon their plans. "Bezir's gone, the business is finished," they'd say. The plan had been to plant bombs in four of the busiest tube stations. The plan was dropped and the bombs were dumped in the Thames. Regaip didn't know any of this. Just like those kickboxers didn't know that, years later, a London underground station and a double-decker bus would be blown sky-high by four al-Qaida militants. They didn't know that in those suicide attacks on July 7, 2005, fifty-two people would die and that seven hundred people would be injured.

In the end, it was left to other people to fuck England. Not to Bezir who had fantasized of blowing London up just because he was angry with himself.

Derdâ was running as fast as she could but she didn't have any idea where she was going. She ran as if she'd been running away from Bezir all her life. She didn't know he was dead. She ran because she hadn't run for five years. She ran faster and faster, her legs feeling lighter and lighter. She sprinted through the spots of light cast on the sidewalks by the streetlamps, through totally deserted back lanes, past bronze statues that made her think that all life in London had stopped to watch her, faster and faster as she was filled with a feeling she'd never felt before: freedom.

The cold night air stung and her eyes teared up, but Derdâ didn't slow down. Her heart—all but sixteen years old—thundered like a military band, a military band celebrating a victory in war. And she laughed as tears streamed over her lips, but there was no one to share in her joy. Just like Stanley had described it before—she neither walked nor ran. She glided, she flew under the city lights like the dark shadow of a colorful butterfly.

When she arrived at the Crouch Hill intersection, she stopped. Not because she was fazed by the choice of five directions, but to listen to the sound of her heartbeat, so loud it was like the sound was pouring out of her mouth. She looked back at where she came from. She couldn't see the apartment building and there was no sign of Bezir. It was all history now, everything, her entire past. She spread her arms wide and fell down on her knees. She looked up at the sky where the stars were living behind the clouds and she let out a cry like she'd done five years ago. "AAAAAA!" This time it was a cry of happiness. AAAAAAs of happiness! She saw the lights go on in nearby apartments, so she got to her feet and started running again down one of the five streets. If she could have, she would've taken them all, to make up for all the streets she'd never taken before. But she had to choose one. She did, not someone else; the choice was hers. She said, "I'll take this one." And she took the one she wanted. She turned and raced down the third street on the left.

When she realized there were fewer and fewer houses and gardens lining the street she slowed down and the smile on her face slowly dissipated like steam off a mirror. She was exhausted. She needed to find a place where she could rest until morning, a place that was both safe and warm. Around the corner, she saw a red phone booth enclosed by panes of glass, a red phone booth, a home for one. Derdâ spent her first night alone in London in a telephone booth, using the space as best she could.

In the morning, she felt a hand on her shoulder and she quickly opened her eyes and covered her face with her hands. Bezir looming over her, his hand raised, always caused the same reaction. Sometimes he'd stretch out his hand for a glass in the cupboard and Derdâ would wince and jump back out of his way, her hand over her face. But this time there wasn't a slap. She slowly spread her fingers and peered out. She saw a little boy no older than five. He was smiling—his two front teeth were missing. Suddenly his mother seized him by the wrist and dragged him out of the phone booth. They bustled off, the boy in tears, the mother scolding him for talking to strangers.

Derdâ tried to stand up but her legs were too numb from sleeping so cramped up. She rubbed them for a minute and then struggled to her feet. With her first stride out of the telephone booth, her chador billowing in the breeze, *Süper Derdâ* was brimming with courage, ready to face her worst enemy—her future.

Crouch End was one of those satellite neighborhoods. Only a few bus lines connected it to the city center. Here, old, cared-for houses and their gardens lined the streets. The sidewalks were never busy, and the walls along the street were covered in moss. Bob Dylan had once lived in Crouch End. It was a neighborhood where the unemployed lived with their kids who weren't able to build a life for themselves, who sat on benches all day, making biting remarks to one another, killing time as they absently stared at the other side of the street. But on that day, Crouch End, for Derdâ, was a place to find a restaurant, a place where she could change her clothes and get some food. She approached an older man sitting on a bench. His blond hair was just beginning to turn gray. He turned and looked up at Derdâ. His back stiffened when he saw it was her. But he couldn't completely trust his aging eyes and he waited for Derdâ to come a little closer. When she was just above him, he studied her eyes carefully. He knew those eyes, those were the black eyes he stared at, transfixed, when he paused the video at the height of a scene.

With Derdâ now right in front of him, he couldn't help but stretch out his hand and take the girl by the arm. Derdâ pulled her arm back and jumped away, but then stopped, turned back, and looked at the man with grayish-blond hair. The man stood up and put his hands up in the air, open palms facing Derdâ as if to say, "I surrender," and he said, "I'm so sorry! It's just that I'm your number one fan. Really, I am very sorry, indeed."

No one had ever apologized to Derdâ in her own home, but she knew all too well the meaning of an apology at Stanley's, as part of her job was to force people to apologize and grovel before her. She kept listening to the man. He stood up and was an arm's distance away from her. He extended his hand for her to shake.

"The name's Steven. And it's a real pleasure to meet you."

Derdâ looked down at his thin, wrinkled hand and then looked at his face. She didn't take his hand.

"Could I speak to you for a moment?" asked the man. "If you have time, of course? We could have coffee somewhere?"

Derdâ looked just how she did in her films. She was short, but somehow seemed taller than everyone else. She was often silent, but it seemed like she was angrily cursing inside.

"I know you from your films," said the man. "Sensational stuff!"

Derdâ recognized the word: film. She chuckled from under her chador.

"Please," the man begged. "Just five minutes. There's a place just around the corner. I promise I won't keep you very long."

Derdâ's voice cracked—it was the first time she had spoken since her rebirth.

"Alright," she managed to say.

The man bowed like a true gentleman and held out his hand to show Derdâ the way. "This way, please."

Derdâ walked three paces ahead of him.

They went to one of the oldest pubs in Crouch End. A group of old age pensioners gawked at Derdâ in her black chador like she'd come from another planet. Soon a waitress arrived and Derdâ hastily asked her where the bathroom was. The waitress gestured toward the back of the pub. Derdâ took her bag and went.

In the bathroom, she examined her reflection in the narrow mirror for some time before she took off her chador and the nightgown underneath. She folded them and put them in her bag. Then she put on a pair of black jeans (clearly an indication of Stanley's goth taste), a black Cramps T-shirt, and a black leather jacket. She unzipped her thick black plastic shoes and looked at them with disgust before chucking them in a can overflowing with soiled toilet paper. Then she put on her new red Dr. Martens.

She was totally transformed. She was a new woman, her hair flowing freely down to her lower back. She touched it and frowned. It made her mad. She wasn't bothered by the jeans or the T-shirt, but having her hair in full view was too much too fast. With her bag slung over her back and her leather jacket over her arm, she took a deep breath and opened the bathroom door.

Derdâ's number one fan couldn't believe his eyes. So many things raced through his mind just then. The girl was much more beautiful than he ever imagined she would be; her breasts were smaller than he'd imagined them, but her face seemed somehow familiar.

He ordered coffee for himself and was pleased when Derdâ asked for the menu. He would have more than just five minutes with her. After some hesitation over words she didn't know, Derdâ randomly pointed to a dish on the menu. Her choice was steak with mushroom sauce and French fries. It was her lucky day and she didn't even know why.

"I'm sorry to say it, but it seems we won't be able to understand each other?"

Derdâ was inspecting the dirt between her nails and marveling at the parts of her body now fully exposed; she raised her head and said, "Maybe." She seemed to have a faint recollection of the man.

"Then let me ask you this, could it be that we've met before?"
Derdâ didn't understand.
"Where are you from? Which country?"
She still didn't understand.
"Spain? Italy? Romania? Somewhere else?"

Derdâ just smiled pleasantly. She really didn't understand a word. Just then the waitress brought Steven's coffee and a paper placemat with a history of the pub, a napkin, a fork, and a steak knife for Derdâ. The man went on naming countries.

"Greece? Turkey?"

Suddenly Derdâ tuned in. She didn't exactly understand what the man was trying to say, but she was sure she'd heard the word "Turk." Now he knew that he had something and he said "*Türkiye*?" Derdâ nodded. He continued in Turkish.

"Alright, OK, now I remember you. You were just a child then. You applied for a visa with your father in Istanbul."

Derdâ squeezed the handle of her steak knife. She knew the decision she'd make at that second was crucial. The son of a bitch who'd opened the door to the past five years of hell was sitting right across from her. Now she recognized Steven. The taste of that horrid chocolate he'd given her that day still lingered in her memory. She imagined driving her steak knife deep into his chest, or skewering his thin, wrinkly hand onto the table. But she didn't. She kept on listening.

"How many years has it been? Five, six? What an incredible coincidence, don't you think?

Derdâ nodded her head, forcing herself to smile a little.

"You do remember me, don't you?"

Derdâ nodded her head again.

"Why don't you come over and see me sometime?"

Derdâ nodded her head for the last time before cutting into her steak. She'd get her revenge out on this guy some other time. But right now she needed someone who could help her adjust to life in London and he was the only English person she knew who spoke Turkish, so she couldn't kill him, at least not yet.

Steven's semidetached house had a garden in perfect trim with stunning red and white roses. It was only few streets away from the pub but Derdâ felt as if each and every person they passed on the way was staring at her hair. Those few minutes spent fantasizing about how she'd gouge out their eyes made her forget her hatred for Steven. Steven unlocked the green wooden door to his apartment and they both stepped inside.

The house was both cozy and tastefully decorated, and it seemed like a happy family lived there. It was extremely neat and tidy. Steven gestured for Derdâ to sit down on the sofa. It had a white and red rose design just like the roses in full bloom in his garden. Derdâ sat down in the armchair beside the couch. She knew that if she sat down on the sofa Steven would sit right next to her. But as it happens he had other plans. He wanted to show Derdâ one of her films.

He picked up the remote and turned on the DVD player. Then he turned to Derdâ, perched on the edge of the armchair, and said, "Please make yourself at home," adding, "you might want to put your bag down?" Derdâ was still clutching her bag. She slowly set it on the floor but she was startled at the sight of her own image on the TV screen. She felt nothing at all.

It wasn't long before the film quickly got violent and Derdâ looked at Steven who was standing over her. As far as she could judge his expression, he was intently following everything. His face went through a range of emotions. First sour, then pleased, then frustrated. Every now and then he chuckled. This old guy was nothing like Stanley or Mitch. But it did occur to Derdâ that Steven was just as mad as Rahime. Derdâ looked back at the screen and was shocked to see her own two eyes staring right back at her, a frozen frame of her frozen gaze. Steven had paused the film just at a close up shot of her eyes.

He gingerly placed the remote control on the couch and said, with a queer smile on his face, "What is it you wear? Would I be able to find one for myself? What do you call it?"

"A chador," Derdâ said.

He snapped his fingers, leaned forward on his toes, then rocked backward.

"That's it!" he cried. "A chador! Where can I find one?"

Unmoved by his surprise, Derdâ simply nudged her bag on the floor with her Dr. Martens.

"I have one in here."

Steven was sixty years old but he had the build of a child, as if he'd been afflicted by a serious illness in his youth that had stunted his growth.

"Really?" he said, and he nearly threw himself at Derdâ's bag before he stopped himself. He looked at her, his face racked with curiosity.

"Could I have a look at it?"

Derdâ remained silent while Steven leaned over and pulled her black chador out of the bag. He wore an excessively courteous expression on his face, as if he were handling a sacred possession of the royal family. He held it up to the sunlight beaming through the window.

"Perfect!" he said in English. And then he continued in Turkish.

"How do you put it on?"

Four hours later, Steven and Derdâ were sitting at the table just behind the sofa eating pasta. He was wearing Derdâ's black chador. Derdâ eagerly ate her food as she spoke. She was much more at ease than she had been before.

"Now your face is exposed. You're eating. But soon it'll be covered, too. Only your eyes will show."

"Yes," said Steven, almost whispering.

"You won't speak permission," Derdâ roared. This was her catchphrase from her latest film. Steven was about to agree, but he stopped himself and covered his mouth with his hand as he made coy circling gestures under his eyes and smiled coquettishly like an Ottoman madam.

"I'll stay here tonight," Derdâ said.

Steven nodded in assent, and he nodded again and again.

"Maybe I'll stay tomorrow, too," she went on.

Seeing Steven now entirely subservient, Derdâ became even bolder.

"Maybe I'll never leave. And you will teach me English. Yes, we'll start tomorrow."

And then with a glance at Steven's empty plate she erupted. "That's enough already. You've had more than your share. Now get up and clear the table!"

As Steven hurried to clear the table, Derdâ had a look around the house. She stopped in front of a walnut china cabinet with crescent moon and star reliefs—clearly it was from Turkey. Tucked away among a set of crystal whisky glasses and souvenir plates from various countries, she saw a packet of Camel cigarettes. Steven had been struggling to quit and though he'd been clean for some time he still kept a single pack of Camels in the china cabinet as a kind of prisoner of war. Derdâ opened the cabinet door and pulled out the pack. She took out a cigarette and shouted, "Rahime!" Steven was now Rahime. He'd fallen in love with the name the moment he'd heard it. Derdâ had learned a lot from Mitch's scripts. The first way to break down a person's sense of self was to deny him his name—it was far more effective than just beating him with rods or bats. The slave was then renamed. The master was the one who named it. Like a child who names his pet, or like the Americans or Europeans who came and arbitrarily labeled a vast geography the "East"—only because the land lay east of their borders—and who forced the people of that geography to accept the name.

Holding up his chador so he wouldn't trip over himself, Steven scurried over to Derdâ who told him to bring her a lighter. Steven raced to the kitchen and came back with a box of matches. Derdâ put the cigarette between her lips and watched Steven light her cigarette. Steven was so excited that his hands were trembling. He clumsily snapped the first two matches in half, but he finally managed to light his master's cigarette. Derdâ began to smoke in perhaps the most unusual of circumstances.

She took her first drag and coughed twice, and after the next drag, only once. After that, she never coughed again. The inside of the china cabinet was lined with mirrors inside and Derdâ's eyes were stuck on the image of her long hair like a fishhook stuck in seaweed. She couldn't take her eyes off her hair. She stared and stared. And stared. She snuffed out the cigarette in a souvenir plate with windmills from Amsterdam and made for the kitchen.

She looked at Steven in the bathroom mirror. She stared at his hands, at the scissors in his hands. First her braid fell to the floor, and then he cut off the rest of her hair. Steven's eyes found her eyes in the mirror. They asked her if he'd cut enough. But her hair still bothered her. As long as she had hair on her head she'd feel naked in public. "All of it!" she commanded. "Cut it all off. And then you'll shave my head."

Steven put down the scissors and finished the job with a razor. He rubbed the remnants of the shaving cream off Derdâ's bald scalp with a towel and tears welled up in the young girl's eyes. But she was determined not to let Steven see her cry. She was, after all, his master. She could not cry in front of him. She slid her hands over her scalp. It seemed like an entirely different person was staring back at her from inside the mirror. For a moment, she wondered what her mother would say if she saw her like this, but she stopped herself, straightened, and lit another cigarette. She could stop herself from staring into the mirror, but she couldn't stop feeling the top of her naked head.

That night she smoked the whole pack. And with each breath she felt a little better, as if she were born again, as if she bore the bald head of a newborn baby on her shoulders. She no longer had hair and so she no longer felt like she needed to cover her head. She wished she'd shaved her head years ago.

For the next few weeks Steven adopted Rahime's role and Derdâ became Bezir—communicating mainly with her fists—and they rarely left the house. Deep down, both of them felt ashamed, though they never talked about it. Indirectly encouraging one another to be more independent in their new roles, they were able to reluctantly venture outside. They went to the local supermarket. Steven had become comfortable with his new identity much more easily than he'd thought he would. After all, only his blue eyes were visible. People only realized he was a man when he spoke. When he asked for an extra bag in the supermarket, or when he couldn't make out the expiration date of a product and had to ask a supermarket employee for help.

But there was another reason why people were staring at Steven. It was something to do with planes. To be exact, planes that were flown into buildings on US soil and caused the death of several thousand people just in New York City alone. The September 11th attacks. That's why he attracted attention, and the attention of his neighbors in particular. Ever since he moved into the neighborhood, Steven had had little contact with them. They despised Rahime from the beginning, but their principles didn't allow them to express their feelings. After all, in Crouch End people didn't have anything against homosexuals or transvestites. Their liberal views and tolerance toward all walks of life and lifestyles was a point of pride. They felt they were an example for all of humankind. They wouldn't have ostracized Steven even if he had dressed up like a little girl. But, like every human being, they had to have someone to outcast. And those planes came at just the right time to satisfy this fundamental need, just at a time when there was nothing left that they could demonize, right at a time when respect and tolerance in society was becoming too overbearing for them, just at that very time in history when it was considered inappropriate to malign someone because of his or her appearance. They hated Rahime the moment they saw her. You could see their true feelings in their faces. Scorning Muslims had become a kind of sport in England, a sport more popular than cricket, even before 9/11. And everyone wanted a part of the game. What's more, the winners were rewarded with a very special prize for initiating a struggle based on the basest urges and a bonus medal for their nationalism. They were both racist and progressive at the same time. Who wouldn't want that?

So the time that Steven decided to don his black chador was at the least ideal point in history. But he quickly learned not to care. And Derdâ got used to her bald head and to smoking. In the daytime, she studied English, and at night, they watched Derdâ's films or other films of the same genre. Apart from that, they remained strangers. Steven had long since given up on his steel balls. For years now his sexuality was only ever manifested when he lay alone in his bed, vacantly staring at the ceiling. So Derdâ had hit upon what might have been the best living situation in all of London, perhaps in all of Great Britain. She ate and she slept and she learned English and she managed her slave. She no longer so desperately despised the commercial attaché who played such a pernicious part in her past. Before long her desire for revenge would vanish into thin air. In other words, everything seemed too good to be true. Then one day there was a knock on the door.

Derdâ opened the door and found Stanley standing there. Her eyes opened wide in utter shock. She felt paralyzed.

Confused at the appearance of a young girl at his house, Stanley asked her, "Who are you? Where's dad?"

"He's inside," Derdâ whispered. She was hardly able to speak. Behind Stanley there was a man in blue overalls holding a stack of cardboard boxes waiting to come in.

"Everything's going upstairs," Stanley said. Then he took a closer look at Derdâ. He looked at her Cramps T-shirt. Narrowing his eyes, he thought for a moment, but then shaking his head he stepped inside.

"Dad! Dad, where are you?"

When Steven appeared at the top of the stairs, Stanley turned and looked at Derdâ in pure shock. He didn't know what to say or think. Which one had been his next-door neighbor until just a month ago? The bald girl who had the same eyes and the right body, or the one in the black chador? Steven spoke and then he knew.

"Why didn't you tell me?"

Stanley took a few steps forward and said, "Dad? Is that really you?" He turned to Derdâ. "And you? Are you . . ."

Steven came downstairs and stood between, like a carbon copy of his idol.

"She's the mysterious mistress of us all!"

The words "Mysterious Mistress" flashed on the screen when Derdâ made her first appearance in her first film. It was Stanley's idea. It had been his idea. Now he lowered his head and stared at the girl standing before him. *Life is such an infernal web of coincidences,* he thought.

Derdâ was in no position to deny it. She accepted the nickname with a nod of her head. And Stanley started to laugh. Soon he was roaring with laughter.

Stanley had moved back home. He moved into his old room on the second floor of his father's house and became another one of the sullen kids in Crouch End who never grow up.

After he got over the initial shock of his father in effect becoming Derdâ—all it had taken was for Stanley to find the transformation entirely absurd and then just laugh it out—he told them about Bezir's murder in Finsbury Park and everything that had happened after that. But he didn't mention that he'd been fired from Stick and that he had to leave the apartment because he'd blown all his money on heroin.

"I was scared, Dad," he said. "The place had turned into a living hell. Think of it, they shot my neighbor!"

Steven shook his head and said, "Then you'll just have to stay here, there's nothing else we can do about it."

Then, pointing out Derdâ to his son, he went on, "You two have met, right?"

"That's right," said Stanley, smiling. And turning to Derdâ, he said, "So we've met before then." All his admiration and respect for his former master was gone. She was no longer covered.

Those feelings blew away like a handful of dust in the wind. She looked like any other girl from London to him now. She looked like any one of those idiots killing time out on the streets. He listened to his father's romantic story. How he'd first met Derdâ in the Istanbul consulate and then their dramatic reunion on a sidewalk bench in Crouch End. He was convinced it was all fated to be. Stanley could understand why Derdâ liked staying in the house. In the kitchen, he told Derdâ the police were looking for her. He made a point of letting his father know, too. He hoped this would encourage him to get rid of her. But his father was now Rahime, and he didn't give a damn about Scotland Yard.

Stanley didn't mind that his father now wore a chador, or that Derdâ ordered him around as her slave. Still somehow it reminded him—if only rarely—of happy days in the past and of his mother. But were those really happy days? First of all, his mother hadn't really been around. She'd left home when Stanley was eight. After opening a ninth anniversary gift Steven had given her she just up and left, just half an hour after thanking Steven for the steel balls chained together, thinking that it was some sort of necklace. Only twenty-five minutes after Steven told her, "But they're for me, not for you." Twenty-four minutes after she heard him say, "I want you to push both those balls into me one by one." In the years that followed, she'd done everything she could to gain custody of Stanley. But the judge in charge of their divorce proceedings was Steven's friend. They knew each other from the London dungeons where Steven had himself whipped on the weekends. In the end, the verdict came quickly enough and it was in Steven's favor. Then the judge pushed those steel balls into Steven as eight-year-old Stanley watched them through the keyhole of his office door.

After that, something happened to Stanley, some kind of strange chemical reaction occurred, and he stopped growing and felt tremendous pain. Like all people who suffer such a life,

Stanley lived in his own fantasies. But when he stepped into the pit and came in contact with reality, he really began to suffer. He got older without really growing and he felt the pain more and more. So he began to fill those voids with the heroin he bought off a fourteen-year-old boy called Black T, whose real name was Timur. He'd used to hang out at the entrance of the Finsbury tube station. Stanley did it so he wouldn't have to deal with reality and break some part of his body, like his heart.

Fourteen years old. That period in human life known by the science of psychiatry as adolescence, that branch of science taught from behind rickety desks with wobbly legs, that period of human life in which symptoms are described by professors as irregular intermittent bouts of rage, inappropriate reactions, exaggerated behavior. All those books on adolescence talk about getting accustomed to oneself and one's environment, and about the difficulties in adapting to society. And the authors of those scientific articles, well, they never knew Black T and they couldn't even remember what the hell they were doing when they were fourteen. But the fact is that it's all pretty straightforward.

You're born and before fifteen years are up you realize just what kind of a place the world is and you know that you're just stuck somewhere between birth and death. It's a feeling more than it's actual knowledge. Then there's the first revolt. You scream as loud as you can. But it's no different than the desperate cries of someone in a crowd who realizes his wallet's been stolen. At first, people in the crowd look at him with contempt or indifference, then they get tired of listening to the noise and they appoint someone to speak to him. The representative comes and says: "So what if your wallet's been stolen? Our wallets have been stolen, too. But we're not making such a fuss." For a real scientific intervention, it's better to send someone with a diploma. So, faced with the indifference of the crowd, the rabble-rouser gradually makes less and less noise. He begins to accept reality and starts filling the void around himself with people. It's called growing up or becoming an adult. But to be more exact, it's about adult compliance or docility. It's an artificial mode of being. It's fabricated. Calculations have been made on its proposed function and it's shaped and designed accordingly.

The founding principle of adult compliance is the belief that each and every individual in a society should be useful in some way so that the existence of society is somehow guaranteed. And, more importantly, in a totally chaotic world, adult compliance is measured with deadly accuracy. It's all about the young tree bending down and kissing its own roots. But a fourteen-year-old kid's outrageous behavior is natural, even though it's frowned upon and classified as adolescent rage. His eyes have opened to the horrors of the world and he's come to understand that all the nasty business in the world is on him. He locks himself in his room. He tries to lock himself away from the outside world. Or he tries to break down all the doors and walls and barriers by screaming as loud as he can. It's the same kind of reaction you'd have to a fire-breathing dragon. It follows that these reactions won't disappear as long as you're alive—that's to say as long as the dragon exists.

But of course, as allowing a band of adolescents to remain in their natural state would lead straight to the disintegration of any societal structure, the transition to adult compliance is seen as a necessity for humanity. A social requirement. But some people are dense and they go on screaming till their dying breath. Because life is a violent process and the world is a violent place and what both life and the world deserve are extremely violent punches dead square in the face. It's why an adolescent revolt is thrusting a knife through someone sixty times to kill him. A fourteen-year-old kid who truly opens his eyes understands that every human is surrounded by at least sixty dragons with smoke bellowing out of their mouths.

Adolescence, in spite of all its stupidity, is the period in which a human being is most free.

When their lives and the world they live in become docile you can expect adolescents to calm down, but not until then. Stanley was one of those kids stuck at fourteen. And he might've seemed like an idiot coming home to his old room with The Cramps posters up on the walls, but at least he was doing his best to pay the world back in full for what it had given him. Not that he knew anything about life on earth. He didn't watch the news and he wasn't a political activist following his conscience. Stanley was doing everything he did without knowing anything about the world, like any other fourteen-year-old would.

Why did you need to know that somewhere in the world there were people bombing schools? This world reeked of burning flesh no matter how you looked at it. And why did you need to know that other kids in the world were dying of starvation? This world has halitosis because it's always hungry. Children's noses pick up the smell and give it back to the world as adolescent rage, till the time their noses are blocked with adult compliance. Would that day ever come for Stanley? It's hard to say. But for the time being he was having himself whipped and taking heroin because of a desperation he couldn't understand. He couldn't pinpoint its origin. Like any other fourteen-year-old, he couldn't express his pain. He felt something, but didn't know anything, so he was unable to see the shit all around him. But it always reeked. So, like most adolescents, he thought he was insane and he was constantly looking for someone he could infect with his madness.

He couldn't have found a better victim than Derdâ, Derdâ who once soiled her black gloves as she stimulated the nerve endings in his asshole. Her gloves smelled like shit. So Stanley became the man to give Derdâ her first heroin injection. It made them even. It settled the score. Derdâ learned that people gave both pain and pleasure to each other. First Derdâ to Stanley, then Stanley to Derdâ. First the children to their parents, then parents to their children; first the past to the future, then the future to the past; first nature to humans, then humans . . . First the dead to the living, then the living . . . In turns, back and forth, both pain and pleasure, until eternity, happy, the *dolce vita,* fuck!

When she heard that Bezir had been murdered Derdâ didn't feel a thing. But an hour later she started to cry when she looked at herself in the bathroom mirror. And she couldn't stop. The tears came from somewhere deep inside her, she was heaving tears. "Why?" she said to herself through her quivering lips. "Why, why, why . . ." Then slowly she pulled herself together. She composed her face and she dried the tears on her cheeks. She answered her own question in a whisper: "Why didn't I kill him myself?"

Then she laughed at herself in the mirror. She wondered what Bezir would do if he could see her now. What would he say? Would he beat her? Would he kill her? Would he throw her out the window?

Derdâ shouted at the mirror: "You couldn't do shit to me! Nothing! I'm right here! Come on you fucking son of a bitch! Here I am! You checked out, you bastard! You got the fuck out of here!"

She went through all the foul language she'd learned from Nazenin. She hadn't had the chance to learn anything new. When Bezir's image in the mirror faded, leaving only Derdâ's own reflection, the bathroom was still and Steven quietly moved away from the door and tiptoed down the corridor.

Derdâ could've stayed for five more years in that bathroom saying to the mirror what she hadn't said for the past five years. But instead she took one final look in the mirror and said,

"Fuck!" And she left. It was her last conversation with Bezir: a conversation without Bezir.

Like all addicts, Stanley could crunch figures faster than a calculator. He was sure that Derdâ had close to three thousand pounds. She was still wearing the same T-shirt, which meant she probably hadn't spent much of the money she'd saved up. Stanley wasn't sure how to approach her about it. So he decided to wait as he slowly finished his last few grams of heroin.

One night Stanley got the lucky break he was waiting for— Derdâ came into his room to bum a cigarette.

"I'm all out," said Stanley, "but I do have this." and he took a bag of heroin out of a metal box by his bed and shook it in the air like a little bell. Taking a step toward the silent bell, Derdâ asked him what it was. The answer came to her in full force ten minutes later. And from then on Derdâ had no reservations whatsoever about spending her money to get the exact same answer over and over again. She went to Stanley's room every day. She didn't wince at the sight of the needle over her arm because she'd been convinced by the almost-two-hour-long speech Stanley had given her. He sounded like a salesman pitching a state-of-the-art vacuum cleaner. Derdâ had been locked up for five years, a total of sixty months, close to two thousand days, almost forty-five thousand hours. And this gave her forty-five thousand reasons! Forty-five thousand reasons why she watched with curious eyes as the needle punctured her skin. She had forty-five thousand reasons to do anything, except suicide. Not that. She wasn't going to die. To compensate for those five years, she was going to live another fifty, no, another five hundred years. But if she kept on visiting Stanley's room, she'd have to make do with only a couple of years before her eyes closed on this world.

Meanwhile, she continued with her English lessons. She had ordered Steven never to speak Turkish again. She remembered the grammar she'd learned from her books. Now she only needed practice. She was in the test-drive phase. But when it came to heroin, the test-drive phase was different. It wasn't like any new car that you could test drive and then just walk away from without buying. A test-drive with heroin only ended in a crash. If the driver was still alive, he had to buy the wreck. He had to pay the price of surviving the accident. The price was a lifelong struggle to never crash again. But for now, Derdâ was still in the early days, just gazing out the window, enjoying the view. There were no obstacles on the horizon and so it never occurred to her that she'd eventually crash. But her money was running out. In a way, that wasn't a problem because Black T at the Finsbury tube station always helped her out. He always gave Derdâ a discount when she and Stanley went up to see him for a fix. They were neighbors.

Then time sped up and it seemed fragmented. Days, sometimes weeks, passed without either of them realizing it, and soon there were obstacles all over the horizon.

Everyone had sat down for dinner. With a smile on his face, Steven looked at his son and Derdâ. He no longer had any idea who Derdâ really was. Both their faces were pale, as pale as northern Europeans. The purple eyes that were once on the young girl's back were now on her nostrils, which had trouble taking in air. Steven was serving pasta.

Sitting down, he said triumphantly, "I have a new idea."

Worried by the enthusiasm in his voice, Stanley and Derdâ exchanged glances.

"What if we gave chadors a local brand name and produced them ourselves. Of course, they'd be the standard black, just like the one I have on now, but we could have a brand somewhere here on the chest, like 'Stevens' . . . Or . . ."

Steven went on thinking with his eyes fixed on the ceiling. Stanley and Derdâ realized that he really wasn't interested in their thoughts on the subject and they both looked down at their food. They absently twirled pasta on their forks. Neither of them was hungry.

"There could be a logo, don't you think? If only Lacoste sold chadors . . . Wouldn't it be nice, with a crocodile just here? Or maybe 'Fred Perry' chadors!"

He went silent for a minute and then continued, "Now I have something important to tell you both. Could you both please look at me?"

They reluctantly raised their heads.

"I'm going to have an operation."

"Are you sick?" Derdâ asked.

"No!" Steven cried and then chuckled. "Of course not. But in a way, yes, I am. I am sick. I am man. And I want to get rid of this . . . So I've decided to become a woman!"

Stanley interjected, "But you don't have that kind of money."

"Of course I do," Steven said. "Who do you think I am? I've worked all my life. I didn't just loaf around like you, waiting to die! More pasta?"

Their plates were already full of his pasta. But that didn't matter. The important thing was whether Steven was telling the truth or not. Did he really have money?

Stanley sprang to his feet and waved his fist in the air. "You're going to give that money to me!" he shouted.

Steven laughed again.

"No, sir, I'm not giving you a penny."

Stanley put his hands around his father's neck and then knocked him and his chair to the floor. Steven crashed into the floor and his feet flung out and kicked up the table, sending two plates of pasta flying across the room. Derdâ was shocked by the sudden commotion, and jumped up when the plates crashed to the floor. Steven might have died from a heart attack or cerebral hemorrhaging. His head had taken quite a knock against the floor. But he went on roaring with laughter before he was seized by a terrible coughing fit.

His son knelt down by his father and put his hands around his throat and screamed, "I'll kill you! You're going to give me that money. I'll kill you, I'm telling you . . . Look Dad, I'm begging you! Please, just give that money!"

As she stood on the other side of the open green wooden door, Derdâ looked at Steven and gave Steven her last order: "Stop crying, Rahime!"

The old man's eyes were full of tears. His master was leaving him. His threats and entreaties couldn't convince her to stay. Knocking down Steven in his chair hadn't changed a thing. His son's momentary hysterical fit resulted in Steven kicking Stanley out of the house. Steven threatened him in a way that was much more severe than Stanley had expected. "How would you like it if I called the police and had you arrested?" Steven asked him. Stanley couldn't handle even one night in police custody so he packed up his things and asked Derdâ if she was coming. Derdâ took her prized possession—her dictionary—and followed him out the door.

Steven grabbed Derdâ's arm the same way he'd done when he first met her on the bench. But she pulled her arm away, quickly turned, and gave him the order not to cry.

When she got to the garden gate, Derdâ turned around one more time and looked at Steven.

"Will you ever come back?" implored the man behind the chador. His words reminded Derdâ of Nazenin. This time she wasn't afraid to wave good-bye.

They headed for Stick. As they passed the Camdenhead pub, the skinheads hanging out by the door thought Derdâ—with her shaved head and Dr. Martens—was one of them.

They called out to her: "What the hell are you doing with that goth fag? Get over here!"

Derdâ hesitated for a moment, but Stanley took her by the arm and angrily pulled her along. He had no patience for those fascist leftovers from the eighties. He didn't even lift his head to look at them. Soon enough they arrived at Stick. A giant green-haired Russian stood at the entrance. They went in and went straight to the bathroom to inject the heroin they'd got from Black T. They'd spent a good half of Derdâ's money. Stanley finished first and when he came out he found Mitch.

"I don't know what the hell I'm going to do," Stanley said, after he'd given him a three-sentence rundown of what had happened.

Derdâ joined them. Mitch didn't recognize her. Stanley introduced them.

"So here's your film star! Ask her if she likes the current hell we're living in."

Mitch bent down and looked at Derdâ's face under the dim pub lights. He couldn't believe his eyes.

"No way!" he said. "Impossible!"

He looked at Stanley.

"Oh, yes," he said, calmly nodding his head.

He pointed at Derdâ. "She still doesn't understand us, right?"

Derdâ could now speak English pretty well, and with a commercial attaché's accent.

"I beg your pardon, but I've always understood you perfectly!"

Mitch roared with laughter and held out a glass of beer for Derdâ. She pushed the glass away and looked around the pub. That night Stick was a perfect madhouse. Transvestites, goths, punks who didn't care what year it was, seventy-year-old rock-abillies who had draped their jackets over their shoulders in the same way for the last fifty years, the Teddy boys who adjusted their hair every five minutes with not one but two different combs, the mods with their heavy jackets, and a lone drunk Japanese girl dancing on the bar. The DJ was playing "Girl Anachronism" by the Dresden Dolls and as Amanda Palmer's voice poured into people's ears, it temporarily blinded them, which was probably why almost everybody was just swaying back and forth in one spot with their eyes closed. Or maybe this was just because Stick was jammed that night and nobody could really move.

It was hard to say what all these people did during the day. But Stick was a place where they could take refuge in one another at night. In the past, they used to chase each other down with knives but this was a place where all dreamers of totally different styles came together because they'd become extinct. Now there was nowhere else for them to go. In a world where everything was changing so fast, they were stuck in the ruts like invariable coefficients. They were there because they felt like strangers on the streets that were once a second home to them. Now their only home was Stick, which was only one-tenth the size of a narrow street.

Mitch looked at Derdâ. "Incredible! So this is what you look like. What do you say? You want to get back in the film business?"

"No way," Derdâ snarled.

Stanley was intrigued.

"Do you really think we could bring her back? I mean, we could make some money if you shot a few new films, right?"

Mitch took a sip from his beer and thought for a moment.

"That's all over probably. We've already sold to every possible person interested. But if she wants to, there are a few guys I know . . . They're doing some stuff for a website. She could star in one of their films. I hear they pay well."

He pointed at two young men at the bar laughing at the Japanese girl. They looked like university kids, two fresh young faces, too clean for Stick.

"What kind of film?" Stanley asked.

"I don't know," Mitch said.

Derdâ broke up their conversation.

"No! Never again! It won't happen again!"

Stanley wasn't listening. He walked over to the men at the bar and started talking. He came back a few minutes later.

"They'll pay three thousand," he said. "Think about it, three thousand pounds!"

Mitch asked, "What are they shooting?"

"Straight porno, a man and a woman, something classic, about half an hour long."

By morning Derdâ came to understand total deprivation and agreed to do what she'd so adamantly rejected only a few hours before. They called the two guys shooting the porno. They'd told Stanley they were students at Cambridge. One of them answered the phone and told them to come over that afternoon. He gave them his address in Covent Garden.

They shivered violently until morning in Mitch's room. Then they took a few Valiums to ease the pain and hopped on the earliest train to Finsbury Park. They started the day by paying Black T everything that Derdâ had left in her pocket. Then they went into the cafe at the Arsenal football shop near the tube station and shot up in the bathroom.

When they came out, they asked Black T for change to buy train tickets. He gave them a few coins from the money they'd just given him, and they went to Covent Garden.

They made it to the address and looked for a place to sit down to rest for a while. They sat for a whole three hours on a street bench without saying a word. Only once Derdâ looked over at Stanley and said, "I'll kill you."

Stanley said, "You better pull yourself together."

With his ear up against the intercom, Stanley stared vacantly at Derdâ. Finally, a voice came through.

"Third floor, the door on the right. The elevator doesn't work."

The front door clicked open. They entered the building and walked up three flights. A man with short hair and glasses was peering out from behind a door. He was naked. Stanley stepped in, but Derdâ stood motionless on the last step.

"Come on," Stanley said. "Come in."

Derdâ took a step and then one more. She heard voices. Then she went in and saw them. Fifty-one naked men. To Derdâ, it looked like a thousand. They all went silent when she came in. Derdâ took a step back and heard the door close behind her. Then she heard Stanley.

"Come on, you have to do this, you know. Don't think about anything, nothing at all. Just let yourself go. None of this means anything. You understand? It doesn't mean a thing. Just go and open your legs and then we collect our money and leave."

Derdâ was silent. The one behind the door with glasses, assuming that she was ready, slowly pushed her forward. He led her through the men to the living room. The floor was covered with a transparent linoleum mat. Derdâ looked into the faces of all the men, including the one who opened the door, as best she could, turning around. Then she flung off her jacket and the men screamed. They were nervous but they began laughing. Soon enough they were clapping and grunting and making all kinds of absurd noises.

Each one was in their first year in economics at Cambridge. They were all there because they'd made a bet with the law students. A week ago they'd all watched a video of thirty-seven law students gangbanging a black girl. They'd watched it twice to be sure about the number and then a plan to break the record was born. Prostitutes walking the streets had turned them down. They'd gone to Stick as a last resort, hoping to find a woman insane enough to go along with their plan. Someone desperate for money. A heroin addict seemed like a pretty sure bet. After all, it hadn't been more than a year since the movie *Requiem for a Dream* had come out. Some of the scenes from the film were still fresh in their minds. They imagined them vividly as they masturbated in the dorm bathrooms.

Derdâ was completely naked. The one with the glasses put both his hands on her shoulders and pushed her down. Her knees hit the linoleum mat on the floor. Then he pushed her down further until she was flat on her back. A blond man stood over her. He looked down at Derdâ like someone on a bridge contemplating suicide, staring down at the water with fear in his eyes. Then somebody pushed him down onto his knees. The crowd started clapping, like one united pair of hands, then two, then twenty. The blond, adjusting his heartbeats to the claps, separated Derdâ's knees like a hunter prying open a trap. The clapping ceased.

Overwhelmed by the weight of the silence and the sight of nothing but naked bodies, the blond man fixed his eyes on Derdâ's breasts. Then he placed his palms somewhere near her shoulders. Everybody in the room held their breath. And the boy lowered himself over her. But it was no good. He couldn't get himself into her. Everyone in the room huddled closer to get a better look at Derdâ, the flower choosing death over blooming, and the boy whose face had gone pale. First there was heated discussion, and then a box was handed down to the blond. A little bit of Vaseline went a long way and convinced Derdâ despite her resistance. The blond replaced his palms back near her shoulders, held his breath, and pushed himself into her. And lost himself. It took four minutes for the harsh lines on his face to dissipate. For Derdâ, it felt like a little less than four years. He took off the filled condom and raised it triumphantly in the air like a champagne glass, making sure everyone could see it. Twenty thunderous claps and thirty screams.

After the first eight men, Derdâ began to confuse the faces and felt like none of it was real. Only in the darkness under her eyelids did she become aware of what she was doing. She wanted to die. She couldn't close her eyes again but she couldn't look at the faces dripping beads of sweat onto her face. So she looked directly into the camera held by the boy with the glasses, but he was moving all over the place. As best she could she kept her eyes fixed on the camera lens. After all, it was the only thing that wasn't foaming at the mouth. She lifted her head like a professional porno star and followed the small, black circle of the lens, never losing eye contact. Of all the things in that room, the only one that couldn't harm her was that lifeless object. So when the boy with the glasses discovered he was a natural porno director and disappeared out of Derdâ's view to take close-ups, Derdâ shouted out to him, "Come over here, come back!" She was surrounded by fifty-two slabs of flesh, one inside her and the remaining fifty-one being made ready manually. No surprise she chose to look at the camera, because Bezir wasn't there to stare at.

After the first twenty men, she started hitting the newcomers as they lowered themselves over her. She hit them on the face, on the shoulders, wherever she could. She didn't even look to see where slaps and punches were landing. But her eyes still followed the camera. And she swore at the ghosts in Turkish.

"Fuck you all! Fuck you! You sons of bitches! What the hell are you doing now? Why don't you come and do something? I'm here, where are you? Where are you?"

After the first forty men, she started crying and begging the camera with her eyes.

She cried, "Please save me! Please someone get me out of here! Help me . . ."

And after fifty-two, she lay unconscious on the linoleum mat, drenched in sweat and tears. She came to when Stanley shook her. Her eyelashes were glued together by her tears and with every breath little balloons formed in her nostrils. It was as if she'd been washed in glue. Fifty-two men had poured themselves into her. Who knows how many kilograms of their white, translucent cum were inside her. How much did it all weigh? Maybe that was why she couldn't stand up. Because of the weight of the bodily fluid all over her face and inside her. She couldn't move, so Stanley took her in his arms.

He went to the bathroom and set her in the bathtub as if laying her in her grave. First he adjusted the water temperature and then he bathed her. Derdâ thought of how Rahime had washed her. Rahime washed her like Stanley was washing her now. And she thought of Vezir, and the conversations that they had had in Rahime's house. She thought of all those fantasies when she'd slip her hand down her şalvar, hiding between the yellow armchair and the wall. In her fantasies, she was often surrounded by naked men and Bezir was forced to watch. She thought of all her myriad fantasies. But only one of them had come true, the one that never should have become reality. She had dared to dream it because she was sure it would always remain a dream. Then her mind fell upon a question: Who's the one to choose which dreams will come true? The one who dreams the dream or the one who makes you dream that dream?

She looked at Stanley as he dried her face with a big, white towel and she asked, "Did you know?"

Stanley remained silent and continued to dry her shoulders. She raised her voice.

"Did you know there would be so many men?"

"Yes," Stanley answered her.

"Why didn't you tell me?"

"What difference would it have made?"

No one was left in the living room apart from four already dressed students packing up the linoleum cover. Everyone else was already gone. There was something strange in the faces of the men still there, something that made them inarticulate. A heaviness akin to regret, a terrible weight that prevented them from lifting their heads. It was a weight a few thousand times heavier than the white and translucent heaviness that was all over Derdâ, and the color was much darker.

While Derdâ dressed she tried to look each one of them in the eye but she couldn't. They shifted their eyes and escaped into themselves, pretending to be busy rolling up the linoleum cover.

Stanley took out a wad of money from his pocket and said laughingly, "Life starts now." Derdâ stepped into the entrance hall, opened the door, and turned around to look at Stanley before going through the door.

"Fuck life!"

Three thousand pounds vanished in thirty-two days. They stayed at Mitch's place and they turned the money into heroin like alchemists. For thirty-two days they stayed locked up at home listening to the same album over and over again. *Off the Bone* by The Cramps. They especially liked their song, "The Crusher." One morning Derdâ took out the CD and tried to break it in two. She couldn't break it so she opened the window and threw it out onto the street and waited for a car to drive over it. Finally, it was crushed by a Volvo and she sat back, relieved. There was a knock on the door. She went to open it.

It was Black T. Though these two kids had been wrenched out of Turkey and catapulted to London, they still spoke to each other in English. They didn't even know the other spoke Turkish. They never got that far. They only talked about heroin. Quality, price, distribution, life on heroin, the fashion of heroin, death by heroin, and Black T's school life, on his heroin sales in the nearby schools. But it seemed like Black T wanted to talk about more this time.

"Why do you shave your head?"

"I have to. Why do you always wear sweatpants?"

"So I can run if I have to."

Black T was breaking marijuana he took out of his pocket into pieces and sprinkling it over the tobacco in the cigarette paper like it was some kind of spice. He stopped and laughed.

"Actually, you know what? One day I'm going to open a restaurant—a cool place. They'll be white tablecloths and everything. It'll be one of those places where the waiters are all old. My customers will be from the royal family. But it'll only be a front, because there'll be heroin in the salt and pepper shakers, or heroin in the salt shaker and cocaine in the pepper shaker, something like that. Some of the customers will know and they'll ask the waiter, "Do you have any salt?" even though there's already a shaker on the table. And the waiter will bring the real salt shaker. And when they ask for the bill, it'll be something like this. Duck a l'orange—forty pounds, wine—a hundred pounds, salt shaker—a thousand pounds. Everything will be out in the open, you know, nobody will be tricking anybody, you get me? I'll expand my business and cook at the same time. You know, I'll go to a culinary school. I think it's a great idea. I love to cook."

He lit his joint and took a deep drag.

"Want to work for me?"

Derdâ took the joint from Black T.

"I hate cooking," she said, inhaling.

Black T laughed.

"I'm not talking about that, idiot! You'll sell stuff for me. I mean, you'll carry it. I mean, if you go on like this, you will either end up a whore or you'll just die here. This'll be a real job and you'll get your share as payment. What do you say?"

"Stanley . . ."

"Fuck that goth fag. The guy came into this world to kill himself. He doesn't care about anything. Anyway, where are you from?"

"I don't know," said Derdâ.

"What do you mean 'I don't know'? How do you not know? Where were you born?"

"In an apartment building."

"Where?"

"In Finsbury Park. Twelfth floor."

"You know where I'm from. I'm Turkish. Do you know what that means? It means that no matter who gets in my way, I'll fuck him!"

"Great," said Derdâ. "I'm sure of that."

"You don't believe me?"

He took a flashy mobile phone out of his pocket and dangled it in front of Derdâ's nose.

"I'll dial a number with this and in half an hour this place will be burned to the ground! You understand? No one messes with the Turks! We'll fuck them all up! Anyway, what do you say? Will you work for me?"

"Any payment up front?"

"I don't want you to go all zombie on me before the job's done. Today's a trial day for you. Let's see if you can make 'employee of the month.' You'll get your pay in the evening."

"I know a little bit about Turkey," Derdâ said. "Which part are you from?"

Black T laughed.

"How in the world would you know? We're not talking about a holiday resort. I'm from Yatırca! Ring any bells? Yeah, right!"

Derdâ couldn't even laugh.

"When did you come here?"

"I had a sister. She died. I was nine years old. That's when we moved here. Actually, almost all Yatırca's here. I have lots of relatives here. Have you heard about the Fighting Wolves? They were on the news last week. For beating up a Kurdish kid in a tube station. But he was one who started it! They hate us, you know? You say that you're from Yatırca, so you're a Turk, and they go after you right away. You're a Kurd, they say. Anyway, that whole gang's related to me. You know, my mother's a Kurd—I think, or something like that. What the hell do I know? It's complicated. If you ask me, I'd rather be Jamaican. But don't say that to anyone. Don't you think they're cool? Right now they have a festival on in Notting Hill. I think they're great guys, always chilled out, but they fight good when they have to. Yeah, that's it, I should've been born Jamaican. Fuck! I wish Yatırca was in Jamaica. If only."

Derdâ was only interested in some of what Black T was going on about.

"Was your sister sick?"

"No, there was this fucking accident. She fell off a bed the day she started school. Off the top bunk. At least that's what they told me. I don't remember very much, though. All I know is that she fell down and cracked her head open in that fucked up school! Sons of bitches! They couldn't even keep a little girl safe! Do you know how old she was?"

Derdâ answered through numb lips: "Six . . ."

"How did you know?"

"Just a guess . . ."

"Sons of bitches!"

Derdâ still held herself responsible for that little girl's death. It was like Black T had been sent as some kind of retribution. Whoever it was who decided which of her dreams would come true, now he'd brought her the brother of the girl she'd killed. She could confess everything. She could stand up and shout, "I made your sister get in that bed! She died because of me!" But she didn't. Because whoever it was who brought Black T to her, he was a little late. Thirty-two days late. Because revenge for all the crimes she'd committed in all her life and all those crimes she was going to commit, had already been taken. Fifty-two naked men had taken revenge for everything. There was no revenge left to take. So she remained silent. Like a convict on a galley ship whose sentence had already been decreed. A Cosette as silent as Jean Valjean.

Stanley had been passed out right inside the front door for some time. Black T had to jump over him to get in the house.

He opened his eyes and mumbled, "I'm not goth. I'm just a fag!"

In the afternoon, Black T came back with a sports bag.

"Take this," he said.

He handed Derdâ a piece of paper.

"Here's the address. They're going to give you an envelope. Don't open it. Have a look on the other side of that."

He waited for Derdâ to look.

"You're going to take that envelope to this address. That's it. That clear?"

It was clear. Black T pulled out some cash and gave it to Derdâ.

"Take a taxi."

Then he leaned over and whispered into Derdâ's ear. He pointed to Stanley.

"Tell him to forget all that stuff I said about being Jamaican. OK? And that goes for you, too."

The first stop was Notting Hill. The taxi could only get so close. Every year the Trinidadians, Tobagonians, and Jamaicans organized a carnival in Notting Hill. It was in full swing. Roads in the area had been shut to traffic. Derdâ got out of the taxi and checked the address. Hundreds of people were moving down the street chugging beers. No one seemed likely to be able to stop and give directions. So Derdâ gave herself up to the crowd. As she moved closer to the carnival, the drums got louder. Ahead of her, she saw a group in the parade wearing red T-shirts, pounding furiously on drums. Derdâ made her way to the edge of the sidewalk and leaned against the police cordon, waiting for the drummers to pass. Then an open-air bus playing West Indian music out of massive speakers rigged on its top loomed into view. A group of topless girls gyrated to the music behind the bus. Derdâ smiled.

People on the back of the bus threw confetti into the crowd. Every so often the women would stop dancing to wildly shake their hips. They wore colorful bikini bottoms, and some had enormous feathers attached to their waists that made them look like peacocks. Spectators seemed less interested in the dance than in their bodies. Eyes were riveted on their quivering hips, their breasts, and the sweat glistening on their bodies. Most of them were men but not a few were lesbians. It was a feast for the eyes. Everyone was getting their fill.

Derdâ remembered she was there to do a job and began to feel restless. She forced herself through the crowd and turned down the first open street. Music was blaring there, too. A reggae band was performing on an open stage and a crowd was dancing to the music, marijuana smoke hovering above them like a low cloud. Derdâ stepped into the crowd and noticed a policeman and a policewoman absently surveying the scene. As if the only duty they might be willing to perform was helping someone find an address. Derdâ was no longer afraid. She held the address out to the woman, leaned toward her ear, and shouted, but the music was so loud that she could hardly hear her own voice. Body language was the only option. The policewoman pointed to the opposite street and shook two fingers for the second street on the left.

The street was relatively quiet. Two-story town houses with front stoops lined both sides. Derdâ could easily read the house numbers. The street seemed completely deserted. Then she noticed a group of people lined up in front of one of the houses up ahead. At least ten people all patiently waiting in the line. As she got closer, Derdâ realized it was the house she was looking for. *No way they're selling drugs like this,* she thought. And she was right: these people weren't lining up to buy cocaine or heroin.

Ignoring the people in line, Derdâ walked straight through the front door and held up the card with the house address to a Jamaican standing inside. He understood that she had something to deliver. "Come on in," he said and he was pleased to tell Derdâ why all the people were queuing up outside.

"Dese people are just a waiting for the toilet. One person, one pound. Not too bad, eh? Not too bad . . . Dey drink like animals and den dey don't have no place to go, man. Every year we take more money like dees dan we do selling fried chicken. And you know how? Wid a hole, man? We just renting to dem a hole!"

They went up a narrow staircase and into a room where three Jamaicans and a pit bull seemed fast asleep. But they were just listening to music, from time to time looking up at the ceiling, at each other, or just into empty space, as they bobbed their heads up and down to the rhythm of the music. Not too fast, not too slow. A record player in the middle of the room was playing Desmond Dekker. The king of ska. "Rude Boy Train" blasted out of speakers in all four corners of the room.

The Jamaican from the front door left to run his lucrative business downstairs. The Jamaicans in the room seemed uninterested in Derdâ, though the black pit bull raised his head to look at her momentarily before nodding off again.

Derdâ said, "Black T sent me. You have an envelope for me."

And she dropped Black T's bag on a low coffee table between two leather armchairs. The Jamaicans looked up lazily at the bald girl, their heads still moving to the rhythm of the music.

One of them said, "It been a long time since a skinhead visit us."

Another one: "It been a long time since we beat a skinhead."

The third: "You go on, Bob!"

As Derdâ jumped back to the door, the three men cracked up laughing and Bob started barking. One of them stood up, saying, "Don't worry, we don't have rabies like you people," and he pulled the bag off the coffee table and unzipped it. Derdâ made a mental note. She had to figure out just what sort of shit these skinheads got themselves into. The Jamaican pulled three half-kilo bricks out of Black T's bag. He looked at the others.

"Anyone wanna try?"

Only Bob answered. Towering over Derdâ, his dreads swaying down around his waist, the Jamaican said, "You wait for me here." He picked up the three bricks and left the room. The other two went back to bobbing their heads. Derdâ wasn't worried. She was sure the man would come back with the heroin. At least she hoped for so much.

Then a Jamaican looked up and said, "Who was dat man?"

"What man?" the other said.

"Dat man just sittin der. He just left. You know him?"

"No."

"Den what was he doing here, man?"

"I don't know, I thought he was your friend."

"I don't know him, man!"

"He seems irie, man."

They looked up at Derdâ and one said, "Black T sent you, right? So give us the goods and let's see how it is."

Derdâ's mind went cold.

"I just gave it to you. Your friend just left with it . . ."

"We don't know dat guy. But you know him, right? Why else would you give the bag to him? You know him. No matter, now give us de stuff and we check it out."

Derdâ's heart went cold.

"What are you talking about? I just gave that guy the stuff and he asked if anyone here wanted to try it . . . You really don't know him?"

"No," the two men said.

Derdâ's entire body went cold. She could feel the beads of sweat forming on her forehead.

She grabbed her head and cried, "What am I going to do now?"

The two Jamaicans looked at each other. But they couldn't keep the act up any longer and burst out laughing.

"You really must be a skinhead," one said.

The other: "How could anyone be so dumb?"

Derdâ wanted to strangle them but she threw herself down in the armchair and asked for a cigarette. Laughing, one passed her a joint. The harshness in her face softened as she lit the joint and soon enough she was laughing along with them. The rhythms of Desmond Dekker filled the room and it seemed, if only for a short while, that they were all genuinely happy. As the joint moved round the room every now and then one of them imitated Derdâ: "And what I going to do now?" And they cracked up, laughing all over again, replaying the scene again and again, laughing every time, until their friend came back with the three bricks of heroin.

"It's alright," the Rasta said, handing Derdâ an envelope.

She stood up and took it. The others got up to say good-bye. Derdâ patted Bob on the head—a dog as mellow as the man he was named after—and left the room. On the ground floor she saw the Jamaican watching the door. As a woman came out of the toilet, the Jamaican turned to Derdâ and said, laughing, "You wanna go? A special price for the lady." Derdâ thanked him for his offer and left the house. She stepped through the line outside and walked back through the carnival where she hailed a taxi and set off for Chelsea. She gave the driver the second address written on Black T's card. After a few blocks they pulled up to a ten-story apartment and Derdâ got out of the car. She found the apartment number on the panel beside the door and rang the bell.

A muffled voice crackled through the intercom, "Who's there?"

"Delivery from Black T . . ."

A sharp metallic snap stopped her before she could finish and Derdâ pushed open the door. She thought of the Jamaicans and everything that had just happened to her on the elevator ride up to the eighth floor. She started laughing. She was still laughing when she rang the doorbell to apartment 33.

Regaip opened the door. Her eyes shot open in shock. Derdâ stopped laughing.

Regaip grabbed Derdâ by the collar and pulled her inside. Then he slammed the door shut.

"Is anyone following you?" he said in a strange English accent.

"No, no," Derdâ stuttered. She noticed the gun in his hand.

Derdâ stood before her father. A man who had nothing but blood on his hands to prove it. *I'll be fine if I just stay calm. Give him the envelope and leave,* she thought. She struggled to stay calm and collected. Regaip hadn't recognized her. In the last sixteen years he'd spent no more than five days with his daughter. The last time he'd seen her was five years ago. Derdâ had shaved her head since then. *He doesn't recognize me,* she thought. And there was something he didn't know. Something else that had come between them: cocaine.

A week after Bezir had been killed, Gido called Regaip and told him to rent a new flat and hole up there with a year's supply of food. "Don't leave until you hear from me," he ordered. They had a cop on the inside who had told Gido that the Dulluhan brothers got the MI5 onto them. His only advice on the matter: "Make yourself scarce."

And Regaip did just that. But he couldn't entirely shut down his past, especially his history as an ex-con. Regaip hadn't taken a shine to prison, just like he hadn't taken a shine to the security cabin at the entrance to Ubeydullah's furniture factory he was confined to his first three months in London. He could hardly breathe in there. So one morning he left home with the other security guards, just as if they were going to work. But instead they went straight down to the underworld as if running to a new-found freedom. He'd never learned the fundamentals of English grammar but Regaip quickly formed his own gang because he knew the rules in the underworld. They were called the Fighting Wolves, a group formed with the children of relatives from Yatırca. The first few weeks Ubeydullah and Bezir tried to hunt Regaip, but they knew he was a forest ranger and this time wasn't just hiding out in the mountains. He was in London. It was futile tracking down a ranger in a city like London. They'd never find him. So there was only one thing left to do. Ubeydullah took the matter into his own hands: he put a curse on the man, and not a small one at that.

So many years in prison and now holed up in his house in Chelsea with nothing to do but stare at the walls and curse his fate, Regaip stayed in command of the Fighting Wolves and he had no qualms investing his earnings in cocaine. "If I can't go out into the world, I'll bring the world to me," he'd say before taking a blow. The coke made him say, "God is great, but fuck his decrees." In his drug world, he met the people who'd shot their own brother, who'd strangled their wife. People who didn't even know their own children. The drug world turned people against each other. Heroin addicts didn't give a damn about anyone else in the world. They themselves were the centers of the universe and they found as many reasons as there were planets to justify their actions. "May God save them," Regaip used to say. But he didn't say it any more. Hadn't said it for five months. In fact, he'd been cooped up like this for the last five years. He no longer had a brother or a wife, so his tragedy now was not recognizing his own child. He had no idea that his daughter had been living the life of a retired trade attaché since he saw her last. He could hardly even remember what she looked like.

He let go of Derdâ's leather jacket and walked into the living room, muttering to himself in Turkish.

"How would a stupid egghead like you even know if you were being followed?"

Derdâ stepped into the apartment and then stopped, holding the envelope, waiting. Regaip called out to her from the living room.

"Come here!"

Derdâ was reluctant to go into the living room. All she wanted to do was deliver the envelope and leave. Regaip stood scratching his forehead with the barrel of his gun. The room was empty except for a television and a sofa. He pointed to the sofa with the gun.

"Sit."

Derdâ handed him the envelope.

"This is for you . . ."

Regaip trained the gun at Derdâ's face.

"I said sit."

Derdâ's felt sick. The poverty and deprivation she had endured in her short life, the weed she had just smoked with the Jamaicans, and the sight of her armed father after so many years. It was all too much to bear.

Her voice quivered, "I just came to drop off this envelope . . . please . . ."

Regaip stepped forward and grabbed Derdâ's ears. She didn't have any hair to grab. The pain was so great she bent over and nearly collapsed on the sofa. There was no way out. Regaip released her and she grabbed her ears as if to regain balance. It felt like he'd torn them off. He'd only pulled them the way any other father would have done. He scolded like a father, too.

"If I tell you to do something, you do it. If I tell you to sit down, you sit down. If I say stand up, you stand up. Now listen to me. Listen. Listen carefully. Take off your clothes."

Tears welled up in Derdâ's eyes. She shouted in Turkish this time, silencing Regaip.

"I'm Derdâ. Derdâ. Your daughter! I'm your daughter!"

For a moment, Regaip froze. A moment later, his body went limp.

Then he screamed in Turkish: "How the hell do you know my mother's name?"

And he struck Derdâ in the face with such force that he knocked her over, leaving her crumpled up on the sofa, hyperventilating like a wounded animal. Like a young dog about to die. Her mind was blank. She was looking through the wrong end of the telescope again.

"Don't waste your time crying," Regaip said. "I'll fuck you either way. Isn't that why you came? Didn't that kid tell you? Timur . . ."

She gave up trying to convince her father who she was. Derdâ cried out through her tears, "Who's Timur?"

"The bastard who goes by Black T," Regaip said, laughing. "I asked him for a girl and he sends me you. But first give me that envelope."

So Black T knows, she thought. *He knows I killed his sister. He sent me here to get his revenge.*

Until then Derdâ had kept a tight grip on the envelope. She stood up and threw it at Regaip's face. It bounced off his shoulder and fell to the floor. Regaip smiled. He leaned over and picked it up. He opened it and pulled out a thick wad of cash. He counted it, his eyes flickering over the bills like a money-counter.

"Now strip. I don't want any more trouble from you!"

And he slapped his daughter's breasts, his bloodshot eyes smiling hungrily like gaping mouths.

"Or do you want a little something before? A little tetanus shot?"

"Dad," Derdâ pleaded. "Dad, don't you remember me? For God's sake . . ."

He caught her by the ears again.

"You freak, how dare you speak that name before God? Look at yourself, damn it! If your mother or father saw you like this they'd die of shame!"

As he dragged her down the corridor, he continued to berate her. He opened the bedroom door and threw Derdâ onto the bed.

"There's stuff there by the bed! Do what you need to do, but just be ready when you come back," he said before locking the door behind him and stuffing the key in his pocket. He walked back to the living room, stuffing his gun back into his pants. Then he grabbed his cell phone off the TV and dialed. He started shouting the second the boy picked up.

"You stupid mother fucker! You pick a junkie up on the street and send her to me, you dog! You flatter yourself, thinking you can find me a girl, eh? And in the end, you find me this whore psychopath! And then she turns out to be fucking Turk!"

He had exhausted himself and paused to catch his breath. Black T broke in the moment he got the chance.

"How should I know? The girl was set on seeing you . . ."

Regaip hurled his cell phone at the wall and scrambled out of the room. It had finally sunk in. He tripped at the entrance and frantically picked himself up.

"Derdâ!" he cried as he pounded on the bedroom door, fishing the key out of his pocket with his other hand. His hands were trembling when he unlocked the door.

Derdâ lay motionless on the bed with a syringe hanging from a dark purple bruise on her arm. Regaip ran over to her and shook her by the shoulders.

"Derdâ! Oh, Derdâ!"

Derdâ opened her eyes and whispered. Regaip leaned over her lips, and he heard something he would never forget.

"Dad, fuck me as much as you want."

The words slipped in through his ear and coiled around his brain like a snake. Regaip took his daughter in his arms and sobbed, pressing her tightly to his chest, staring up at the ceiling. He sobbed as much as his breath would allow. The same painful pitch as the cacophony unfurled on judgment day. Regaip was sobbing so loudly he didn't hear the SAS commandos and MI5 smash down his front door as they raided his apartment.

Regaip screamed as the officers pulled him away from Derdâ, as they pulled his gun out of his pants, as they cuffed him on the floor. He kept screaming, but his voice was cracking.

"Forgive me, oh, forgive me, please forgive me!"

The MI5 needed just one more call from his cell phone to get a fix on his location. Regaip had made that call just to bawl out Black T.

An officer checked Derdâ's pulse and called an ambulance.

As Regaip was dragged out of the apartment, his voice echoed through the halls: "Derdâ!"

Regaip had almost fucked his own daughter, the daughter his wife Saniye had given up just four days after she was born. Even when he put his hands over his ears, he could still hear Derdâ whispering those words to him. He saw her bald head, the dark purple bruises on her arms. He saw those words in the cracks of the prison walls. When he paced his cell her ghost was there beside him. He shared his life story with her and he tried to explain why he'd left her. But he kept returning to the same refrain, "I had no other choice," and he begged her forgiveness just as many times. But Derdâ's ghost never forgave him. Those whispered words kept swirling in his ear: "Dad, fuck me as much as you want . . ."

He tried cutting off his ears on the steel edge of his bed. Regaip hanged himself the moment he had the chance, leaving behind nothing but a sentence chiseled on the wall of his cell:

GOD PROTECTED US FROM THE VERY WORST.

It was the only thing he could be thankful for in this world. He was spared at least from fucking his own daughter. That was enough. So when he left the world, his eyes closed in peace. He was thankful for that.

Derdâ woke up in the intensive care unit of St. Mary's Hospital. She'd been in a coma for three days. She looked up at the bottle of serum on the steel hook beside her bed and watched it drip like an hourglass.

She thought that she was alone until a nurse leaned over her and quietly said her name. Derdâ looked up to see a plump redhead smiling down at her.

"So the little lady has woken up. Good morning," she said.

Then she pointed to a button at the end of a cord dangling near Derdâ's motionless arm and said, "If you need anything just press this button. I'm going to get the doctor now. So you don't go anywhere."

Derdâ looked at the hourglass again and began counting the drops, her mind completely blank. The nurse reappeared with a young man holding a clipboard.

"How are we feeling?" he asked with a smile on his face.

"Alright, I guess."

The doctor handed the clipboard to the nurse and pulled a penlight from his shirt pocket to examine Derdâ's eyes.

"I guess, you say, but to me you look just fine. Do you remember what happened to you?"

"I screwed up, I guess . . ."

"We could say that," the doctor said, laughing. "Right, so do you remember what you took?"

"Heroin . . ."

"No. You injected a critical amount of cocaine, enough to put you in a coma for the last three days. You were lucky. Your heart stopped beating twice. Do you understand me?"

He looked over his file.

"Derdâ. That's a pretty name. Where are you from?"

"Turkey."

"Good . . . Now look, in a little while the police will come to ask you a few questions, alright?"

Derdâ nodded.

"Ok, then. I'll be back a little later," he said and turned to leave, but then he stopped and smiled.

"Yes, that's right. Fethiye! I was there just last summer. What a wonderful country. You're a very lucky girl!"

Two MI5 officers stood on either side of Derdâ's bed.

One looked up and said, "Look, the only thing we're asking you to do is testify in court. That's all. Nothing else. Nothing about your personal life. And we'll do everything we can to see that you can stay in England, because, as you may or may not be aware, you're now residing here illegally. All you have to do is tell the judge what you know."

"But I don't know anything," Derdâ said.

"But you know Bezir, right?" the other officer asked. "The one who brought you here and kept you locked up in that apartment."

"Yes . . ." she whispered, softly.

"Ok then, so just explain what happened to you in that house. And of course there's your dad. We need you to talk about him."

"But I only saw him once," Derdâ said. Her voice was louder.

"Look Derdâ, we're here so that we can catch all the people who have hurt you since you came to London."

He was lying. For the past five years they'd been after everyone from the Dulluhan brothers to Gido Agha, from the Tariqat leader Hıdır Arif to Bezir's kickboxers. And if it had been at all in their powers to do so, they would have extradited Sheik Gazi himself from one of his guest homes in Turkey and put him on trial in London. But for the time being, people at the London headquarters were preoccupied with this dramatic new trial. What could have been more dramatic than the plight of a young girl taken from her village in Turkey at the age of eleven against her will, a girl who eventually ended up living and working with a London sadist and drug addict? And her father was the man who had organized it all from the beginning.

Derdâ was now the linchpin in the Turkish underworld in London. The claim in court was that she was somehow involved with radical Islamic gangs working with London drug lords. In making this connection, they hoped to kill many birds with just one stone. All the related persons could be added to the suspect list, their bank accounts subject to inspection. At least a few would receive life sentences. To be able to pull it off, MI5 officer James Bond had to do what James Bond would never do. He had to lie to a sixteen-year-old girl. Derdâ believed everything he said.

Derdâ was sent to a private drug rehabilitation center in Brighton. At the end of week five in her treatment the MI5 came and took her back to London. The Queens Court building—known in most other countries as the Palace of Justice, for the sense of intrigue that the name evoked—was submerged in a mask of snow. Derdâ quickly learned that although the building went by a different name it still hatched the same kind of intrigues.

In an historical court room in an historical building, Derdâ appeared before the judge. She was a protected witness so Hıdıf Arif would never know who had testified against him in a court of law.

"They took my picture in a village in Turkey and they sent it to Hıdıf Arif in London. He was the one who picked the girls. And he picked me. He picked the man I had to marry, too. Rahime told me all of this, you know, that woman who jumped off Tower Bridge . . ."

Derdâ was happy to tell them everything she could remember. She even told them about Black T.

"I bought heroin from him. He was a member of a gang called the Fighting Wolves. They fought with rival Kurdish gangs. He worked for my father, Regaip. And the kid said he wanted to be Jamaican."

They weren't too concerned with the Jamaican angle. All the same, Derdâ was tireless in her account of everything she could remember. She even told them about the spittle that would fly out of Vezir's mouth during his religious lectures on the eleventh floor of her apartment. But she didn't mention Steven, Stanley, or Mitch. It was strange, but somehow she felt that they had played a part in saving her life. The truth was she despised Stanley, but there was no need for him to go to prison. He already led a life confined by the walls of his heroin addiction, or so she thought.

And she was right, for the next six years he lived within such walls and the harsh reality on the street. After his father died, Stanley returned to his family home—it was finally his—but soon died of a heroin overdose. The walls had come crashing down around him. As for Steven, he was buried in his chador, as specified in his will. Only Mitch managed to turn his life around. He returned to his native California where he married a man then quickly divorced him. Then he married a woman and they started shooting documentary films together. Most of them traced the plight of Muslims in the various countries where he had lived. In a speech he gave after receiving an award, Mitch said, "I'm not sure where she is right now, but I owe so much to a particular Muslim girl who was always a source of inspiration."

Unaware of such future notoriety, Derdâ mistakenly mentioned one of Mitch's films during her testimony, but the content was so grotesque that the judge didn't believe her and put it all down to delusions formed during Derdâ's days of heavy drug use. So she changed the subject. When it came to the story of the fifty-two Cambridge students, he only said, "there's no need for this, no need." It was almost time for lunch. Derdâ understood those types would never believe her story.

When they asked her if there was anything else she'd like to add, Derdâ asked about her dad.

"I'm afraid he's passed away. He took his own life."

"My mother would always say, 'God willing they will kill that man one day.' Now I can tell her she doesn't need to wish anymore," she said with a faint smile.

The Brighton rehabilitation center was ten stops from the city center. The main building stood in the middle of a lush green lawn as big as the campus of Derdâ's old boarding school. It was called Hope.

Reading the name on a sign over the garden gate, Derdâ thought about all those people in the world that lived with hope. *So people who just passed by the center, maybe only once a day, felt good just reading the word on the sign,* Derdâ thought. And she smiled to herself. But her smile wouldn't last long. She wouldn't smile again until week twelve in her recovery program.

The treatment for heroin addicts lasted eighty-five days. It was a difficult journey that was mainly about staying in one place as the body purged itself of the drug. A user completed the treatment with the help of three people. A psychiatrist, who could use mild sedatives as a last resort to help the patient deal with psychological pain. A therapist, who worked to re-establish the spiritual landscape of the patient. And a nurse, or companion, who never left the patient's side, providing all the support the addict needed, preventing him or her from committing suicide or harming anyone else.

At the center, a psychiatrist and a therapist worked jointly with twelve patients. The number of companions depended on the season. Most of the addicts tended to come in the fall. Junkies slept outside during the summer, oblivious to the desperate nature of their situation. They were only worried about their lips drying out in the setting sun. But once the weather started to cool off, they dragged themselves out to rehab centers, settling in by the first autumn rains.

In the rehab center there were at least as many companions as there were recovering addicts. And all of them were volunteers. People willing to do such a job for no pay were either atoning for personal sins or already believed they had been absolved. It required a superhuman effort to spend twelve weeks with a heroin addict. Over the course of the treatment, a companion only slept when the addict slept. A superhuman effort meant closely following another human being, sticking to them like air. Companions were like air when they walked arm in arm with a recovering addict, always by their side, never judging them. They had to be sure the addict was always breathing, pick her up when she fell, wipe away her tears. Pay no heed to her foul language. A companion had to take hold of her wrist as she pounded her fists onto a table, and wipe her chin if she spat or drooled, always with the same smile. And if the addict threatened a companion's life, there was nothing they could do but wait until one of the two hospital directors intervened. They had to do all this and they had to be everywhere at the same time. Just like air. The managers at Hope called them saints. That was easier. It would break the hearts of all those women—mostly retired nurses—to look them in the eye and praise them using the words "you're like air" every time they succeeded in curing an addict.

Anne was Derdâ's companion. She had worked with her last addict four years ago and left Hope with no intention of ever returning. But Derdâ showed up quite suddenly and because there was a shortage of companions at Hope they had no choice but to call Anne. She told them straightaway she wouldn't come. She told them that even though she was only fifty-three years old her heart felt old and that she couldn't handle the work anymore. And she hung up. She stared at the phone for four minutes thinking of the last four years away from the job, before she called Hope back and asked which week the addict was in. She promised herself she wouldn't go if they told her week one. She knew it was the most difficult week. Watching an addict suffer through the first week locked up in a room, going through countless visits with the doctor, was like witnessing the end of the world. But they told her week two. She'd trapped herself; Anne told them she'd come in the next day. She kept her promise. The next day she found Derdâ. She wasn't suffering in the throes of immediate withdrawal. She only stared at her with vacant eyes, with Anne smiling back. Anne was living proof of someone who would never retire. She would always continue to volunteer.

"Hello. My name's Anne. I will be with you for the next twelve weeks. What's your name?"

Without even looking up: "Fuck off."

Pleased she at least got a response, Anne said, "Ok, but I won't go very far. I'm now your companion from now on. So I'll just stay right here. If you need anything, all you have to do is look up," and she took two steps back and stood there. This was a tactic she'd developed over the years at the center, a tactic to bring out any shards of humanity left in an addict, with the hope they would rub together and make a spark.

Derdâ sat on the park bench gnawing at the flesh around her nails while Anne stood just two meters away, her hands crossed over her stomach, her feet firmly planted on the ground. She looked like a kind of sentry guard keeping watch. In the past, she'd stayed in this position for up to four hours. She called it the invitation pose. In the invitation pose, she often thought of her time as a nurse—the endless hours up on her feet—and she tried to leave her body behind, traveling only in her thoughts. And she did just that. But soon enough she found Derdâ's humanity. Ten minutes. Derdâ couldn't bear the thought of Anne in that uncomfortable pose and she said:

"Derdâ. My name's Derdâ. Come sit down here. Don't just stand there."

"Thank you," Anne said, smiling as she sat down. It was the first question that she asked all addicts. She always wrote down their answers in a little notebook, doing everything she could to better understand them.

"Why don't you tell me about your experience with heroin?"

Derdâ turned and said, "Why? You thinking of starting?"

Anne smiled.

"Oh no, I'm just wondering what it feels like, that's all."

Derdâ stood up and stormed off. Anne followed just behind her. In about a hundred steps, Derdâ stopped and leaned over to Anne to whisper, "You know fireworks, right?"

Coming closer, Anne said, "Of course."

"They explode like this."

Derdâ raised her hands and flung open her fingers.

"Yes, I know. All the different colors. I love watching them," Anne said.

"That's what it's like when you're on heroin . . ."

Anne interrupted her.

"So you see fireworks, then?"

"No," Derdâ said. "You are the fireworks!"

Anne hadn't heard such a powerful description of a feeling in some time. She jotted it down in her notebook later on. She never forgot the expression. She found it incredibly moving.

"What a beautiful way to put it. You know, you should be a writer."

"Yeah, right," Derdâ said, sarcastically, with only half a smile on her face.

"Why not? Isn't writing just another mode of expression? Do you go to school?"

"No."

"Do you want to?"

Derdâ thought of Fehime from Yatırca.

"Maybe, I don't know."

Derdâ turned to Anne.

"I read your file. You're still young and, believe me, you can do whatever you like. You have a whole life ahead of you."

Derdâ stopped to think and so did Anne. Derdâ spoke and Anne listened.

"I'm already dead. Can you understand that? Dead! I just haven't been buried yet, that's all."

Anne smiled.

"You seem to be breathing a bit too much for someone who is dead."

Derdâ was silent. She didn't think this woman would be able to understand all the things that had happened to her. So she walked away. Her mind was hazy. They had started a new Naltrexone treatment at the center.

She turned and asked, "How do you spell your name?"

Anne knew how addicts suddenly changed conversation. She spelled out her name without hesitation.

Derdâ quickly replied, "In my language, 'mother' is written the same way."

"I know," said Anne.

"How would you know?"

But suddenly she was sick and the only thing she'd managed to eat at breakfast, some strawberry yogurt, dribbled out of her mouth. She was also on Revia and the side effects included impaired vision, dizziness, fatigue, and nausea. Derdâ could hardly keep anything down, even her own stomach bile. It purged her body, but also her mind of the profanities and the physical suffering she had endured.

After Derdâ gave her last testimony at court, she came back to Hope to start her tenth week of treatment. She occasionally came to group therapy sessions but never spoke to the other addicts. She participated as little as possible in the discussions and waited impatiently for the end. To her mind she had nothing to say. There was no one there capable of understanding her anyway. Only Anne, she thought, only Anne could understand her, if only a little. Anne could understand her suffering, her regret, how she hated life and how she wanted to die, as if Anne had felt the same way too once in her life. Anne could finish Derdâ's sentences using just the right words. Derdâ hadn't really loved anyone for years. She couldn't explain the feelings she had for Anne. She loved her but she didn't understand why.

Anne had long since accepted the fact that she couldn't even begin to imagine the weight of all the tragedies Derdâ had suffered. What she saw in Derdâ was a silently flowing waterfall.

Anne wanted to wash her weary hands in that waterfall. She thought of this as love.

"Do you see that tree?" Anne asked as she pointed out a hundred-year-old plane tree whose roots were bursting up out of the earth. She paused and then laughed. "They look like bell-bottoms."

Derdâ was ready to smile but held herself back. A concern emanated from a deep, dark place. If she exposed positive feelings perhaps she would be punished. She was scared of the punishment she would get when Anne left. If she got better, Anne would disappear. So she only nodded.

Anne noticed her silence and putting her arm in Derdâ's she whispered, "I've always wondered about your hair. Did you know that?"

Derdâ ran her hand over her head.

"Do you miss it?" Anne asked.

"I don't know. I'm afraid of it."

Following a long silence together, Anne was as convinced of her love for the young girl as she was of the offer she was about to make.

"Do you know what we should do? We should go to your room right now and cut off all my hair. And you'll do the same. We'll shave it all off."

"Are you crazy?" Derdâ said.

"Of course not," Anne said, smiling. "It'll grow back. But this time you'll let yours grow out, too. We'll do it together. What do you say?"

"I know this trick!" Derdâ said. "It's no different than the way you just stood there beside me when we first met, trying to pull some pity out of me."

"Not at all, my dear lady, nothing of the sort. And that wasn't just a technique. Anyway, what do you say? How about being promoted from skinhead to hippie?"

Derdâ felt ten years old, thinking only of herself, of her own happiness. She thought, *if Anne cuts her hair she won't be able to leave me till it grows back, so she won't leave me.*

"It's a deal. Let's go. You ready now?"

Anne pretended to be scared, covering in mouth in surprise. "Oh no . . ."

"Too late now," Derdâ said and then, taking hold of a lock of Anne's blond hair, she shouted, "we're cutting it all off!"

When everyone at Hope—the therapist, the psychiatrist, the two enormous security guards, the three women in the kitchen, the four cleaning women, and the six members of the board who came every month to inspect the facility—saw Saint Anne's shaved head they thought that perhaps she had finally lost her mind after so many years of unfaltering service. But when she walked in the garden with Derdâ, her eyes smiling, she was far from insane. Both women felt a strange feeling of pride in their baldness. They stroked each other's heads, like two children afflicted with leukemia, enduring the sessions of chemotherapy together without the slightest fear of death. Two days later a therapist brought dark sunglasses from Brighton.

Anne put on her pair and handed the other to Derdâ, saying, "Now we can take our picture and send it to a magazine. We look pretty sexy!"

On the fifth day of the twelfth week they sat silently together with their backs against one of the bell-bottom plane trees.

"Have you noticed?" asked Anne.

"What?"

"How much stronger you are. I've seen so many people in your situation who would never do the things you're doing now. You're the bravest person I've known here, and the strongest. Do you know what this means when you get back to real life?"

"I don't," Derdâ said, running her hand up and down a black thorn jutting out from one of the branches above her head.

"I do. So tell me, what are you planning to do when you get out of here?"

Derdâ's testimony in court covered far more than what the MI5 officers had ever hoped for and had a dramatic effect on the judge who, instead of granting a residence permit, offered Derdâ UK citizenship. She would live out the rest of her life as an English woman. But the MI5 had acted too early. At the end of the seven-month trial, only nine members of the Fighting Wolves (all minors, including Black T) and a few of Bezir's kickboxers had been convicted. They had planned to extradite Gido Agha from Turkey, but he had fled to Iran. As for Hıdır Arif, he was bound to let the world know all about the charges leveled against him.

Every time he was interviewed on TV, he reverted to the same old refrain: "This bogus trial has nothing to do with me. It's an attack on all of Islam, and it is fated to lose."

The Dulluhan brothers made plans to move their Westminster base to Dublin. They first cut a deal among themselves, and later Hıdır Arif made a deal with the British, suspecting they wanted to bring them down. But it wasn't long before Hıdır Arif's office was raided. During the raid, Hıdır Arif tried to take cover behind his glass globe. He took eight bullets, but survived. He believed that a piece of the holy black *Hacer-ül Esved* stone that was knocked out of the shattered globe had saved his life. Three years later, he died of a heart attack on top of a thirteen-year-old girl whose photograph was too good to turn down. It was just three days before he planned to announce himself as the new prophet.

The Dulluhan brothers tried their best to manipulate politics in Ireland. But they were frustrated in their efforts and began fighting among themselves, down to the lowest-ranking foot soldiers. One brother was gunned down by a rising IRA militant—someone they had recently supplied with two thousand

Glocks. The brother didn't die but lived out the rest of his life with a bullet in his skull, a bullet that wouldn't grant him access to his own name, the ability to stand up, to move his fingers or blink his eyes.

So the best thing that came out of Derdâ's trial was UK citizenship. Many countries, the US included, saw citizenship as something that could be offered through a lotto played out on the Internet. But the reality was that citizenship granted to someone like that—just given away—was never a source of true happiness. You can see this in the faces of all the immigrants that somehow ended up in England. Or in the surprise most Americans would express if you told them that the miserable lives they were eking out in their own country were given away as the top prize in an Internet lottery.

Noticing her silence, Anne asked again, "What are you going to do when you leave?"

Derdâ answered, as if ashamed of confessing her love.

"I'll miss you."

"Anything else?"

"I'll find out where you live?"

"And?"

"I'll come and sleep in your garden."

"And?"

"No, I'll just stand there. I'm going to stand in front of your door with lowered head and my hands crossed, like a miserable child."

"Ok. And then?"

"Then you won't be able to stand it for very long and you'll have to let me in."

"Fine, but tell me this. How long would you wait outside like that?"

"How long could you make me wait?"

Anne nodded her head. There were tears in her eyes. She put her hand on Derdâ's shoulder.

"We're going to finish this together," she said and then hugged her.

Tears fell from their eyes. From then on Anne had a daughter and Derdâ had a mother. Just then, Saniye felt a sharp pain pierce her heart. She didn't know why. *It must be all this hard work with the animals,* she thought, *all this damn work at the house and with the animals.*

Derdâ's face between Anne's hands beamed with her first smile in twelve weeks.

Derdâ got dressed and left her room. She had finally freed herself of heroin. She took the first step in the right direction on her last day in Hope, when descending the stairs to the first floor. Making her way down the winding staircase, she saw the crowd below. She felt like the mysterious and beautiful girl who had come late to the ball. They all looked up at her with pride. But there was something akin to jealousy in the eyes of other addicts. And there was a hint of hopelessness in the eyes of the doctors and therapists, because they had witnessed on countless occasions such celebratory beginnings end in countless addicts lurching back to their former lives before finishing even the first week of treatment. But hope always prevailed so now they applauded. They applauded Derdâ with smiles on their faces. Some of them slapped her on the back and others embraced her.

Of course none of them would be there at all if a chemist by the name of C. R. Wright hadn't invented heroin when he added various acids to morphine in his attempt to develop a new kind of painkiller. Back then there wasn't a place known as Hope. But heroin was born. And there was no going back. Maybe they could have used a time machine so that people could go back in time and stop Wright from proceeding with his experiments. The man had little difficulty discovering the drug. The year was 1874 and he was in London, in St. Mary's Hospital. In the building in which Derdâ died twice and came back to life twice. Heroin was invented on the third floor and now every year seven thousand heroin addicts were committed to the second floor where they lay on the brink of death.

Holding a cracked leather bag and wearing her black sunglasses and her white uniform, Anne waited for Derdâ in the garden. She smiled when she saw her step out of the building and she waved to her. But not to say good-bye. Derdâ took ten steps forward and Anne took one. They met one another and stopped. The young girl took her sunglasses out of her pocket and put them on. And the Blues Sisters stepped under the Hope sign on the front gate.

In a gray Seat parked only fifty meters away from the main gate, two MI5 officers watched Derdâ and Anne get into a taxi.

"Now what?" one said.

"We wait and see," said the other.

A young blond sitting in the back seat stuck her head between the two officers and said, "And what if she complains about us, Dad? You know, she did mention us in court. What if she tries again?"

Without taking his eyes off the Hope sign over the main gate, the driver answered, "Don't worry about it. The case is closed."

The driver was looking at the Hope sign. Perhaps this was why he felt overly optimistic. Didn't everything begin with hope? Considering all that Derdâ had talked about in the trial, the officer thought he could uncover a child porno ring. He went to the address in Covent Garden where fifty-two men and a woman had been filmed. He found a camera left in the apartment and the boy with the glasses who had shot the scene, too. Watching the film he felt his heart nearly stop, as if it had been crushed in a door. His son, for whose sake he had been working overtime to support his education at Cambridge, was the first of fifty-two boys to have fucked Derdâ. No matter how much the son insisted, they had no idea how young she was, and the father could never forgive him. He even considered initiating some kind of legal action against his son.

But the day they first examined the crime scene he and his partner destroyed the camera and the memory card. They prevented Derdâ from saying too much about the event during her trial. But there was something else: They didn't know about the camera boy's nosey younger brother. He had already made a copy of the film off the memory card and emailed it to all his friends. The MI5 officers heard about it later. One week before his son and the other fifty-one were due to graduate. The scandal shamed them into leaving school. It blew up when the younger brother brought the film to the Cambridge campus to share with some of the first-year students. He was caught by campus security. A radical feminist professor refused to let the scandal be contained. The university authorities struggled to keep the story from spilling over the campus walls. But to no avail; the scandal came to an end and was sealed with the sentence: "We won't dismiss you from school, but you will choose to leave your-selves." So that year's graduation ceremony at the economics department was sparser than anticipated.

But for now the officer seemed perfectly content as he sat in his gray Seat looking at the Hope sign above the main gate. We are all too willing to be deceived by appearances. Nothing is more important than being resilient enough to cope with life.

In the end, the MI5 didn't just walk away from Derdâ's life. They ran.

Derdâ and Anne arrived at Anne's one-story house in Newbury Park in northeast London.

"Here we are," Anne said. "My palace!"

Big sparkling windows at the front of the house let in the glowing sunlight. The curtains and the front door were white. A low picket fence ran from the back wall to the sidewalk, framing the back garden. The architecture of the house was simple, giving the impression of a doll house that had been magically enlarged a hundred times. And Derdâ was enchanted. Not because the house was extravagant in any way. For the first time, she was stepping into a real home.

They went inside and threw open the windows, breathing in the fresh air. Three bedrooms and a living room. Anne took Derdâ's hand and led her to a small bedroom.

"This one is for you."

A single bed and a small wardrobe. Derdâ turned and hugged Anne.

"Thank you," she whispered.

Anne and Derdâ sat together in chaise longues in the back garden, drinking tea in the setting sun.

"So, my little lady," Anne said. "Now let's see, when would you like to start school?"

Derdâ put her tea down on a low table and pulled off her dark sunglasses. She rubbed her chin and said, "I think I'll just rest for ten years and then let's see."

Ten years flew by.

The University of Edinburgh's main garden was full. People were there to celebrate the graduation of the English literature department, established two hundred years before. It was the first English literature department in the world at a university level. An enormous copper plaque in the corridor of the historic building was inscribed with more than a thousand names. At the end of every academic year the names of the top five students in that year's graduating class were inscribed on the plaque. With Anne's surname, Derdâ was now the last name on that list.

For her eighteenth birthday, Derdâ received a dossier of official documents. Realizing what it was, she began to cry. As she signed the adoption papers her tears smeared the ink. With this signature, she effectively divorced herself from Saniye and began a new life with a new mother. The court decision came back three months later. Derdâ celebrated her eighteenth birthday one more time. But this time there were two candles on the cake. For Anne, Derdâ was born in the rehabilitation center. Saniye's daughter may have been eighteen, but Anne's daughter was only two. And soon, two-year-old Derdâ, the most successful of all the top five students that year, would step up to the platform to speak. Anne sat beside her, adjusting her long black hair.

"I'm so proud of you," she said.

"I wonder if you'll still be so proud when I tell you the subject of my graduate thesis," Derdâ said, smiling.

"How bad could it be?" Anne asked.

"Donatien Alphonse François's influence on English literature."

"Who's that?"

"The Marquis de Sade!"

DERDA

"Derda?" said Isa.

"My dad had this friend. It was his name."

"So? What's it mean?"

"How should I know?"

"So ask your dad."

"He's in jail," said Derda, getting to his feet.

He brushed off the dust. Isa's excitement got the better of him.

"What'd he do?" he asked.

"He killed that friend."

But Isa didn't get it. He was staring blankly at Derda when they heard the sound of a car. They turned toward the sound. Then they looked at each other. Isa jumped to his feet and took off running. Derda followed right behind him. But Isa didn't know the cemetery so well and was soon lost. He sprinted randomly down the cemetery paths. Derda made it to the fountain in the square first, winning the race, and there wasn't anything Isa could do about it. He was new. And he was embarrassed he'd lost. Isa had to sit and watch while Derda filled up his plastic tanks and approached the parked car.

Derda had never seen these people before, but he knew the tomb they'd stopped in front of very well. It was where he got his best tips. Practically every day, someone would come and read the Koran at that tombstone. And afterward, they'd be sure to give him something. And sure enough here was someone else reciting the Koran in front of the tomb. An old man. With a long robe, just like all the others. But this time there was also a girl at the tombstone. A girl his age. *Has she been here before?* Derda thought. He didn't recognize her. He went up to the old man and held up his tanks.

"Should I pour water over the grave, uncle?"

He was so used to it, it must have been the thousandth time he'd heard a voice like this. The anguish in the reader's lilting voice was palpable. Derda spoke the language. He also knew that he had to persevere. Perseverance was an absolute. It was the first condition for getting money from these types. He waited patiently, not moving an eyelash, and with an ever so slight change in his voice reciting the Koran, the old man gave him the answer he was waiting for. Derda dashed to the head of the tomb and began pouring water over the earth, following the girl, who was pulling out weeds. They moved around the tomb and then, as he was filling up the birdbath, the girl stretched out her muddy hands. Derda watched the water stream out of his tank and over the girl's hands.

"Thank you," she said.

It was practically a whisper. Derda was going to say something too, but as soon as he opened his mouth, his feet were cut off from the ground and he landed in a heap on the path near the tomb.

When the dust settled, he saw a man the size of a giant looming over him. "What did I do?" he wanted to yell, but he didn't.

162

He pulled his knife out of his pocket, thinking he could drive it into the giant's knee, but he let that thought go, too. Then the old man growled some kind of command and the giant reached into his pocket and Derda watched him pull out some change. The money meant nothing to the giant. But Derda really needed it. He hadn't had a thing to eat all day. But he wasn't going to get a thing from that giant with the beard. Especially because of the girl. He saw the girl's face as he turned to leave. It was like she wanted to say something to him. Almost as if she wanted him to save her. But maybe Derda's hunger was making him see things.

Isa had watched everything from a distance. He ran over to Derda. He had lost both the race and the customers and he wanted to rub it in.

"You did it wrong."

"What?"

"You shouldn't have gotten so close to the girl. Those guys don't like that kind of thing."

"Fuck them!" said Derda.

He walked past fast. Faster. Deeper into the cemetery. Straight into the darkness of the thickening shade of more and more trees. Isa was following him.

He shouted, "Where are you going?"

Derda stopped and looked over his shoulder.

"Home," he said. "You go, too. No one comes later than this. No point waiting around for nothing."

Isa watched Derda's back disappear for a few seconds. Then he stuffed one hand in his pocket, grabbed the empty tank with his other, and walked down to the cemetery gates, the tank bumping against his knee the whole way. As for Derda, he slipped through the shadows and arrived at the wall. His house was right on the other side of that wall. On one side his house, on the other side the cemetery. Just the way his father had wanted it. "It'll be easier to build," he'd said. "Here's a beautiful wall already built. We'll put up three more, and then just stick a roof on top. There you have it. Home sweet home."

His mother had done her best to protest but his father wanted to make the most of the little money he had. And so he built their house right up against the cemetery wall because the total cost of the house would be one wall less. It was just like the other houses around them. Some people called this sort of house a *gecekondu*, a homemade house built illegally under the cover of night. But his mother could never stop saying it was "just like a coffin." She lived cooped up in that house until her death, from cancer, just the day before. Just one of the two hundred thousand who suffer from eye cancer. Maybe looking at that wall did it to her. The cancer made the woman forget how to see, made her forget her own name, then even how to breathe. The only thing she didn't forget was how to say the house was "just like a coffin." Even after she went blind, she still could see the wall by running her hand over the contours of its stones.

She died on her floor mattress with Derda by her side. She called him to her side just before she died. "Come here." Derda came to her side, and then she died. As if she wanted to say, "Come here and see how a person dies." And so Derda saw. He even cried a little. But then he pulled himself together and got to his feet. His plan was to go to their cemetery wall neighbors and pound on their doors until their doors broke down. But he stopped at his first step as if in revolt. He'd remembered Fevzi. Fevzi who'd run away from the orphanage. Fevzi who'd run away from the orphanage and started living in the cemetery. "Don't tell anyone, but . . ." He remembered the beginning of his story. "Ten guys jump a guy, you know? They'd say they'd be back to do it again. I was so scared I never went into the bathroom again. I hid bags behind the closets. Then I'd shit in them at night." So ended his terrible tale of shameful cowardice. *What if . . .* Derda said to himself. *What if they find out my mother's dead? They'll send me to the orphanage, too. My dad's already in jail.* But instead of sitting and worrying, Derda came up with a plan. No one knew his mother was dead. Well, then, there was no need for anyone to find out. *I'll bring her to the cemetery and I'll bury her!* he thought. If the floor of the house hadn't been poured concrete, he would have buried her then and there. But it wasn't a shovel that was going to make her coffin.

He clambered up the wall, gripping the hand-sized hollows worn into the surface, then jumped down to the other side and walked along the side of his house, fighting his way through the tangled branches of a fig tree. He turned the corner and came to the front door of his house. He took the key from his pocket and was about to insert it into the lock when a creeping scent hit his nostrils. When he opened the door, the source was all too clear. His mother was rotting. He had to find a way to get the corpse to the other side of the wall, and fast, and then bury it in the first loose earth he could find. But Derda's mother weighed twice as much as he did. She could rot all she liked, but she'd still be eighty kilos. He had barely been able to roll her off her mattress and onto the floor. The night before he'd pushed her onto the floor and slipped into her bed. He hadn't cried too much. The woman had been sick for eight months and for eight months she hadn't been to a doctor or a hospital. She'd been dying right before his very eyes. Derda had gotten used to it. The woman had prepared him. "If anything happens to me, tell the neighbors," she said. "They're good for nothing, but tell them just the same. They should tell your dad, too, he should know. Have them bury me somewhere around here. No point sending me back to the village. And tell them I hope God damns them all!"

Since her husband had gone to prison not one of them had come over to see them. Even when they knew she was sick, they couldn't take the twenty steps to go visit her. What Derda made working at the cemetery didn't really let them live, but it kept them alive. In a word, they'd been abandoned. To themselves and to their own survival. "It's all your father's fault," the woman would say. "Because of him they won't even look us in the eye!" Before she fell ill, she'd sold dill at the market. Yasin, the guard at the cemetery, got the dill from a relative of his. But when that relative started asking for the woman instead of money, she dropped the dill and the market.

Derda's father had been in prison for six years. Like he told Isa, his father had killed his best friend, his blood brother, Derda the Arab. They met at a cockfight. They'd both bet on the same cock. But it turned out to be the wrong cock. Both of them were incensed they'd lost the last lonely *kuruş* rattling around in their pockets, and they both got the idea into their heads to cut up both the winning cock and its owner. So they were both lying in wait, behind the warehouse where the cockfight was held. Each was oblivious of the other. One waited at the warehouse's left corner, the other waited on the right. The cock owner left the warehouse by the back door to get into his van. Both men jumped him at once. But in a deft turn the cock owner broke free and they plunged their knives into each other's legs instead. They were both too drunk for their knives to penetrate very far, but still they slumped down on the ground. The cock owner got away with his cock, and the guys on the ground got up and tried to figure out just what had just happened. But when they found out there wasn't much to find out, first they started to laugh and then, leaning on each other for support, they went off to drink. A hospital won't dress wounds on credit, but Derda the Arab knew somebody who had a taverna where they kept your tab in a notebook and served you *rakı* just the same.

According to the recollections of people who lived behind the warehouse, it all started with a proclamation: "Now we're blood brothers." Then they worked together in their great struggle against poverty. As representatives of the oldest crime tradition—mugging—they'd hang low in the same shadowy spot then jump out at the pedestrians most likely to have fat wallets. Mugging means excessive violence for little money. Mugging means jumping out in front of guys who might be armed themselves, who might not even have fat wallets. Mugging means jumping out with your eyes closed and wishing for just a shred of luck. In the old days, in the oldest style of mugging, it was only children and idiots who would even try it.

One drunken night, at the end of a few years of filling the world's quota of dim-witted muggers, Derda's dad and Derda the Arab decided to hold up one last guy on the way back to their cemetery homes. But before they were deep in the deed, Derda's dad remembered having kissed their victim's hand a week before on a holiday visit. He was an old man. So he said, "It's ok. Let him go." But Derda the Arab wasn't having it. He cursed the old man and beat him up, but then the soberer of the two men stabbed his partner in crime in the heart. Derda's dad was left standing. He pulled out the bloody knife, looked around him, and saw the old man struggling desperately on the ground. Then he heard someone, a witness, running toward him. One from a knife wound, the other from a heart attack. There he was in the middle of corpses, calculating which way he should run. He didn't realize he was surrounded by six sweaty young men fresh from a match on the astroturf pitch. They'd lost 8–1 and they worked out their revenge by pummeling Derda's dad until the police came. Who could believe that Derda's father killed his partner to save an elderly neighbor? And so he was damned by the law and damned by his neighbors in the cemetery houses. Derda's curse had been that his father had gotten drunk enough to name him Derda. And it was only a matter of time before his wife was infected by the curse, too. A few days.

Derda looked at the house's cemetery wall, thinking. Mostly he was thinking about how he'd be able to hide a bag behind the closet and then shit in it in a dark dormitory. That and exactly what Fevzi meant when he said, "They hold you in twenty places and fuck you in one."

He needed a knife. A big one. Then he gave up on that idea. *This isn't a job for a knife,* he thought to himself. *I need a saw.* Then he gave up on that, too. An axe. "That's it," he said. "I'll chop up my mom up with an axe. Then I can bury her. Piece by piece."

But it wasn't that easy for Derda to find an axe. First he asked the neighbors. And he didn't lie. "I need it for my mom." No one had one. And even if they'd had one, they would have shut their doors and buried themselves inside one way or another just the same. "What are you going to do with an axe? Is your mother still sick? Is your bastard of a father still alive? Tell your mother, nothing before he pays his dues!" He always answered in the same way. He just nodded. There was only one person left to ask. The cemetery guard Yasin. Derda ran. He wiped the sweat on his forehead at the door to the wooden guardhouse near the cemetery gates. He didn't know how to knock at the door so he just yelled, "Brother Yasin!" He waited at the door. Yasin stuck his head out of the window. He'd just woken up from his afternoon nap and whenever he just woke up he was in a foul mood. There was nothing in this world worth waking up for.

"What?"

"Brother, do you have an axe?"

"What're you going to do with an axe, boy?"

It was like "yes" and "no" weren't in the language.

Derda gave an exact copy of what he'd heard his mother say—that is, when she could still speak—countless times.

"To chop the branches off the trees near our house. We can barely walk through the garden . . ."

First Yasin tried to get what he was going on about. But he realized he hadn't been listening to what the kid had been saying anyway, so with a "No axe!" he pulled his head back inside the guardhouse. Derda watched the empty window for a few seconds before he ran out of the cemetery. He ran to the end of the street and straight into the hardware store. But as soon as he went in he came right back out. There, in front of the display window, arranged in metal buckets in a row on the sidewalk, he saw them. Axes. He went inside again.

"How much are the axes?"

An old man lost in a drawer full of screws said, "Price is on them." Derda went out again and grabbed an axe and looked at the price tag on the handle. He stared and he stared and he stared. And then he bolted, the axe still in his hand. He ran down the sidewalk on the other side of the street. He didn't have to go as far as the cemetery gates. Every ten meters or so the cemetery wall had collapsed, like a rolling wave. He jumped over a collapsed concrete wave and ran, skipping over the tombs.

By the time he got home he was gasping for air. Insects were crawling out of his mother's open mouth and streaming into her nostrils. He felt nauseated but he didn't puke. He forced himself to hold it in. It came all the way up to his throat. *That's as far as it's going, but I'm not going to let it get any further.* A few belches, but nothing else came out. He pulled the sheet off her floor mattress and covered the woman up so her blazing white eyes wouldn't be able to see. Standing with his shoulders level, he grasped the axe in two hands and held it high above his head. He closed his eyes. "I'm not going to that orphanage, mom!" he yelled as he drove in the first blow. His eyes opened. He had tried to aim right for her neck but the axe had hit the woman's chest. It was lodged deep in her chest. Soon the dirty white sheet changed color. Red. He put his foot on her chest, took the axe in two hands, and yanked it out of her flesh. He raised it again and dealt another blow. Then another. For hours he drove the axe into her, yelling "I'm not going!" with every blow.

Then there were ten gangrene-colored lumps sticking up from under the sheet. The sheet made bridges, sagging toward the floor between the ten pieces. He smashed those bridges again and again to break the lumps into ten separate pieces. But still some bits, some pieces held together. He took a deep breath and with a single swift movement pulled the sheet away. He opened his eyes slowly and looked over his mother-in-pieces. He couldn't hold himself any longer and the puke that had only come up his throat before now spurted out. Whatever was on the floor, he puked all over it.

He poured three full tanks of water over his head. Both to wake himself up and to wash himself off. His blood went cold as ice when he got near those ten pieces spread out over the floor, what was left of his mother. His mothers, that is.

Pieces of his mother's flesh were welded inside the şalvar and shirt she had worn for the last two months. He got a knife and started to cut the fabric. The pieces opened up like he was unwrapping presents. Inside each one, his mother's nakedness was exposed, dripping with blood and bone. This was the way Derda saw his first naked woman. By first chopping up his mother, then by undressing her.

He ripped the sheet into pieces and wrapped all his mothers up, one by one. Then he piled them up one on top of another just inside the front door. He grabbed three empty water tanks and left the house.

Everything was bathed in darkness; the sun had gone to rise in other places. He stuck one of the empty tanks under the cemetery fountain and waited for it to fill up. Then he heard a voice:

"Derda!"

He looked all around him, but he didn't see anyone. He thought he'd die from fear when a thin branch stretching out from the thicket bent revealing Isa behind it. He was carrying a full tank. Derda was so terrified that he felt like he was looking at the world through the wrong end of a telescope. Everything and everyone seemed so far away. Even those closest to him. Even Isa, one step away.

"It's overflowing," the kid said, pointing to Derda's tank. If he had looked at Derda a little more closely and not at the tank, he would have seen the change in his eyes. Isa didn't see the tears in his eyes. Whatever else there was, there was darkness. Derda wiped the tears from his cheeks with the back of his hand, pretending he was wiping away sweat. Then he snapped back to life and nudged the full tank away with his foot and stuck an empty one under the fountain. Then he realized Isa was still there. He'd been watching him in silence for a while, but he didn't think he could have seen anything.

"What're you doing out here at this hour?"

"My dad kicked me out," said Isa.

"Where to?"

"What do you mean, where to?"

"Where'd your dad kick you out to?"

"He didn't say. Get the fuck out of here, he said. I'm just wandering around."

"What'd you do?"

"Told him I was going to drop out of school."

Derda felt water at his feet. He bent down and saw his second tank was overflowing. He put the third one into place.

"Why?"

"You don't go to school either, you said so!" Isa said.

"That's different," Derda said. "I never went to begin with. What year were you up to?"

"Fourth."

"Ok, then you only have one year left. It's over then anyway, right?"

Isa laughed.

"Over? Then there's middle school, high school, university."

He stopped laughing.

"Why didn't you go? Didn't your parents make you?"

"No," said Derda. "I'm waiting."

"For what?"

"University. I'm going to start from there."

Isa couldn't tell whether Derda was serious or not. He could understand as well as he could see in the darkness. Then at once both started to laugh. Like when they carried water tanks together. Then their laughs tapered off and they both fell silent. Like when the fountain was turned off.

"Come on, help me out here," said Derda. He hauled the tanks up by the handles and started to walk. Isa took the third and followed him. It was no easy task to get the tanks over the wall. At one point Derda said, "I'm going to break open a hole in the wall so I can go in and out. I'm tired of jumping over."

"We have an axe," said Isa. "It's my dad's. Maybe we can smash the hole open with that."

They were on the other side of the wall. Their hands on their knees, catching their breath. Between gasps for air, Derda asked:

"You have an axe?"

After Isa left the cemetery, Derda went home and tried to scrub the blood off the concrete floor with pieces he ripped off the foam rubber mattress. When he saw a piece of mattress wasn't absorbing any more, he tossed it into a trash bag at his side and ripped off another. He used the entire foam rubber mattress to erase all trace of the blood. Its stench had seeped into the sheets wrapped around the rotting flesh, and it was in every corner of the house, never to be removed, although the blood itself was no longer there. Derda was exhausted. A kid of ten and one years old. All the strength in his body and all the innocence inside him had been used up. He took off his T-shirt, balled it up, put it under his head, and lay down on the concrete. He rolled onto his side and pulled his knees up to his stomach. A while later, because there was no mother's womb to curl up into, he stretched his legs out, and stretching for the last time, he fell asleep.

He knew the first lump he picked up was his mother's left foot. It was the last piece he'd wrapped up so it was at the top of the flesh pile. As much as he could see of the world through the house's two small windows, the world was light blue. Those hours when the sun's color mixes into the night. He left the house and jumped over the wall and landed in the cemetery with the lump of flesh and the lid of a pan in his hand. Twenty meters ahead, twelve tombs were all lined up in a row. It was the row of tombs closest to the cemetery wall. No doubt one day those twenty empty meters of space would be filled in, but for now the dead didn't quite reach Derda's house. From where he stood, Derda saw nothing but marble tombstones. Marble slabs inscribed with the names of the dead. Marble signs showing where their owners lay on the other side.

The morning *ezan* from the cemetery mosque was thrown into the winds by the loudspeakers hung in tree branches. Derda was scared. He knew he had hardly any time left. He thought he should put some sort of marker to remember where he'd buried the pieces. But he had no time to figure out what and now the light blue world was starting to wrap around him. Then it came to him. The idea to use the tombstones as markers. Marble slabs. On one side of the tombstones lay the buried coffin with the owner of the tomb. And behind it on the other side he could mix his mother's pieces into the earth. He went to the foot of the tomb farthest to the left facing the wall and started to dig like his life depended on it. Holding the pan lid with both hands, he dug out the earth until he had made a hole an arm's length deep. He dropped his mother's left foot in and pushed the dirt back in

173

with the pan lid. It was covered up. He got to his feet and took two steps back. He was trying to see if you could tell someone had been messing with the dirt. Then he looked up and stared at the tombstone's inscription. Letters and numbers. A few seconds. He didn't bother staring at it any longer. Whatever he did know, Derda did not know how to read or write. He turned around and ran and reached the wall in one bound, leaping over it like a creature of the night. Like nothing had happened. Like an insect scurrying into his home.

That morning he went over the wall eight more times. Four times out, four times back. When it was really morning, he knew the cemetery kids would start coming. He couldn't risk digging any more holes so he stopped for the day. Half of his mother was at the foot of the first five tombstones from the left. The other half was in a pile behind the front door. Derda took two steps and collapsed. Letting the dirty pan lid fall to the ground, he curled his arm into a pillow under his head. He didn't sleep; he passed out. He hadn't eaten for two days.

In his dream, he was in the orphanage. He'd never seen it. He didn't know where it was or what an orphanage looked like. All he knew was what Fevzi had told him. Beds, closets, toilets, and the bigger kids who beat you up. And the hands that would grab you by the neck or ankles at any moment. He didn't stop for even a second, the whole dream long. He ran between bed and closet and closet and bed but the threat of getting beaten up was always there, following right behind him. Just once, just to see how far away the fingertips clawing at his back were, he looked over his shoulder. And at just that second, he smashed into something with the whole weight of his body. He collapsed, then looked up to see what he'd run into. He saw his mother looming over him. Her eyes were red and swollen, like they'd been the weeks before she died. She was standing and looking down at her son at her feet. Then the woman's mouth opened and two insects slipped out between her two lips. Derda tried to get up but it was like the palms of his hands were stuck to the ground. He was forced to watch the insects fall from her face. Then his body straightened like a switchblade springing open and he woke up.

He tried to stand up. But his head was spinning and he couldn't get up. Blinded by hunger, slowly he planted himself over his feet and stumbled to the door. He took the key and stepped outside. Three meters away, eight-year-old Süreyya sat on a rock. She had a candy bar. It was like Derda was transfixed. Süreyya was small for her age and couldn't do anything but cry, but Derda didn't even notice. He tossed the thick, rich candy bar into his mouth and watched the little girl as he chewed. And then he started to hear again. First Süreyya's tears, then Süreyya's mother's screams.

"You trying to be like your dad, you dog?"

The woman could have reached him in four steps, but she took the fifth to get more momentum to slap Derda. The slap jolted Derda awake.

"Where's your mother?" the woman yelled.

Then she turned, looked straight at the house, and yelled, "Havva! Get out here and look what your shit of a son did!"

She held Süreyya's elbow while she kicked at Derda on the ground. But she was wearing slippers so her kicks weren't too fast or too hard.

"She's not there!" Derda managed to say. "My mom's not home!"

"What do you mean, she's not there?"

The woman stopped kicking and pulled Süreyya onto her lap.

"She went to the hospital," Derda said. He hadn't even considered what he'd say if anyone asked about his mother. "They put her in the hospital."

175

All at once the woman pitied Derda. It must have been a record of going from crying to smiling. Like a seed flittering through the air, the journey from hate to pity in under a second.

"What are you going to do?"

Derda got up and, like all the kids did, brushed off the dust that kicked up and fell all around the cemetery houses. Whatever there was in the earth there; there was death. The dust of death was in the air. He didn't want to infect anyone with it.

"I'm going back and forth. She's Ok now. They say she'll be out soon."

"Do you have food and everything?" the woman asked. She was still rocking the whimpering Süreyya on her side. Then she got fed up and gave the girl's cheek a light slap and chided her with a "quiet, you!"

"There's some, but it won't last long," said Derda.

"Come over tonight. I'll give you something."

Derda said "Ok" out loud to her, but "tonight?" inside to himself. Tonight wasn't soon enough. There were hours still before the sun would set. Derda watched Süreyya and her mother walk away and slip inside their house and decided he needed to find a job. He had to earn some money. With money, he could buy bread. Maybe even a little cheese. Whatever he could. He realized he'd forgotten his work kit, his tanks and brush, and he went back home. He felt so faint he swayed as he walked. The candy bar hadn't been enough. His head was still spinning.

The cemetery kids gathered in the shade of the trees around the central fountain, laughing. The boys joked with each other, sitting on the marble borders around the graves. The girls picked the blooms off the stems of flowers that relatives of the dead had left and were sticking them in their hair. Some still weren't old enough to go to school. Some had never been to school. Others came to the cemetery after school. There was no time for homework. Everyone had some reason why they had to work. But there wasn't any industrial park, nor any busy main street where they could sell packs of tissues anywhere near there. All they had was the cemetery. Their world was the cemetery, thousands of square kilometers of cemetery.

If they'd lived in a country where people burn their dead and only have to look up at the sky to remember them, they couldn't have made even 5 *kuruş*. But in the city where they were born, those still living remembered their dead by going to the last place the dead were seen—the cemetery—and standing at the head of their graves, blowing their noses a few times, and giving a little money to have the marble washed and scrubbed. This was where the kids came into the picture, armed and ready with their plastic brushes and tanks of water. They were opportunists who knew how to watch the visitor for that moment of weakness as they stood remembering the dead. They knew just when to plant themselves in front of them and stick out their little hands to collect money from the pity tree.

Their business was a side industry to life. Like the bond between life and what comes after, an added layer of communication between the living and the dead. People expected that the children, less than a meter and a half tall, blinking their eyes meaningfully, would pray for the peaceful rest of the dead, in exchange for the tips. If that's what they were hoping for, then people must not rest, in peace or otherwise, when they die. In many cases it's not until they die that they wake up, their eyes as wide as life preservers. For these people, there's no such thing as "resting in peace." Especially since they can't even sleep anymore. But for everyone, the situation two meters under is totally different than the situation up top. The truth down below: worms, bugs, and lots and lots of flesh. The fantasy on the surface: "Rest in peace, Dad," "Sleep in light, my love," and lots and lots of prayers.

And so no one thinks they're being entirely absurd. They think they're speaking honestly when they say it, right in front of the dead. The dead who don't know anything about it and who couldn't care less. "Come on then, pour some water, and get rid of those weeds." Humanity's fantasy world, the cemetery remains intact. And children were the Peter Pans of that fantasy world. They all looked so much alike that brothers couldn't be told apart. In the eyes of the adult world it was like they stayed the same, never growing up.

A child, so it is said, grows up when he learns about death. But such sentiments were meaningless at the cemetery. Because if you grow up by learning about death, what happens if you make money cleaning tombs? Do six-year-olds hope to grow? Will it make Süreyya taller so she can jump down off the wall? How big could they get? They're like the dead themselves. They don't grow or change. And if they are the dead, then the world underground is the mirror equivalent of the world above it. Everyone's dead and that's that. But that's not the way it worked out. The kids fell asleep on the tombs they cleaned, but nothing was going to happen. While they started up a game of hide-and-seek as the sun went down, nothing was going to happen. They didn't feel a thing. Nothing was missing, nothing was wrong. They were the first to notice. Maybe the thing that was missing or wrong was just that they never felt anything.

Whatever it was, they just didn't think that a cemetery and its tombs were that important. They weren't afraid of the dead coming back to life or of ghosts. The only thing they were afraid of was bad weather on a holiday. The only thing they were afraid of was a rainy holiday when people who normally flooded into the cemetery would say, "It's going to be nothing but mud there," and not bother to come to the fantasy world they called a cemetery. Besides that, they could care so little about the dead and anything about death, that, sticking flowers left on the tear-soaked earth behind their ears, they tried to break the record for hopping from one tomb to the next without touching the ground.

The oldest was twelve years old. The littlest ones were six. They were a thousand dark years away from mothers holding their children as they watched horror films set in cemeteries. The cemetery wall was always there right behind them. Maybe later on they would all come together somehow. Those inside the walls and those outside. One would be a teacher, the other a school janitor. One a judge, the other a clerk. One a doctor, the other a blood salesman. One a prosecutor, the other a lying witness. One an architect, the other a laborer. One a pianist, the other a piano mover. One a member of parliament, the other selling *simit* at rallies. One a mistress, the other a son of a bitch. But which would be which? Has any research ever been done? Any scholarly article written? Has any work been done to compile the statistics that mark the relationship between people who spend their childhoods washing tombstones and their future career choices? Or do they even know the word "career"? They don't have a choice, anyway. In short, if a person starts to earn money from the dead from the age of six, what do they do later in life? Derda had an idea on the topic.

"I'm going to search for buried treasure. There's treasure buried around here. But no one knows where."

The others were quiet, listening. The topic was sufficiently intriguing.

"What treasure?"

Derda grinned like he was the master of all the world's secrets.

"You'll find out when you're older."

The kid he said that to was two years younger than he was. His name was Remzi and if he ever took an intelligence test, his family would be called into a special meeting to be told their son was a genius. But Remzi had never even been to school. He'd taught himself how to read and count and add by reading the inscriptions on the tombstones. He'd memorized all the names, birth dates, and dates of death on all the tombstones. Without even really noticing he was doing it. Now he was listening to Derda, but at the same time his busy mind was trying to add up the number of letters in the sentence he'd just listened to with the number he was about to say.

"That's great but . . ."

"Incoming! Incoming!"

Remzi's calculations were left up in the air. Four cars rolled in through the gate. The first to see them sounded the alert. The kids leapt up; many started to run. Remzi could have finished his sentence, but he needed money, too. Just as much as the others. He got up and ran after the others, shaking the numbers out of his head. They were all gone. In any case, in a few years, not very many, if he just kept doing what he was doing, his talents would evaporate one by one and he'd be nothing more than any other ordinary man. Anyway, it wasn't anything to be afraid of. But he didn't know that. And then he couldn't really stop his mind from racing even if he wanted to. Even now he was thinking about which of the cemetery's 7,226 tombstones the treasure could be buried under. Then he visualized each and every one, one at a time. Maybe that's why he didn't see what was in front of him. He ran straight into the marble of a family tomb and fell down.

He looked at his bleeding elbow then looked up and yelled, "Hey, wait for me!"

Everyone heard. But no one waited.

"What else can we do, Hasibe?" said the woman.

She couldn't think of anything else to say. She put her arms around Hasibe's shoulders, but she herself was crying, too. She couldn't stop herself. It was like all the pains had compounded, crashing over her like an avalanche. Her head was lowered, like the sun would never rise again. But actually, the dearly departed was not her daughter. Nor had she even seen the girl, not even once. But, whatever the woman whose shoulders she held felt, it hit her heart just as hard. If nothing else, she felt love. Maybe she wasn't her child, but she did love her husband, and so she transferred the love. And just think, a girl like that, just twenty-six years old. She killed herself, so far away where she was working in service of the nation. For the nation's children. She had met the mother of the deceased at a teacher's association event. It was an evening organized for family members of teachers who were serving so far away. They were fond of one another instantly. It was like they already knew each other. How could they not? Both of their loves were posted at the same school. One a daughter. The other, a husband. One was Yeşim. The other Nezih. One a new teacher. The other the assistant principal. One was a wren and the other the cat that caught her.

Yeşim realized that her life's search was for death. And in the end, like not a few people, she succeeded in getting her corpse buried. What she wasn't able to do in a letter, she worked out with a pistol. With her retired colonel of a father's ancient pistol. She crumpled. The old man who owned the gun now held the marble slab with two hands and kissed it. After her attempted suicide at school, Yeşim was released from her post and she returned to Istanbul. For the first few days she didn't speak. The next few days she laughed too much. Then the next day she shot herself.

Now she was lying in a brand-new tomb while two meters above her they couldn't care less about what had happened. If she could have, she would have sprung back to life. Nezih's wife held out her phone to Yeşim's mother, and she set it against her ear. "My condolences, my friend," he said. Nezih's friendship was artfully orchestrated. He gave his condolences from the other side of the phone.

At just that moment if Yeşim could have, she would have opened her eyes as wide as her eyelids could open. She'd have ripped open her shroud with her fingernails. She would've scratched and dug at the earth above her like a beaver until she reached the surface. Then she would have torn the telephone out of her mother's hand. If she could have done it, she would've opened her mouth as wide as she could and screamed, "Fuck you, you son of a bitch!"

But Yeşim couldn't do any of that. She couldn't even flutter one single eyelash. It had been twenty-six days since she'd been buried. She probably didn't even have a single eyelash left. Hasibe didn't know what else to say, so she said "thank you" and handed the phone back to Nezih's wife. The woman shut her phone and wrapped her arms around Hasibe. They cried together.

Derda, for his part, was waiting for the moment when they would fall silent. The moment when they would begin to collect themselves. But which one should he stretch his hand out to? The old man, or one of the women? *If they give me chocolate instead of money, I'll throw it back in their faces,* he thought to himself. The greatest counterstrike in the arsenal of the cemetery visitors was just that: candy or chocolate. Their hands would dive into their pockets, and getting hold of the three or four candies they'd positioned earlier, they'd take them out and hand them over with a "Here you go, son."

The first to stop sobbing was Nezih's wife. Despite the fact that the woman was becoming like family to her mother, Yeşim was a stranger to the woman. Not so the case with her husband, Nezih. So her tears were the first to dry. Derda didn't miss the chance and stuck out his palm. Looking at the child's disheveled face, Nezih's wife opened her handbag and took out her coin purse. No spare change. She was forced to go for paper money.

The least valuable, of course. She wanted to pull out just one note, but out came two. She regretted it, but it was too late.

"Just out of the blue, we gave good money to some strange child. Anyway, may it be a blessing on our heads," she said later when she went home, to her son, a university student five years younger than Yeşim.

Just as fast as Derda snatched the money he ran out of the cemetery and straight into the closet corner shop. He got a sandwich with sautéed meat and ate it then and there. He ate three of them, one right after the other. He practically choked himself. He grabbed a soda from the refrigerator, cracked it open, and downed it all in one swift move. Down the hatch. Then he started to come to. He remembered he had the last pieces of his mother back home to bury. That's the first thing that came to mind as soon as his stomach was full. The five pieces of his mother, right behind the door. As soon as night falls, he said silently to himself. He paid the grocer and left, but he turned right around and went back inside.

"Give me a pack of cigarettes."

"Which ones?" the grocer asked.

"The cheapest," said Derda, "and a box of matches."

And that's how he started to smoke, with the last money left in his pocket. He was eleven years old.

Isa caught Derda at the cemetery gates and couldn't hold himself back a second longer.

"Buried treasure! We have it in my new cemetery."

He must have been one of the unluckiest kids in the world. His family had moved from living next to the city's biggest cemetery to living next to the second biggest. Isa was still cleaning tombs. Cleaning the tombs there reminded him of his old cemetery he'd left behind. But he wanted to forget it. *The easiest way to forget was to focus on the new,* he thought.

"And in the fight over the treasure, someone died . . ."

Derda started to walk away. Seeing that he wasn't going to say anything, Isa kept talking.

"Our cemetery is really big. Bigger than here. Anyway, there's these two brothers. They hate each other. They both have their own gang. I'm on the younger brother's side. He doesn't look big, but whenever they get into a fight he beats up his big brother. Anyway, each gang has its own territory. We don't get mixed up with each other. Everyone stays on their own side. It's like here, you can't just claim a tomb and stand there. Then, one day, there was this rumor about some treasure. But it wasn't buried on our side. It was on the other side. So we snuck over there. We dug everywhere. But somehow we couldn't find anything. Then, the next day, one of our guys found this weird tomb, like a mausoleum. But no one knew what it really was. Then they said, yeah, that must be it. But how are we going to dig for the treasure? It's on the other side. So then we said, let's go, if we have to we'll fight, then we'll dig and get the buried treasure. So we went over there and then there's this kid from the other gang sleeping on top of it, guarding it. One of the little guys. Lying on top of the tomb, asleep. So we wake him up. He's terrified. No, don't do it, he's begging us. We didn't listen, of course. You're going to dig! So he started to dig. Then . . ."

"Fuck that," said Derda. The story was flying out of Isa's mouth so fast that it smashed right into Derda's two little words and shattered.

"Who cares? In the end did you find the treasure? No! So fuck it."

Isa's face went hard like marble. Cemetery marble. His veins stuck to his skin like the green veins running through marble. He understood then what no one had been able to really explain about life. For some, death is a permanent condition. For another, it's just dust in your eye. Isa looked around at the tombstones and thought it was good that they were dead. That day he believed that humanity died because that was their right. Till the day he died he never believed anything else. Maybe that's why he became a marble engraver. He walked into one of the workshops on the road going to the cemetery as an apprentice and walked out a master. All because that day Derda cut him off. Because he didn't let him tell the story of his life. Maybe that's why Isa only spoke to marble for the rest of his life. If only he could have told his story. Maybe he could have told it to one of the kids at school who listened so carefully to the teacher but somehow never heard him. But it didn't work out. In the final days of his apprenticeship he made his own tombstone. He hid it in a corner. Every now and then he'd go by and speak to it. To tell it the story Derda had cut off. Over and over again. And then he died. From all the marble dust he had inhaled. Just up and died one day. And his story? Who cares? Especially not after Isa was dead and buried.

They walked silently to the square. Side by side. Neither could have guessed what was passing through the other's mind, not even if they'd had a thousand chances. Derda's dark mood, Isa's words. Since Derda had chopped up his mother, words just got stuck in his mouth. How would he know, he asked himself. Then, to be forgiven, he took the pack out of his pocket and pulled out a cigarette.

"Light one up."

Isa didn't refuse. He took the cigarette like he'd been waiting his whole life for it. He lit it like he'd discovered fire. He sucked down the smoke like he'd been smoking for a hundred years. But it was his first time, too. Who knows how many more children started on cigarettes that day? All over the world.

Derda took a few steps then kicked a pebble with the tip of his toe. The pebble hit Isa's arm, so he got a free kick. They drove that pebble like they were in the World Cup. Sometimes it went off the road and onto the paths but they kept after it. Who knows, on that day, how many kids kicked a pebble. And who knows how many felt like a kicked pebble themselves.

The morning *ezan* slid off the houses' rooftops and into Derda's ear. His two black eyes opened and saw the ceiling. His nose wrinkled from the smell as he straightened himself over his two feet and stood up. He was late. It was so hard to wake up. His belly was full; Süreyya's mother had given him a dish of rice. But if he didn't hurry, he wouldn't be able to get all five parts buried.

As he buried the first four parts at the foot of the marble tombs in the row, the sun, outlining the tree branches, had already risen enough to prickle the nape of his neck. He took a deep breath.

"Just one piece left."

He ran to the row of tombs by the wall. His mother's right hand was under his arm. It was the first piece he'd wrapped in the sheet. He collapsed at the foot of the tombstone. He looked around. He could make out a figure in the distance. In his excitement he'd forgotten his shovel, that is, the pot lid. He dug with his hands but the earth was hard. Somehow the hole wouldn't get deeper. Then he looked at his mother's hand. At the hand wrapped in seven layers of fabric. He thought he could fit the hand into its little grave without the extra padding. So he peeled off the hand's shroud and tossed it off to the side. The naked hand dropped out of his hand like it was on fire. He couldn't take it anymore. He looked up and looked around again. He looked off to the side of the slab in front of him, to see where that person he'd seen before had gone. But he didn't see anyone. *Must have left*, he thought. *Who knows who it was.*

He nudged his mother's hand into the hole and then pushed the dirt he'd dug out back in to cover it. Then he stood up and started walking. Walking fast. He walked past the front of the tombs lined up side by side, the row where behind each tomb a part of his mother lay. Actually, to be more correct, he passed behind them. Because the tombs' owners lay in the other direction. On the other side of the slab. When Isa began his apprenticeship he told him, "They're called *şahide*," the marble tombstone's other side.

Soon enough he was worried that he hadn't buried his mother's hand deep enough and so he turned and looked over his shoulder as he sped away. Just to check he hadn't left the hand uncovered. But out of nowhere he ran smack into something and fell to the ground. He looked up to see what he'd run into and he saw a man. A man with a beard. In a long robe. Derda knew the cemetery mosque's imam and this wasn't him. It was Tayyar. And he was meeting him for the first time.

Tayyar silently watched Derda get to his feet like it was the most interesting thing he'd ever seen. Like he wouldn't have been able to take his eyes away even if it was the end of the world. He watched the boy brush off the dust. But this time he wasn't just brushing away the dust of death, he was also chewing his heart, which had leapt into his mouth. And he was asking himself, "Did the guy see what I did?" He didn't dare look up. He couldn't look the man in the eye. He kept looking down at himself, trying to look like he was looking for more dust to brush off. Then Tayyar spoke. Derda listened with his eyes still lowered. Still afraid.

"Next time, be more careful."

Then he stepped to the side and walked away. Derda turned around but the man was gone. *What did he mean? What am I going to be careful about? What did he mean by that?* Derda stood frozen. It was like the dirt under his feet had turned into a marshy bog. He was rooted to the spot. Then the marsh dried up and he took one step. No way, he said to himself. *Is that even possible? You went and ran into a guy in a huge cemetery. What's he going to say? Of course, he's going to say be more careful.* He laughed. He was sure he had been afraid for nothing. He shook his head and told himself he was an idiot. *If he'd seen me bury the hand there, wouldn't he come running up to me? Wouldn't he grab me by the neck and haul me to the police? Who would see something like that and just say, "Be more careful"?* He laughed again, walking away. Then he stopped and turned to look back at the tomb.

He wanted to die. Tayyar had stopped where he'd just buried the hand and was looking back at him. He had no hope but to turn and walk away. He left his steps behind him faster and faster until he was running. If he'd heard any sound behind him he would have found a way to sprint even faster. But behind was only silence.

He got as far as the cemetery gates and stopped to catch his breath. He shook his head. "For nothing," he said, "you're scared for nothing!" And he laughed.

"What are you laughing about so early in the morning? Take this and go get me some bread."

Yasin's hand stuck out of the guard shed's window. Derda took the money and asked, "Keep the change?" He was still laughing.

"Keep it, boy, keep it," Yasin said.

Once again waking up had put Yasin in a foul mood. Also because he was hungry. Also because he'd given his money away to Derda. He'd only been out of bed for two minutes but he'd already been ripped off. He hadn't even had a bite to eat yet. Fuck the change from the bread and Derda with it!

"Bastard," he said. Then he got back into bed. "I'll just sleep a little till he comes back," he said without really thinking about it. He fell asleep.

"Anything else?"

Derda didn't answer the grocer. He didn't even hear him. Because his mind had gone back to the fabric he'd peeled off his mother's hand and tossed aside. Did the man see it? Is that why he stopped there?

He shot out of the grocer's like a guided missile. A rocket was smaller, but he was more agile. There were at least ten corners to turn on the way to his target. He flew through the whole cemetery until he got near the last row of tombs closest to the wall. He hadn't planned what he was going to do when he got there, but when he got there he found a surprise he hadn't been expecting. The man in the robe was standing at the head of the tomb where he'd buried the hand.

He stopped and hid himself behind the first tree he saw. He hid behind it and peeked around the trunk. But it didn't do him much good. There were at least fifteen rows of tombs between them. Forty meters. He thought he shouldn't get too close to the man, but he could watch him from an angle. He figured he should leave twenty tombs between them, just to be safe. He made a quick survey of the trees. He looked at their branches, winding around each other. He had to get over there and hide in those branches. He would be able to see everything from there.

He ran like a squirrel, leaping, quick on his feet. He hid behind every fifth tree to survey the scene. Finally, he bounded behind a mess of green leaves that, from the number of branches and their closeness to each other, seemed like one tree from three roots. He held his breath.

He straightened his back against the tree and peeked around the trunk, his left eye peering between the branches. It was as brave as he could bear to be. But he had to at least be able to see what the man was doing.

He was leaning against the base of the tomb, burying a large white envelope in the grave bed contained by the marble edging around the tomb. There were two red roses on the tips of the branches coming out of one single trunk near the tomb's front side. He measured and buried the envelope five hand-spans away from then. Close to where birds were drinking water from the birdbath in the grave bed. He smoothed the dirt with his hand and looked around. Derda's single eye disappeared behind the trunk. He could hear his heart thumping in his ears. It was beating like it wanted to break out. He collapsed to the foot of the tree trunk again. He couldn't bear to turn around and look again.

He stayed there for about half an hour. He'd taken root there, he'd become a part of the tree. Only his hair rippled in the light breeze, like the leaves around him. He knees were pulled up to his chin. His arms were around his folded legs. He was entirely motionless.

When he'd decided he'd waited long enough, he stood up slowly, scooted over slowly, then stuck his head out and checked to see if the man was gone. The coast was clear. He left the trees and walked, his eyes scanning thirty steps ahead of him, when all of a sudden he bent over with the pain of a fist smashing into the back of his neck.

"You ass, did I not tell you to go buy me bread? You animal!"

It was the first time in his life that he was happy Yasin was hitting him. That morning Yasin had left the house without having eaten his breakfast and he was in such a bad mood that he never wanted to stop pummeling Derda.

After three punches he got up and ran out of the cemetery to get the bread from where he'd forgotten it on the grocer's counter. He dropped it through the open window of the guard's house. "The window's open. Stick your arm in and drop it on the table," Yasin had told him. So Derda did as much. He stuck the bread in under the curtains and left it on the table by the window, then kept running. He had to find the bloody fabric and get rid of it.

It was the same scene; the same day all over again. There was a man in front of the tombstone. But it was a different man. A man wearing a short-sleeved shirt. A man with glasses. The man looked around and adjusted his necktie. A man in his late fifties.

Derda hid in the same place again. He watched the same white envelope with the same eye. He watched the man pull the envelope out of the ground and leave a yellow one in its place.

Covering the top with dirt and looking around once more, the man left, walking down the road to the cemetery gate. He didn't walk slowly like the man in the robe. His movements were hasty. He'd finished his work within a minute. And now he was leaving. Derda could see his face but he didn't look like anyone he knew. He was slim, and his hair and skin were fair. His face betrayed no emotion. His wrinkled face seemed impenetrable.

Derda waited for the man to be out of sight. Then he got out from behind the tree and ran straight to the tomb. He walked behind it. He fell to his knees and searched for the fabric. He found it. He gave a long deep sigh. He hadn't been caught. He laughed. He took out the box of matches and lit one. The skinny little match roared into a fire and he held the fabric by one corner and held it away from himself. He gave the loose end of the fabric to the fire. The fire burned furiously, devouring the fabric. He held onto it for a while until he had to drop it. Then he stomped it out. The pitch-black ashes flew away and the bloody sheet was no more.

Then he went to the tomb. To the envelope at the tomb. He got into the grave bed of the tomb and looked around. He didn't see anyone. With a quick movement he drove his hand into the earth and pulled out the envelope. It was taped closed. Happily it was same kind of tape they sold at the corner grocer so he knew he could reseal it if he needed to. He opened it slowly, cautiously. He opened the envelope without damaging it at all.

Then he knew that this couldn't possibly be real. Because inside the envelope was a thick stack of money. Derda's trembling hand pulled five banknotes out of the stack and slipped them into his pocket. Then he took out five more. As long as that enveloped stayed open he couldn't help himself. He was afraid of taking too much so he closed it up and ran his fingernail down the tape to reseal it. He looked at the hole he'd pulled the envelope out of and covered it over with dirt. He had to run. He ran. He had to run fast. He ran even faster. He ran out of the cemetery gate and to the bus stop on the dingy street. He waited, terrified. He was terrified he would see the man who'd left the envelope or the other one with the long robe. He didn't stop looking to the left, to the right, or behind him for even a second. He was like a dog chasing his own tail.

The old lady sitting at the bench at the bus stop even said, "What's got into you, son? Sit down like a man!" gesturing to the empty spot next to her.

But Derda didn't hear her and he fidgeted relentlessly until the bus came.

He got off the third bus he'd gotten on to. The name of the stop he'd gotten off at was the same as the name on the sign on the huge building. He walked up to the gate. People just called the stop "Prison." "Drop me off at prison."

He walked up to the private at the gate.

"I have something to give to my father, my mother sent it."

The private banged at the big iron door behind him and a few seconds later a prison guard stuck his head out from behind it.

"What?"

"It's for my dad," said Derda. "I wanted to give him something, my mother sent it."

"What is it?"

He showed him the five banknotes he'd taken out of his pocket. He kept the others in his pocket. The guard glanced at the money in the kid's hand and quickly added it up.

"Who's your dad?" he asked.

Derda said the first and last names of the man he hadn't seen since he was five years old and whose face he couldn't remember.

"Ok," said the guard. Only his head was visible through the crack in the door. Then a hand stuck out. He took the money and while he was closing the door he heard the kid and stopped.

"How is my dad? Is he Ok?"

"This is a prison, son. You think anybody's "Ok" here?" he said, disappearing behind the door.

It went in through the kid's ears then welled behind in his eyes.

At the sight of the spring of tears about to be punctured, the soldier said, "Don't listen to him, your dad is fine, don't worry."

Derda swallowed, raised his head, and looked at the private.

"He's good, right? And would you tell him, my mom died," he said, and walked away.

He believed that his father in prison loved him enough not to send him to the orphanage. He couldn't tell anyone his secret. Derda's biggest secret would isolate him for the rest of his live-long days. Because his secret was that he had chopped up his mother and buried her in pieces. But you could tell even from the way he walked. From the way his hands were jammed into his pockets. From the way his head was bowed. From the way his feet shuffled against the ground at his every step. From the way he walked slow, like he had no place to go. Or the way he walked fast, like he was late for everything. And then from his smell. Sweat and loneliness. Maybe people across the street or in passing cars couldn't understand why, but once they looked in his face, it wasn't long before they noticed. The gendarme who watched him walk away noticed. Maybe that's why he shook his head and muttered, "Life's a bitch. Fuck it!"

And so the news received into the soldier's ear and the money received into the guard's pocket were gone and forgotten.

Neither reached their destination. But Derda, on his way back home, said with silent lips, "Wait and see, Dad, wait and see how much more money I'm going to bring you!" For three days, he didn't leave his post near the tomb that people seemed to be using as some sort of mailbox. But no one came, and no one left an envelope.

But on the fourth day it happened. Just what he was waiting for. He saw the man with the long robe. But this time the man passed the tomb he'd used before. He was in front of the tomb to its right. From behind the trees, Derda, if he didn't remember incorrectly, was thinking that at the base of that tomb was another piece of his mother. The piece of her right leg, knee to ankle.

The man in the robe buried a white envelope and, staring straight ahead, walked away. Derda didn't lose a second. He ran to the tomb. He opened the big white envelope trying to imagine what could be more valuable than money. Inside was a stack of papers. Papers and photographs with writing on them. Photographs of groups of men with beards and robes. Some of their turbaned heads were circled with red pen. There was something written close to them. With the same red pen. But Derda still couldn't read. If he could, he could have read names like "Sheik Gazi" and "Hıdır Arif." But even if he could read he still wouldn't have understood anything. Because he'd never heard of MI6, the British intelligence service, or of the members of the Hikmet Tariqat in England. In fact, even if he could have read every single one of those papers, he still wouldn't have understood a damn thing.

The stack of paper he held in his hand, in exchange for money, became the information property of the intelligence service. Even if he had known what post at the consulate the man with the glasses who came through the cemetery gates to this row of tombs held, he still wouldn't have been able to get what

194

was going on. Because, of course, Steven's business card didn't say he was MI6's man in Istanbul, but that he was the commercial attaché. The swapping technique he used with Tayyar was called a *dead drop* in MI6 lingo. It was a method of exchange where the giver and the receiver never met face to face. It saved them from having to use a safety deposit box or something like that, like they had had to before. But there had to be some sort of signal to show if the drop point was empty or full. Steven had chosen a streetlamp on the street leading to the cemetery. A streetlamp post, to be more precise. After leaving an envelope, he put one of two bike locks around the post. One was blue, the other red, two bike locks. They passed between Tayyar and Steven, back and forth. The result was first and foremost that the exchange was secure. The safest place to do such an exchange was a cemetery where hardly anyone ever went. There are no casual passersby in a cemetery. Because there, the majority of eyes are underground. But maybe Steven chose the cemetery on account of his own personal style of dark romanticism. After all, it was called a *dead* drop.

The reason for Tayyar's treason was a lot simpler. It amounted to nothing more than a mere sentence Sheik Gazi had said years before: "Know that Hıdır Arif is my only successor." But Tayyar had devoted his life to Sheik Gazi. Tayyar, when he was just eighteen years old, threw himself into the middle of a missile assault orchestrated by a man known as Tehran Selahattin and saved Sheik Gazi's life. He was in a coma for seven days. And then he acted as witness as Sheik Gazi and Tehran Selahattin made peace, kissing each other's cheeks and agreeing to divide the region between the two of them. The result was, like his spiritual father had said once upon a time, there was no reason for him to cry anymore. Steven was experienced enough to know how to find the rotten tooth in a mouth of tens of thousands of teeth, and to know how to pull it out. In the end Tayyar accepted

Steven's offer. In any case, since the day the successor had been indicated, that is, for years, Tayyar had been waiting for such an offer. What he did wasn't treason exactly. It was taking his due. In cash. It was impossible for Derda to have known about any of that.

He was putting the papers back in the white envelope and burying it where he'd found it. If he didn't, maybe Tayyar would catch him. But Derda, with the mugger's instinct he'd inherited from his father, with some strange unconscious motivation, decided to take half of the papers. He stuck them up under his T-shirt, securing the corners in the waistband of his pants. He quickly buried the rest and ran away. While he was running, he thought that if these papers were really worth money, then he wasn't going to have to clean tombstones anymore. But he wasn't going to take money from the yellow envelope that day, he said to himself. Two misdeeds in one morning were enough for the kid.

With the five bills in his pocket he ate and smoked cigarettes for five days. Eventually he even forgot to knock on Süreyya's mother's door at night. He hid the papers he'd taken from the white envelope in his pillowcase on the floor mattress, and every night he lay his head on them and dreamt of being rich. But it wasn't long before he realized he didn't know who he could sell the documents to. "That's Ok," said Derda. "I'll find a way." Then, after waking from dreams of becoming a professional thief, he slipped into sleep like a child.

While Derda was sleeping, Steven was sitting in the consulate's safe room, typing a cryptograph into a keypad. Each typed letter was encoded into holes punched into a paper ribbon inside a machine. The yellow ticker tape was vomited out of the machine like a snake emerging from its hole. It curled and coiled. While he finished the code, he inspected the ribbon like it was the receipt from a cash register. Using his thumb and his index finger, he counted out eight figures. Then he put it into an envelope, sealed it, and waited for the M16 courier to come. They came from London twice a month. With diplomatic passports in their pockets, of course. For an intelligence service, a courier was an arrangement as antiquated as messenger pigeons. But Steven was like that. Old-fashioned enough to write a letter. Nothing had pleased him so much as the fact that the Internet program specially designed for cryptography they'd loaded into his computer had been a terrible failure. Thinking of the choice words to write in his text, he fondled the yellow ribbon hanging out of the side of the machine in front of him. As for what he wrote, this was the header:

SURVEILLANCE REQUIRED FOR BEZIR, MEMBER OF HIKMET

And he continued:

Notwithstanding the arrangements made on your orders to process with due order the visa requests of a laborer previously convicted of murder and his daughter, I believe that having more comprehensive, continual profiles of Ubeydullah and his son Bezir would be ultimately profitable for our cause. In light of the most recent documents I have obtained, it appears to me that Bezir has become a fanatic inclined to violence. As for Ubeydullah, he is attached to Hıdır Arif with an unshakeable allegiance. Accordingly, in my view, approaching him with the offer was a mistake. In sum, given my assessment of him as a potential mudjahadeed, I would request that as soon as feasible Bezir be placed under strictest surveillance.

Steven didn't return to his Beyoğlu home till it was practically morning. Knowing he wouldn't be able to sleep, he turned once again to Thomas Edward Lawrence's *Seven Pillars of Wisdom*. Maybe for the thousandth time. As he read, he still couldn't quite put his finger on why he was such a great admirer of the man known as Lawrence of Arabia. He wondered why for maybe the ten thousandth time. Perhaps because he had been a spy, too? Or was it because he too had been a masochist like himself? There he was, between the two reasons, smiling as he rubbed himself through the fabric, back and forth. Steven was sitting on the sofa in his living room dressed like an Arab sheik, like Lawrence. He felt happy inside the white fabric a Damascene tailor had sewn for him.

He had read some twenty pages when the telephone rang. He answered like an Arab sheik. He didn't care it was four in the morning.

"Dad!"

Then Steven hung up in his son's ear. He didn't care if it was the first time in four years he'd heard his voice. Then the phone rang again. Three times, right in a row, like it was coming from close by. Steven turned a page and silently looked at the phone long and hard, as if from far away.

When Derda passed through the cemetery gates the sun was about to set. He stopped in front of the guard's house.

"Brother Yasin!"

"Why are you yelling, boy?"

He stopped in place. Yasin was behind him. He handed him the *bağlama* he was carrying. Inside its black case.

"The man fixed it. They did just what you said."

Yasin asked as he took the *bağlama*, "Was it enough money?"

"Yeah, was enough."

"Any change?"

"You said keep whatever's left. I was out all day for you. I already . . ."

"Fine, boy, fine," said Yasin.

Then he walked inside his guard's house. He shut the door and sat on the divan. He unzipped the case and slipped it off the *bağlama*. Two days before he'd fallen against the wall during a bout of heavy drinking. He was holding the instrument by its round body, and the handle had snapped when he'd slammed against the wall.

"If anything had happened to the body, they'd be no saving it," the master had said to Derda. Then he'd put on a new handle. The handle that was now cradled in Yasin's palm. He was about to touch the strings but he stopped. "I'm sorry," he said in a small voice. The *bağlama* forgave Yasin and the sound of a *türkü* emanated from the guard's house. It was a *türkü* Derda knew: "I Did it Myself, I Found it Myself." There hadn't been anyone else for Yasin to blame. Ever. But there was someone Derda was angry at. Yasin.

"He sent me off at the crack of dawn!" Derda said. Then he wondered if anyone had come. He wondered if anyone had come and gone to the tomb he'd watched from the base of the tree, never letting it out of his sight for a whole week until this morning. There was only one way to find out. And that was to go and see.

He came to the row of tombs closest to the wall and stopped to think. He looked at the tomb where the first envelope had been buried. Then at the one to the right. Where the second had been buried. Then he turned to look at the tomb to the right of that one. "Do they go from left to right?" he asked himself. "I mean, are they using the tombs in a row? Yes," he said. *They had to be. They must have to constantly move their hiding place so there's no risk of someone discovering their system*, he thought. *But they're going down the row. Left to right.*

He was so sure of his theory, he stepped right up to the tomb, stopped in front of the tombstone, and stuck his fingers into the soil in the grave bed. He loosened the soil, searching, until he felt something hard. But this was no envelope. He sank his hand in even deeper until he could grab onto what seemed to be some sort of box. He pulled it out. A white box emerged from the earth. It would have been impossible to find a kid more ecstatic than Derda was just then anywhere on the face of the planet. Who knew what sort of treasure was inside the box? Maybe more money than could fit inside an envelope!

He took a quick look around him, then opened the box. But as soon as he opened it he wanted it shut, and fast. But he couldn't get the lid to fit back on. He lost his grip jostling the pieces of box and lid, and everything tumbled to the ground. Derda practically fell himself. The box, lid, and his mother's left hand dropped into the dirt. Well, whatever was left from his mother's hand. A bit of flesh, and lots of bone. Derda knew it was her left hand because he'd buried it at the base of that tomb. He swallowed to keep from vomiting, he took deep breaths to keep his heart from stopping in its tracks, and, holding it gingerly with the edge of his T-shirt, he put the hand back in the box and set the lid on top. Then he took four steps to the other side of the tombstone and, dropping to his knees, looked for the hole he'd dug before. But there was no need to look far. It was there, gaping open between his knees.

Someone had found his mother's left hand, put it in a white box, and buried it in the earth in the grave bed. But who? Derda didn't know Tayyar's name. "He saw!" was all he could say. "That man must have seen. That morning he saw what I did. That's why he said to be more careful. Be more careful or you'll get caught!"

He was right. Steven's directive had been: "Write a list of the documents inside the envelope, and put that into the envelope, too. That way I'll be able to confirm what is supposed to be inside."

Steven, taking advantage of this basic preventive measure, had informed Tayyar of the missing documents. And he, for his part, made a list of those who could have seen him bury the envelopes. And there was only one person on that list. That kid who'd been secretly burying something at the base of the tomb. Tayyar dug where he'd seen Derda on his knees and when the piece of flesh appeared before his eyes it was enough to turn the stomach even of a hardened warrior like Tayyar. He shook it off, though, and prepared a line with one single bait. One hook, one bait, one fish. He wasn't about to run after the kid, who came from who knows where and who went who knows where. He was going to catch his prey with one single shot. He only had to decide which tomb to use as the trap. The tomb where the kid had stolen the documents? Or, as if everything were following its normal course, put it in the next tomb to the right that was going to be used? Two possibilities, one gamble. Tayyar banked on his suspicion that the kid was clever enough, and that he had been watching them for some time. He buried the box in place of the papers.

It was perfect; the perfect bait. *In just the right place and in just the right measure,* thought Derda, *it couldn't have been anyone else. It must have been that man in the robe! If it had been someone else a ton of police would've come. They would've grabbed me before I even got into the cemetery. But that white box, this business with burying.* "What am I going to do," said Derda, out loud. Practically yelling.

"I am in so much fucking trouble!"

Then he looked at the box in his hand. First he had to get rid of that. That before anything else.

He ran to the base of the wall and dug a hole as deep as he could, threw the box inside, and covered it up. He got up and turned around without looking. This time he didn't even want to remember where he'd buried it. He didn't care anymore about knowing where he'd buried his mother. Did it do him any good to know? It wasn't like he was going to go up to each tomb and say a *Fatiha* for her in each place. "Whatever," he said to himself.

201

Whatever. But now what am I going to do? What do these guys want from me? he thought. "Money!"

"They want their money. Fuck, they want their money back. But it's gone. I already spent it all. But wait, the papers are still here. I'll give them those back. Maybe they'll forgive me. When I give them the papers maybe they'll stop following me. But what if they don't?"

That night he brought a box to the hole and put the papers wrapped in his pillowcase inside and buried it, smoothing over the dirt as best he could. That night he didn't sleep. He waited with a knife in his hand, hardly daring to blink, alone inside his dark house. Until the morning *ezan* came like a lullaby and put him to sleep.

When he woke up he left the house barefoot, ran to the wall, and jumped over. He went to the grave bed and dug. Then dug some more. And some more. He dug away at the dirt in the grave bed until he'd flung it everywhere. He laughed while he flung it away. And in the end he was sure. They'd taken the papers. *They're gone! The man in the robe must have come and taken the papers. And maybe he'll never come back. But the money,* thought Derda, his face hanging. *And if they come back for the money? But it wasn't that much, right? But what if the man in the robe does come back to get the money? I'll be so screwed then,* thought Derda, terrified down to his core. *He'll kill me. Because I can't give that money back, not for my life. I couldn't get it together, even if I had months.* "Shit!" yelled Derda. "Fuck!"

After that day, Derda became like a hermit. And day after day he grew older. Because the pain is not the fear itself, the fear is in the waiting. And waiting for fear is worse than fear. Just like someone once wrote.

"What's up?" Isa said. "You waiting for someone?"

"No," said Derda.

But he wasn't very convincing. He kept looking around, stretching his head out to see past the trees. Even standing up then sitting back down again. He'd been acting this way for just about a month.

"Then why do you keep looking around?"

"What's it to you?" barked Derda. Then he regretted it. "I'm going to say something. But it's a secret."

"Ok," said Isa. "Tell me."

"If you see a guy in a long robe around here, tell me."

Isa pointed to someone over Derda's shoulder. "There's one," he said.

Derda jumped to his feet and looked behind him. It was Ubeydullah's brother Yakup, wearing a long robe; he stood at the head of the tomb that looked like a mausoleum, his hands opened in prayer. Derda turned to Isa.

"Not that guy! Yeah, he's wearing a robe, too, but look: You know where he'd be? You know our wall, right? Our house wall? There, those tombs closest to the wall, right? You know, the last row? There. If you see a guy there, you better tell me. If I'm at home, come get me. Wherever I am, come find me, I mean. For the love of God, look, it's really important."

Isa laughed.

"Ok, but why's it so important? Is this your secret?"

"Look, recently, I did some work for that man in the robe. I washed a tomb. Then he didn't give me any money. So I cussed him out. Then the guy beat me up. Get it? Now if that guy finds me, he's going to really shit in my mouth. I really cussed the guy out bad."

"Really?" said Isa. "You think the man has nothing better to do than chase after you? He probably forgot. He's not coming back."

"*İnşallah* that's true," said Derda. Then he got to his feet, used his hand to block the sun, and surveyed the scene. Sitting down at the base of the tomb and leaning back against it, he took the cigarette Isa was offering him.

"Anyway, if there's anyone walking around back there by those tombs you tell me, Ok?"

Isa lit Derda's cigarette.

"Sure, don't worry," he said.

Then he lit his own cigarette, adding, "But if you ask me, you're scared for nothing."

Isa took five drags before he asked, "You know Fevzi, right? That kid who ran away from the orphanage?"

Derda nodded his head.

"I saw him yesterday. That guy's weird. You know, he's always carrying a bag around. And you know what's inside it? He showed me. It's a doll. You know, like a toy for girls. It's got this dress on. Then Fevzi took its clothes off. It's got boobs and an ass like a real woman. Like a real grown-up woman, you know? Anyway, he said that doll was the reason he ran away from the orphanage. What do they call them? Barbo, Barba, anyway, something like that. Barbie, Barbie. And you know why? Because the guys there saw him there, feeling up the doll, then they jumped Fevzi, you get it?"

Derda, still keeping an eye out, stubbed his cigarette out against the tombstone.

He asked, "Yeah, but why'd he take the shit for a doll? Why didn't he just get rid of it? Throw it away and not get beat up?"

"Wait, listen," said Isa. "Guess who gave him that doll. Do you know?"

"Why would I know?"

"Man, the prime minister gave it to him!"

"Fuck!" said Derda.

"I swear, man. They were in this town, this village, whatever, the prime minister came. So they all went. He was smaller then. The prime minister was giving out toys. The kids were all scrambling around, grabbing and pushing. He found it on the ground. First he didn't really get what it was. Then somehow he couldn't give it up or throw it away. I mean, if nothing else, the prime minister did give it to him, right? But the kids in the town, they saw him and it's a girl thing, right? They started to touch it. Fevzi couldn't do anything about it of course. Then they started touching Fevzi. And he . . ."

Derda turned and looked at Isa.

"Man, did you do something?"

Finally Isa answered. With a question.

"You want to?"

"Go fuck yourself, man," said Derda. "What do I want from him?"

"You get bread and give it to him, and then Fevzi . . ."

"No way," said Derda.

"Everyone's doing it. That's what Fevzi said. The kids from the football pitch come, too. But you should see the doll, it's like a real woman. And Fevzi, with his hand . . ."

"Man, go fuck yourself!" said Derda. He felt sick to his stomach. Not from what Fevzi did to Isa in exchange for his loaf of bread. For believing what Fevzi had told him about what happened at the orphanages. Maybe all of it was true. Maybe they did jump Fevzi in the toilets. But Derda wasn't about to carry around a Barbie. For a second he thought he'd done everything for nothing. He'd been afraid of the orphanage for nothing. He'd chopped up his mother and buried her for nothing. He'd stolen the money from that man in the robe for nothing and for nothing he'd gotten into a shitload of trouble. And all because of Fevzi. And all because of that stupid doll. Because he got a doll and went crazy.

"I'm going to fuck that Fevzi!" said Derda out loud, without even realizing it. Then Isa looked him right in the eye and he corrected himself.

"Not like that, man."

"Wake up, wake up!"

He was stretched out in the shade of the cypress trees, sleeping between two graves in an empty plot waiting for death. Derda opened his eyes and saw Isa leaning over him.

"What's going on?"

"There's someone at one of your tombs. But it's a woman."

Derda jumped to his feet. Out of habit, he grabbed his plastic tanks and his brush before he set off after Isa. His heart was in his mouth and he pressed his lips together to force it back down. But when they came close enough to see the woman standing in front of one of the tombs, he knew he'd have to open his mouth to say something.

"It's Ok, you can go."

"Are you sure?" asked Isa.

"Yeah," said Derda. "Go back to work."

Isa walked away, leaving Derda to hide himself among the trees at his lookout point. He trembled like a leaf as he watched the woman.

The woman stood in front of the tomb where his mother's left breast and rib cage were buried, those parts that'd given him so much trouble to chop apart. She stood entirely still, staring at the marble slab. Derda thought she might just be a regular cemetery visitor. She looked like she was about to cry. She touched the tomb's marble edge and then covered her mouth with her hand. Derda was almost totally convinced. This woman wasn't the fear he'd been waiting for. Then just as he was moving out from his hiding spot in the trees, he saw something that practically made him faint. He rubbed his eyes, then spread open the curtain of leaves in front of him and watched the woman pull a white envelope out of her bag and lay it on top of the earth in the tomb bed. "Fuck!" reverberated through him like a scream.

The woman dug a hole with her hands. She dug it deep enough to bury the envelope inside and then she looked around. Derda ducked his head behind the tree. *What should I do?* he asked himself over and over again. *What am I going to do? What am I going to do? What am I going to do?* Then a thought occurred to him. *What if I go up and talk to her? What if I go and explain everything to her? If I tell her I can't give them their money back? If I fall over her feet and tell her I'm sorry? If I beg for forgiveness? Maybe I could persuade her. Then she'd go talk to the guy in the robe. Yes, yes!* he said to himself. *It's got to work. I'm sick of being scared. I don't care what happens.*

Derda left the security of the trees like a falsely condemned man going to his execution, who, despite his innocence, holds his head high as he walks toward his legally sanctioned death. With each step, his fear diffused a bit more. Approaching the woman from behind, he took a deep breath and spoke.

"Excuse me."

The woman had just covered over the buried envelope in the hole and she turned and looked at the kid as if she'd been awoken from a dream.

"It was me who took those papers. And some of the money. But I gave the papers back. But the thing is, I don't have any money. Please, forgive me! I'll do anything you want."

The woman looked him over from head to toe as he spoke. His shoes, hair, his tanks and brush, his eyes, and his teeth. She seemed both lost in thought and intent to size up the boy. It didn't seem like she was going to say anything, so Derda continued.

"Please, for the love of God!"

The woman shook her head and gestured at the tombstone with her hand. Derda didn't understand. He asked her the first thing that came to mind.

"You want me to clean the tomb?"

The woman pointed toward the tomb and nodded again. Derda didn't ask again.

"Ok," he said. "Just a minute, I have to get water."

He ran as fast as he could. He was ecstatic that the whole thing could be resolved so easily. He'd wash a tomb, and his debt would be cleared. He ran to the fountain in the square and caught his breath while the tanks filled with water. Then he ran back without stopping, taking the shortcut paths instead of the main road going down to the cemetery gates. But when he got to the trees between the tombs where he'd hid before, he stopped dead in his tracks. The woman was gone. He spun around looking for her. Nothing. He took off toward the cemetery gates. If she was on her way out he'd catch up with her for sure. He had to catch up to her and talk to her. He had to be sure that they'd agreed, that everything was okay. He wasn't scared anymore. He dropped his tanks as he passed the fountain. They were weighing him down. He ran as fast as his legs could carry him and stopped at the cemetery gates. But there was no one there. No woman, no one at all. He stepped out of cemetery gates and looked both ways down the main street. It was like she'd vanished into thin air. *Maybe she got in a car and drove away?* he thought. But then he didn't know what to think. He was totally confused. There was only one thing he could be sure of, and that was that he wasn't going to touch that envelope buried at the foot of that tomb. But he really didn't know anything anymore. He didn't know what they expected him to do; he didn't even know if he and the woman had come to an understanding or not.

"She pointed at the tomb," Derda said aloud. He tried to remember what she'd looked like as he imitated her gestures.

"This is what she did. She pointed to it like this. Then I said, should I wash it? And she nodded . . . That's how it went, right?"

That was as far as he could extend his monologue with her. It was easy to understand. And fairly certain. They'd clear his debt. But on one condition: Derda had to clean the tomb. He laughed. He broke into a run, only slowing down to grab a tank when he passed the fountain. He didn't stop until he was in front of the tomb. He looked around. He was sure someone was watching. They must be watching to make sure he fulfilled his part of the agreement. He started pouring the water little by little over the tombstone. And he looked up and into the distance.

"Look, here I am, doing what you wanted me to do!" he wanted to cry out, and he wasn't doing a shabby job at that. One by one he collected the leaves that had fallen over the tomb from the surrounding trees. With his brush he scrubbed the dirt and dust off the tombstone after he'd poured the water over it, and he tried to work as respectfully as he could. Respectfully and pains-takingly. *It must be the tomb of someone important,* he thought. If it wasn't, how could just cleaning it clear his debt?

Derda felt a growing sense of independence as he cleaned the tomb. He was conquering his fear. One by one the knots in his throat were untied, the permanent tension in his face mellowed into a smile, and for the first time in a long time, he felt good. Even happy.

The morning sun seeped into his eyes and he woke smiling. He had dreamed of his father. In real life, he didn't even remember what his face looked like, but in his dream he knew it was him. He was out of prison and they were having breakfast together. Derda got up and got dressed. He ate some bread and a bit of cheese left over from the day before. He got his tanks and his brush and walked out the front door. He turned left and followed the house's wall until he came to the cemetery wall. He bent over and went through the hole he'd smashed open years before and stepped into the cemetery. The dead had multiplied and now the tombs were ever closer to the wall. He weaved his way between them and went to the new fountain. He filled his tanks and walked to the front of the tomb and stopped. He washed the tomb as if he were performing a sacred devotion. He had no idea if the envelope was still in the grave bed or not. Because he didn't want to know. He only did what they wanted him to do, and kept the tomb sparkling clean.

When he saw that there wasn't a speck of dust remaining he ran his hand over the tomb and smiled. Then he looked down at the stone path under his feet. Under the path beneath his feet lay his mother's left rib cage and heart. The path ran between all the tombs, covering all the buried pieces of his mother. He leaned over the tomb and caressed it, whispering, "See you tomorrow."

Derda was sixteen years old.

"Hey, what's up?" said Remzi.

"I'm good. You been waiting long?" asked Derda.

"No, no, come on, let's go."

They walked out of the cemetery gates. The bus was pulling up to the bus stop and they ran to catch it. They leapt up the two steps onto the bus then stood facing each other, hanging from the leather straps. The first one to speak was the would-be genius of his age, Remzi.

"They pay good money, but the work's kind of tough."

"That's Ok," said Derda.

"They're a bit, well, you know, so don't try to push it or be stubborn or anything."

"No way, man. What am I going do? Act like an ass? As long as they give me my money, I don't care. I don't care about anything else."

"And," said Remzi, "if you get on their good side, they'll give you a sales point, too. And then you'll earn more."

"What do you do?"

"I work the machines. In the depot."

The employers quickly learned the value of Remzi's talents when they saw him comfortably working with all the complicated machines and mechanisms.

"For now, I'll just be doing loading, right?" asked Derda.

"Yeah. You get the stuff from the depot and load up the van. Then you deliver the stuff to the sales points. Come on, this is where we get off."

They got off the bus and started walking down a dismal street off the main road and stopped in front of a three-story building. Remzi grabbed Derda, who was rushing up to the front door.

"Not there, down here," said Remzi, pointing to a flight of stairs at the side of the building leading down to the basement.

They went down the stairwell. Remzi banged on the iron door at the bottom. A voice answered them from inside. A gruff, muffled voice.

"Who is it?"

"Remzi."

The door opened and the strong smell of a printing press hit their noses. As the odors rushed out, Remzi and Derda went in.

A man with glasses stood beside the open door. A man who'd aged when he was still young. Like age had just fallen on him all of a sudden one day.

"Is this your friend?" His words seeped out from the spaces of his missing teeth. It was like they'd all escaped from his mouth one night.

"Yes," said Remzi. Then he turned to Derda. "This is Brother Süleyman," he said. "My boss. He looks over everything."

He made a sweeping gesture indicating all the machines of the printing press: everything. The building's basement was bigger than it looked from outside. It was probably twice the width of the building itself. Or maybe all the books piled on top of each other gave it that impression. Thousands of books and enormous printing machinery.

"No one else's here yet?" asked Remzi.

"Nope," said Süleyman. "I just got up myself. Get the tea on, let's have some. What's your name?"

"Derda."

"Look, son, do you know what kind of work we do here?"

"Remzi told me a little about it," said Derda.

Remzi was in front of two waist-high cupboards against the only wall in the warehouse not covered by piles of books. On top of one was a stove. On top of the other was a kitchen sink with a faucet that never stopped dripping. There was a refrigerator next to the cupboards. Remzi put the water on to boil in the makeshift kitchen of the depot that doubled as Süleyman's home. The smoke curling out of his cigarette mixed with the steam from the teapot. Süleyman cleared his throat with a hearty round of morning coughs and then spoke.

"I don't want to hear about you doing anything stupid, not even once, you understand?"

"I understand," said Derda.

"Israfil will be here soon. He'll explain the job better than I can. But let me tell you loud and clear. Now, you might wind up in trouble sometime but if you tip the police off to what's going on here, they'll get you. You understand what I'm saying?"

"Don't worry," said Derda.

"Wrong! I can't even worry about worrying. You have to think about it. If you do your job like a man, if you keep your mouth shut, then you'll get your money."

"Fine," said Derda.

He didn't care about the depot or about anything Süleyman said. The only thing he wanted was to make a bit of money. Because he was way too old for the cemetery now. His pained expressions didn't fool anyone. And after all, the hand reaching out for money didn't reach up anymore. Now more often than not the hand came down to the customer. Derda was taller than most cemetery visitors, who were, after all, bent over in mourning. And besides, the cemetery walls had almost entirely fallen down, and they were being rebuilt. They were saying that Yasin was going to be let go and private security guards would be brought in. And they weren't going to let the kids inside anymore.

It wouldn't be long before the cemetery children would be history. The dirt roads had been covered in paving stones; the widest ones had been paved with asphalt. The times were changing. The children were going to be left outside, on the other side of the walls rising around the cemetery. There was no bread to be won from the dead anymore. Soon there'd be no children left there. Within a month at most. So the pursuit of gainful employment had come to each and every one. Isa had gone to the marble engraver as an apprentice, Fevzi had disappeared into the city, and Remzi, through connections from relatives, had found work in a depot that printed pirated books.

When he'd told him about it—"book work"—Derda shouted at him, "Man, are you making fun of me? You know I can't read." But Remzi had told him, "Man, you're not going to be reading the books, you going to be hauling them around."

They were eating a breakfast of the *simit* Remzi ran out and bought and tea, all laid out on top of a box spread with the uncut pages of one of the day's bestselling novels. They ate in silence.

Then the iron door swung open and a monster of a man came in. Süleyman picked up the pages loaded with sesame seeds from the *simits* by their corners and crumpled them in his fist. He looked up.

"Look, Israfil's here."

When Israfil took off his coat, the butt of his pistol flashed at his waist. Remzi stood up and Derda followed his lead.

"Brother Israfil, this is Derda. The friend I told you about. To do the loading work . . ."

Israfil looked over Derda and his guilty eyes and asked, "What's your father do?"

"He's in prison," said Derda.

"Fine."

It was the first time Derda had seen someone register absolutely no surprise at his answer. Israfil nodded like being in prison was a totally ordinary existence, but Derda waited for him to ask more. But he didn't. Because for Israfil, prison was a just another reality. He drank the tea Remzi brought him in one gulp and spoke.

"The van comes around nine. They'll tell you what to load. Then you'll go with the van and deliver the goods to the sales points. Depending on the situation, you'll do the rounds three or four times. In the evening, you'll pick up the stuff from the sales points and bring it all back here. That's the job. And you'll work fast. There'll be no lingering around in front of the sales points, understand?"

214

"Ok," said Derda.

Israfil lit a cigarette and gave his empty glass to Remzi, adding, "Look, you are here because your friend here vouched for you. Work hard and earn your keep."

"I understand, brother," said Derda.

Then Israfil stared at Derda with a crushing glare and took three long, deep breaths. There was no need for him to speak. Because the threat came out of Israfil's body like a cloud and fell over everything in the depot. When Israfil felt that Derda had been sufficiently impressed by the cold damp of the cloud, he turned around and was lost in the labyrinth of books.

Half an hour later, Derda was carrying two boxes loaded with forty books each. He passed through the iron door, climbed up the twelve steps, and loaded the boxes into the back of a windowless van pulled up to the top of the stairs. It took him seven trips to learn that it took fourteen boxes to fill the van. He turned the jug next to the refrigerator upside down, filled up his glass, and drank the water in great gulps. He wiped off his sweat, yelled "Coming!" then ran up the stairs and jumped into the passenger's seat where he was greeted with a cigarette thrust right up under his nose.

"Light this."

He took the cigarette and lit it with a lighter on the dashboard. Then he and Abdullah, a man he'd met an hour before, pulled out of the side street and onto the main road. As soon as they were on the main road, it became all too apparent that Abdullah was a closet blabbermouth. Like all secret talkaholics, it was only when there was just one person stuck by his side that he really started up. He'd sit in deep silence at a crowded table in the coffeehouse, but when everyone else had left, he'd bore a hole in the ear of the only man left. He'd tell any story that happened to cross his mind. Or he'd talk about whatever he'd held bottled up inside until that moment. He'd gossip about the people who'd just gotten up and left, he'd even answer questions that people who weren't even there anymore had asked earlier. All this was only more evidence about why no one wanted to be stuck alone with Abdullah. But Derda didn't have the benefit of choice. Every day in the van, for hours on end, he was alone with Abdullah. Starting from his very first "light this" he was doomed to listen to Abdullah's unending jabber all day long.

One of their first stops was a sales point set up on a pedestrian overpass near a university. This was when Derda understood why Remzi said the work was a bit tough, and he hated that sales point with every single step of the sixty-four steps he had to climb to get to the top of the overpass. He didn't know what he was getting himself into when he tripled up the boxes. When he dropped off the last box clutched between his fingers, his legs smarted with pain. A young man with a beard named Saruhan was standing in front of the sales point. He was a student at the university you could see from the overpass. According to what he said, he was studying math. It took Derda two weeks, and countless trips up and down sixty-four steps, to find out that much.

Their deliveries brought them to spots in all boroughs of the city, in all the shopping areas and neighborhood centers. The salesmen were usually about the same age as Saruhan. As soon as they saw Derda come up, they peeled themselves off the walls they were leaning against and opened the boxes Derda set down on the tarps they'd spread on the ground, working quickly to take the books out. They rarely looked at Derda's face. But when the work was finished they always gave him a "Thanks, man." The only one of them who said any more was Saruhan. Sometimes he'd ask, "What's up?" Sometimes he'd say something like, "It's freezing cold out here!" Depending on the weather, the boxes would either be left at the sales points or, if it was raining, they'd ride around in the van until nightfall.

At the end of the day, Derda, sometimes with Remzi, sometimes alone, returned to the neighborhood where his cemetery house stood. He had to wake up even earlier now to carry out his five-year-old duty of washing and tidying around the tomb. For the first two years he'd been genuinely afraid that the man in the long robe would come back. But in later years the man's face began to fade from his memory. Eventually all that was left was the tomb. The fear that had made him start washing the tomb had long since crumbled and disappeared. Now Derda didn't see it any differently than breathing. It had become a sort of habit. A type of dependence that didn't do anyone any harm. Maybe if his case had been brought to the attention of some committee of professors, he'd have been able to identify with their explanation of his behavior. A short series of words starting with "obsessive" and ending with "compulsive." But Derda wasn't brought into the presence of anyone, besides the tomb, that is. And to tell the truth, he never felt anything remotely like presence or peace of mind except for when he was cleaning that tomb. Maybe he really did see it as compensation. Compensation for stealing someone else's money while burying the pieces of his chopped-up mother.

"I really got off cheap," he'd say sometimes, looking at the tombstone. He'd been talking to the tombstone since he was thirteen. He didn't even know who he was talking to. God, his dad, his mother, or maybe to himself. Maybe he talked to it because it was just a stone. A marble stone. And maybe Derda talked to a marble stone because he was so totally alone. For three years, every morning.

He planted flowers for every season. But he stayed clear of planting anything in the grave bed. He planted a row of daisies in front of the tomb. Who knows what the family of the deceased lying under the tombstone thought when they came and saw the

217

flowers. But Derda never even saw them once, because he'd finish cleaning in the early hours of the morning. Then he'd stay as far away from the tomb as possible, in the farthest corners of the ever-expanding cemetery. Always in the pursuit of bread. In the mornings, he'd always return and ask, "How are you?" But he had to supply the conversational material himself: "I'm fine." Then he'd continue for himself, "I'm not bad myself. I got a bit of work yesterday. And so, you see, last night I didn't go to bed hungry. Do you like the daisies?"

Derda had to answer for the marble stone every time. And every time he left he said, "See you tomorrow." No one was aware that he'd formed a sort of friendship with a stone. But anyway, who was there to know about it? He was too scared to go see his dad. He thought that maybe he'd lead them to him, the men with the long robes, and they'd hurt him. But over time it became easier to be patient. He'd be patient and wait for the day when his dad got out of prison and came home. Five years had passed, five years for Derda to become a machine made for waiting. First he waited for the man in the long robe, then he waited with a yearning for his father. Waiting, he acquired the aspect of a patient stone himself. A white stone, a patient stone, a white and patient piece of marble.

"Is he always like that?"

"What?" asked Saruhan.

Derda was looking at the spread of alarm clocks set out for sale nearby. To be more precise, although he was looking at it, he was actually listening to it. Some twenty randomly set alarm clocks didn't leave one molecule of air undisturbed by their electronic cacophony. The man at the stand sat above them reading a newspaper like he didn't have ears. It was as if the clocks didn't even exist in the same space-time continuum as he did.

Saruhan knew who Derda was looking at.

"Him? That guy's crazy. A few times we practically came to blows, he's a real wild card. The bastard must be mentally ill. He sets those clocks like some sort of maniac and then just sits there from morning till night."

"How can you stand it?"

Saruhan laughed. He showed him the headphones dangling from his overcoat's pocket.

"With these. I listen to music. The batteries just never fucking die. I'd pimp your mom on it. I tell you, even if I had some cash I wouldn't go up to the guy and see how much he's asking. He never sells anything anyway."

The man in front of the clock stand flipped the page of his newspaper and, feeling the others' eyes on him, nodded in Saruhan's direction. Saruhan laughed.

"Nothing, nothing!" he said. "We were just saying how nice they sound." Then he turned back to Derda.

"What's Abdullah doing?"

"He said he was going over to collections. He told me to wait here. Who knows when he'll come back."

"Now that guy's crazy in a totally different way. Let me tell you something, Derda. Thing is, everyone and everything is crazy. Take this job, for example. What kind of work is this, man? But what can you do? Here we are, just standing here, because we have to. We're telling ourselves at least we're going to make our three *kuruş*, right? Come rain and mud, hell or high water, we're right back standing here."

"Can I ask you something?" said Derda. "Why's it illegal to sell these books?"

"Long story," said Saruhan. "Fuck it. You want one? I'll give you one to read."

"No, that's Ok. Thanks anyway, though." He was too embarrassed to say he couldn't read.

"Take one, man. It's on me!"

Saruhan was leaning over the tarp spread with books. He picked up a thick book.

"Take this. It never sells anyway. No reason for you to haul it around back and forth, breaking your back. Wish I could choose the books we sold. If I could decide which books they printed, I would have made a fortune a long time ago. Anyway, they go and print the most ridiculous stuff. Ok, some of them sell well. But this? It'd be a fucking miracle if you sold one a month. And it's as heavy as a block of gold, I mean, shove it. Look at it!"

Derda reluctantly took the book Saruhan was holding out to him. But he didn't even dare look down at it. Because if Saruhan said something about what was written on it, it would quickly become apparent he couldn't read. He changed the subject and asked how much it sold for. But Saruhan was rummaging around in his pockets, not paying any attention.

"Wait, I'm going to get a light from the crazy guy," he said, and walked over to the mad clock seller.

Derda was left alone. He looked at the cover of the book in his hand and froze. He was staring at the two words in the whole world he might possibly have been able to recognize. Because for the last five years he'd been on his knees in front of the marble stone where those two very same words were engraved. Because those were the very two words that were engraved on Derda's brain. He didn't know them as letters, but like indentations carved into his memory. And he knew every curve of the images by heart. They had no sound to him. He had no idea how to pronounce them. And up until now he'd never wondered how to either. It didn't even occur to him to wonder. A man only learns the names of those things people say. And no one said the name on a tombstone out loud. In any event, now those two words were there, staring back at him from the cover of the book. Staring right into Derda's eyes.

"What happened? You going to take it?"

He couldn't understand the question because he didn't even hear it being asked. He raised his head and looked right into Saruhan's eyes.

"Teach me how to read."

The next morning, he went to the tomb, book in hand.

"Look," he said. "I found you. What's your name, do you know?"

He smiled. He drew his finger across the first word, saying "Oğuz . . ." Then he touched the second word.

"Atay . . . Oğuz Atay."

After work, they'd meet at a coffeehouse near the overpass. After they'd delivered the last box to the depot, Abdullah would drop him off at the nearest bus stop on his way back home. And knowing that all the busses passing there went to the overpass, he jumped on the first one that came by. Of course, Saruhan wasn't giving him lessons for free. They agreed to what amounted to a fifth of Derda's salary. So Derda went to bed five nights a month hungry, but he didn't care. He wasn't exactly untalented at being hungry, nor was he too bad at Saruhan's reading lessons.

"First," Derda had said to Saruhan, "say the name of this book to me."

"*Tutunanmayanlar—The Disconnected.*"

Soon, Derda started to dream about *Tutunanmayanlar*. Who knows what was written on those pages, he said to himself. He held one section of the book tight with his thumb and watched the other hundreds of bent pages flip through like a film strip. Sometimes he'd hold it close to his face and feel the wind from the pages. Closing his eyes and feeling that wind on his face, his dreams were filled with visions of *Tutunamayanlar*.

When Saruhan said, "Boy, what are you going to do with that beast of a book? You can't even write your name yet," Derda smiled. "Forget it," he said.

They were set up at the coffeehouse's lowest table, and he was trying to memorize the letters that he had, until that day, perceived as nothing more than meaningless shapes. When he'd been negotiating terms with Saruhan, he'd even had to agree to a predetermined number of teas included in the price. They'd agreed that after five, Saruhan would have to pay for any additional teas out of his own pocket. But he never drank a sixth.

In the mornings, Derda would practice by reading the marble slabs in the cemetery. Once he'd learned their names, he found himself imagining the lives of the dead. Before, he'd considered tombs nothing more than stone and earth. He was also learning his numbers. He surprised himself by connecting the whole of a fifty-year life span by the single narrative thread between life and death. It was as if just at that moment, even if only for a moment, the dead were brought back to life.

In the evenings back at home, he'd read the picture books Saruhan gave him. He was practically burning with passion to start reading *Tutunamayanlar,* but he'd promised himself and Saruhan that he wouldn't. Until he could read without making a mistake, he wouldn't touch it. But Saruhan had one and only one reason to insist on the promise, though, and that was that he wanted to prevent Derda from realizing that, as a teacher, he was useless. If Derda realized Saruhan had no talent for teaching, then maybe he'd stop taking lessons.

But in the end, Saruhan's shoddy teaching only meant that Derda had to take lessons for longer and that Saruhan earned more money. What he should have been able to do within two months, Derda learned to do in five. Of course, he considered that he was the one with a problem, and he took to considering any seven-year-old who could read as some sort of genius.

He reported his daily progress to Oğuz Atay every morning at the head of his grave and he read him chapters from children's storybooks. Daisy season had long since passed, and violets now bloomed around the tomb.

In the evenings, he walked around reading all the street signs, feeling like he owned the world. Like he flew home on a carpet woven with letters. His mouth was thirsting for knowledge dried out by the wind.

Then, one evening, despite all desire to extend his profitable lessons, Saruhan said "Ok." Saruhan closed the children's book that Derda had read completely, without error, to the very last line, and he looked at his pupil.

"Well, there you go, you can read."

And it was true. Derda could read. But that was all he could do. Saruhan, who had, despite himself, accomplished something practically impossible, had only taught Derda how to read. Derda had memorized letters and syllables, but had never once taken a pen between his fingers. Because, according to Saruhan, his fee didn't cover that. And if he wanted to do another round of lessons to learn how to write, well, that would mean another agreement. Saruhan wanted to make more money. Saruhan's appetite for money had been whetted over time. He'd noticed his lack of success as a teacher and also how Derda forgot how letters were written. Now the time had come to profit from it.

"And writing? Do you want to learn how to write?"

Derda smiled.

"Why would I need to know how to write? What am I going to write? Like I need to learn how to write!"

"Ah, shove it," Saruhan said to himself. Then, "Hey, another tea over here!"

It was the first time he'd had the sixth tea. When it was all said and done, it was their last lesson.

Derda had slept like he was paralyzed. He lay on the concrete floor, his arms stretched open wide like a man crucified on an invisible cross. Every time he breathed in and breathed out, the copy of *Tutunamayanlar* on his chest rose and fell. He'd read a seven-hundred-page book. And now he was staring at the ceiling. It was the first novel he'd ever read in all his life. And all that he'd understood of it could fit inside one speck of dust. There was one speck of dust rattling around in his mind, but there were many more left behind in the *Tutunamayanlar* rising and falling on his chest. And all the weight of those specks of dust made it very hard to breathe. Even if he hadn't understood the sentences, Derda did understand the compounding feelings he got from the book. Derda couldn't understand Oğuz Atay's words per se, but he sensed something even beyond what was written. And maybe he continued into the beyond, passing out of the realm of mere understanding, passing out of the realm of not understanding. The names, events, the conflicts, the speakers in the novel, everything was spinning around his head, making even the walls of the house seem like they were changing colors.

Derda watched the ceiling like it was a rainbow, like he was a drunk lying out in the rain.

He saw a man pass before his closed eyes. Each time he closed his eyes. One solitary man. He came to Derda like he was one and the same with all the names in the book, like they were all him. Turgut, Selim, like everyone was contained in just one man. A man constructed from goodness. Or maybe from pieces of shattered glass. Maybe carved out of the air itself. Then he smashed into a stone of darkness. The man was broken into a thousand and one pieces. Or maybe he just dissipated. Whatever he experienced, the darkness became a stone and the man was crushed like he was built out of sand. He melted like ice; he was left behind in the book. That was everything that Derda had understood. And he was one to understand those people who are left behind. He would have called them tombstones. He believed in the book rising and falling on his chest and he closed his eyes, without even bothering to blink first.

THE TRANSPLANT

The door to the cemetery house was forced open with one swift shove of the shoulders and three men in white aprons filed in. With a gurney. They filed in and stood around Derda, who lay as if dead and stuffed. One of them leaned over him and pressed his jugular vein to make sure he was still alive. Then he reached over and picked up the book resting on Derda's chest.

Just then, Derda's eyes opened and he tried to shout, "What's going on? Who are you?" But he couldn't. He couldn't work his vocal cords any more than he could raise a finger. Only Derda's pupils listened to his unconscious commands. Derda couldn't do anything but look. That, and breathe in and out. He took three breaths in and three breaths out while he watched the book being put into a box. The titanium box and the man carrying it directed themselves to the front door and the others shifted Derda onto the gurney. It was all one coordinated assault.

The gurney slid into an ambulance waiting in front of the house and Derda's eyes watched an oxygen mask being lowered over his mouth. His eyelids started to feel heavy. Then the weight was too much to bear and his eyes closed.

When they started to feel lighter again, Derda blinked his eyes open and saw that he was being pulled out of the ambulance and put into the cargo of a plane. And then another oxygen mask lowered over his face.

The medivac was in flight for nine hours and fifteen minutes before it landed in Bangkok. After refueling, the wheels of the plane lifted off the tarmac, scraping the breast of the earth like razor blades, and in four hours they were in Manila. Throughout the trip, Derda's eyes and Derda's consciousness kept opening and closing.

Derda was pulled out and loaded into an ambulance just like the one in Istanbul. First the road was asphalt, then just dirt. The ambulance pressed on through the damp and the bugs. The journey was not an easy one. It ended like a dream, the gurney left on a moss-green hill behind trees that opened like two curtains at the end of the road. At the peak of the moss-green hill there was a cloud-white house with a black hole for a door. And in front of it, on the wide slope, thousands of people were lined up like an enormous snake. Each person carried something in their hand or at their side. Something . . .

Passing the line of people and their things, the ambulance cut its siren and slowly climbed the slope. And it came to a stop when it arrived in front of the white building. Derda was carried out of the ambulance like he was as light as a feather and then they shot him through the building's door like he was a projectile missile. After him, the line of people and things filed in, closing off passage from the corridor.

226

They stopped when they came to a closed door at the end of the corridor where the line began. Before them, at the front of the line, stood a small girl. She carried a tabby cat in her arms. Clearly, it was her turn to go through the door that would soon open to receive her. One of the people pulling Derda leaned down to the girl's ear and whispered "emergency."

The small girl, with a maturity unexpected for her years, stepped to the side, and Derda's gurney went in through the open door.

Inside the room were a surgery table and two elderly men. One was a Jivaro Indian, the other was Filipino. They were changing the white sheet on the surgery table. They spread it out and smoothed it flat with the palms of their hands and then looked up. This was the signal the men bringing Derda in had been waiting for. Without any hesitation, the elderly men dumped Derda, wearing nothing but pants, onto the surgery table like he was nothing but a lump of dough.

The Indian went up to the man carrying the titanium box and waited for him to open the lid. Seeing the book, he asked, "Isn't there a pocket edition?"

The man carrying the box shook his head. The Indian gave an exhausted sigh and took the book in his right hand and flipped through the pages. Then, holding his left hand over the book and rubbing his fingertips together, a gilding powder rained down over the book. As the book underneath took on the color of the gilding dust, it began to shrink and narrow until Tutunamayanlar was no bigger than a fist.

The Indian took the shrunken book and showed it to the Filipino man. He nodded his head and closed his eyes. Then he plunged his scalpel-like nails on his heart-like left hand into Derda's left rib cage. Derda screamed when they pierced his flesh. But he hadn't felt anything. And he only thought he'd screamed. As it was, he hadn't felt enough pain to warrant a scream, nor could he even open his mouth wide enough to scream. In his terror, he looked at the puckered face of the Filipino. The others watched the elderly man spread open the cleft, holding it open with his two hands. There wasn't a single drop of blood, and Derda's breath continued as normal. But there was plenty of reason for blood or shortness of breath, in fact, there was even good reason for him to die right then and there. In fact, one such reason was right in front of his nose. Derda's eyes met Derda's heart, just a hand's span away.

The Indian took the heart from the Filipino man's hand and placed the book in the man's empty palm in its place. The Filipino man raised his head and closed his eyes, looking only with the tips of his fingers. He spread the cleft in Derda's skin open like he was pulling a curtain open, and with his free hand he buried the book into Derda's flesh. All that had been connected to his heart before, all his veins and valves squeezed around the pages, covered over the book completely. When the man took his hands away from the cleft, Tutunamayanlar pumped blood and Derda was returned to life. The Indian watched his lungs fill with his first breath, and, pressing the pedal to open the garbage bin under the surgery table, he tossed Derda's heart into the trash. Because the piece of flesh was of no use.

THE BUILDING

The white building situated ninety kilometers to the north of Manila was neither a temple nor some palace of miracles. It was just a white building. A big building with one narrow room and a long corridor. It looked like a skyscraper without windows. A monument the width of an apartment building with only one room inside.

It was in 1985 when the building appeared out of nowhere, when the Philippines was turned upside down by an earthquake. People from all around the world crowded together to get a look at the building, trying to understand what they were looking at. But no one, not a scientist nor anyone else, could come up with a feasible explanation for its existence. It didn't even have a door. In time, the boredom of not knowing made interest wane and the hordes that had once surrounded the building ceased to come.

One summer morning three years later, the already aged Filipino man came to the front of the building and, perching himself against his outstretched palm and leaning against the building, he began to wait. To those who asked, he answered, "I'm waiting for someone. But who that is, I do not know." And claiming that he had performed bloodless surgery with his bare hands, he became known as nothing more than one of the country's thousands of forgers and crooks. He waited for two years, never once taking his hand away from the wall, and without aging a day.

Later, on another summer morning, an Indian at least as old as the Filipino man, with a skull shrunken to the size of a fist hanging off his belt, came to the building. He came from the Andes. As protection against the revenge of the souls of those he'd killed, he shrunk their heads and carried them on his person. He was an Indian who lived deep in the green Amazon, an Indian of the Jivaro tribe.

It must have been that he already knew what he was going to do, because there wasn't any hesitation when he came within four meters of the Filipino man's hand, his palm against the building. At just the spot where he pressed with his two hands, the wall broke in and disappeared inside the building, the piece sliding to the right. And such it was that the building's door was opened, just like the mouth of an enormous cave, never to be closed again. The two old men stepped into the corridor that appeared before them, and when they arrived in the room at the end, the building whispered their purpose into their ears.

"Wait!" it said. "Wait here. They will come to you."

"Who?" asked the Filipino man.

"He who has found his life's meaning. Those who have found the thing to which they will dedicate their lives. They will come.

You will take out their heart and put that thing in its place. And then you'll throw the heart away."

"But," protested the Indian, "how can someone live without a heart?"

"You'll see!" said the building.

"And what if no one comes?" asked the Filipino man. "Who would be so dedicated to something they'd be willing to forgo their own hearts?"

"That, too, you will see!" said the building.

"But what about those who never find their life's meaning?" asked the Indian. "What will happen to them?"

"As for them, they will rot whilst they still live, and so will that piece of flesh in their chests. And they will continue, but they will not be truly alive."

The Filipino man had the last question: "But why now? Who knows how many people have dedicated their lives to something before now. Why has this happened now of all times?"

The building spoke for the last time: "Because a boy named DERDA has been born!"

"Who?" the Indian was going to ask, but it was as if an invisible lasso had caught him, and he was dragged outside the building.

THE FIRST

The elderly Indian ran down the slope and followed the dirt path disappearing into the forest. Slipping through the walls of trees, he arrived at a village to find people crowded around a motionless child lying on the ground, struggling to draw breath. Two ends of a piece of paper stuck out from the top and bottom of his clenched fist. The Indian, requesting the assistance of the onlookers, carried the child to the narrow room in the white building. The Filipino man pried the child's fist open and took the paper. Then, tearing his heart out, he put the paper in the empty cavity in his chest. The first thing in the white building to be inserted in the place of the first ripped-out heart was one American dollar bill. It was the crumpled tip the child had gotten from a tourist a few hours before. The moment the Filipino child had seen the banknote in the palm of his hand was the moment he found the meaning of his life: MONEY.

The villagers who had come to watch saw that the child was healed, and two elderly among them dropped to their knees, prostrating themselves before the miracle child. And then the Indian told them that whoever had dedicated their earthly lives to something would become known to themselves, one by one. In time, they'd teach others the way, and thus the so-called FINDERS would form an army of thousands.

All over the world, the millions of people who had found the meaning of their lives were transported to the white building where their hearts were ripped out and thrown into the trash.

Some time later, the World Health Organization made an offer to store the hearts to use for critical transplants. But the building answered in no uncertain terms: throw away the hearts!

THE LAST

Derda's eyes and mind opened again when he came back to his cemetery house. The three men with the white aprons left him just where they'd found him, then left the house, closing the door behind them. His hand searched for the book on his chest but there was nothing there. He scrambled to his feet and went over the house with his eyes and his fingers. But somehow he couldn't find Tutunamayanlar anywhere. Then all at once he stopped, and he started laughing, a strange hiccupping laughter. Why do I need it? he thought. If I lost it, what's the worst that could happen? Anyway, I already read it.

From that day on Derda never searched for Tutunamayanlar again. And he never ever thought of the white building, which he *remembered in fragments as if from a dream. In any event, on the very day Derda had been born, that building sprung up in the very spot where Derda had found it. And in any event, after Derda had gone in and come back out again, that building was swallowed anew by the moss-green hill. It sank back into the place where it had risen from years before with a slow deliberation, slow enough to give the two elderly men and the hundreds waiting in the corridor chance enough to escape. People waiting in the corridor had time to pour out of the black hole of a door and save themselves and the meaning of their lives. But the two elderly men were content to stay in the room, looking at each other with a smile. As it was, their work had reached its end, and the time had finally come for them to rest in death. The respite of death. They both understood. That knew that the last heart they'd torn out was Derda's: Derda, whose name they had heard years before. There was only one thing they didn't understand. And the Indian asked: "What was that book?"*

The Philippine smiled. Then he spoke.

"I don't know, but it must be such a book . . ." He swallowed and continued. "Such a book that, on account of it, millions of people found their life's meaning in it."

"Did he ever write anything else?"

"Yeah, probably. We don't have anything else, but they'd be at a bookstore," said Saruhan.

Then he told him how to get to a bookstore near the overpass. Derda set off running. He had to be back before Abdullah came. It was the very first time he'd gone in a bookstore. A woman popped out in front of him.

"Yes?"

"I'm looking for Oğuz Atay's—"

Before he could finish his sentence, the woman turned around, and with Derda following in her wake, she walked deep into the store. They stopped in front of a shelf and she pulled out *Tutunamayanlar*.

"I have that one," said Derda. How could the woman have known that he meant he had it inside him?

"Alright, then," said the woman, handing him *Waiting for Fear* and his published journals.

"That's all we have."

Taking his crinkled, crumpled money out of his pocket and practically tossing it at the cashier, he paid for his books and left. Running, he just made it in time to catch Abdullah's van pulling up to the sidewalk. Abdullah gave Derda such a look at every red light all the way to the depot that Derda learned how much Abdullah hated having a reader at his side. You can't talk to someone who's reading.

That night, Derda finished *Waiting for Fear* by the light of the only light bulb in the house. That night, Derda finally heard the voice of the stone he'd spoken to for three years. The last sentence in the last story in the book, "Railway Servicemen—A Dream," was this: *"I am here, dear reader, where are you?"*

"I'm here!" cried Derda.

Then he left his house and slipped through the hole in the wall and ran through the darkness straight to Oğuz Atay's grave. He dropped next to the tombstone, whispering, "I'm here."

"Look, here I am. I'm here. Next to you. I was always here by your side. Always. Look, now I'm here . . ."

Derda was crying. He didn't know why he was crying, but he was crying. Maybe because he'd been alone for so many years. Maybe because the man himself had looked at people, saying, I am here, where are you? Maybe because he could only cry when he was alone. Maybe because he could only cry when he was at Oğuz Atay's side. Derda was crying. And at the same time, he caressed the violets growing around Oğuz Atay's tomb. He cried even more, because he didn't know why he was crying.

Between his sobs he whispered, "I'm here, I'm here, I'm here . . ."

He couldn't have been able to explain what the stories in *Waiting for Fear* were about, even if he'd wanted to. He couldn't have listed the names or the themes. He didn't have enough words at his command, or sufficient capacity of thought in his intellect that those words could carry. But, just as he said, he'd be there until death. Or maybe even beyond death. There. Forever. In the sky or on some other invisible stratum, side by side, in secret, set in stone in a peacefulness beyond goodness and beyond names. In a place reached by feeling, on the other side of not-knowing. A place where musical instruments whose names he couldn't know played classical music he was hearing for the first time, and the light fragmented the sprinkling drops raining from his eyes into a prism of seven colors. In a place that neither ignorance nor knowledge would be able to explain. Wherever Oğuz Atay is, it's there. When he couldn't hold on any longer and fell, it's there he fell. Maybe he didn't fall, maybe just that moment was exempted from gravitational pull. Not a place you grab hold of to get to, but a place you fly to.

That night, Derda slept between two graves, caressing the violets.

Derda was reading Oğuz Atay's *Journal.*
"*These days I feel a hopelessness . . .*"
Derda felt miserable.
"*It doesn't matter what happens, all I want is to be shown a little respect . . .*"

And he felt frustrated. "Of course!" said Derda. "Of course he has to be shown respect."

"*Progressive, regressive, every sort of movement holds a monopoly over a small half-enlightened gang, so that over the years they don't feel the need to renew their reality for today, to not lose their place, now they play games like a greedy merchant trying to stay in business . . .*"

Derda didn't understand who he was talking about, but he got even angrier.

"*They are like rotting gums, like a tooth that's fallen out . . .*"

"Yes!" said Derda to himself.

"*The world is contrived . . .*"

And again Derda yelled, "Yes!"

"*If only there were a tomb or two on this street, if only every day on our way to work we could greet death . . .*"

He laughed. He felt he had an understanding with Oğuz Atay; he believed there was an invisible bond between them.

"*Why don't they understand my writing, why isn't there anyone around me . . .*"

He was angry again. "I don't understand either. But look, I'm here at your side," he said.

"*Every country has its fools—I mean, among the people in every country who understand literature. They scramble after foreign books. They don't even know I exist. And I, apparently, am waiting for a crowd of fully formed readers to emerge out of these men. How idiotic . . .*"

And Derda's spirits were dashed once again.

"*I suppose that here, I feel like I've been left on the outside . . .*"

And Derda, from deep inside himself, said, "Me, too."

"*I'm afraid that in the end, I'll give in, too; that would be even more tragic . . .*"

Derda was crying. He had to wipe his tears off the pages at the end of Oğuz Atay's *Journal* that had photographs of the author at each stage of life, drying them again after each drop. He felt like Oğuz Atay was so close to him, and he couldn't have felt the unhappiness any more deeply.

He believed that Oğuz Atay was as lonely and unhappy as he was himself. It must have taken him half an hour to subtract 1934 from 1977. When he got the result—forty-three—he thought "so young." He glared at all the tombstones of the dead in the cemetery who had lived beyond forty-three with a strange animosity. Maybe, he said to himself. Maybe, some of these people were the fools Oğuz Atay talked about. He calculated the age of one resting in peace and yelled, "The jerk lived for seventy years!" Then he did some more calculating. "That's twenty-seven years longer." He raised his head and looked toward the sky. There, whomever he might see, he understood. Another of Derda's dreams had been dashed. For the nth time.

Inside his dark house, he stacked three books one on top of another and made himself a headrest. Lying down on his back and staring at the gray ceiling, he told himself, "More. I have to learn more. Everything. I have to learn everything about him."

Why did he die at forty-three? In his *Journal* he talked about an illness. About the hospitals he went to. About surgery he'd had. He couldn't have died like Derda's mother did. There was no way. Oğuz Atay had to have closed his eyes for the last time in a different way. Maybe he died by looking at people too much. Looking through to the other side of other people's eyes. But how could he be sure? Who could he ask? Saruhan, of course.

"Say you want to learn about a writer's life, what do you do?"

"Well, there are biographies," said Saruhan.

"Where?"

"Where do you think? At a bookstore."

"This biography thing is a book?"

"Derda, for the love of God, get out of my face. I'm already going crazy because of those insane clocks."

Derda went back to the same bookstore, just five steps from the foot of the overpass. The same woman popped out in front of him. This time she was smiling. After all, now Derda was a good customer.

"How may I help you?"

"Just . . . one second . . ." he said as he pulled a piece of paper out of his pocket. Not paper exactly, but a palm-sized corner of a box top. Saruhan had written on it. He showed it to the woman.

"Biography. All right, but whose?"

Derda said it as if it were his own name: "Oğuz Atay."

"Let me see," said the woman. She slid in front of the computer at the cash register. She typed something then looked up at Derda.

"Yes, we have one left."

She walked past Derda, scanning the shelves. Running the fingers of her right hand down the spines of the books, she found one and pulled it out. Then she handed it to Derda who had followed her to the shelf. Derda realized thick books were expensive. And he knew that the money in his pocket wasn't enough. He asked like he was a small child.

"What if I read it then bring it back?"

The woman laughed. "Do you really think that sort of thing is allowed?" she said.

Then she yelled, "Hey, where are you going? Stop!"

Derda was four long steps away from the bookstore and cutting through the crowd. He started to run. He knew that the woman herself wouldn't be able to catch him but still he didn't dare slow down. Saruhan was the only one who saw Derda escape up the stairs like a huge cat. At the time, he was propped against the edge of the guardrail, smoking. He watched him get lost in the crowd, slipping through without knocking into people, running with a childlike agility. Then Saruhan saw the woman come out of the bookstore and look around anxiously.

"That boy is crazy," he whispered to himself. He turned around and looked at the clock seller. He was pulling them out of a box, setting them one by one, then putting them on display on his tarp on the ground.

"Oh, God," said Saruhan, shaking his head. It didn't escape the man's attention.

"What do you want? You got a problem?"

"No, nothing, no. I just said I hope you have good sales today."

Saruhan put the headphones dangling out of his coat pocket in his ears and cut off the sounds of life with a bit of Slayer. With a knife from the "Raining Blood" line.

Derda was just about to walk through the cemetery gates when he heard a voice.

"Where you going?"

A young security guard in a navy blue suit was standing in the door of Yasin's guardhouse.

"What do you mean where you going?"

"Where are you going?"

"Home."

"There'll be no more going through the cemetery to get home anymore. It's forbidden."

Derda stared at the young security guard for a few seconds. In silence. Then he spoke.

"Where's Brother Yasin?"

"I don't know any Brother Yasin or anyone else."

Derda hadn't gone through the cemetery gates for a few weeks so he hadn't found out yet. Yasin and the job he'd held for twenty-four years had been terminated, and so he took his *bağlama* and left. It was the first thing that Yasin had done that he regretted. He thought that anything would be better than waiting around with the dead and gone. So he'd returned to his village and embraced his aging mother.

"Son, what have you done all these years?" the woman asked.

"Nothing," he said. "I just stood and waited."

"Well, what are you going to do now?"

"I got tired of standing around. I'll do something, that's all."

"Fine, but what?"

"Mama, I just got here, don't make a man regret coming home."

But Yasin continued doing nothing but just standing around. Up until the day he died. He stayed there for a while, underground. It was like he'd never come, like he'd been different from all the other people on the face of the earth. Because all the others had done something, were doing something, and would do something. Even after they'd died. Some of them would go to heaven, some would become a part of nature, some would be reincarnated. No one could risk going and disappearing completely like Yasin. No one would have the courage to be lost without leaving a trace. Someone has to witness another's passing over this earth. To grace the presence of their existence. Everyone but Yasin has a pyramid buried inside them. In some way, everyone has a plan for immortality. But Yasin had seen too much death, like he'd lived all his life on a battlefield. Like he'd seen death up to the very last person left living on the face of the planet. Maybe that's why he wasn't afraid of going. Because he was scared enough of existing at all.

Derda ran around the perimeter of the newly erected cemetery walls, past the front door to his house, and continued in a walk. He walked around the corner, fighting his way through the tree branches. Just as he'd suspected, the hole in the wall had been filled in. Now it was closed up, but that very morning he'd passed through that same hole twice. Once out, and once back in. But now, the wall in front of his home was fully intact. They had poured concrete between him and Oğuz Atay. He turned around and walked toward the trees. He held his book tightly against him, protecting it from the branches, and he wondered what he'd do in the morning. Apparently, the new height of the walls wasn't enough to secure the cemetery. They'd also laced the top of the walls with barbed wire. Now there was no way he could jump over.

"I'll just break open a new hole," he said, pulling his key out of his pocket. "If I have to, I'll put a hole in the side of the house."

He opened the door to find a man wearing nothing but long underwear on top of the floor mattress. A thin man with white hair, a wrinkled nape, and naked except for white long under-wear. A man with his toes and palms pressing against the floor, rising and falling, like he was doing push-ups. On both sides of the man Derda saw thin, scrawny legs. And tiny little feet. The heels were raised off the ground. Both people were yelling. One from pain, the other from pleasure. Neither of them could have heard the door open. But when Derda screamed a glass-shattering scream, they flew apart like two pieces of wood flung by the wind. One covered himself with his hand, the other covered herself with the sheet.

"What the hell are you doing here, you fuck?" said Derda.

"Derda, I'm your father!" the man said.

"Man, why are you yelling?" said the small girl.

"Süreyya?" said Derda.

He watched in silence as his father counted money into Süreyya's outstretched palm. He was sitting on the only chair in the house, his elbows leaning on the only table. He looked at the Oğuz Atay books stacked near where his elbows were leaning. He was embarrassed. Of Oğuz Atay. Of them and for them. He couldn't bear to watch any longer. Once Süreyya saw the agreed upon amount in her palm she closed her hand tight. He watched her mouth, opening like a spoiled child.

"Good work barging in like that, like some ox."

Derda didn't answer, and the girl left. The white-haired man, zipping up the pants he'd slipped over his long underwear, but without bothering to button them, walked straight to his son with his arms wide open. He was grinning from ear to ear.

"My son! My lion!"

Derda shoved the approaching man back with his two strong hands. His father took a step back. His face twisted bitterly and he shouted.

"You ass, you animal, so many years and this is the way you greet your father? What, so we tossed a woman around in the house. I mean, it's only too clear you're familiar with the girl yourself."

At once he felt abashed and he laughed.

"You ass, what, is that it? She your bitch? Hmm? Come on, tell the truth, out with it. Is that why you got so angry? Ok, man, we won't touch her again. Get up, come on. Come here, let me hug you."

He took Derda by the elbows and pulled him toward him. He cried "son!" and threw his arms around Derda. But the son's hands hung down at his sides like he was a corpse. Then the man righted himself and held his son by the shoulders.

"Stop, let me take a look at you. You've grown into a big man now, eh? Man, you're strong as a donkey now. Good for you, man, you look great."

At the same time, he threw soft punches into his son's cheek. Trembling lightly at every blow, Derda finally spoke.

"Mom died."

The man's fist hovered in midair.

"She died? I thought she went back to the village. That's what the girl told me."

242

"That's what I told everyone," said Derda. "I said she went back to the village. But she died. Five years ago. Then I cut her up."

The man let his hands drop off his son's shoulder as he took a step back.

"Cut what?"

"My mother. Then I buried her."

"What are you saying, boy?"

"I chopped her up so they wouldn't send me to the orphanage, and then I buried her. So no one would even know she was dead."

"Man, what are you saying?"

"You're not at all what I thought you'd be, you know that?"

"Son, tell me straight. Where's your mama?"

"That girl's only thirteen."

"Look, Derda, I'll give you what's coming to you . . . Speak like a man, where's your mom? Man, what did you do to that woman?"

"Well, did she at least give you a good fuck?"

And when his father replied with a "motherfucker!" Derda buried his fist into his father's still open mouth. Derda felt his fingers bust his father's teeth. He pulled his fist away and leveled another blow with the same speed. This time, his fist landed square on his father's nose. He must have broken it in several different places. The old man's face was streaming with warm blood. The man tried to step back but he tripped over the floor mattress and fell down. Derda dropped to one knee and with one hand he pulled his father up by his hair, and with the other he landed one last punch clear in his face. And then everything went silent. The man hadn't once put his hand up in defense, nor had he cursed his son when his teeth were smashed out of his blackening bloody mouth. There was complete silence.

Derda loosened his fingers' grip on his father's hair and asked, "What, did you die? Eh? You dead?"

He stopped and listened. He couldn't tell if his father was breathing through his barely opened lips or not, nor whether he understood what he said to him. He started to curse the man. He grabbed his father under the armpits and dragged him onto the mattress and stuck a pillow under his head. Not so long ago the white-haired man had been rising and falling on that bed, feeling a thousand pleasures. Now he lay there like a corpse. A corpse who could breathe, short and jagged breaths though they were. Father and son were face to face, eye to eye. They had to have felt something, but neither could really see into the other's eyes.

The white-haired man's name was Celal. He had a nickname leftover from his days as a mugger: The Tick. But nothing was enough to save him from the assault of his son's marble-hard fist. Not his name, not his nickname, not his years in prison. Eleven years on the inside. Eleven years his hand hadn't felt the flesh of a woman. And so, as he took the key out of his pocket where it had waited for eleven years and entered his house, out of the corner of his eye he had caught a glimpse of Süreyya. Süreyya, sitting out in front of her door, two houses down. "Get over here," he had said. And Süreyya had come. The girl named her price before he even asked. Just like her mother had taught her, and just like she'd been doing for the last year. When they put an end to their work at the cemetery, Süreyya had simply switched sectors. And anyway, there was more to be earned in her new job. Her father didn't care. Because he wasn't awake enough at any hour of any day to even be able to care. Anyway, if he had been awake, would it have made a difference? In the end, this much money for just lowering your şalvar and pulling them back up again, who'd go and sell packs of tissues on the street? And, just to sweeten the whole thing, weren't all the men in the neighborhood in love with Süreyya? Weren't they all lining up at her door with boxes of chocolates in hand?

Süreyya had also asked Celal, "Do you love me?"

"Of course," Celal had answered. "How could anyone not love a girl like you?"

Süreyya loved men, too. It was only Derda she hated. Because Derda looked away when he walked by. He was the only one that didn't see Süreyya. The most he ever said to her was a cold hello as he walked past. "Is he a fag?" she said behind his back to whoever was around. To two colleagues her same age. They laughed as she glared at Derda's back, her eyes burning with hate. Because she was in love with Derda and he was the only man on the street left who hadn't seen her naked. In fact, that was why she'd been so pleased when he caught her with his father. She relished it even more later, when she heard curses coming out of their house. *He's jealous,* she thought. She walked over to their house and knocked at the door. Derda opened the door.

"What?"

Süreyya at eight years old and Süreyya on her back under his father, it all flashed before his eyes in a series of images.

"I heard some noise. Thought I'd find out what's going on."

"How long have you been doing this?"

"Doing what?" Süreyya laughed. She wanted to hear Derda say it, say what her job was. She wanted it to sting him. Maybe she wanted it to hurt her, too. Maybe she wanted it to hurt the whole world. But Derda didn't say it. He asked again without saying a word, just by his look. The question's beams pierced into the girl's eyes.

"What's it to you anyway?" said Süreyya, finally. "Why do you care? What are you, my boyfriend or something?"

"Does your mother know?"

Süreyya laughed.

"You're so stupid, you know that?"

Derda didn't know what to say. None of the words he knew would suffice. He felt so small in front of this thirteen-year-old girl; he couldn't do anything but be silent. Nothing but silently watch her laugh. He thought that every single person, everyone, even babies born that very instant, were bad. Everyone, he said to himself. Everyone! They were all so miserably bad. So bad and so revolting. Kids, old people, cripples, sick people, everyone.

"Where's your dad?" the girl asked. She stretched her neck to try to see around Derda.

"I'm going to destroy all of you."

"Eh?"

The door hit her so sharply that she staggered a few steps back.

She shouted, "What did you say, you fucking maniac?"

Derda turned away from the door and walked over to his father, lying on the floor. Right over to his bloodied head. He raised his right foot and held it in the air just a hand's distance away from Celal's face. If Celal had come to at that moment and blinked open his eyes, he would have seen that the world had been blotted out by the bottom of his son's shoe. But he didn't. He just groaned softly. For a minute that felt like a year, Derda wavered between wanting to smash his father's face in and not. In the end, he settled on mercy and took his foot away. He sat on the chair by the table and took the stolen book in his hand. On the cover was one of Oğuz Atay's caricatures.

Bringing it up to his lips he whispered, "Forgive them."

Then he opened the book and started to read. "Stop moving your lips," Saruhan would have said if he'd been there. "When you read to yourself, don't mouth the words." But Derda wasn't reading the book to himself. He moved his lips so that the whole world would hear and he whispered the words he read. As he read he looked up at the cemetery wall.

"Sons of bitches," he said. "I'm going to destroy all of you."

He read three pages, then abandoned the house without even bothering to close the door behind him. He took his books with him. Süreyya and her mother watched Derda leave, and they picked up stones from the ground and waited for him to move on like he was a rabid dog. Then they ran inside his house, and releasing a death's wail they dropped to the ground by the man's head. But they saw the man was still alive and they stifled their wails.

"Go, get some cotton," said the woman. Süreyya went. Whatever else, Celal wasn't a mugger anymore, he was a promising new customer. And he hadn't even been back from prison for a day. Who knew how thirsty he was for a woman?

Süreyya's mother turned Celal's pockets inside out, but they were empty so she shouted toward the open door, "Someone come help us!"

She thought someone else might as well bring the hydrogen peroxide. She had a point. Cotton bandaging was expensive.

"Where have you been, boy? Last night we had the kids hauling all the stuff."

He couldn't well say that the first time he saw his father, after eleven years and thousands of dreams, he'd beat his face in until it was good and bloody and then left home for good.

"I'm sorry, Brother Süleyman," was all he could manage.

"Well, what's going on, what are you doing here at this hour?"

At least he might be able to say that he didn't have a place to stay.

"I left home. Maybe I could . . ."

Süleyman cut him off. Opening the door and clearing the way, he said, "Get inside." Derda went inside the depot. A question followed in his wake.

"You hungry?"

Derda remained silent. In the language of poverty, "Yes."

"There are some buns left over from breakfast over there. Sit, eat them if you want."

Süleyman had created a world out of empty boxes for himself in the depot. He'd laid out a spread with vodka and food and would be in his little world until morning. He slipped to the head of the table where he'd been when Derda had knocked, and he took the glass in his hand. He bit the top off a pastry almost entirely buried in the grip of his two hands, and he looked at Derda. He sighed, then took a gulp of vodka and spoke.

"So what are you going to do?"

Derda was trying to get the stale pastry, as hard as smashed rock, down his throat. He swallowed and asked, "Could I stay here for a little while?"

"How little?"

"A few days. Then I'll find something."

Süleyman didn't believe it. But he didn't think it was important, either. Whatever else, a person to talk to had emerged out of the nothingness of night. He looked at the books Derda had pulled out from under his arm and set on top of the box.

"Son, a man who leaves home usually has a bag in his hand. You left with just these books?"

"Yes," said Derda.

"And what books are these?"

He couldn't see from where he sat. If he could have seen them, he'd have recognized them. Among them was a book he'd been printing for years. Derda said its name.

"There's *Waiting for Fear*, Oğuz Atay's . . ."

"Hmmm. Oğuz Atay . . . They laid that man to waste," said Süleyman.

Derda asked like he was going to learn a secret about his own past.

"Why?"

"In those days I was deep inside the movement, you understand? Anyway, one day one of our guys brought us *Tutunamayanlar*. We take a look at it, at its psychology and all. Fuck that, we said. We, we said, are here shoulder to shoulder at war for the homeland, and this guy goes and explains it all, going only by whatever's going through his head, we said. We couldn't have known of course . . . And what a mind, you know? Anyway, here you go, drink some of this. It'll warm you up."

For a moment Derda remembered the fools Oğuz Atay had talked about.

He asked, "That movement you mentioned, what movement was it, brother?"

"Issues between the right and the left, son. You don't know anything about the world. Shit. The people were eating each other up, arguing over which sidewalk is yours, which is mine, men knifing each other, then he goes and explains it all jagged like that, anyway, that's what we said, you get it. Against us, I mean. Not just against us, against everyone. Against time, even time. Come on, son, don't just stand there. Go get yourself a glass from over there."

Derda took one of the tea glasses lined up by the sink and went back to Süleyman's dinner spread. He watched the man hold the bottle upside down as high as his mouth and he watched the vodka pour out.

"Come on, let's see now," said Süleyman. He raised his glass and clinked it against Derda's tea glass. Derda's face and throat winced at his first swallow. But his mind winced, too.

"Then what happened?"

"What could happen? The guy wrote more of this type of thing but no one cared. Then he was dead and gone. When was that now?" he said, looking at the ceiling, and when Derda answered he stayed like that, staring up at nothing.

"'77. 1977."

"You see?" said Süleyman. "Look how the time's passed. How old was I then? Twenty-three, twenty-four? Something like that, anyway. Anyway, then we were on the inside. In prison. And there I discovered him again. Then I read him, as a man. I read and I understood. Like I said, this guy understood, he knew. Look, I still don't really know, but I do know that this guy had something like a vocation, he had something to say, that much I know, you understand? Just once, there was this man like a genius. He was going to write something else . . . that's what they said, anyway. What was that, anyway?"

Derda knew. What Oğuz Atay would have written if he hadn't died. Anyone who'd read his *Journal* would know.

"*The Soul of Turkey*."

"Hah," said Süleyman. "That's it. *The Soul of Turkey*. The name itself is nice. But look at what happened then. Does Turkey still have its soul? Turkey's soul has been sold. Years ago they sold it. They sold it like a pimp. You'll see, the soul of this country went to the coffers of sons of bitches. Son, bottoms up!"

Derda winced all over all over again. The vodka sparked the fire, and his fatigue extinguished it.

"Brother, is it okay if I go to sleep?"

Süleyman nudged his chin in the direction of Derda's resting spot.

"Pull out those there. Lie there."

The things to pull out were collapsed empty boxes, the spot where he could lay out to sleep was on top of them. Derda did what he was told and lay down. As soon as he closed his eyes, he saw Oğuz Atay's photographs. *They laid that man to waste*: the words echoed between his two ears.

He opened his eyes and asked, "Brother Süleyman, if you saw them, would you recognize them?"

"Hmm?"

"Well, the men who laid him to waste, like you said. Whoever they were, if you saw them, would you recognize them?"

"Lie down, man, go to sleep," said Süleyman, and he laughed. "Why man, what are you going to do?"

"I'm going to cut them down, all of them," said Derda. It was like he was talking about cutting a loaf of bread. Maybe that's why Süleyman didn't know what to say.

"The kid's going to sleep here?" asked Israfil. Then he turned to Derda.

"You're going to sleep here?"

"If it's okay, just a few days," said Derda.

"Fine," said Israfil. "Stay. That way you two can keep an eye on each other." Then he added, gesturing to Süleyman, "Don't let this one have too much to drink." He looked at Süleyman.

"Süleyman, for God's sake. Look, you're the one heading up these operations. Don't do anything to yourself you won't be able to reverse. One day you're going to doze off drunk, and you're going to burn the place down with those cigarettes, sucking on them like they're some sort of teat."

"Okay, okay. Just mind your own business," said Süleyman. He wandered off toward the machines. Israfil threw a hand onto Derda's shoulder and smiled.

"You know how to use a gun?"

"No, brother," said Derda.

"Well, seeing as you're going to stay here, you're going to watch the place at night. Süleyman doesn't know his ass from his face. So we're going to trust in you to take care of any nonsense, should it arise. Anyway, hang on, we'll arrange everything. Abdullah isn't here yet?"

"He hasn't come yet, brother," was what he was going to say, but then he heard two raps on the depot door so he ran over and asked, "Who is it?"

"Remzi, Remzi."

Derda threw the bolt and pulled open the iron door. Remzi was laughing.

"Derda, man, you really turned Uncle Celal's head a ripe shade of red! Boy, how many years you haven't seen the man and you throw yourself on him as soon as you see him?"

"Your dad's out?" asked Israfil.

Derda was forced to admit it. He hadn't wanted to mention anything about his father being out. Or his beating him up.

"I was going to wish him all the best, but it won't help much now, I think."

"We had a little fight," said Derda, practically in a whisper. He was embarrassed. But Israfil didn't react at all like he'd expected.

"Good on you!" he said. "Before you become a real man, you have to fight with your father." His thoughts on the matter were clear and he added, "Derda, man, you're one crazy kid." Then he turned to Remzi, "Come on, don't hang around like that. Go help Süleyman."

Derda was going to follow Remzi, but Israfil caught him by the arm.

"You have any money?"

He didn't, but he said "yes." Israfil pulled a pistol out of his pocket and handed it to Derda.

"Anyway, take this, keep it at your side."

"Thank you, brother," said Derda. And he held the door open for Israfil. Abdullah was parking the van near the top of the stairs. When he came to the top of the stairs, Israfil laughed and called out to Abdullah.

"Apo, watch out for this kid! Check it out, the bastard practically destroyed his own dad!"

Abdullah responded with a feigned smile, pushing it as wide as it would go. Then, as Israfil walked away, he dove right in with his usual "Derda, hurry up, we're already late."

That night, as the illegal printing world came down and a cardboard box castle was erected in its place, the first thing that was put in place was the after-work vodka spread. But this time there was only one glass next to the bottle.

"You're not going to drink anything?" asked Süleyman.

"No," said Derda. He showed him the book in his hand. "I'm going to read for a while."

"You know best."

Since the night before the ghosts of the past were still very much inside him. Maybe if he talked about them more, then he'd be able to fall asleep like everyone else. But Derda didn't know about Süleyman's ghosts. *How would he know,* he thought, *how could he know about the revolutionaries of those times? How could the kid know?* He tipped the glass into his mouth with a greedy violence. He wanted to get drunk, drunker than he usually did. But Derda interrupted his drunken reveries, coming in to ask some names from the book in his hand. He asked about Oğuz Atay and *The Men Who Saved the World* who didn't even have the power of speech. He asked some questions about a small group of people who called themselves socialists but wanted to be perceived as social realists by others. And Süleyman spoke of it all so vividly that the enormous depot was transported back in time. He talked about anything he knew. He even tried to explain some of what he didn't know.

But after every name, the same question: "Is he still alive?"

"What do I know, he died, probably," Süleyman would say. "Look, a new book came out. There, I printed it yesterday," he would say sometimes. Derda was marking the book with a pen. He was creasing the pages of the book in front of him and flipping the pages violently. He was drawing in oxygen and exhaling poison into the growing pyre of the endless names. All at once Süleyman realized that Derda was making out a hit list.

"Hey, what are you doing, man?"

Derda looked up but he didn't say anything. No matter how drunk he was, Süleyman was going to remember.

"Boy, are you crazy? Of all the people in the world, what are these men to you? Don't let me hear you say that you're going to cut them down or anything else ever again!"

Derda looked at the floor and spoke.

"Didn't you say they laid him out to waste?"

"Yes, but—" said Süleyman. He was going to continue, but Derda was getting to his feet and Süleyman saw he was going to speak.

"What's written here, do you know? Look, you know what's written all over this book? They killed the man. They say Oğuz Atay had this brain tumor, right? Then he went and died at such a young age. That's just it, this tumor is bullshit, it's those bastards you were talking about, they were the tumor. The man died of sadness. You still don't see it? Look, it's written here. They didn't get up and curse the man down. You know what they did? Nothing! They didn't do anything. Just like that, like some dog just walked past them or something, they didn't even turn back and look. That's why the man died. No one turned around and looked. How'd they get away with it? You tell me. Can anyone with a conscience do this? Fuck! The man died right in front of their eyes."

Derda was crying like a child. Because he was still a child, a newborn in fact. His world was as wide as his swaddling clothes.

He couldn't hear Süleyman telling him, "Calm down, son, sit down! Go splash some water on your face." Because Derda the newborn had just opened his eyes, but his ears had yet to start to hear.

"I'm going to find them one by one and fuck them all!" he said in the end.

Süleyman's voice came on top of him.

"Sit down like a man. Don't make me get up and stop you. Are you on drugs, boy?"

Derda looked at Süleyman like he was the wildest creature to come out of the most untouched jungle of the most remote corner of earth.

"No," he said. "I'm fine, in fact I'm more than fine."

After that they didn't talk anymore. Derda buried himself in his book, muttering to himself as he read. And shaking his head. And wiping his tears with the back of his hand. And swearing. And all the while whetting his desire.

In the morning, Süleyman woke up coughing and saw Derda was still reading. There were some things he wanted to say, but he gave up. Derda reminded him of himself, of his life, in the deepest days of the revolution. Torture, fights, those nights when they handed out pamphlets, all the swindles they ate and all the swindles they served. What does someone learn from life, what does it teach Derda? "Fuck it," he said to himself. "Fuck it all."

Every night that week Süleyman and Derda sat side by side in silence. One drank vodka, the other never stopped reading. Then, one day, Derda went into a shop in an industrial park and came out with a can of spray paint in his hand. He had asked for black. They were all out. In the end he was willing to settle for red. That night he left, telling Süleyman, "I have to go do something." And Süleyman had told him, "Get cigarettes on your way back."

Derda walked forever until he made it to the overpass where Saruhan sold his books. It took him a good hour of walking. He pulled the scarf he'd gotten from Remzi off his neck, wrapped it around his face, and shook the can in his hand. That's how the man who'd sold it had told him to do it. It was five steps to the door of the bookstore where he'd stolen the book from. He checked the stairs on both sides of the overpass then looked around him to make sure no was there, and then he sprayed a big O. Right on the glass door of the bookstore. Everywhere else was covered by metal shutters.

There were only four words he knew how to write: His name, his last name, and Oğuz Atay. But he had drawn the letter O too big so there wasn't any space left to put the rest of it. No room for either Oğuz or Atay. So much for writing the whole name, now he was forced to content himself with just the initials. But he hadn't even left enough room next to the O to stick one measly A. Derda had let his excitement get the better of him. He had been too hasty.

But he had no time to waste standing around, making a decision. There was only one empty space near the O to put the A, and that was inside the O. He spray painted an A inside the O and took two steps back to admire his work. A letter A inside a letter O. Bright red. It was a symbol that perhaps for others would signify something entirely different, but for Derda it was the signature of Oğuz Atay.

An A inside an O looked so nice to him that it was some time before he could tear his eyes off the sight of it. But then noticing oncoming blue and red lights flashing from the end of the street, he took off running in the opposite direction. He couldn't get caught by the police. Not yet, at least.

He'd chosen to mark a bookstore of all places with Oğuz Atay's signature because he was under the impression that all the names of the men he wanted to take revenge on for Oğuz Atay could somehow be found there. True, perhaps, that he didn't know where any of them lived, if they lived at all, but all of them must appear somewhere in the books in the bookstore. Resting on the shelves of that bookstore. Lined up side by side.

A twisted smile flashed across his face. Streets passed, stairs changed. His smile turned into laughter. And as he laughed he ran faster. The streets rang out with the sound of him as he passed. Finally, finally! he was able to really do something for Oğuz Atay. He couldn't clean his tomb anymore, but at least he could plaster the bookstores with his signature. He started to pay attention to the shops he was running by. By chance he passed two more bookstores and started the can in his hand shaking again. He hardly needed to—as it was, it was well shaken from his run. He drew two more A's inside of two more O's, and left them to mix with the night.

"Where were you, boy?" Süleyman asked.

Derda smiled.

"It took me two hours to find a shop open to buy your cigarettes."

Abdullah, relieved to see there was no book in Derda's hand, barked "Light this" at him. *There's something different about the kid,* he thought. He was smiling and looking out the window. Despite the weather being cold the window was open, and he was rubbing his arm against the van's hood and swinging his hand holding the cigarette.

When they arrived at the overpass he saw three people gathered in front of the bookshop's door. One was the woman he'd taken Oğuz Atay's biography from. The van had drawn near the opposite side of the overpass so there was no way they could see Derda. They were looking at the symbol on the door and talking to each other, their hands at their waists. *They must be deciding who's going to wash it off,* thought Derda. *Maybe they're talking about how they can wash it off.* Laughing, he started up the overpass's steps, with two boxes in his hands.

"What's up?" said Saruhan. "I see you're in a good mood."

"I'm good, I'm good," said Derda. He even tossed a hello to the clock seller when he passed him on his way back down. Usually he couldn't even look at him because of all those alarms going off. But that morning, nothing was as usual. He wished it were that night again. He wanted to be running down the streets, seeking out all the bookstores, and spraying Oğuz Atay's signature on them all over again. On all the bookstores' windows, on all of them, and maybe on all the walls of every street.

He was leaping down the stairs two by two thinking all this, when for a second he thought his eyes were playing tricks on him. He stopped, staring at the symbol, willing himself to believe. There, on the building across the street, on the wall, was a symbol spray-painted in pitch-black. It was the letter A inside the letter O. Barely different from Derda's symbol, only that the legs of the A slipped out a bit from inside the O. He didn't know what to think. But who? was the only thing he could say. Who did that?

He heard Abdullah's voice loud and clear, but as much as Abdullah spoke, he stayed motionless. He eyes fixed on the symbol.

"Hey, ding-dong, get over here, why'd you stop there? Come on, get down here, we got more work to do."

"I knew it," Derda said. He was smiling. Squeezing his fists tight, jumping down the stairs.

"I knew it! I knew it!"

"Boy, what did you know?" said Abdullah, crossing in front of the van to the driver's side.

"Nothing," said Derda. He got into the van and shut the door. This time it was he who held out a cigarette.

"Light this."

"Well, all right then!" said Abdullah.

After his first drag, Derda leaned his head back against his seat and thought. For the first time in his life he wasn't alone. *Yes,* he said to himself. *There's someone else out there. Maybe a whole slew of people. People just like me. People out on the streets taking revenge for Oğuz Atay. Maybe they're on every corner.* He sighed. *If only I could meet them.* He still couldn't completely believe it. He couldn't believe he'd known how to draw the correct symbol. That means it works like that, he said to himself. That means that however someone feels, their hand knows and just does the right thing. When they were stopped at a red light he watched the faces passing in front of them. *Which one,* he thought. *Who could it be? Maybe it's everyone,* he thought, laughing.

Just a few short days earlier Derda had thought that every single person who crossed the face of the earth was bad to the core, and now, if even for a split second, he believed in the possibility that everyone could be good. He fantasized that all people and all of mankind could love Oğuz Atay. Because Derda believed that Oğuz Atay was everything good. Everything that touched goodness originated in him. The photographs at the end of his *Journal* passed before his eyes, especially the very last one. The one where Oğuz Atay looked straight into Derda's eyes. Maybe it was only his own voice ringing in his own ears: I am not alone.

Meanwhile, he wasn't listening to anything Abdullah was telling him. But the guy must've been talking nonstop for the last half hour they'd been stuck in traffic. He talked about all the phlegm he was coughing up at night ever since he was forced to stop smoking, and he just kept talking. Derda was paying so little attention to Abdullah that he took the packet out of his pocket, took out a cigarette, and offered it to Abdullah. And even with great joy. As if to celebrate his not being alone. Like it was his birthday. As if because there weren't candles to blow out, he wanted to light a cigarette instead.

"Light another one."

Abdullah looked at the cigarette, then at Derda's smiling face.

"You're right, boy," he said, taking the cigarette. "If we're going to die, may as well die doing this."

Maybe life is beautiful when it's misunderstood. But only when it's misunderstood.

Then there came to pass three more nights of signatures. The windows of newspaper stands, bookstores, bus stops, whenever he found himself alone with a wall before him, he tagged it with Oğuz Atay's signature. For three nights, Derda put Oğuz Atay's seal on whatever place he could. And he passed his daytimes looking for more places he could tag, always on the lookout from the windows of Abdullah's van. He saw four more symbols that weren't his. He had four more dreams. *I wonder who did them?* It was like he was suddenly part of a secret underground organization. So secret that even the members of the organization didn't know each other. He wondered about the name of the organization. *What could it be?* he thought. Then, all of a sudden, he remembered the name of one of the children's books Saruhan had had him read. It was called *The Oğuz Turks*. Derda smiled. *Why not?* he thought. And he thought about that for a while. Then he forgot about it totally and didn't think about it anymore. Anyway, he said, the most important thing was that he was not alone. Because up until that day, the most important thing had been that he was alone.

On the fourth day, there was no work. Israfil had said, "There's no going out to work today, everything's too mixed up out there."

Later, when he'd asked Süleyman, he'd said, "Look, son, you think we're the only ones out there doing this kind of work? There's a ton of rabid vagabond hounds frothing at the mouths out there."

There was a whole day ahead of him waiting to be filled. Then Derda remembered his old friend Isa who he hadn't seen in a long time. Not that he really wanted to go anywhere near the cemetery neighborhood. But not because he was afraid of his dad. He'd entirely erased him from his mind. Or that's what Derda thought anyway. His mind had pushed it as far as it could into his skin. And maybe on top of that, he'd stomped on it. In the end, he'd forgotten. There was another reason he didn't want to get anywhere near the cemetery. He was embarrassed. Because of Oğuz Atay. Who knew for how many days now his tomb hadn't been cleaned? Who knew how much the dust of death had wrapped around it from all sides? And what about the violets? Who knew what had happened to them. Were any still standing? Had they all wilted?

And so, changing buses twice and walking clear across three main avenues, he made it to the marble cutter's shop and found Isa inside a cloud of marble dust. *He looks like a baker,* he thought, *with his face all white.*

"Derda! Where have you been, man? I said to myself, I said did that bastard die or is he still around?"

They hugged each other. The marble dust got all over Derda.

"Sorry about that," said Isa. He started brushing the dust off his bare arms hanging out of his T-shirt. As he brushed the dust away the color of his skin took on darker shades. His left arm especially seemed dark. As the whiteness dispersed, tattoos on his arm came into focus. Tattoos made by his own sleight of hand. With sewing needles.

"What's that?" said Derda. He grabbed Isa's left arm and looked at it. With difficulty, he read it: "'I have no power over the dawning day, nor can anyone understand it.' What's that supposed to mean?"

"Fuck it," said Isa, looking at his tattoos. "I was out of my head, I just wrote it, that's all."

Then at once he looked up.

"You can read?"

"Yes," said Derda.

"Good for you, man. Now you can get your primary school diploma."

"Nah," said Derda. "What am I going to do with that? Anyway, I'm still holding out for university."

They laughed. Then Derda took Isa's arm again and looked at his tattoos.

"Did it hurt?"

"It must have hurt, but like I said, I was out of my head."

That much was obvious from the way the letters slid and curved. They got smaller as they went from his elbow to his wrist. Like it had been done by some simpleton sign painters. Just like Derda the night he'd discovered Oğuz Atay's signature, Isa hadn't calculated the empty spaces correctly. The space got narrower and narrower, and to be able to squeeze in all he wanted to write he'd had to make his letters smaller and smaller.

"How'd you do it?" Derda asked.

"With a needle," said Isa. "Just a normal needle."

"How'd you do the color?"

"You know those oil paints? For the astroturf pitch? I used them. You use black, and it becomes like this blue color. Anyway, tell me what you've been up to. Remzi told me some. I saw him the other day. You're working for some pirated book thing?"

264

"Pirate?"

"That's what they call it."

"No way!"

"Derda, you ass, you haven't changed a bit. You still don't have a fucking clue. You don't even know the name of what you do. Anyway, hang on."

Isa yelled into the workshop.

"Master, I'll be right back!"

There was nothing but a cloud of dust in the direction where he yelled. And behind that, two men with masks. They were working at a block of marble with saws. One of the men inside the cloud raised his free hand.

Isa said to Derda, "Come on, move it. Let's go have a couple glasses of something."

Isa slipped a leather jacket on over his shirt. Then they left the workshop, walking without talking. Whenever they looked at each other they started to laugh. A hundred steps later, Isa said, "Here." Derda stopped and looked up.

"Isn't this a hardware store?"

"That guy died, man," said Isa. "His son turned it into a bar. Come on."

And so this was the way that Derda returned to the hardware store where years before he'd stolen the ax from their spot in front of the display window to chop up his mother. But now there weren't any drawers of nails or metal buckets to be found. In their places were four little tables, each swaying on its pedestal, with two stools set across from each other. The hardware store owner's drunken son jumped out of nowhere.

"My, my, my, Isa, you're an early bird today."

"So it goes, Mahmut. Look, here's an old friend of mine. From when we were kids."

As it was, he was still a kid. They both were. Derda took Mahmut's outstretched hand and gave him a nod. They sat at the stools around the fourth table. Mahmut got two beers from the rickety bar near the entrance and took two steps to their table and set them down in front of them. Then he slapped his forehead with the palm of his head.

"Ah, shit, I didn't even ask what you wanted to drink."

Isa smiled.

"Don't kill yourself over it. Beer's just the thing."

Then he looked at Derda.

"Beer's all right, right?"

"Sure," Derda said.

Mahmut walked away and took up his perch on the stool behind the bar. He reached under the counter and brought out a glass of vodka. Three glasses raised high in the hardware store-cum-bar called NAIL. Mahmut called it that in memory of his father. And in memory of his father he drank. Just like he did every time. Even if he didn't say anything about it.

"Come on, so tell me," said Isa. "What the hell are you doing over there? You just up and left us."

"Man, it's not like that," said Derda. "What do you mean I left you? My dad just showed up out of nowhere. We got into each other pretty fast. Then I just left and slammed the door behind me. Thank god Remzi had helped me get some work, otherwise I'd really be down and out right now. I'm staying there, too, now. What are you up to?"

"What can I do? I mean, shove it. I'm working like a donkey. Then I come here and drink like a donkey."

At first, they'd had to stop themselves from talking to glug down their beers. Now they drank because they had nothing left to talk about. Which one of them could have said something, anyway? Was Derda going to talk about Oğuz Atay? Or was Isa going to pick up his story where he'd left off? That time when Derda told him to fuck it? The story about the treasure hunters he'd started when he was ten and had never been able to finish.

In any event, it was because of that story that he'd started to talk to marble. And it was because of that story that he'd carved into his own skin. And he'd filled every hole he pierced into his skin with tombstone paint. All because of that story. But why did it matter now anyway? Didn't everyone have a story like that? Something they'd started and never finished. Because no one ever listened to it. But why bother telling it when you could just flush it away. When you could just flush it down the toilet. A toilet brimming with alcohol.

The second beers came without them even asking, even before they'd finished the first ones. The third ones came that way, too. Before they'd even emptied the second ones. At one point, Isa went to the workshop to talk to the master. To say, "forgive me for today." To bargain with a "tomorrow I'll stay until late." He was smiling when he came back.

"It's okay, the master didn't say anything."

They smiled. And three glasses were raised once again at NAIL. During those minutes when the hours fall into night, the door swung open seven times and closed seven times. Seven more marble cutters came in. And among them, Isa's master. He sat far from his apprentice. So he wouldn't have to see his face anymore. He was sick of it all. Most of all he was sick of home. Of his wife at home. As he sat far from the faces he was sick of seeing. And he got drunk enough to be able to stand the face he was sick of looking at.

Then Isa called out, "To marble!" and raised his glass high. And then, because every man at NAIL had no thought in his head except the thought to drink, they could care less they were toasting a stone and they laughed and drained their glasses. Some guys hit the bottom of the empty glass and yelled "Mahmut!" But he was at least as drunk as his customers. He yelled, "I'm coming," and took one step, but discovered one foot was missing from beneath him and crashed to the floor. Everyone laughed. Two marble cutters pulled him up. Over the course of four beers, Derda and Isa had run out of talk and just looked around NAIL, chuckling. One was listening to whoever was talking. The reminiscences of a marble cutter. One to the stories of a tombstone in its most exhausting days of mourning.

Then, one by one, the stools were left empty. Only Mahmut and the two boys were left. And only then did Derda begin to speak.

"There's this guy called Oğuz Atay . . ."

"Yeah, who's that, man?" said Isa. "Your relative or something?"

"No, man . . ."

So many liters of beer had left Derda's throat squeezed for air, and he gasped like he was out of breath. He was trying to explain it to him, but it wasn't working.

"No, that's not it. The man . . ."

"What?" said Isa. "What man? Your boss?"

Derda almost died laughing.

"What do you mean, boss?" he said. "Look, what did I say. Oğuz!"

Then he started tapping on the fingers on his left hand with his right pointer finger, spelling out "O Ğ U Z" as he knocked each one. All of a sudden, he stopped and sat completely still.

"Yeah, we got it, Oğuz," said Isa.

Derda was staring at his fingers like he'd never seen them before. Like he was trying to figure something out. Then he looked up at Isa.

"It works, man!" he said.

"What are you yelling about, for fuck's sake."

"Man, it works!"

"What works, come on."

"Now look," Derda said, and then using his left pointer finger he started from his right pinkie finger, tapping one finger after the other. At the same he yelled, "Look, look. O Ğ U Z." Then he went over the fingers on his left hand with his right pointer finger, crying "A T A Y!" Isa didn't understand anything.

"Boy, are you out of your head? What are you talking about?

"You have a needle, man, a needle?" Derda was yelling.

"What do you mean a needle?"

"For a tattoo, man!"

"Fuck that, man, you're drunk," said Isa.

Just then Mahmut came staggering up with two more beers. He plunked the brimming beer glasses on the table, then the owner of NAIL bar said, slurring his words, "One more drink never screwed anyone."

The high-pitched sound of an oud was coming out of the one speaker that hadn't blown out of an old, beat-up cassette player whose make and model had long since rubbed off. The cassette was just as old as the player itself, and its sound encircled the three bare bulbs hanging down from the ceiling and mixed with the dust of the workshop. Then the voice of Münir Nurettin Selçuk rose over the oud. It rode over the oud like it was flying. "*I have no power over the dawning day . . .*" it said. Isa had first heard the song playing from his master's tape. It was like the first two lines had been written for him; he believed they were meant for him, and he carved them into his arm himself. He couldn't have heard of either the poet Cahit Sıktı Tarancı, nor the composer Münir Nurettin Selçuk who set the poem to music. "Cassette tape" he would have known, and that was all he needed to believe. "Master, leave the tape, I want to listen to it tonight." And now he was playing it again. But this time, he was having Derda listen to it.

"Man, that hurts!"

"Of course it's going to hurt," said Isa.

Meanwhile, Isa was holding two needles gingerly pinched between his fingertips, heating them over the flame of the stove. Then he dipped the points of the needles into black paint mixed up on a plastic plate, and swiveling around on his stool, he took Derda's outstretched left hand. He started to pierce Derda's pointer finger as fast as a sewing machine, with two needles bound together with a rubber band. As the painted points of the two needles pierced the skin, the black mixed with blood. Every so often Isa wiped Derda's finger with a filthy rag. Otherwise he couldn't see where he was going. When he wiped the finger the letter "A" jumped out like a beacon.

Isa's forehead was sweating out all the beer he had drunk. But Derda couldn't be bothered to notice; he was looking intensely at what Isa had done on his right fist. There was a letter on each finger on his fist. And his fist said OĞUZ.

"That's all done," said Isa. Wiping his forehead with the back of his hand, he said, "But it won't work this way. Make your hand into a fist, make your skin good and tight."

First Derda looked at the bleeding letter A, then he made a fist and dropped his hand onto the table between him and Isa. Next was the letter T. Isa's back and neck ached from leaning over and trying to focus his two crooked, drunk eyes. He stretched out then hunched back over the table. He started to pierce into the middle finger of the fist before him with the painted needles. Again and again.

"Ok, now you can't wash your hands for at least three days," said Isa. At the same time he was holding Derda's fist, admiring his work.

"Eventually it'll scab over. But be patient, don't pick at it. If you do, it'll make it come off. Just leave it alone, or it won't set."

"Thanks, Isa," said Derda. "I'll never forget this favor, what you've done for me."

"Fuck that, man, what favor? Just show up every now and then and buy me a beer, that'd be enough."

Derda returned to the warehouse with the morning *ezan*. They slipped in side by side. But as soon as he went in, he met eyes with Süleyman. Still drinking. Sitting at his vodka table.

"Israfil came. He asked for you."

Derda's bright idea had been to hide his drunkenness by not speaking, but he was forced to break his silence.

"What did he want?"

"He said you shouldn't be out at night, that you should stay where you're staying."

"Why?"

"They're going to smash this place up. That's what he said."

"Who?"

"Who do you think? Some thug, goes by the name Hanif the Trashman."

Derda couldn't hold himself back and he laughed.

"I don't get it, is the guy a trashman or a thug?"

"Yeah, keep laughing," said Süleyman. "But where are you going to be when these guys are up against the door?"

Derda tried to act serious but he couldn't quite pull it off. He was still smiling when he said it, but still he managed to ask, "What do they want?"

Süleyman rolled his glass back down his gullet. Derda folded up boxes and set up his bed.

"This," said Süleyman.

Derda turned around and looked at the man, his eyes as blood-red as the base of a terra-cotta pot.

"This?"

"Yeah, this," Süleyman said, gesturing to all the books. And to all the machines. "Everything. Boy, there's a lot of money in this business. And when there's a lot of money, there's a lot of problems. Get it?"

Süleyman fell silent. He bent his head down, like he was tracking some thing with his eyes. To be more precise, four things. Four fingers. Four letters. He couldn't quite see them from where he was sitting, so he asked.

"What's that?"

Derda raised his right hand and first looked at his tattoos himself. He looked at them like it was the first time he was seeing them. Then he turned his eyes toward Süleyman.

"This? Yeah, these are letters, it's nothing."

"Let's see!" said Süleyman. "Let's just see what you got written there."

"It says Oğuz." Then he raised his left fist and showed it to him. "And this one says Atay."

Süleyman laughed. "What an ass. What kind of man are you? And Israfil was going to give you a gun! Son, you'd take off all our heads!"

Derda stood facing him, still trying to make his sagging face look stern.

"Come on, lay down, get some sleep. They'll be here soon."

During his two hours of sleep, Derda punched everything that tried to get in his way with an OĞUZ and an ATAY. Deep in the dreams of a moment.

"What's up, you cold?" Israfil asked. He was looking at the black gloves with the fingertips cut off that Derda had on.

"No," Derda answered. "It's just that my hands get sweaty and the boxes slip, so I put these on."

But he'd really put the gloves on because he was being drowned in all the attention and questions about his tattoos. He'd bought them from the street bazaar they set up near the warehouse on Sundays.

"Well, okay," said Israfil. "Now come with me."

"But Brother Abdullah will be here soon," said Derda.

"Don't worry about him, they'll be fine, you come with me," Israfil said, leaving the warehouse.

Derda followed two steps behind him. They got into a twenty-year-old Mercedes and pulled out onto the main road. From there they turned into major traffic, and they moved forward slowly in fits and starts. Israfil was totally silent. And so Derda didn't say anything either. But as soon as they'd made it onto the highway around the city, Israfil's grating voice cut into Derda's ears.

"How old are you?"

"About seventeen."

"Where's your mother?"

"She's dead."

"Have you seen your father again?"

"No," Derda answered.

"Now, look, you can count on me like a big brother. So don't feel uncomfortable or shy. Is there anything you need, any problem you have?"

"No, brother," said Derda. At the same time he was looking at a face of Istanbul he'd never seen before. He was looking at glass-faced skyscrapers.

"In that case, Derda *efendi*, seeing as you don't have anything to ask me for, would it be okay if I asked something of you?"

Derda was sitting up straight in the leather seat, his eyes overflowing with the view from the windshield. It was the first time he'd even seen the Bosphorus. The first time in his life. And to add to that, they were headed straight for the bridge he'd always heard about, but had never crossed.

"Derda!" said Israfil. "I asked if it would be okay if I asked you for something."

"Of course, of course," said the kid without even thinking. He was looking into the Bosphorus as if it were a mirror of waves reflecting from deep inside Istanbul.

"There's a guy," Israfil continued. "A thug, goes by the name Hanif the Trashman."

Derda had both hands on the dashboard. His back was straight as a bolt, his lips pulled away from his teeth. His pupils were playing a game of tag with what he was seeing. If he looked to the right, he regretted losing the view of what was on the left. And if he looked to the left, he regretted the loss of the view out the other side. Just then the traffic opened like an accordion's bellows and the front tires of the Mercedes lunged onto the Bosphorus Bridge. And just then his heart started pounding so loudly that Derda closed his mouth so no one would hear its deafening beat. He saw white islands floating on the water below. White ships. He looked out to the horizon. Everything was so beautiful. The sky looked so beautiful. He looked at Israfil, seated at his side. He wanted him to look at it, too. Just for a moment, and he'd be so happy and then he'd smile until it hurt. And in that moment he could hear Israfil. Sixty-four meters over the deep blue waters, kilometers and kilometers under the snow-white clouds.

"So, you're going to shoot that guy. For me."

Derda didn't get it.

"What?" he asked. There was still a smile on his face.

"That guy called Hanif. You're going to shoot him."

That time he got it. That moment of clarity was the moment the bridge ended and Istanbul made everything ugly once again. Even Derda.

"Yes sir, brother."

Israfil chuckled and lowered his fist onto Derda's knee.

"Good for you, man."

Israfil laughed again.

"Hey, man, what's your hurry? Wait at least a second there, we're on our way."

Derda was rubbing his tattoos through his gloves with his fingertips. Just a little bit longer, he said to himself. To Oğuz Atay.

"There's just a little bit longer, anyway," said Israfil. Derda smiled.

They turned onto a dirt road leading to the vineyard covering the slope across from them, and they stopped at a gate with iron spikes that loomed before them. Israfil opened the garden gate with a remote control he slipped out of his pocket, and the Mercedes pulled inside. The first thing Derda heard was the barking, then he saw the slobber smeared across the windows. Two leaping black dogs running alongside the slowing car were looking at Derda like they wanted to kill him.

"Those are my babies," said Israfil.

When the car stopped, the dogs ran to Israfil's door. They were so impatient to be under their master's control that they were butting into each other, trying to get ahead.

Derda got out of the car and looked first at the two-story house, then at the man in the black suit coming out of the house's French doors.

"Brother Tayyar, we're here!" yelled Israfil, as he stroked the dogs' heads with his palms. Derda didn't recognize Tayyar. For one, he wasn't wearing a long robe, and he didn't have a beard covering his face like a veil. But Tayyar didn't take his eyes off the boy; he thought that for sure he knew that face from somewhere. But from where? Anyway, there was no hurry. It would come to him eventually. Whatever else, they had two days together before them. Two days that they'd spend together, face to face, at the house. Two days out in the country, at this house, to teach Derda how to use a gun. The closest person to the house would have to spend an hour and go a hundred kilometers from the highway out on the horizon to get there.

"Look, this is Derda."

Israfil was holding the boy by his shoulders and pulling him to the steps going up to the front door.

"He's like a brother to me," he was saying, with a wink at Tayyar. Tayyar's bulging physique covered half the front door. Derda shook Tayyar's outstretched hand.

Israfil spoke again.

"And this is our brother Tayyar."

Tayyar didn't let go of the hand in his and looked into Derda's eyes in silence. The boy didn't know what to do, but he couldn't well pull his hand away. It was like his hand was buried inside firm, dense, flesh. They seemed clamped together by their hands and their frozen, staring eyes. Finally, Israfil untangled them. He put one hand on each of their shoulders.

"Come on, let's go inside."

They went inside. In the house's ample living room there were two couches, two big coffee tables, at least six easy chairs, two or three televisions, and a round dining table with chairs around it. That was as much as Derda could see in his first two steps inside. He couldn't be exactly sure of the numbers or of how big the living room was. It looked like there was just too much furniture. Like everything already had its spare lined up next to it.

"Derda, have a seat, I'll be right there," said Israfil. Then he walked deep into the living room, went up, and was lost from sight. Only then did Derda realize where the stairs to the second floor were. Only when he saw Israfil disappear from view after going up two stairs.

Tayyar hadn't yet spoken. "Sit down, let's see now."

Derda pulled his eyes from the spot where Israfil had disappeared and looked at the couch Tayyar was pointing to. He took two steps and sat down. Tayyar took his hands out of his pockets, spread open his jacket, and displayed two butts of two pistols at his waist.

"Where do I know you from?"

"Me? I don't know," said Derda.

"You ever been to Çemendağ?"

"No."

"Anyway, we'll figure it out," he said, sitting down on the couch opposite Derda. He spread his arms out like wings and leaned the back of his head back against the couch and threw one leg over the other. His eyes, like a net made of iron, fixed Derda in their trap.

"What's your father's name?"

"Celal," answered Derda.

"Celal? That's right, Israfil mentioned him. Just out, right?"

"Yes."

"I'm going to remember where I know you from, just give me a minute. How old are you?"

"Seventeen."

Derda didn't want to calculate the months and make things any more complicated than they needed to be. From the very first moment he'd seen him, he'd felt the crushing pressure of Tayyar's jet black eyes. Like twin pistols. Like he was under the weight of reinforced concrete. After he answered a question, he quickly lowered his head and his eyes. He couldn't get free of the weight of the iron net. At the same time, he was thinking about why he could possibly know Tayyar. If I'd seen that man before, I'd definitely remember him, he said to himself. He didn't hear Tayyar's questions. Because at the time he was talking to himself.

"Any at all?" Tayyar was saying, this time raising his voice.

Derda looked up all of a sudden. "Any at all what?" he asked.

"Any clue! Do you have any clue about what you're going to do, I said."

"Yes, brother," said Derda. "There's this guy . . ."

"What guy?"

"A guy called Hanif the Trashman."

"And what is it that you're going to do to him?"

"I'm going to shoot him."

"And how do you know that I'm not from the police?" asked Tayyar, the question flowing from his mouth like a river. It fell out so fast, it stung Derda's face and made his forehead break out in a sweat. As soon as he heard the word police, he forgot the rest of the question and Derda's temples started to throb. He didn't know what to say. First he lowered his eyes, then his shoulders collapsed like he wanted to be small enough to squeeze in between the thick tufts of the carpet under his feet. His head hung low below his shoulders.

"If someone asks you something like that, are you really going to say you're going to shoot a man?"

Derda buried himself even deeper.

"Ok, then. Who is this guy? What is it you're going to do?"

Derda's voice barely reached his lips, but he just couldn't get it through his closed mouth. Even as it was, he was only going to say, "I don't know."

"That's exactly right," said Tayyar. "Do not speak. Just listen. If you're going to learn anything, you're going to learn by listening."

He shifted his legs, crossed them the other way, and lowered his arms. He held one fist at his waist and the other against his knee.

"Now this Hanif, he's the kind of guy that, if we don't shoot him, he's going to shoot us. Only he's not going to shoot me. He's going to shoot Brother Israfil. He's going to shoot you. He's going to shoot up everyone you've got in that warehouse, you understand?" he said.

Derda hesitated. He didn't know if he should respond or not. He just nodded. He did the right thing.

"Good! He lives on the coast, in Maltepe. Israfil will show you his house. First you're going to learn everything you can about where and how he lives. Then, when Israfil tells you to go, you're going to go in the morning and you're going to wait there. You been out there before?"

He shook his head right to left. Tayyar leaned over the coffee table in front of him and started to mark on it with invisible ink. With a pointer finger as thick as the barrel of a gun.

"So there's a road along the coast. There are houses on this side, and the sea's on this side. There's a sidewalk along the coast, too. You understand?"

He signaled his understanding with a rise and fall of his chin.

"Hanif leaves his house around noon, but you're going to be waiting there from early morning. He leaves the house from the front door, he crosses the street, then he has his walk along the coast . . ."

As Tayyar spoke, Derda started to think that maybe it was possible that he had met the man across from him before. But it was just a feeling. A feeling that had a lot to do with the man's face and physique, but most of all with his voice. He was sure that he'd heard that voice sometime before. But somehow he just couldn't place it. Now he looked into Tayyar's eyes as he listened.

"Don't bring anyone with you. There's a streetlight in front of the house. Cross the road there. You'll wait on the sea side."

For a second Tayyar felt the boy's eyes glaze over and to test him he asked: "So, what is it you're going to do?"

"I'm going to wait on the other side of the street by the sea."

"Right. Good."

Then Derda heard the sound of a pair of feet behind, a sound that got louder as they approached. It was Israfil, coming back. When he passed by Derda he grabbed his shoulders and said, "Listen up good to Brother Tayyar." Then he sat in the easy chair diagonally across from him.

Tayyar continued, "Then he's going to leave his house. He'll cross the street to where you are, then he'll start to walk. You're going to get up and follow behind him."

Tayyar suddenly broke his focus and turned to Israfil.

"Get the kid some sweats and some sport shoes. He can't go around there like this, Hanif will know something's up."

"Ok," said Israfil, "leave that to us."

Tayyar turned back to Derda. Like he'd just thought of it, he straightened his back and took out one of the revolvers at his waist.

"There are six shells inside this. You're going to approach him from behind and plug him with all six. Two in his head, the other four between his shoulder blades. Understand?"

"I understand," said Derda, but his mind was all a blank. So he decided just to stay silent. He didn't understand where the blades were. What blades? His mind had gone blank since the moment Tayyar had pulled out the gun; his eyes had been glued to it. And, as a consequence, his ears had gone blank, too.

The weapon Derda couldn't take his eyes off was not just a Smith & Wesson 38-caliber, short-barreled revolver. It was the machine for Derda's revenge. With that, he would make reparations for the past. Tayyar realized that Derda was daydreaming.

"Watch," he said. He opened the cylinder and knocked the six shells into the palm of his hand. With one flick of the wrist the cylinder was back in place. He handed the empty weapon to Derda.

"Take this."

Derda took the revolver.

"Now get up."

He got up.

"Israfil, you get up, too."

Israfil got up.

"Israfil, now just walk like you're going for a walk. And you, track him from there at the door. Then like I told you, put two in his head, four in his back. Ok, come on, let me see how it works."

Israfil started walking, plodding around the living room. Derda followed after him. Three steps later he raised the revolver and pulled the trigger. One time right after another.

"No, not like that," Tayyar said. He got up and told Israfil to stand still. Then he pointed to a region of Israfil's back with his hand.

"Look, this is where between the shoulder blades is. Not any lower. Ok, go back there, both of you, to the door. First Israfil, you start to walk, then you. Let's do it again, let me see now."

They did as Tayyar said and after Derda had taken three steps, he raised the revolver. Six times his fingertip fell on the emptied trigger, then he looked at Tayyar.

"This time was better. But next time, be more careful."

All of a sudden Derda remembered that morning in the cemetery. He remembered running into that man. And he remembered what the man had said. He had said the same thing then. "Next time, be more careful." And his jet-black eyes had bored into Derda. And now he was looking at Derda again. Derda didn't want to believe it. But he had to believe it. Because it was all true. For years, he had lived in fear of the man in the long robe, this man called Tayyar, with every breath he drew. Hundreds of drops of sweat appeared all over his body. The sweat of fear emptied out of his every pore. A cramp in his stomach that felt like it was going to burst spread all over his body. The revolver in his hand trembled.

Tayyar stood up and Derda thought that the man had understood what he'd been thinking. He knew that Derda had recognized him. As Tayyar approached him, Derda scanned the room for a way out. But he couldn't find an escape route. He didn't walk nor run nor scream out. He only trembled and waited for fear.

"Come with me." Tayyar took the revolver in Derda's hand by the barrel. "Let's go outside and take some shots. Let your hand get used to the feeling."

Israfil had locked up the dogs in their kennel in the front garden. He knew all too well the way they went crazy at the sound of a weapon firing. And added to that, Derda was a stranger to them, and they were trained to rip off the hand of any stranger holding a gun. But their knowing how to take off a hand from the wrist down couldn't be entirely attributed to their training. They'd just kept up with the life their owner led, that's all. Like dogs trained to be seeing-eye dogs for the blind, these dogs burned with passion to take out someone's eye. They were just like the hundreds of thousands of child soldiers all over the world. Just like them, the dogs in the front garden had no choice how to lead their lives. They were encouraged to develop their natural, God-given brutality to an even higher level of brutality. The only difference between child soldiers as tall as their rifles and all the attacking dogs in all the gardens of the world was their reward. But if you think about it, the rewards weren't so different after all. One was given cooked meat, the other raw. Children cannot eat raw meat. If they could, they'd eat the corpses of their enemy child soldiers. And they would that much more affordable to keep.

They went to the back garden so they wouldn't have to hear the dogs barking. They walked between two old plane trees and stopped at a distance of five steps from a high sand dune. Tayyar took the shells out of his pocket and inserted them into the round in the revolver's cylinder. Then he handed the weapon to Derda, holding it from the barrel. Israfil was a couple steps away, trying to light the cigarette pressed between his lips despite the wind. Derda looked at the revolver he was gripping from its hilt and heard Tayyar's voice.

"Ok, now let's see you hit the sand dune there. Let's see how you place your hands."

He watched Tayyar take two steps to Israfil's side. Both men were now standing behind Derda. Derda turned and looked at the sand dune. There was nothing between him and it.

"Just stay calm," said Tayyar. "Don't bend your arm. Just before you pull the trigger, take a breath and hold it, okay?"

Derda didn't say anything and Tayyar asked again: "Did you hear me?"

"I heard you," said Derda as he slowly raised his arm. He took aim at the sand dune.

"Take one step forward," said Tayyar. "This is the amount of space you should have between yourself and Hanif."

Derda did what he was told and took a deep breath and held it in. He was afraid. Tayyar saw his hesitation and yelled, "Don't be scared. Fire!"

Derda turned around in place and pulled the trigger. He didn't lower his arm, nor did he bend it. Three bullets in Tayyar's chest and two between the shoulder blades of Israfil as he tried to run away. The last one plunged into the back wall of the house.

He opened his narrowed eyes as wide as he could and saw the two men sprawled on the ground like two crooked lumps. As soon as he saw them he shut his eyes. He expected some sign of life from Tayyar or Israfil. But the garden of the house was as silent as the vineyard. Even the dogs had stopped barking.

Derda raised his head and released the breath he'd been holding. He looked up at the sky. One raindrop fell onto his left cheek. Then another one onto his forehead. "Just stay calm," Tayyar had said. He'd done just what he'd been told. After so many years, Derda was breathing easily for the first time. Without the fear burning his throat. Two steps from two corpses. Under a naive rain.

First he stuck the revolver into his waistband. Then he tore off his gloves and threw them to the ground. He raised OĞUZ and ATAY to the sky. So that there would be no one left who had not seen them.

The dogs sensed they'd been left ownerless, and they started to bark and whine. Their eyes filled with blood. Because, just like child soldiers, they had no tears to cry.

The very day Steven's mission at the consulate was completed and he left Istanbul, Tayyar had called Hıdır Arif to tell him about his suspicions about Gido Agha. This is what passed in their conversation: "Gido has something going on behind our backs. He came to see me recently. He's looking for the man at the head of your Istanbul operations. Someone known around here. I took a look, put out some feelers. I'll have us a look myself I said. Then he asked about our contract. It was obvious he was going to take me into his confidence, and take me on as an informer."

"The man has no god."

"Absolutely."

"So what exactly are you going to do?"

"Give him the go-ahead, I'll go under his orders. Let's see what he's up to."

"Good idea," Hıdır Arif had said. "But we can't let my father find out. He absolutely cannot find out that you are going after that bastard."

"You just play it cool. I'll find some excuse. I'll say, may God forgive it, I'm going to take a look at operations abroad."

Tayyar hung up the phone and picked it up again. This time he called Gido.

"Yes, Brother Tayyar!"

"Forgive me, brother. Brother, there's something I have to tell you."

"Go ahead."

"This Hıdır Arif has double-crossed me so bad, if my father weren't in the middle of it I'd strangle him. And I'm saying, I don't want this whole thing to blow up. If you arrange some things in Istanbul for me . . . if I could leave this to you."

"Of course, Tayyar, think nothing of it. It's a good thought," Gido Agha had said.

Then, lastly, Tayyar called Steven. For the British residence permit that he'd been promised in exchange for services provided to MI6. Steven had had told him, "Not to worry, we'll have it sorted in no time at all." But that no time at all got longer and longer. In that ever-lengthening period of time, Tayyar had left the Hikmet organization, liberated himself from his beard and robe, and had manipulated both Hıdır Arif and Gido Agha into thinking that the other was an informant. But then he started to get himself into trouble. Because both Hıdır Arif and Gido Agha got wise to the situation, and when it got to that point, Tayyar's judo skills were not going to be much use to him. And, seeing how Sheik Gazi had appointed one of his own sons as his successor anyway, the others started to distance themselves from Tayyar. That meant the old man knew something. Maybe when he told Tayyar he wouldn't cry again, what he meant to say was, "You're not going to cry again, because you're going to make others cry." And no one wants a man around who's going to make them cry.

Tayyar, first sliding out from beneath their rules, and then being sidelined by the clan and from the order, invested all the money he'd gotten from the MI6 into all sorts of criminal activities he'd always thought about doing. One of these was the illegal printing press printing pirated books that Derda did the hauling for. And, to protect that business, he invested in having Hanif the Trashman killed.

How could Tayyar have known? That a kid he'd seen years before for half an hour at most would be the one who, thousands of days later, would kill him within another half an hour?

How could Derda have known? That by killing Tayyar, he took revenge not only for himself, but for everyone?

How could Israfil have known? That he should never have brought Tayyar and Derda together?

How could Hanif the Trashman have known? That because of Derda, he was still alive?

How could mankind have known the results of existing?

And to all the same answer: They couldn't have known.

Maybe that's why life can go on. Because no one can know in advance just what it was all about. If a person could foresee all the outcomes of all his actions, surely he'd stop living right then and there. He'd stop himself from living, he'd stop life. In horror. In fear of committing any action while his heart was still beating. For the stark end result of every action is pain, and if women and men really knew this, maybe they wouldn't perpetuate the human race. But maybe it's worse than that. Maybe they do know and still they continue. But in the end, he was a human being, and it was his nature to cling onto life. He would have done anything for life. If necessary he'd abandon his mother's corpse in the maternity ward, he'd even go forth into the world still bonded to a twin, because at least he'd still be alive.

Derda wasn't eleven years old anymore. He didn't have to cut up bodies anymore to be able to carry them. It wasn't easy, but he managed to drag first Tayyar then Israfil to the bottom of the sand dune. He went through all the pockets of both men. He found a packet of money, a revolver, a box of shells. If he had known how to drive, he would have taken the keys to the Mercedes off Israfil, but he didn't, so he didn't.

On his second trip circling around the house he found a shovel, and returning to the recently departed, he started churning up the sand that was turning into mud in the increasing rain. Within a few minutes, there was no dead man left lying. Maybe it wasn't in the soil of the earth, but at least they had been buried somewhere.

He went back into the house and shut the door behind him. As long as it rained, he had to wait inside. First he went into the large living room. He stepped onto the staircase rising from beside the far wall. When he arrived on the second floor, he walked down the corridor and turned the doorknob of the first door he came to. He entered a room with a double bed and, above it, a large photograph. A black and white photograph inside a gilded frame. Israfil was standing with his hands on the shoulders of a woman seated in front of him, and she held a baby in her arms. All three were smiling. Even the baby. Derda stepped onto the bed like he was going upstairs and he bounced and bumped as he walked across the bed, straight to the photograph. He was a nose's distance from the baby when he started to cry. Tracing over the baby with the fingers of his right hand, he said, "I'm sorry."

Whatever had happened, there was no reason for Israfil to have been killed. He was like someone who stumbles onto a battlefield. Of course the truth of the matter was that Israfil had arranged everything so Derda would be the one to shoot the man and rot in prison. But Derda's mind was so full of thoughts of Tayyar that that didn't even occur to him. Looking at the OĞUZ on his fingers, he said, "You, too. Forgive me," and he crumpled down onto his knees. His sobs shook the bed. He cried looking at the photo, pressing the palms of his hands against the image again and again. When he had no more tears left to cry, he curled up like a child and slept in the bed of the man he'd killed. In his slumber, there was no trace of the regret that had risen like a great flame.

He took all the frozen meat he could find in the freezer in the kitchen and dumped it out onto the living room floor. Then he took a ball of string he'd had to turn the house upside down to find and went out into the garden. He propped the front door open with a chair so it wouldn't swing shut. As soon as they saw Derda, the dogs started to bark. Their barks got even louder and more frantic the closer he got to their kennel. They started to jump and butt their heads against the chicken wire.

Derda tied one end of the string to the sliding iron bar on the kennel's gate, then started pacing backward until he reached the iron fence surrounding the garden, feeding the string out as he went. Then he dropped the now slim ball of string to the ground and grabbed onto the fence. He jumped over the fence and landed outside the garden. He crouched down and pulled the ball of string through the iron bars of the fence. The first time it didn't work, but on the second tug the iron bar slid open and in one leap the dogs jumped out the open gate and flew into the garden. In one fell leap, they were out of the kennel and lunging after Derda. They were going to kill the stranger. They stuck their muzzles through the iron bars and tried to jump. But they couldn't reach him. The stranger was half a kilometer away, smiling. "Go on," he was saying, "go on inside, there's food in there." Then he turned around and walked away. To the highway on the horizon.

When he reached the highway, he saw there were lanes going in three directions, but he didn't know which direction he wanted to go in. But despite his state of panic he managed to remember which way the Mercedes had come from, and he crossed to the other side. He was going to go back to Istanbul. There was only one thing he had left to do. The last thing he was going to do in this life. After that, he didn't care. But first he had to flag down a car. Or a truck would do. A red one stopped.

"Where you going?"

"Istanbul."

"Hop in!"

The driver was an old man.

"What are you doing in these parts, son?" he asked. "There are wild dogs around here, this place is cursed."

You couldn't tell that Derda had two corpses to account for. He was just a kid who, at the age of seventeen, had the last spark of life he was ever going to get. That, and he was just a tad afraid. Because he hadn't had time to clean himself up.

At first he didn't answer, then all at once he asked, "Do you know a place called Beyoğlu?"

The old man laughed.

"Aren't you listening to what I'm saying to you? What are you going to do in Beyoğlu?"

"My dad's waiting for me there."

"What's your dad do?"

"He's a writer," said Derda.

"What's his name, maybe I know him."

"Oğuz Atay."

"Never heard of him."

For a second, Derda thought of pulling the gun out from under his shirt and shooting the man. For not knowing Oğuz

Atay. But he gave up on the idea. It's not his fault, he told himself. Those guys who ignored Oğuz Atay wouldn't be driving a truck now. So he forgave the old man.

"You will," he said. "Pretty soon you'll hear about my dad."

The driver laughed again.

"Yeah, why not, let's see."

They didn't speak again.

When he got out of the truck, the sun was just starting to leave Istanbul behind. The old man had told him how to get to Beyoğlu but it didn't help him out any. He didn't know any of the roads or the square he'd mentioned. He only knew Beyoğlu. And that was only the name. Saruhan had told him: "All the stuff he wrote about and the drawings, they're all in Beyoğlu. There was one *meyhane* in particular, it's famous. What was its name ... Çolak? Çorak? anyway, something like that."

He flagged down the first taxi that passed. "Beyoğlu."

When they arrived in Taksim Square, the driver said, "Well, this is it."

Derda was searching out of all the car's windows. "Where?" he asked.

The driver released a deep sigh to calm himself and then, jabbing a finger toward Istiklal Street, he said, "Go down there. All of that is Beyoğlu."

Derda got out of the taxi and walked into the crowd, thinking about just how many people lived in Istanbul. For years he'd lived in a cemetery that only saw people on the holidays. He was totally thrown off balance by all the noise and the crowds. Actually, Derda had gone precisely there to find the place where he would lose his balance. But Beyoğlu was too much for him. People were passing in great streams all around him and all the lights on Istiklal went in one eye and out the other. He didn't know what direction he was walking in, nor how many people's feet he was stepping on. He just kept moving forward. Even if he didn't know where he was going, at least he would keep going forward.

He stopped at an intersection and asked the nearest ruffian sputtering out of the mouth of a side street.

"I'm looking for a place called Çolak, you know it? It's a *meyhane*."

It was a kid Derda's age. He looked at the hand pressed against his chest to stop him, then at the face across from him. Derda's face looked like those people in Beyoğlu who people are afraid of. He was scared, too.

"A *meyhane*?" he said.

"Çolak, Çorak, something like that."

"Huh, I don't know," the kid said.

"That's okay. Do you know Oğuz Atay?"

The kid was taken off guard. He was so surprised he started to stammer.

"Uh, yeah . . . yes, but . . ."

He was going to ask Derda why he'd asked, but Derda was gone. If he had known he could have saved a life with just one yes, would he have stammered and nodded like that? He watched Derda go for the first ten meters, after that he couldn't see him anymore. Derda got mixed in with the people. And the people with Derda.

After he'd asked seven more people and gotten the answer, "Huh, I don't know," seven more times, he went up to a chestnut roaster at the head of a side street that smelled of sewage and asked him the names of the *meyhane*. And he got a different answer.

"There's a place called Çorak down there. Go down, take a right at the third street."

Then Derda bought some chestnuts. He walked, ripping off the husks. He went down the street he was supposed to go down. He turned right where he was supposed to turn right. He took five steps, and then he saw a sign stuck out on the sidewalk staring right back at him. A lit-up sign. With ÇORAK written on it. He crumpled up the paper bag in his hand, tossed it on the ground, and went inside.

As soon as he entered, a waiter whose red tie poked out from the collar of his blue sweater approached him.

"Yes?"

Derda pushed the waiter's chest with his left hand and pulled the revolver out from his waist with his right hand and fired two bullets close to the antique chandelier hanging from the ceiling. Just like Tayyar had taught him. Without bending his arm.

The sound of the shots reverberated so loudly through the storied *meyhane* that, for a moment, people couldn't even hear their own screams. Their ears started to come back to life as they knocked into each other, trying to get under the tables. As soon as their ears worked again, what they heard was Derda. He was yelling at the waiter who stood, frozen.

"Pull away those tables, get everyone out in the open! Fuck you, hurry up!"

The waiter felt the hot barrel of Derda's gun against his forehead and he stepped back gingerly. "Okay, brother, okay!" He turned around and started to pull away the tables where people were hiding between and below.

"Stand up, you ass! Stand up!" Derda shouted.

"Let me see your face. I want to see everyone's face."

And from the place he stood, as much as he could see, he came eye to eye with a young man. He'd come out from under a table but he was still folded over in fear. His hands were up and he was shaking his head. He had had seven *rakıs* but the two shots had made his mind clear as a bell.

"Fuck off!" said Derda. "Go, get out of here, fuck off!"

At first the man didn't understand. Then, followed by the revolver that help him clear his mind, he walked past Derda and out the front door without lowering his hands or stopping his shaking head. As soon as he was gone Derda was eye to eye with another young man.

"You, get out of here. What the fuck are you looking at? Fuck off!"

And he ran out of the *meyhane*. Derda was pacing in between the tables, driving out any young person he saw. "Go fuck yourself, asshole!" Twelve men and nine women left Çorak in tears. The only ones left behind were three men between the ages of sixty and seventy-five sitting around one single table.

Derda walked up to them and asked the man with the beard, "What's your job?"

The man with the beard opened his mouth to say, "Now, look here!" but Derda screamed.

"I said, what's your job?"

When a man with glasses next to the man with the beard said, "Whatever your problem is, we'll solve it. Look, he's a journalist. But don't do it like this!" Derda laughed.

"Is that so?"

When he saw Derda smile like he was going to take the barrel of the revolver away from his face, a wave of relief washed over the bearded man for a second. "Of course, son, I'll help you with whatever you want to say. Just tell me!"

"So for you to listen to his problem, there had to be a gun pointed at your face? Is that it?" yelled Derda.

"Whose?" the bearded man and the man with glasses said together.

"If I say his name, will you remember, you fucks?"

The only one who hadn't spoken until that moment, and, interestingly enough, the only fat man among them, yelled, "You tell us, tell us, who is this about?"

Derda held his breath, directed the revolver's barrel to the bearded man, and pulled the trigger. He shot the journalist in the mouth. The bullet went right into the mouth opened to say,

"Don't do anything crazy." The bullet went in his mouth and through the back of his neck and lodged into the wall behind all at once. The man crumpled like his knees were broken and the man with the glasses tried to get under the table. The only man left standing was the fat man. Derda looked straight at him then shot him through the left eye. His two hands flew to the blackening hole where his eye had been, then as he fell into a heap, Derda bent down and shot the man with the glasses under the table. The man raised his hands in an attempt to protect himself, and the bullet that spun out of the revolver pierced through his palm and into his knee.

Derda stood up and yelled, "Today, you have been slain for Oğuz Atay, sons of bitches! For Oğuz Atay!"

Then he turned around in place and ran to the door, knocking over chairs as he went. He pointed his gun and yelled "Out of the way! Out of the way! Fuck you!" at the people who'd gathered outside of Çorak. The people scattered and Derda started to run, not knowing where he was going. When he heard a police siren, he turned into the first dark street he saw.

That night, Derda ran until morning. It was a miracle that he wasn't caught, because all the police in Istanbul were after him.

By some coincidence or twist of fate, all the streets he went down led him to the overpass where Saruhan sold pirated books. In the first light of day, he went up the steps like King Kong climbing up the Empire State Building, and at the top he saw the clock seller. He'd come early that morning for some reason. Their eyes met and the clock seller nodded his head in greeting. Then he turned away and started setting the alarm of the clock in his hand.

Derda dropped to the ground where Saruhan would set up his sales point and he leaned back against the guardrail and stretched out his legs. It was the first time for hours that he'd stopped moving. His hand went to one pocket. Then to the other. He was looking for cigarettes. He looked up and called over to the clock seller.

"You got a cigarette?"

The clock seller looked up. "Hang on." He set the clock in his hand on display and walked over to Derda while he stuck his hand in the pocket of his raincoat. He pulled out a pack of cigarettes. Then when the man was two steps from Derda, he pulled out a revolver from his other pocket and pressed it up against the head of the boy, who was still seated on the ground.

"Lie down," he said, calmly. As if he were telling him to lie down and have a little nap.

Derda did as he was told and got down on the ground.

Derda, having been to all corners of Istanbul that night in one form or another, had one more question as he was arrested by the undercover police assigned to the university environs.

"Well, are you going to give me a cigarette or not?"

Even as he was still completing his deposition to the police, before he'd even left the presence of the prosecutor, Derda's story was being printed in all the newspapers and broadcast on all the television stations. The man with the beard whom he had killed had been one of the most prominent journalists in all the country. And the others, the injured ones they were trying to keep alive in the hospital, were two writers. Two writers of novels. The fat man wasn't of any particular note, but the one with glasses practically ate prizes for dinner. So everyone wanted to learn every detail. First and foremost the question was: Was this attack in any way connected to terrorism?

At first, the deposition Derda gave the police seemed so ludicrous that they were convinced he must be a terrorist. But with the details he gave them, the tattoos on his fingers, and the clarity in his confession to the point that he himself led them to new developments in the case, they finally came to believe what he said and they accepted his testimony.

"I," Derda had told them, "I shot them for Oğuz Atay. I don't know who they were. I didn't care. I was looking for a writer to shoot, or a journalist. They were there. I pulled the trigger and shot them."

"But who is Oğuz Atay?" a policeman close to retirement asked him. Derda was handcuffed at the wrist but still he jumped to his feet. "You asshole!" Two policemen behind him pushed him down by the shoulders and forced him to sit down and shut up. Then one of them asked, "What does this have to do with Oğuz Atay?"

"Do you know why Oğuz Atay died, do you know? From grief! And who drove him to despair? Who made him so depressed? Everyone alive then who didn't care about him. If you don't believe me, go and read all his books. Then go read about his life. I shot those bastards to get revenge for him."

"Well, do you regret your actions in any way?" they had asked him.

"If they have no connection to Oğuz Atay, I might feel some regret." Then Derda stopped and thought.

"But actually, no, shove it, I don't. Because everyone who lived at that time and knew about Oğuz Atay and didn't see what was happening to him, no matter who they are, they're guilty. So I don't regret it or anything like that. Do you know what I do regret, though? I thought those two bastards were dead when I left."

"And what is your connection to Oğuz Atay?"

Derda smiled at the question.

"What do you mean, what is your connection? We're the Oğuz Turks!"

This response immediately engaged their renewed interest in the inquest. The police were excited to have uncovered a previously unknown terror organization.

They asked, "And who are these Oğuz Turks? This is an organization? How many of you are there?"

"Look, even I don't know. I mean, I know that they're out there somewhere, but who they are, how many people, I have no idea. But I see their symbol tagged everywhere."

When they asked, "And what symbol is that?" Derda drew an A inside an O on a piece of paper. One of the policeman started to say, "But isn't that . . ." but the other grabbed his arm to silence him and asked, "You made all the young people leave the *meyhane*. Why?"

"Oğuz Atay died in 1977. At that time, those people may not even have been born yet. Or maybe they were just kids. That's why I let them go."

"And where did you get your weapon?"

"From a man named Tayyar."

"And where is he?"

"I buried him somewhere, but if you asked me where, believe me, I don't even know. I mean I know where, but I couldn't tell you how to get there."

"Is there anything else you'd like to say?"

"I also shot a man called Israfil. Actually, I wasn't going to shoot him, but he was there, so . . . But really, I wish I had thanked him, he brought me over the Bosphorus Bridge."

"What else did you do?"

"I don't know. I also beat up my dad. I smashed in his mouth and broke his nose."

The prosecutor took especial interest in Derda's case. He reviewed the police deposition and tried to figure out if the kid was mentally ill or not. But he couldn't figure it out alone so he forwarded the case to a psychiatric clinic he knew. And there, too, the panel of highly educated professors was divided. Some thought Derda was the sole inhabitant living in a world of his own creation, while others decided he was nothing more than an ordinary killer. But some time later, when they learned how many pieces Derda had chopped up his mother into, and at what age he had done it, the opinions of the panel went from two to one. It was still too early to make a definite diagnosis, but it was apparent that Derda's mental situation could not be that of a normally functioning, healthy individual. If nothing else, normal people who have normally functioning brains keep it to themselves or sue someone when faced with difficulty. They don't go and gun people down.

The case was heard by the Juvenile Court, where each and every hearing was besieged by television reporters. The television channels aired documentaries about Oğuz Atay, and *Tutunamayanlar* was discussed in panel discussions. The same discussion was also alive and kicking in the divided psychiatric clinic. Some thought that while he lived, Oğuz Atay had indeed suffered injustices, but others thought that connecting such a thing to his death was impossible, and that his death had absolutely nothing to do with literature. If even for a brief interval, Oğuz Atay was so widely discussed that even the driver of the red truck heard his name on the radio and learned who that kid he'd picked up a while back had called "my dad."

But then, after a while, the programmers realized that these and similar discussions weren't garnering the viewership they once did, so they shifted their focus to Derda himself. They had guests on their shows to talk about the problems of illiteracy, about children who worked in cemeteries, and about childhood violence. And then, even if it had nothing to do with it, they talked about substance abuse and addiction. Because paint thinner and huffers are the poisonous words that paralyze a viewer on one channel.

"How could a name like Oğuz Atay go hand in hand with such a violent act? It's hard to even believe. Just think about the state of our streets." This type of sentiment was built up, then brought down. Everyone seemed to have an idea about Derda's frightening imagination. Especially after everyone heard what Süreyya and Celal said to the cameras. Celal revealed all through his tears.

"He shot me! My only son, I hadn't seen him for years and then he near well killed me! That's just how the boy is, it's just not right. I'm talking to those with experience here, bring me my wife, let me have a proper funeral for her. Every night she haunts my dreams."

Only Isa refused to speak. He didn't answer the questions of any newspaper journalist or TV reporter. As much as they pressed him, he pressed the words back down his throat. Maybe it was because the only person he was ever going to tell any story to was hidden behind all the people pressing the microphones in his face.

When they were released from the hospital, the fat man was left with only one eye, and the man with the glasses had lost his physical symmetry. He was going to limp to his dying day. And when they got out of hospital, both of them were in a hurry. To write their new books. One of them wrote *A Single Bullet* and the other *Çorak Life*. And both of them wrote on the first pages: *In memory of Oğuz Atay*. Because, as soon as they both could speak again, both the fat man and the man with glasses talked incessantly about their deep respect for Oğuz Atay. But they worried the people listening weren't sufficiently convinced, so they dedicated their books to the man just to make sure. Of course, *Çorak Life* became a prize-winning novel. And of course, the book release party was held at Çorak. And as for the fat man, once again he didn't receive the interest he might have hoped for.

But beyond these developments, the event that garnered the most attention was the funeral for the man with the beard.

300

Anyone who had anything to gain by talking about his life, his writings, or by organizing readings of his work, each and every one gave teary declarations into whatever television reporter's microphone they could find. One of them called him "a martyr for literature," which was copied clear enough in the headline in the bearded man's newspaper:

THOUSANDS WALK FOR LITERATURE MARTYR.

And right below it, Derda's photograph. Taken as he exited the court building. Between two police. His fists handcuffed together, stretched out in front of him. He looked straight into the lens above OĞUZ and ATAY. "Scandal in the court" was written next to him. And below that, "Murderer gets off with twenty-four-year sentence!"

Although they were presented throughout the court case, the medical reports about the suspect's mental health didn't do him any good. The court decided first and foremost to appease the roar of public opinion, so instead of sending Derda to some sort of treatment center, he was sentenced to juvenile penitentiary. Until he was eighteen. After that, he'd be transferred to a regular prison. But no one was happy with the twenty-four-year sentence. He was expected to be sentenced to life in prison without parole, but he only got life, which meant that after serving twenty-four years he could be released on parole. Dependent of course on good behavior. His punishment was nothing more than the immediate result of group hysteria. The hysterics were operating under the delusion that, if Derda received three times the life sentence—each one worth thirty-six years—they could rest assured that Derda would rot and die in prison and they could go back to their homes and live in peace and harmony forevermore. But the hysterics had overlooked one thing. And that thing was that Derda had committed the murders the week before his seventeenth birthday, so he had to be tried as a minor. Maybe if he had tested his patience for another week, his crimes would have been piled on his adult back and the courts would have been forced to process Derda as an adult. But that's not the way the legal calendar turned. It worked another way. In a way that helped no one.

At the unveiling of the sculpture of the man with a beard in front of his newspaper's building, the speaker made this speech: "This attack was a speech against freedom. That the sentence received was only twenty-four years amounts to nothing less than an official endorsement of the act."

Two years had passed since the event, and if people wanted to remember, they could do it by monumentalizing the martyrs to literature. They didn't want to remember it by thinking they had lost a child from their very own families; it was easier to believe that a very, but very, secret organization had struck and killed. No one wanted to reject that theory, anyway. The bearded man was killed for his beliefs. And that was that. And maybe because of that, they'd made the statue of him more handsome than he had ever been in real life. That's how people wanted to remember him. But don't we all have a job on the side, as long as we live? Designer and Director of the Past are positions of such honor after all.

Derda had explained all the details about how Tayyar and Israfil had given him the gun to kill Hanif the Trashman, but the court practically overlooked the deaths of those two men in their decision. They turned details that should have worked in Derda's favor into incriminating evidence. Anyway, it wasn't like anyone got up and went on television to cry and say what good people they had been. But once Israfil's son did try to attack Derda as he left the courts. But police held him back and he couldn't get to the boy who had once apologized to his photo. And as for the members of the Hikmet movement, they took it as some sort of sign. They attributed all that had happened to Tayyar as consequences of his leaving the order, and for years to come in their conversations they told his tale. May it be an example to the children.

The last thing was for the pieces of Derda's mother to be dug up from all the places they'd been buried and sent for autopsy. When it could be concluded that Derda had had nothing to do with her death, all the pieces were put in a cardboard box and returned to Celal. Her aging husband walked meaningfully past all the television journalists and got into a taxi, the box in hand. Then he got out two streets later. He tossed the box in the first dumpster he saw without even breaking his step.

Every year Derda was in prison, he received a mysterious package. The prison wardens would slip it to him secretly. Sometimes there was money inside, sometimes drugs. Hanif the Trashman was sending them. He had followed the whole case very closely and understood that it was all because of Derda that he could still draw breath. He'd have paid whatever he could; the debt of a life is not small. The man was true to his nickname—he lived on the streets. For years he'd collected paper from trash cans to scrape out an existence, piling them into the sack bigger than he that he dragged behind him and cashing it in by weight. When he was Derda's age he'd killed a man for the first time so he could sleep under a dry roof. He knew all too well what prison was like. And also the value of a life, scraped out from childhood by sorting through the trash.

Derda never found out who was sending him the packages. For the first few years, he really believed they were from Oğuz Atay himself. From his soul. Then after some time he stopped thinking about it. Actually he stopped thinking altogether. Up until the day he pulled a cell phone out of a package. In his nineteenth year in prison.

There was no one he could call. So for the first few weeks he barely even touched the phone. Then one day, he took it in his hand and started pushing random buttons. He knew nothing about the technology before him and he had no idea what he was doing. So when he heard the sound of a film starting up on the screen he was scared. He panicked until he figured out how to shut the thing up. He practically smashed it to pieces and threw it down the latrine. He went about it all wrong, but eventually he hit upon the place to press and the sound went off. Only then could he take a look at the screen with a little more attention and care. A film was playing, some ordinary film. He smiled. After spending twenty-two years on the inside, he could watch the world on the outside from palm of his hand. He got so excited he even started laughing and chuckling. Then he covered his mouth with his hand to silence himself.

Hanif the Trashman hadn't sent Derda a package for three years. It had been three years since he'd been killed. And at the most unexpected moment, too. He'd been shot during an argument in traffic. Now it was his son who prepared the packages. He had listened to his father tell Derda's story like he was a fairytale hero from another time. Time and time again. Now he was carrying on his father's legacy. Hanif had never actually told him, "After I'm gone, you will send him the packages." It wasn't like he had planned to die or something like that. But in any event, the son considered it his very own mission and kept sending the packages to the fairytale hero.

But he had no idea what would make a thirty-five-year-old man who'd been in prison for nineteen years happy, so he tried to put himself in the other man's place. In the end, he decided that the only thing that could soften the explosive boredom of being stuck between four walls would be a phone with a hard drive loaded with countless films and songs. He chose the films and songs himself. It was the only electronic mechanism Derda had ever had in prison. And he couldn't actually use the phone as a phone, but nevertheless, Derda was pleased. And so, in the end, the son had decided on the right gift.

Once Derda had figured out how to use the machine, and once he understood that there were hundreds of films stored in the telephone's memory, Derda dove into the fantasy world contained in a screen the size of his palm. He stayed there for hours on end. When they were called out into the courtyard so that his one-person cell could be aired, he came back burning with desire to bury himself in the films again.

Derda couldn't believe how much the world outside and people had changed. He just couldn't believe his eyes. And for the first time in nineteen years, the thought of the day he'd be released scared him. There had been no decision on it as of yet, but Derda was convinced he'd be released on parole. Anyway, his record since entering prison was spotless. He hadn't killed anyone, he hadn't fought with anyone, he hadn't even cursed the wardens. The other prisoners considered Derda some sort of madman, and by what they'd been told about him, they decided he really was part of a very, but very, secret organization so no one bothered him. No one would touch him. No one dared fight with OĞUZ or ATAY. With such stellar behavior, he was sure to leave prison after twenty-four years. But if the world he went into after he left his cell looked like it did in those films, it would probably take him another twenty-four years to get used to it.

One morning he came back from breakfast and started the next film in the line of the hundreds he had watched. A young woman appeared on the screen. And then a man beside her. Derda knew what sort of film this was because they were both naked. But the truth was that Derda had never watched a porno, nor had he ever touched a woman. The last naked woman he'd seen was his mother's chopped-up corpse. Süreyya didn't count because when she jumped up from the floor mattress in the cemetery house, Derda had turned away, turned around completely and stared at the door. For whatever reason, he'd stared into the keyhole.

Derda paused the film and went back to the menu. He touched the place to start the next film in the lineup. Two women caressing and kissing each appeared on screen. Derda skipped that one, too, and went on to the next film.

First he saw a girl with no hair, then he saw a man. A blond man. Then he saw other men. Derda turned away. He didn't want to watch. He wanted to skip ahead to the next film, but his eyes had left his fingers blind and he didn't know where his fingertips were touching. They slipped over the screen and touched the image of the girl. And he was looking straight into the eyes of the hairless girl.

The sound was down to a whisper's volume. At one point, the girl was obscured from vision and only the back of the man on top of her was visible. Just then Derda heard a sound. The cameraman must have heard it, too, because just then he jerked the camera to the direction the sound came from. The screaming, crying girl was in the center of the frame. Derda couldn't believe it. He went back and rewatched the same sequence. He heard it again:

"Gel buraya! Gel!"

The girl was speaking Turkish. Like she was calling out to Derda to come to her. Then another man took up position between her legs. But the girl kept staring straight at Derda. She was shouting.

First she was just cursing, but then she said this: "Why are you just standing there? Come and do something. I'm here, where are you? Huh? Where are you?"

The consequence of a most entrenched habit, Derda called out "I'm here!" without thinking. The sound of his own voice scared him and he paused the film. He felt like that frame of the film had been filmed for no other reason than to provoke him. He looked at the frozen frame with tears in his eyes. The hairless girl's cry was just the same as the call to action that had led him in pursuit of Oğuz Atay so long ago. He'd forgotten that cry until the beating of his heart against his rib cage reminded him. He felt its pulse in his fingertips. And one of those fingers, without ever taking his eyes off the eyes of the girl, set the image in motion again.

There were countless more men, and Derda cried with the girl and listened to her pleas. She couldn't bear it any longer. Then men fell over the girl one by one like a filthy rain, and Derda looked on, hopelessly. He paused the image and went back.

He watched the girl yell, "I'm here, where are you?" countless more times and every time he answered her. "I'm here!"

"I'm here!"

Not one more, he never watched any other film.

He just listened to that girl.

That crying girl.

That girl who beat the men on top of her with her listless fists.

He listened to the sound of the girl's high voice as she
  screamed.

He didn't want to, but he counted.

Fifty-two men who went in and out between her legs.

He closed his eyes, and pressed the cry to his ear like a seashell.

He knew all the contractions in her voice by heart.

He engraved the letters formed by the girl's lips onto the walls
  of his mind.

Sometimes he watched with his eyes filled with tears right up
  to his pupils, sometimes he spoke as he watched.

He spoke to the girl like he was speaking to Oğuz Atay's
  tombstone.

Whatever he knew, he told her.

Whatever he was afraid of, he listed them one by one.

Whatever he imagined, he whispered it to her.

Whatever he had forgotten, he remembered.

Whatever he dreamed of, he told her.

Then he asked the wardens for something.

To teach him how to write.

Because now he had something to write.

He worked for months to learn how to write.

And months to perfect his penmanship.

And in the end, each letter that fell from his pen onto the page
was a painting.

And each of those paintings was a pledge.

That's why he wanted to learn how to write.

Because he thought that if he wrote his pledge it could never
be erased.

Not from his life nor from his future.

When he was forty years old and there were forty days left
until his release from prison,

As many years as from the last time he cleaned Oğuz Atay's
tomb,

After five whole years spent looking at the girl without hair
and crying, "I'm here!"

Derda wrote a letter.

With all the love he had.

DERDA'S LETTER

You asked, Where are you? Well, I'm here.

My name is Derda. When I was sixteen years old, I commit-
ted three murders and left two people permanently disabled. Some
of them were for Oğuz Atay, and some of them were for me. Or
maybe because I'm crazy. Later, I realized it didn't make much dif-
ference. Now I'm forty years old and I've lived for twenty-four years
in a prison cell.

You don't know me. You couldn't even have known that such
a person existed. But I saw you. I saw how you were beaten. I also
saw how you begged them. I've been looking at you for the last five
years. Every day for five years.

There are forty days left until I'm out. I don't know where you
are. I don't even know if you're alive. But in forty days, this letter
and I are setting out on a journey. This letter and me, we're going
to go all over the world so we can find you and give you this letter
ourselves. This journey will start without you, but will end with us
together. If need be, it will be a journey to the death.

I thought about your name a lot. None of the names I knew
seemed right for you. I'll hear it from you the day I find you. So I

stopped trying to guess. For now, I just call you "my dear." I hope that doesn't make you mad.

I've made a pledge to you. No matter where you are, I'll find you. If you're dead, I'll be running right after you. If there's no life after death, I'll create it so I can find you.

Because I am in love with you.

Derda

JOURNEY

After his last night sleeping in prison, he woke up and opened his eyes. He looked at the ceiling. All he needed to do to start the day he'd been dreaming of for years was to sit up in bed and press his feet against the cold concrete floor. But he didn't do it. He waited. He eyes were watering but he never blinked. When his cheekbones got wet, Derda saw his dear's face in a mist on the ceiling. He raised his OĞUZ hand up toward her. Like he could touch her face. Like his fingers were being tossed by ocean waves like coral, like he was caressing a ghost. When his tears reached his chin from both sides Derda whispered "I'm coming" and like a dead man coming to life, he slowly sat up on his bed.

He stood up and wedged his hand into the split in the spring mattress and pulled out his telephone.

"When you're leaving they won't search you," the courier wardens had told him. "We'll just say someone else was on duty. So don't worry about anything."

Derda slipped on the pants and shirt that had waited a week to be worn. He put on the jacket and dropped the telephone into the inner pocket. He had never had any interest in how he looked. He didn't comb his hair. He let his moustache grow out. Washing aside, he didn't do anything. The wardens had brought him the suit. They chose the color, too. They chose black because they knew just how Hanif—who had paid them more than the Justice Department—looked when he wandered the streets. They believed that Hanif the Trashman's path to immortality was in his name. Maybe they were right. Maybe all secrets are hidden inside names. But the order the wardens received was crystal clear: "Derda will not learn our name." So he would never learn why the suit he had on was black.

He buried his feet one by one into the black shoes in front of him. Then he pulled out the letter he'd kept hidden beneath the spring mattress. He opened his jacket and slipped the letter in next to his telephone. He took four steps and looked at his reflection in the mirror above the cell's sink. He was forty years old but he felt stronger than ever. He put up his fists and posed like a professional boxer. He smiled, looking at OĞUZ and ATAY. Then his smile dissipated and he waited without lowering his fists. Like the statue of a professional boxer. Like a boxer who would wait in the center of the ring all alone for the chance to knock out all his opponents the world over. Like he was going to smash the wall behind the mirror, and the walls would fall and the prison would be destroyed.

He didn't break his pose until he heard the cell's door being opened. He had to hear, "Come on, Derda, you're out."

He was taken to the prison gate by two wardens, passing through the corridors going to the place he'd been taken from, the place he'd be delivered unto once more. The wardens stopped and looked at Derda. One of them said, "It's all behind you now."

Derda smiled.

"And it won't happen again. It all starts now."

They shook hands and Derda turned to the door and took his last breath as a prisoner.

The gate was four meters high and weighed tons. It started to slide to the right like a magical wall. As it slid open, life slipped inside. The sunshine. Derda walked toward the light and when it had opened wide enough for his two shoulders to pass through, he stepped through the gate.

It was the first step in the journey of his life. At his second step, his way was blocked. By a man in a suit.

"Are you Derda *Bey*?"

Derda didn't answer. He used his hand as a shield against the sunlight that dazzled his eyes and he tried to make out the man's face. The man spoke again.

"If you could spare me a bit of your time, I'd most appreciate it."

Derda grabbed the man's wrist as the man slid his hand into his jacket. He didn't know what that hand was going to come back out with. The man said, "I was just going to give you my card." Derda loosened his fingers and as he took the card stretched out toward him, he heard: "Sefer Baylan, attorney at law. I have a client who would most like to meet with you."

Derda handed the card with the same name that he'd just heard back to the man.

"Please, keep it."

Derda didn't know what to do with the card so he let it drop to the ground. He wasn't accustomed to being given business cards. The attorney smiled as if he hadn't seen it.

"Derda Bey, my car is just there. If you could come with me, I'd most appreciate it. And it really won't last too long."

Derda was prepared to take any necessary action to remove obstacles on his journey to his darling. Ready to fight, to injure, even to kill. But he hadn't been expecting an attorney. And he especially didn't expect one to come up to him and make him an offer. He didn't know what to say, and anyway, he never was any good at talking. He only knew he had to set off on a journey.

"I have to go," he said. "There's some place I have to go."

"Please," said the attorney, "first let me introduce you to my client, then I will bring you anywhere you need to go."

Derda didn't want to listen anymore. He took two steps away and let the sun fall on his face. Then he heard the sentence that changed everything.

"Derda Bey, look, it's a matter related to Oğuz Atay and it's very important."

Derda pivoted around and faced the man.

"Where's your car?"

The attorney was so pleased that he'd been able to pull off this most difficult part of the task he'd been burdened with that he smiled with all his heart.

"Yes, please, right this way."

The car wove through the streets where once upon a time Derda had raced down the sidewalks. When they passed under the overpass where the clock seller had arrested him, he asked, "So who is this who wants to talk to me?"

"It would be best if my client explains, Derda Bey."

"How did you know what day I was going to be released?"

"We've been following your case, sir. And let me say, that we were most pleased with your release on parole."

"Why?"

Like anyone who doesn't know what to say, the attorney changed the subject.

"Once we get out of this traffic here, the rest will be easy."

"Where are we going?"

"There's not much left, Derda Bey. Please forgive me, but I forgot to ask you. Do you smoke?"

The driver was an accomplished defense attorney. He was young and didn't have very much experience, but he was prepared for any kind of self-sacrifice in the defense of a client. Just so he wouldn't have to say any more than was necessary, and to answer Derda's question before he could himself, he lit a cigarette. Sacrificing his car that had never been exposed to smoke before.

Derda lit the cigarette the attorney handed him with the lighter that had followed it, blowing smoke into the upholstery on the ceiling and remembering Abdullah. Apo, who'd say, "Light one up!" Who knew where he was now? Who would know? When they are alone and they lit up and talked, who knew who regretted being born? Derda smiled, remembering those days.

And Sefer, turning his head for a moment and seeing him smile, asked, "Please excuse me for asking, but how does it feel?"

"What?" Derda asked.

"Being reunited with freedom after twenty-four years."

Derda sucked half of the cigarette between his fingers down in one drag and spoke.

"You should ask the other prisoners. I don't have a place to go, myself. I mean, if you left me on the outside, I'd go back and stay there for another twenty-four years."

His answer surprised Sefer, and he remembered the first thing Derda had said to him.

"But didn't you say there was someplace you had to go? I thought that's what you'd said."

"Yeah, there's that," said Derda. "Prison was hard only when I had someplace to go. Otherwise, I didn't care."

While Sefer was thinking about how a person, halfway through a seventy-year-old's life span, who'd spent twenty-four years between four walls, could not care, he turned into a wide avenue. Derda recognized the street immediately. It was the street that led to the cemetery. Nothing had changed. Of course the sidewalks, the color of the asphalt, the walls, the buildings, and the people had changed. But one thing hadn't changed at all, and that made all the other things not count. And that was that the street went to the cemetery. Just to the cemetery and nowhere else. So he didn't even bother to ask, "Are we going to the cemetery?" Instead, he leaned forward to look out of the windshield to look for a sign. He looked toward the sidewalk on the left hand side. He was looking for a sign that once said NAIL. But he couldn't find it. He didn't see any marble workshops nor any bar. He looked at the tattoos on his fingers and thought of Isa. *Thank you*, he said inside. *Wherever you are, thank you.*

They slowed down as they passed through the cemetery gate and Derda's eyes searched for Yasin's guardhouse. But his eyes came back empty because the guardhouse had been knocked down years before, and a two-story building with a glass facade had been built in its place. There was no gate with iron bars now. The cemetery was just closed at night. There was a barrier that opened automatically. There was no guard or anyone else to see Derda. He wondered how they kept the kids out. Was a barrier really enough? He didn't know what to think. He couldn't even have imagined that the *gecekondu* neighborhood of houses stuck right against the cemetery wall had been totally destroyed. When he lived in one of those houses, it had been like hell to Derda. And no one could destroy hell. At least, no person could. In any event, there was nothing left of that neighborhood or of the kids who would hop over the wall or pass under the barrier to work in the cemetery. They were all at school now. The school that somehow Derda never made it to.

When they arrived at the square where there'd once been a fountain, the attorney stopped the car and looked at Derda.

"After this, I think you know where to go."

Derda opened the door and got out of the car and watched everything that had belonged to his childhood pass before his eyes and go. In and out in one breath, everything in the cemetery passed. He was seeing the one place that in all of his twenty-four years in prison hadn't been touched. The same tombs, the same tombstones, the same trees. Maybe a bit older. Like Derda. But that was all.

"It was very nice to have met you!" the attorney yelled behind him. But Derda didn't hear him. He was walking deeper into the cemetery where he knew the tombstones as well as the dead. His feet knew just where he was going but even so, Derda felt drunk. He touched the tombstones as he slowly made his way through the shade of the trees.

And then his feet stopped like they'd sunk into the earth. Because at the head of Oğuz Atay's tomb was a woman, standing, with a white envelope in her hand. A white envelope.

Derda didn't do what he'd done all those years before. He didn't hide. He didn't hide himself among the trees or hold his breath. He just walked. Straight to Oğuz Atay and the woman.

The woman turned around when Derda's shadow fell over her, and she asked, like a dream wrapping around him, or like they were the only two people left on the face of the earth, "Derda, right?"

His squinted as he answered her. "Yes." He looked at her with the same hope as the sailor, lost on the seas, looks at the sight of the mainland on the horizon. In two words, the woman's voice already seemed so familiar to him, and the way she looked into his eyes . . . Derda had to tell himself it was impossible. He practically shouted it to himself.

"I'm sorry," the woman said. "I've exhausted you in bringing you all the way out here."

Derda's two ears and two eyes were so full that he couldn't hear what she was saying. Maybe if time had stood still he would have been able to figure it out. Especially this strange similarity. But the minute hands and the hour hands didn't pay any attention to Derda.

"I know what you've been through," the woman continued. And she took Derda's hand. The OĞUZ hand. Then she put the envelope into his hand. "If you will read this, you'll understand everything. I wrote it to you. It's a letter."

Derda fell down onto his knees at the base of Oğuz Atay's tomb like he was eleven years old. Entirely blind to the dust of death everywhere. He wasn't in any state to stay on his feet. At that moment, Oğuz Atay's tomb was the only reality he could trust. He felt better when he leaned his back against it. And taking a deep breath, he opened the envelope.

When he pulled out the sheet of paper inside, he looked up at the woman and patted the earth next to him. The woman sat down on the ground. At Derda's side. And she leaned her back against Oğuz Atay, too. She pulled her knees up and rested her chin on them. And she planted her eyes on a faraway tree. On a tree where, once upon a time, Derda had slept in the shade and dreamed.

DERDÂ'S LETTER

Dear Derda,

I know how to start but I have no idea how this letter will end. But first of all, I will call you "you," nothing formal. Maybe the first time I see you, I won't be able to do that. But for me, you are you, someone I know. And anyway, the first time I see you I'll be so excited that it's highly probable I'll even forget your name. But one of the things that gives me courage to write you this letter is that. My name. Our names. Because they are both the same. They're both Derda. Anyway.

I was born in a small village called Yatırca. When I turned eleven I was forced to marry and I was taken to London. I stayed a prisoner for five years in an apartment there until I escaped one night. I started doing heroin, then I started doing everything to be able to keep doing heroin. To the point where once I even slept with fifty-two men. It was filmed and now I know there are millions of people out there who saw me like that. I'm telling you all this because I want you to know me. Know me completely, with nothing left out. Up until today, I haven't been able to tell all this to anyone like this, openly and simply. But now, it's like I'm telling it all to myself and I can write everything calmly. Actually, I'm probably calmer than if I had been telling it to myself. I'm writing to you with a strange peace of mind. Anyway . . .

When I was sixteen, I met a woman named Anne at a rehabilitation center where I went to get off heroin. She was a retired nurse. She treated me with a love that I'd never known until that day and she took me into her home. Then years passed and I became her daughter. Anne's daughter. Her name was written like that, anne, like "mother" in Turkish. Was written, I say, because two years ago she died of a brain hemorrhage and I, in losing her, lost everything.

The first thing I did when I was able to feel alive again was to read her diaries. She hid her diaries like buried treasure. In her diaries I read that Anne had once worked in London at the Atkison Morley Hospital in Wimbledon.

In the year 1976 on the 22nd of December, Anne, at the time twenty-eight years old, was on night duty in the intensive care unit when a patient was brought in. It was a patient who'd just come out of surgery for a brain tumor. It was a Turk. And who was it, do you know? Maybe you already know. In any event, his name is written on your fingers. It was Oğuz Atay.

Oğuz Atay stayed in intensive care until the 31st of December with Anne always at his side.

The first thing Oğuz Atay said to her was this: "Your name is written the same as the word 'mother' in Turkish."

Oğuz Atay couldn't sleep because of the horrible pain in his head. Apparently he even called his head "Ağrı Dağ," a joke of course about it being a "mountain of pain," and also the Turkish name for Mount Ararat. Of course Anne couldn't have deciphered the meaning of that but she did Oğuz Atay the favor of writing it down on a piece of paper. Then she copied out the sentence in a language she didn't understand, letter by letter, into her diary.

They talked until morning every night for eight nights. At first, Anne just listened. Because in those days the only thing in Anne's head was death. Suicide. Not for any particular reason. The reason was everything, her whole life. From everything she had lived. Some people are like that. They're just much more sensitive than other people. They carry death around on their back like a bag and when they get too tired they're the first ones to tire of the weight and open it up. Anyway . . .

For whatever reason, Oğuz Atay sensed what Anne was thinking about. Maybe he could just feel it and so he told her only about life. About his desire to stay alive. Those eight nights were so affecting that Anne was convinced to let herself live. Because across from her was a man struggling with life like Don Quixote, and he was telling her how to live with all the words he had felt in his heart until that day.

Anne talked about his English.

"It was like Shakespeare was across from me, and I listened to him speak like I was reading from a book. I can't write his words here. The moment I write them the meanings of all the beautiful things he made me believe would be ruined. He didn't give me any chance. There was nothing I could do but believe in him and what he was saying."

After Oğuz Atay was released from the hospital they never saw each other again, but Anne never forgot him. If you ask me, I think she fell in love with Oğuz Atay. But she never mentions anything like that in her diaries. There's only this one sentence: "He was the only man I met in all my life that I might have been going to fall in love with."

Then years passed and Anne came to Turkey. And she came, if you are reading this letter, exactly to the spot where you are standing right now. The Edirnekapı Şehitliği Sakızağacı Cemetery. To the head of Oğuz Atay's tomb. She mentions a letter in her diary. A letter she wrote to Oğuz Atay. Who knows what she wrote? Anyway . . .

And so, Anne came to bury the letter in Oğuz Atay's tomb. This is what she wrote in her diary:

"I buried the letter above him today. Maybe years will pass and it will only mix in with the soil. Or maybe as soon as I leave, his soul will read it. Then a boy came up to me. He looked so poor, so terribly downtrodden. I suppose he was working in the cemetery washing tombs. He said something to me. But of course I couldn't understand what he said. I gestured that he should clean the tomb. If only I had given him a bit of money. But I was so sad that I started to cry and I left running. I didn't even look behind me."

I found out that you worked in the cemetery. Could that boy have been you? I doubt it. But who knows, maybe it was.

After I had read Anne's diaries, I understood that it wasn't just her that had saved my life. Maybe Oğuz Atay counts, too. Maybe he also saved me from that hell. Because Oğuz Atay saved Anne's life. And if there hadn't been any Anne, I would have been destroyed.

So I figured that much out but I didn't even know then that a man called Oğuz Atay had even existed. And here I am at the University of Edinburgh, a professor of literature, did you know that? How embarrassing it was not to know who he was! And I should say here, I apologize for my Turkish. It's the first time in my life that I'm writing a letter in Turkish. And this will be the first time in twenty-nine years that I return to Turkey, to ask you to read this letter.

As soon as I finished Anne's diaries, I started to read everything that Oğuz Atay had written and do all the research I could to find about him. And then you jumped out in front of me. And all the news to do about you. Your photographs, what you'd said during the court case. I couldn't believe it. Especially when I read your name.

Now I've read the letter over again from the beginning and I can see how badly I've written it. There's an "anyway" at the end of every paragraph. Anyway, not anyway! If I kept going beyond every "anyway" there'd be thousands of stories I couldn't possibly write now.

I feel like a young girl. It would have to be an eleven-year-old girl who would write all this to you like this. Anyway!!

Like I explained at the beginning of this letter, we've arrived at the section where I don't know where its thread is going. We've arrived at the end. Because I'm not sure what I want from you. But it's like, there's you and me. I don't know what I'm going to say.

If you're still reading this you're still beside me. But if you believe all this is just some coincidence, you can go right away. Let's go on with our lives and forget everything.

No, I can't lie. I can't go on with my life and I can't forget anything.

Because I also read Oğuz Atay, and I've met you.

Maybe you'll say, how much can you know someone through photographs and news clips? You're right. Maybe very little. In that case, let me say this: I know you *az*, just a little.

Do you see it, too? *Az*, it's such a tiny word when you say it. Just A and Z, just two letters. But between them there's an entire alphabet. There are tens of thousands of words and hundreds of thousands of sentences you can write with that alphabet. The thing I wanted to say to you and all the things I couldn't write are between those two letters. One is the beginning, the other is the end. But it's like they were made for each other. So that they'd be brought together and read as one. It's like they climbed over all the letters between them, one by one so they could meet. Just like me and you.

And so maybe there's a lot more than just "a little." Maybe life and death are like *az*. And maybe, I know you just "a little" means I know you better than I know myself. And maybe "I don't know" means maybe I'd do anything to learn. Maybe a little means everything. And maybe it's the one and only thing I can say to you.

I couldn't think of a better place to meet you than at the head of Oğuz Atay's grave. Because if you read it and leave without even looking back, I'll bury this letter in the soil.

Derdâ

DERDÂ AND DERDA

They woke up at the same time. They turned and looked at each other. Derda stretched his neck out to reach her lips and he stayed there where he kissed her.

That day they wandered the streets of Edinburgh. Night fell fast and they returned home.

Derdâ went to the living room. Derda went to the bathroom.

He shook the can of spray paint in his hand and he drew a big, red O on the big bathroom's big wall. Derda looked at it for a few minutes, smiling. A blood-red letter on a snow-white wall. Then he added an A inside the O. He looked at it like it was the first time he was seeing it. Or like he'd spent his whole life looking at it.

He went into the bedroom and slowly began to peel the clothes away from his body. He undressed and then he was naked. Music floated in from the living room. He closed his undulating lips. It was the most loved album in the house: *Altre Follie, 1500–1750.*

Derda stood in front of the full-length mirror in the bedroom and raised his fists, posing like a boxer. He looked at himself above OĞUZ and ATAY. Until Derdâ came in and broke his pose. She was also naked. She was also smiling.

Derda offered Derdâ his hand like he was a gentleman of another age and he showed her into the bathroom. With a bow. Derdâ walked in and stood near the bathtub. She bent her knees and put two fingers into the water to test it. Then she straightened up and with one movement she took out her hair clip and shook out her hair. Her hair fell over her shoulders like a river. She put first one foot, than another, into the hot water. Her naked body losing itself in the hot water.

Derda brought two champagne glasses to the side of the bathtub and set them on the checkered tile floor. Then he lowered himself slowly into the hot water.

They looked at each other, smiling at each other from behind clouds of steam and then, closing their eyes, they listened to the music.

The notes got slower and slower and their eyelids opened and they looked at each other. They both stretched down and picked up glasses of champagne. Without taking their eyes off their love, they took a sip. Like taking a breath. A breath of poison.

"I love you a little bit," said Derdâ.
"I love you a little bit less," said Derda.
They spoke no more.

But just once they looked at the symbol on the wall and together they thought: *It began with Oğuz Atay and it will end with Oğuz Atay.*

And accompanied with the endless melody called *La Folia.*
They looked at each other for the last time before they fell
    asleep.
Fell into death.
They were eighty years old.
For both of them.
Forty years to be together.
And forty years to die together.
For another forty years, they could not have survived.

(music)

Forever La Folia XVI